BLOODY SOIL

— A Kolya Petrov Thriller —

S. Lee Manning

Also by S. Lee Manning

The Kolya Petrov Thriller Series:

Trojan Horse

Nerve Attack

BLOODY SOIL

— A Kolya Petrov Thriller —

S. LEE MANNING

Encircle Publications
Farmington, Maine, U.S.A.

Paperback ISBN 13: 978-1-64599-404-6
Hardcover ISBN 13: 978-1-64599-405-3
E-book ISBN 13: 978-1-64599-406-0

Library of Congress Control Number: 2022942966

Editor: Cynthia Brackett-Vincent
Cover design by Deirdre Wait
Cover photograph © Getty Images

Published by:

Encircle Publications
PO Box 187
Farmington, ME 04938

info@encirclepub.com
http://encirclepub.com

To Jim, Jenny, and Dean

1

HAMBURG, GERMANY

LISETTE KNEW HER FATHER'S murder wasn't her fault but knowing that and believing it were quite different things. She still blamed herself. If she hadn't had asthma, her father wouldn't have gone outside every evening after dinner to smoke his pipe. He'd have been inside on that warm summer evening instead of sitting on the wicker glider on the porch. If he'd been inside, maybe the three men would have just passed by the house and found someone else.

Of course, she didn't blame herself quite as much as she blamed the man with the wolf tattoo.

They lived in Blankenese, on a hillside in a house that her father would teasingly compare to a hobbit hole, a comparison that would make her mother roll her eyes. After all, it was one of the most expensive neighborhoods in Hamburg, and their home, with a view of the river, had cost in the millions.

Lisette knew all this because her mother repeated it whenever her father would make the hobbit hole joke.

He'd just laugh. "Bilbo Baggins was rich. Although he got his money more honestly than I did."

Of course, her mother was pragmatic and not all that interested in the exploits of hobbits, dwarves, and elves. Lisette's father, though, loved Tolkien, and would read the stories to Lisette, even though parts of them were scary. But they were German. Lisette was accustomed to scary fairy tales. In the German version of Cinderella, as told by the Brothers Grimm, the birds peck out the eyes of the stepsisters.

Lisette's father was a lawyer. She didn't know exactly what he did at his job. She did know that he was older than her mother by almost twenty years. She did know that he'd made a lot of money, enough to buy their house on the hill. She did know that he'd left his high paying job when she was five for a job defending Turkish immigrants. He'd told her that he needed to do something to pay back.

"To pay back what?"

He'd tugged on her braid. "When you're older."

"I'm nine."

"Maybe when you're ten."

He'd said the same thing when she was eight.

She had trouble sleeping. Partly because of her asthma, which she outgrew by her teen years. Her mother or her father would give her medicine to breathe, take her into the shower, and run hot water. One of them would sit with her until her breathing eased and she fell asleep. Sometimes there was no real reason that she couldn't sleep, except an undefined dread from being alone in the dark. Many nights, after her father or mother read her a story, kissed her goodnight, turned off the bedside lamp, and went downstairs, she'd creep out of bed into the hall, listening to the rise and fall of their voices. Most of the conversations weren't that interesting. Some were. It was how she discovered that her mother and father bought her the presents that she thought came from *Weihnachtsmann*, the German Santa Claus, on Christmas Eve.

She didn't tell them that she knew.

It was also how she learned that her grandmother—her father's mother—wanted to see her, but her father had refused. Her mother and father argued about it, but it wasn't too serious an argument. After all, it was her father's decision. He had a right to determine whether he wanted his mother to have contact with their daughter. Lisette's mother had made a little noise about the rights of grandparents, but her heart wasn't really in it. After a few minutes, she let it go.

There weren't that many fights.

Except for those about her father's job.

Her mother wanted her father to go back to the corporate job he'd left. She brought it up numerous times. Lisette remembered the night when he'd shouted that he was done with that life. It was the only time Lisette had ever heard him raise his voice.

The next morning, she asked him about it. "Why do you and Mama fight over your job?"

They were eating breakfast—breads and jams, nougat cream. She drank orange juice; her father drank coffee. From the windows of the dining room, she had a view of the backyard that wasn't so much a backyard as just a hill covered with flowers.

"Your mother is scared."

"About what?"

"There are bad people who don't like what I do."

"What bad people?"

Her mother carried a pot of coffee and her own cup to the table, refilling her father's cup before sitting down. "Tell the child, Dieter."

"When she's older."

"She's old enough." Her mother turned to her. "Have they taught you anything about Nazis in school?"

Lisette nodded. "A little."

"There are still people who believe what they believed."

"Enough." Her father's voice was rising.

"No, it's not enough. You're putting yourself in danger. You're putting all of us in danger."

"Not now."

"It's not all on you."

"I said, not now!"

He finished his coffee. Then he kissed them both and left for work.

Two nights later, when her father was smoking his pipe on the porch, Lisette heard voices. She pressed her nose to the glass of the living room window and saw three young men surrounding the wicker glider where her father was sitting. One man, wearing a white T-shirt without sleeves, glanced her way, but the room behind her was dark. While she could see his face clearly, she didn't know if he'd seen her.

He turned his gaze away, and she noticed the tattoo of a wolf's head on his upper arm. The men were speaking, but she couldn't hear the words. Her father attempted to stand, and one of the men shoved him back onto the glider.

The man with the wolf tattoo lifted his hand. There was a gunshot, and her father's face shattered—along with her world.

2

FIFTEEN YEARS LATER
NUREMBERG, GERMANY

THE NAIL HAD PIERCED her bicycle tire, and the air was completely gone. Lisette carried an extra inner tube in her backpack and although she knew how to detach the front wheel, she acted as if she didn't. She was struggling with the brakes, which needed to be held in just the right way, when the man jogged up to her and offered to help, as she'd hoped he would.

She was on the path that circled the park at the center of the town. It was a popular place to bike. Or to run. It was her first time biking there, although the man, whose name was Karl, told her that he ran there every day.

He wasn't bad looking, short-cropped light hair, a fit body for a man approaching middle age, good features, a man who knew that women liked his looks. She assumed he liked her looks as well. Most men did.

There was a very small chance he'd recognize her. If he did, and he made the connection between her and Frederick, it could be bad. Karl could walk away. Worse, Karl could call Frederick. If he knew what she was doing, Frederick would kill her.

Knowing that made her nervous, not that she showed it. Besides, part of her enjoyed the risk.

With a mixture that would wash out with one shampoo, she'd

dyed her hair blue for the day. She had distinctive green eyes, but the contacts she was wearing turned them brown, and she had a healthy dark tan. But it was her figure that men especially liked. He seemed to appreciate it as well. He gave her body a once over, his gaze lingering for a touch too long on her breasts.

Under other circumstances, a man ogling her breasts would be degrading and infuriating. But right now, she was focused on the goal. If the breasts did the job, she was fine with it.

"Blue hair?" He commented after he examined the bike, the nail in the tire, and her. "Different."

"So I've been told."

"Because it's true. Do you have tools?"

She offered him the small pack on the back of the bike. It took him less than ten minutes to remove the wheel, insert the tube, inflate it, and reassemble the bike's front end.

"You're very good at this."

"It isn't difficult."

"Impossible for me. Can I buy you a drink to thank you?"

He looked her over again, focusing on her breasts. "Why not?"

They walked her bike to a nearby beer garden and sat outside. They ordered beers and shared a bowl of pretzels, exchanging life stories that only vaguely resembled the truth. He was divorced. He worked for a software company. She knew what he was leaving out, that he'd failed at almost every job, that he'd abused his wife, and what he had done that merited her special attention.

He didn't know that everything she said was false. Including her name.

Over his third beer, he looked at her puzzled. "You look vaguely familiar. Have we met before?"

Did he recognize her? That would ruin everything. And possibly put her in danger. But she had confidence from doing this before.

"I don't think so. I would've remembered."

The danger passed, and they moved on from pretzels to dinner, from beer to mixed cocktails. He drank lemon vodka, and she drank gin and tonic. He noticed that she lingered on her drink while he reordered.

"If I drink too much, I throw up." Her voice was light. "That would ruin the evening, wouldn't it?"

"It might. It depends on what you would like to do after dinner."

"Let's see where it goes. I like to keep possibilities open."

Don't promise too much. Don't seem too eager.

But as anticipated, they wound up at his apartment, the bicycle locked to a lamppost. The apartment was small, decorated in Danish modern. It did have the type of artwork, though, that men like Karl often had. Nazi pictures. The rallies at Nuremberg. Along with a pair of crossed swords hung on the wall. She walked around his sparse living room.

"Aren't those pictures from the Nuremberg rallies?" She gazed at one large poster of thousands of people carrying torches.

"Bother you?"

"Not at all." She was careful not to touch anything. "And the swords?"

"My grandfather's."

"Nice. What do you have to drink?"

He produced a bottle of peppermint schnapps and poured two glasses. He drained his glass while she took a delicate sip. Then he pulled her down onto the couch. "You're very beautiful." His words were a little slurred; he was clearly feeling the alcohol.

He had another two drinks, poured by her, while she toyed with her glass. He didn't seem to notice how little she was drinking. They moved to the bedroom where she performed a little dance as she stripped down to bare skin. Then she placed her clothes on a chair at the far end of the room. Far enough? From experience, she expected it to be.

He grinned, his gaze wandering from her breasts to her pubic hair. "Nice."

"Thank you. Now you."

He tried to undress but he was so drunk, he tangled his arms in his sleeves. She laughed and helped him remove his shirt.

She pointed to the image of a sword on his bicep. "Nice tattoo."

7

"Thanks."

He pulled down his jeans and fell backwards onto bed. She helped pull off his pants. He lay on the bed naked, but the alcohol had had its effect. He thought he was going to have sex. His body said otherwise. Which was fine with her. She would have screwed him if necessary, but it wouldn't be.

"Are you a member of *Der Dritte Weg?*" The Third Way was a group of neo-Nazis who were connected to the anti-immigration movement.

"Not anymore. They weren't doing anything. Just talking. Talk. Talk. Talk. Come down here with me."

She lay next to him and let him put his hand on her breast. It did nothing for her. It did nothing for him, either. He was going through the motions, but he had the rigidity of a wet noodle. The wonders of alcohol.

"I was thinking of getting a tattoo." She traced fingers on the sword tattoo. "Maybe a wolf's head. I like wolves."

"I knew a guy who had a really nice one. Don't know where he got it. Haven't seen him in years. Don't know where he is." His words were slurring more and more. He would be asleep in a minute.

"What was his name?" She ran a finger around his nipple.

"Don't remember." He was definitely drifting towards sleep. "I'm falling asleep, Elizabeth. Drank too much. Damn. Damn. Stay. We can play in the morning."

"I'll stay."

He was already snoring. He didn't respond when she leaned in and whispered in his ear. "By the way: my name is Lisette, not Elizabeth."

Another snore. She slid off the bed and took one of the swords off the wall. She checked the blade. Still sharp. Carrying the sword, she approached the bed and positioned herself.

"Karl?"

He didn't stir.

He wasn't the right man, and she wasn't any closer to finding the man who'd killed her father. The killer could be the guy Karl knew. Or any of a hundred other assholes with a wolf tattoo. Still, she knew that Karl had murdered people—she knew about a Turkish street vendor whom five years earlier he'd bludgeoned to death. She'd overheard him talking about it, at the one meeting where she'd encountered him. If he'd killed one person, he'd probably killed others. Maybe he hadn't been on the porch the night her father had died, but he would've applauded the deed. And, just as important, he had already told her everything he knew about the man with the wolf tattoo.

She didn't go after the casual assholes, the ones who just talked. But the killers who had gotten away with it—she exacted justice.

He was the sixth man in the past eighteen months.

She raised the sword over her head and brought the blade down hard onto his throat, almost severing his head from his body. Blood spurted from the artery, soaking the bed, spattering her. One of the reasons she liked to be naked when she killed. Can't walk out with bloody clothes. She watched the final twitching of the dying body, feeling revulsion as well as a grim satisfaction. *Another for you, Daddy. Another for all the people murdered by these assholes.*

There was a slight whisper of conscience. She'd just taken a life. As repulsive as Karl was, he had been a human being. But she silenced the whisper. Had Karl felt anything for the street vendor he'd murdered?

Yes. He'd felt proud.

So did she.

Then she found lemon juice and baking soda in the kitchen, the recipe for removing spray-on tan, and took them into the bathroom, where she rubbed a mixture over her body and let it sit for minutes before turning on the shower. It took ten minutes to shampoo the blue from her hair and wash the tan from her body. Then she dried herself, dressed, and removed the tinted contacts, becoming once again a green-eyed, pale blonde woman, before wiping down all the hard surfaces, washing her glass, wiping down the shower, checking the drain for any trace of her hair, and leaving, using her shirt to close the front door behind her and carrying the towel in a garbage bag. She unlocked her bicycle from the lamppost and rode it to her car. On the way, she dumped the towel in a garbage can, far enough away from Karl's apartment that it wouldn't be traced to him. She would spend the night at her grandmother's house in Bayreuth before returning to Berlin.

BAYREUTH, GERMANY

When Lisette came downstairs the next morning, the old woman was seated outside in her wheelchair in front of a wrought iron table, the surrounding garden resplendent with red and gold fall flowers. Helen, her caregiver, sat on a matching chair and read out loud. Lisette could see the two of them through the kitchen window. She had slept in her usual room upstairs, letting herself in at midnight with her key, and now she placed a teapot, two cups, and a platter of scones onto a tray. Then she carried the tray outside and set it on the table.

"I'll take over for a bit, Helen. Why don't you go for a walk?"

"Thank you." Helen closed the book and stood. The old woman's eyes fixed on her with an expression of hatred. Helen patted her on the shoulder. "It's your granddaughter. You remember her, don't you?"

"Still not speaking?" Lisette hadn't seen her grandmother for several months. There could have been a change. She hoped not.

"We saw the doctor last week. He thinks she'll never speak again. But she seems to recognize people."

"Can she swallow?" Lisette nodded at the tray.

"She can. You have to hold the cup."

Helen left, and Lisette poured the tea into two cups. She held a cup up to her grandmother's lips. Her grandmother refused to drink.

Lisette replaced the teacup on the tray and seated herself. She chose a scone, delicately picked out one of the raisins, and ate it. "I'm not going to poison you, grandmother."

The old woman's eyes still shone with terror and hatred.

"Although it would be just, wouldn't it? After all, don't you support the poisoning of handicapped people who take up resources? Along with killing Jews, Roma, and gays? That's what you told my father when he was a child, didn't you? That what Hitler did was right."

She replaced the scone and picked up her own tea. She drank. "See. Not poisoned."

The old woman's mouth moved, but no sound came out.

Her grandmother had been ten at the start of World War II. She'd lived with her father, Lisette's great grandfather, who'd been the commandant at a concentration camp in Poland, where those designated as subhuman by the Nazis had been gassed, shot, hung, burned, or starved to death. She had been too young to participate in the Third Reich killings, but she'd approved, and continued to approve, thirty years after the war.

She continued to adore Hitler and mourn the loss of the German Reich, even after neo-Nazis murdered her only son.

Lisette had learned this in her teenage years—when she'd asked her mother why her father had been opposed to her meeting her grandmother.

But as far as Lisette knew, her grandmother had never killed anyone. She was a repulsive human being, but not a murderer.

Following a massive stroke just after Lissette returned to Germany, her grandmother was helpless. Even if Lisette hated having a Nazi sympathizer in her family, she paid for Helen's care and the upkeep on the house.

Of course, keeping her grandmother alive and under her control did have its appeal.

Lisette picked up the book that Helen had been reading out loud: *The Diary of Anne Frank.*

"I hope you're enjoying the book. I picked it out specially for you." Lisette replaced the book and returned to her scone. "Would you like to know what I did yesterday?"

The old woman's mouth moved again.

"I did something for my father. He always said we have to pay back. I'm paying back." But she didn't give details. She knew her grandmother suspected that she'd killed people; she certainly hinted at it, and her grandmother wasn't stupid. A Nazi, but not stupid. Still, Lisette was not explicit. Just in case the doctor was wrong about her never speaking again.

Lisette finished her tea and scone and saw Helen peering into the garden. She waved at Helen and rose. "Until next time, grandmother.

Frederick will miss me if I don't leave now." She kissed her grandmother's cheek, feeling the old woman try to pull away.

3

RONALD REAGAN AIRPORT, WASHINGTON, D.C.

IT WAS A QUICK drive from Georgetown just outside downtown D.C. to the Reagan Airport, especially at one o'clock, when traffic was relatively light. He ran the name through his mind. Michael. He was Michael. Only respond to Michael.

He'd intended to take an Uber so that his fiancée wouldn't have to take off from work and because saying goodbye at home might be less difficult—on both of them—but she'd insisted on driving him. As an attorney, she was self-employed, and unless she had a meeting or court, her time was flexible.

"It's a short drive. And I won't see you for a while." With her eyes on the road, her expression was hard to read.

"Maybe a month. Not that long." Although it could be longer, and there was at least a possibility of it ending in his death. He could feel it in the pit of his stomach, an anticipation, both excited and apprehensive, at what he'd be facing. The apprehension would ease once he was there and in the middle of the action, but it wouldn't completely go away. There were also the shadows that waxed and waned from his PTSD but never completely disappeared. He hoped the shadows were under control, but he was never sure. Not that he'd mention it to her. Not that she didn't know, either.

"Still. I wanted a few last minutes. Just in case." Her voice caught.

He glanced at her while she drove. Long dark curly hair obscured part of her face, sunglasses hid her eyes. But he knew she was upset without seeing her expression—or the tears that he suspected she was fighting. He loved her dearly, but what he was doing mattered. To him—and to more than him. Still, he wondered if he'd made the right decision—both about letting her take him to the airport and about going at all.

"I'll be fine." Probably. Still, he never knew.

"Sure you will, *Michael*. You're always fine. Until you're not."

The use of the name Michael amused him. "You looked at my passport?"

"I know where you're going, too. Berlin. And I have a pretty good guess at what you'll be doing."

"And you looked at my phone." He didn't really mind, although she shouldn't have. Then again, it was hard to keep secrets from someone that smart. Her intelligence was one of the many reasons he loved her.

"Maybe. I have other resources as well. You're not the only sneaky person in the world. Are you up to what I think you're up to?"

"That's a little vague," he said.

"Just playing your game. You and I both know there are only a few reasons you would be heading to Germany."

"Would you disapprove—if your theory were correct?"

"No. Of course not. You know I'm proud of you for fighting in a good cause. I just worry."

"I'll be careful." He always was, even if being careful wasn't a guarantee that he'd survive—or survive intact.

"I know you'll try."

They passed the Lincoln Memorial and took the bridge over the Potomac. He looked down at the blue water. A sailboat emerged from under the bridge, one woman in a yellow bathing suit steered while another in red adjusted the sails. A safe topic. "I never understood the attraction of sailing."

"I like it. It can be fun if it's not too hot. I bought a great new swimsuit last week. You haven't seen it yet." Her voice lightened.

"If you'd like to sail, we can go. Sometime. If there's also the prospect of a swim." Swimming was active and had sensual possibilities. He wouldn't mind seeing her in the new swimsuit either. Sailing, though, was nothing more than sitting and sweating in the hot sun while floating. Pretty, but it held no appeal—except if she wanted to do it.

"No, that's okay. I know you're not a fan of water sports," she said.

"I like skiing, downhill or cross country." He'd always liked cold weather sports, although they hadn't been skiing for over a year.

"Not the same."

"It's still water. Just frozen," he said.

"Only you would consider downhill skiing a water sport." Her tone was teasing. "Maybe we should go this winter, even if it's not a water sport. If your leg is okay."

Skiing was a safe topic. For the remaining five minutes of the drive, they discussed both past trips to Vermont and a possible future expedition. At the airport, she pulled over at the curb in front of international departures. He took a harder look at her face. A tear rolled down her cheek.

Sometimes he forgot that he wasn't the only one battling shadows.

"This is upsetting you too much. I can still cancel."

"We've talked about this. I'm going to worry, and you know it, and you're going to put yourself in danger, and I know it, but what you do matters. When you were working as an attorney, you were safe—but really unhappy. If we're going to work long-term, you have to do what calls to you, even if I'm sometimes frightened for you."

"You matter more than anything else to me," he said.

"I'll be fine."

"Sure you will." He reached over and touched her cheek. "I'm calling it off."

She clasped his hand and then brought it to her lips and kissed the palm. "No. Really, it's okay. If I can accept you putting yourself in danger, you can accept me getting a little weepy. Goodbyes are hard."

"Why I didn't want you coming to the airport."

"As you said—a month isn't that long. I have a case scheduled for trial—I could be working fourteen hours a day next week, unless it settles. And my mother's coming this weekend—she wants to take me shopping at the Bridal Room. I'm assuming you're not interested

15

in helping me pick out a wedding dress."

"Good assumption." He checked his pocket for the passport, found and opened it. His face stared back at him along with the name: Michael Hall. "Although I did enjoy buying you a ring."

It had taken them almost a year after their initial engagement to get around to it, for reasons that had nothing to do with their feelings for each other but had quite a lot to do with why she was so worried and the shadows that never completely left him. For the past year, he'd been recovering from broken bones, beatings, and gunshot wounds. But three months earlier, they'd spent a weekend in New York, culminating in a trip to the diamond district. She'd teased him about buying her the biggest diamond in the store, and he'd intended to do so, even if it took all his savings since he was not rich, calling her on what they both knew was a bluff. Instead, she chose a delicate sapphire ringed with tiny diamonds in the fifteen-hundred-dollar range. It was much less than he'd been prepared to spend, but she liked it, which was all that mattered.

She glanced at the dashboard clock. "You need to check in."

"If you're sure."

"Like I've said repeatedly. I love you for who you are—and this is who you are. I'll worry, but I'll live."

He leaned over to kiss her. She tasted of coffee and cream. She was right: He was who he was. He wanted to go, despite the risk, but even so, he'd miss her. The perpetual tension between what he felt called to do with his life and the woman he loved. "I'll text when I can. You know the drill."

She stepped out of the car as he collected his bag from the back seat. He set it on the curb and then wrapped her in his arms for a longer and deeper kiss.

"Go." She leaned in to whisper in his ear. "Just don't do anything stupid. If you die, I'm going to be really pissed."

4

WEIMAR, GERMANY

FREDERICK BAUER LOVED THE city of Weimar. A small city, Weimar had the look and feel of old Germany, narrow streets, buildings that had been standing for centuries and mostly spared in World War II, a town rich in German culture. Bach, Goethe, Wagner, among others, had wandered the streets. Frederick had spent a few years there as an adult after growing up in what had once been East Berlin, filled with ugly architecture that the communist party had insisted on building for the inhabitants. He especially liked the Weimar market square, which looked much as it had 500 years earlier, except for the residents and the omnipresent phones, and the walking paths on the Park An Der Ilm, which had been landscaped in the time of Goethe.

He lived in Berlin, but he traveled around the country, for meetings with members of Germany Now. Walking paths were his preferred meeting place. He could see if anyone was following or watching, and there was less chance of being recorded.

That was where he met the man he referred to as the Leader, who'd had business in Weimar and had set up the meeting. Frederick used the English word for Leader, not the German word. The German word was still viewed with suspicion, as it had been the title for the man whose name was considered a curse in most corners of the world, although not by Frederick.

The Leader was in his early forties, just a touch of gray in black hair cut short. Today he wore a baseball cap and sunglasses. It wasn't really a disguise, but it did help conceal his face. "I sent you the speech for tomorrow. Have you read it?"

"Brilliant as always," Frederick said. "I just wish you could come out in the open so that everyone will know that these words are yours, not mine." The organizers in each district were informed about the Leader, although they didn't know his real identity. Still when giving the speeches written by the Leader to large crowds, which probably contained those working against them, Frederick was more circumspect.

"After Day X, everyone will know who I am. Up to that point, it's best that I remain in the shadows. You've slowed down on the recruiting."

The words sounded less like a reproach and more like an observation.

"I have to be careful. Check people out. That takes time. And then there's that damn Equality Institute. They've doxed some of us. People have lost jobs. But it's worse. Just when we need every person—we're being attacked. Did you hear: One of my recruits was murdered a few days ago."

"Yes, I know about that."

"Karl's the sixth in the past eighteen months to be killed. He'd been doxed by the Equality Institute, just as most of the others had. Then yesterday he was found naked in bed—and the police said he'd been drinking. No sign of forced entry. No sign of a struggle. He was just lying in bed naked. I think some woman let him pick her up, and she killed him—before or after they fucked."

"Unless he was gay."

"None of our people are gay."

"Sometimes they hide it."

"Not Karl. Karl liked woman. Attractive women."

"It could have been personal."

"With six in eighteen months murdered?"

"I'll check with the police. Maybe a camera caught him with a woman—somewhere—and we can track it down."

"We have to do something about the Equality Institute. They could be behind all the killings. The Jew director needs to be taken down."

"Of course, he does. But check our own house as well. We could have a traitor in our midst."

"I will. And if some woman in our group did this—I'll kill her personally. Slowly and painfully," Frederick said.

"Meanwhile—we still have the problem of recruits. And time is running out. Day X is coming."

"I have people who've signed up, but a lot of them are students. Workmen. Never handled a gun. How many people in the army are with us?"

"Some but not enough. Training, Frederick. You have a little over two weeks."

"The various groups will be training this week. And we have a former American soldier coming to the Berlin rally tomorrow—I was planning to use him to help with our newer people."

"An American?" The Leader frowned.

"We have a lot of supporters in the United States."

"I know that. Is he a member of any of the American groups?"

"Not officially. Although he posts regularly in chatrooms. That's how we made contact, several months ago."

The Leader stopped and watched two women jog by. He didn't speak for a moment. "So no one we know actually met him?"

"No."

"That's concerning."

"He has posts going back years," Frederick said.

"But he hasn't committed?"

"Not until now."

"Send me his name. I'll check on my end. If he's a spy, the BfV will know about it. Americans wouldn't be operating on German soil without government authorization. Unless he's one of those anti-Nazi crusaders."

"Heinrich did the search on him. The man is hiding from the Americans, using a fake name. We found his real name."

"Maybe a test, to see if he's who he says he is—and whether he's up for what is to come. If he's okay, we need every man we can get."

What was to come—Day X—a day that Frederick had waited for his entire life—the day when Germans would take back their country from the immigrants and from the Germans who had betrayed their heritage and their country. It would be glorious. "I have something in mind that would both prove whether he's really with us and take care of the Equality Institute at the same time. Don't worry."

5

BERLIN, GERMANY

FREDERICK WAS PLEASED THAT Lisette was cooking dinner at his apartment on his arrival back in Berlin. She had her own apartment, but she often spent several days a week at his—and she liked to cook. Frederick liked a woman who accepted her role. She was good at it, too, as well as beautiful, the shoulder-length blonde hair, the firm breasts, the amazing green eyes. A good cook—smart, vivacious, hardworking—and to top it all, superb in bed. A perfect example of German women's superiority.

"How was your grandmother?" He'd never met the old lady, but he knew she'd had a stroke.

"The same. Can't walk. Can't speak."

"Nice of you to visit her."

"I'm her only family. Help yourself."

She'd cooked his favorite dish—Zurich ragout—a stew with veal, white sauce, and mushrooms. They ate at his kitchen table, the meal complemented by Schwarz Riesling, a light white wine.

"How was your trip?" She poured the Riesling.

"Fine. Made a few contacts." He hadn't shared information about the Leader—or Day X—with Lisette. He trusted her, they'd been together for almost two years, but she was a woman, and women talked too much.

"Good. And you like Weimar."

"I do. It has the feel of old Germany." Frederick broke off a piece of bread and soaked it in the sauce. "We have that American coming to the rally tomorrow."

"Yes, I remember."

"You lived in America. Talk to him, make him feel comfortable."

"Of course. Are you sure he's okay?"

"I'm not sure of anything, anymore." He drained his wine glass and filled it again. "I'm a little worried that we could have a traitor in our midst. How many women have joined us in the past year and a half?"

She poured wine into her own glass. "There's quite a few. Women believe in the cause just as much as men. What makes you think there's a traitor?"

"Karl was murdered."

"Karl?"

"You might not have met him. He only came to Berlin a few times."

"And you think a woman who supports the cause killed him?"

"No, a woman who pretends to support the cause. And I think she may have killed before."

"Horrible." She drank her wine. "Do you have any idea who?"

"None."

"Are you sure it was a traitor?"

"Pretty sure, but it's not definite. The Goddamn Equality Institute doxed him as well, and maybe they have some Israeli assassins working for them. I'm checking it out. And checking out whether a woman in the group could be killing our people. Karl is number six in the past year and a half."

"Six? My God, Frederick."

He nodded. "I'm not sure they're all connected. Possibly."

"A scary possibility." She started eating and pointed at his plate. "It'll get cold."

He picked up his own fork and took a bite. Delicious as always. He nodded his approval at Lisette, savoring both the flavor of the stew and the thought of getting her into bed.

"If it is some woman who's attached herself to the group, she'd have joined around the time of the first murder," Frederick said.

"I'll chat up some of the newer women in the group." Lisette took a sip of her wine. "If you'd like me to."

"Of course. You're a big support to me."

An unwelcome thought forced its way into his brain. Hadn't Lisette also joined a little before the first murder?

It couldn't be her. Could it? No. Couldn't be. But the doubt once aroused wasn't as easily suppressed. She did take those periodic trips to see her grandmother. Still, it couldn't be. Not Lisette. And they were together for six months before the first murder.

But he had to be sure.

6

BERLIN, GERMANY

HIS PASSPORT IDENTIFIED HIM as Michael Hall. It was the name his fiancée had jokingly called him as she dropped him at the airport. It was the name that he'd used online to comment on posts. It was the name he used to communicate with the man he was meeting at a demonstration near the Brandenburg Gate. It was a typical all-American name of English origin, and he looked the part of an Englishman, if not a German. Blond. Blue-eyed. Customs officials didn't give his passport or him a second glance.

Except it wasn't his name.

And the passport was fake.

He'd taken a taxi from the airport. His hotel, while not cheap, was at least not exorbitant. He'd reserved a small room, which he didn't mind because the size made it easier for him to search for cameras and listening devices. He could have saved money by sharing a bathroom, but a private bathroom was not a luxury. Still the room was clean and the bed was comfortable. He also liked the location, just across from the Museum of Natural History, close enough to his afternoon destination that he could walk.

He didn't bother to unpack, but he did check his luggage and find everything in order, and then he quickly assembled the gun that he'd hidden inside various innocuous-appearing objects.

It might not help him if he got into trouble, but he didn't feel comfortable without it.

The gun went into a holster on his hip, concealed by a pullover sweater. With the temperatures outside in the lower fifties, he added a jacket. As he shrugged into it, he noticed his hands shaking.

Jetlag. In the past day, he'd slept only a few hours, and he hadn't adjusted to the time change. Except that was another lie. He knew it was more than jetlag.

He closed his eyes, took deep breaths, and ran the mantra through his mind. He felt the beginnings of calm. He added words of reassurance. *I'm fine. I can do this.* The shaking eased, and he was back. He picked up his phone and checked for a response to his text: *Here safe. Love you.*

It was there. *Love you too. Stay safe.*

The message disappeared as if it had never existed.

He hadn't told her about the shaking, but there was no point. It would just worry her. He thought about her at the airport, the tear rolling down her cheek and then about holding her close and kissing her. She'd said she was fine. He hoped it was true.

He grabbed his room key and headed out.

It was a bright if chilly day, his favorite kind of weather. He walked down Invalidstrasse, then along the Spree River and over a bridge where he bought a cappuccino with two extra shots of espresso. Carrying his coffee, he wandered into the Tiergarten where a violinist and a guitarist played versions of tunes that had originated with the Roma. He paused and positioned himself so he could watch as well as listen for the next twenty minutes. Before moving on, he placed a ten-Euro bill in the guitarist's case.

He headed to the Memorial to the Murdered Jews of Europe, a vast field of concrete slabs, over four acres in size.

He walked up and down the aisles, looking at the gray slabs with no words. Some flowers here and there rested against the concrete, as if the slabs were tombstones, which in a way, they were. He laid a hand on a spot where sunlight hit the concrete of the slab. It was warm, almost like a living person.

In one aisle, a teenage girl did a handstand against one of the slabs while her friend took a picture with her phone. They were laughing, enjoying themselves.

He wondered who the girl would send the image to, and what the reaction would be. He tamped down his unwelcome surge of emotion. Getting angry wasn't going to accomplish anything.

Returning to the park, he sat on an unoccupied bench and stretched out his right leg. Physical therapy had done the trick for the most part, but he had a long day ahead of him. No reason to push it. And he had an hour before the demonstration began. Fighting the exhaustion from the travel and the change of time, he read a few stories on his phone, went to social media where he posted comments, and then around two o'clock pushed up from the bench.

By the time he reached the Brandenburg Gate, the demonstration was underway. From a small platform, a man with a bullhorn shouted words in German that were roared back by the crowd. Michael could understand the German even though his speaking ability was a little halting. The speech was about immigration, but not just about immigration, about Germans taking pride in being German, in no longer having to apologize to the world.

He drank his coffee and watched the police nearby. They were alert but not overly concerned; still he decided to shift his position so he could easily retreat into the park, should the mood change. The gun, while offering some protection, also increased the danger—police wouldn't appreciate an armed foreigner walking around the city. Best to avoid confrontation.

But his concern was unnecessary. The speakers concluded. The crowd began to dissipate, and with them, the police, even as young men and women circled through the crowd.

A young woman approached him. Blonde straight hair falling to her shoulders, the features of a model, and eyes of an unusually vivid green, she smiled at him and offered a pen and a clipboard. Pretty, but probably not an important player in the group, given what he knew about Germany Now and Frederick Bauer.

"*Nein. Danke. Wo ist Frederick Bauer?*" He asked for the man he had arranged to meet.

His accent gave him away. She responded in English with a Texan accent. "You're the guy he was expecting?"

"Yes. Michael Hall. And you are?"

"Lisette Vogel."

"You're an American?"

She laughed. "No, German, but I lived in Austin. Came home a few years ago."

"Austin used to be a nice place. Going to shit like everywhere else."

"At least there's good barbeque. Pleased to meet you, Michael. Your first visit to Germany?"

"Yes." It was true. Although he was a seasoned traveler, he'd never been in Germany except on stopovers to other destinations.

"Is it everything you expected?"

"Hard to say. I just arrived. I'll let you know."

"Fair enough. I'll take you to Frederick."

* * * * *

Frederick Bauer was younger than Michael had expected, maybe somewhere in his late twenties, a shock of brown hair, dressed in jeans and a blue button-down shirt. Frederick broke off his conversation with a middle-aged man, who was arguing with him, and stretched out a hand to Michael. "Welcome. I was hoping you'd make it." His English was excellent, but he, unlike Lisette, didn't sound like he'd spent ten years in America. He didn't look much like his online images, either, but then neither did Michael. Both by design.

"I said I would."

They shook hands. Frederick had a firm grip. His tone was friendly, warm, in strong contrast to the anger expressed during his speech. One was an act, but which one? "Have you seen anything of Berlin yet?"

"Not much. I walked around the garden."

"Did you visit the monstrosity over there?" Frederick waved towards the Memorial to the Murdered Jews.

"Yes. A lot of wasted land."

27

"Worse. It's a blight scarring one of Berlin's best-known monuments and gardens. More than that I won't say here." Frederick glanced around. Michael assumed he was checking for police. "Have you eaten? Join us."

Michael hesitated. "I didn't realize there would be a crowd."

Frederick was surrounded by maybe half a dozen young men—and three young women: Lisette, a woman with dark hair in a long braid, and another blonde in a flowered dress. Frederick waved a casual hand. "You need to get to know them as well. You'll be working with them. And you'll like the restaurant we go to—good hamburgers." Then he placed a hand on the back of Lisette's neck, a possessive gesture, sending a distinct, if unnecessary, message to Michael.

Still, Michael almost smiled at the stereotype of Americans, especially since he was not a big hamburger eater. "Good beer too, I hope?"

"Of course. You are in Berlin."

7

BERLIN, GERMANY

LISETTE LIKED THE BIG rallies for Germany Now. She circulated, passed out literature, and got a good view of the attendees. While always on the alert for the man with the wolf tattoo whose features were burned into her mind, she hadn't seen him yet. At least she didn't think so.

But while she hadn't yet spotted her father's killer, she'd located other targets.

She noted those who interested her, placing a barely perceptible dot next to the name of those interested in violence or whose appearance raised questions. Former members of *Der Dritte Weg* merited attention. But she was deliberate, and she was always sure before she finalized a decision. After she had a name, she'd check out the social media and police records.

The Equality Institute had been a good resource. They had published information on almost all her targets. Surprisingly, or perhaps not so surprisingly, quite a few of her targets had been mentioned in police reports as suspects in unsolved killings. But the police had done nothing.

She had.

It took time and effort, and she had to be careful not to leave any search history, in case Frederick ever checked her computer, but the effort was worth it.

As much as she wanted to hunt down and kill Nazi murderers, she didn't want to kill the wrong person by accident. She was proud of her record. The future was equally promising.

She had a few names on her list from which to select her next kill.

If the murderers were too close to Frederick, she'd left them alone—so far. Right now, in the aftermath of killing Karl, she was a little worried that Frederick might be watching her. She'd take her time choosing the next target. Someone not so close to Frederick so that he might not find out about their murder right away. Or... she could change her methods, so the killing wasn't obviously a murder.

The rally in front of the Brandenburg Gate had been useful. She'd noted a few potentials. And now, as she stood with Frederick and the others, chatting with the American, she ran the prospects through her mind.

She'd do more research later to narrow it down.

Then she turned her attention to the newcomer.

The American, Michael Hall, had not displayed the usual signals that she relied on in making her selections. No tattoos. No boasting. Good looking, tall and blond, he seemed polite and a little reserved. No official membership in a white supremacist organization.

Frederick probably knew more. He always did, and he didn't share much in the way of information with her. She was not part of the planning circle, even though she was sleeping with him. As a woman, she was there to support, not to plan. She cooked for Frederick, and she fucked him when he wanted it. At rallies, she gathered names, listened adoringly and applauded his speeches. And she had access to information. Not everything, but enough.

If that required her to applaud, act docile, and fuck Frederick—she was okay with it. Under other circumstances, she might have found it humiliating, but even if she otherwise considered her role degrading, it gave her the chance to eliminate Nazis. And she did get some amusement out of playing the submissive woman, while secretly killing Frederick's followers. Eventually, she'd kill Frederick, but not yet. Although she liked the idea of telling him exactly how stupid he'd been before she slit his throat when the time came.

However, the conversation from the previous night required some adjustment in her plans. Was Frederick suspicious of her? Could she have slipped up?

Wouldn't he have already killed her if he suspected her?

The thought gave her a small trill of fear. Not that fear was bad. It sharpened her, kept her focused. A little fear was her friend.

And, if she was honest with herself, she enjoyed the sensation. Like being on a roller coaster—only more intense.

She turned her mind back to the present and to the new recruit.

Was the American a killer? Frederick knew something about the man, and she'd probably find out more over dinner.

If he was—she'd decide whether eliminating him was worth the risk.

8

FORMER EAST BERLIN, GERMANY

PRENZLAUER BERG, IN WHAT used to be East Berlin, had mostly been built up in the nineteenth century, offering workers apartments that lacked amenities like bathrooms. In the aftermath of World War II, the buildings were not modernized. The residents preferred the concrete monstrosities built by the East German government, which at least offered modern conveniences like toilets. By the late 1980s, the area was largely deserted—with the East German police cracking down on artists and musicians squatting in the empty buildings. In the years following the fall of the Berlin Wall, young people began trickling back, searching for affordable housing, making Prenzlauer Berg trendy, with bars and eclectic restaurants. Michael knew much of this from tour books, but he nodded politely as Frederick recited the history on the drive to the restaurant.

They wound up in a private back room at Der Zauberberg—a restaurant named for Thomas Mann's famous novel—where the group shared a long table. Frederick sat at the head of the table, waving Michael to a seat next to him, and without a signal or a protest from the others, Lisette took the seat on Frederick's other side.

Hamburgers with bacon and sides of French fries were ordered for the group, washed down with a local beer. Frederick ordered for the entire table, one of the apparent prerogatives of leadership. Michael did wonder what would happen if anyone preferred dumplings or bratwurst. He also wondered if the meal choice was in his honor.

They made small talk while they waited for the food and the beers. Frederick, his hand possessively closed on Lisette's, asked Michael about his flight and his hotel. Lisette asked him if he had a girlfriend, and what he thought of German women. He answered the questions about the hotel and the flight and deflected questions about a girlfriend, although he did express appreciation for the beauty of German women. After the food arrived and the server disappeared, the subject changed.

"What made you decide to join us?" Frederick waited until he was between bites of burger to ask the question.

"I already explained."

"Tell me again." He fixed his gaze on Michael.

Michael drank his beer, noting that it wasn't helping his exhaustion. "The whole world is going to shit. Fucking immigrants. Fucking global elites."

"Global elites? You mean Jews, don't you?"

"Jews and the people who collaborate with them in destroying the white man. Can't get good jobs. Can't buy a house. I wanted to join up with people who think like I do. Maybe learn stuff I could take back home."

"Yes. You know when I was a kid, just starting to think about the world, I didn't worry about Jews." Frederick finished his beer and looked around for the server, a young dark-haired woman. "Wait a minute, let me order another round."

She served the beers, disappeared, and Frederick continued. "We were all told the lies in school about gas chambers and six million murdered and ordered not to question it. I didn't, not at first. I was angry that the Turks, who came here as temporary workers in the '60s, just kept staying. And staying. And then brought more of them here. They brought their culture, their language, and we were just supposed to accept it. And I was supposed to be ashamed of being German—and they kept coming in, more and more.

"Then I realized that it was all about the money. Cheap labor for big international businesses. That the Jews I thought were gone—

weren't—and they were orchestrating it as they had orchestrated so much misery in the past, just as they created a fake story about being murdered in gas chambers. Now there are about two hundred thousand Jews in Germany, and they're up to the usual. And to add insult to injury: a Jew's running an organization called the Equality Institute, helping the scum who have flooded this country from Arab countries, and attacking patriots like us. Exposing our members and costing them their jobs. Putting out propaganda."

It was a long speech, but Frederick obviously liked to give long speeches.

"You're planning to do something about it?"

"Of course we are. Germany Now is going to get the right people elected." Frederick smiled. "Five supporters of Germany Now are members of the Bundestag. Did you think we were planning violence?"

"The thought occurred to me—since you were interested in my knowledge of weaponry."

Frederick waved a hand. "We're not the Nazi party of the 1930s. We want to accomplish our aims peacefully. But our members are under attack. Some are even being murdered. They need to know how to defend themselves."

"I understand. In America, we know the importance of self-defense."

"And you learned about weapons where?"

"Learned to shoot as a kid. That good enough for you? I always carry a gun."

"Even now?"

Michael nodded.

Frederick leaned over to whisper in Lisette's ear. She smiled and shook her head. He returned his attention to Michael. "Do you have family in Germany?"

"Not now."

"But you did."

"Years ago."

"Years ago?" Frederick grinned. "Maybe eighty years back? Are you ashamed?"

"Not at all."

"Then why are you being cagey. I don't understand. You agreed to come here. Offered your services." He gestured at the table. "Don't you trust us?"

"I don't trust anyone very much. This could all be a trap. American intelligence can be very clever."

The table erupted into laughter.

Michael tensed. "What's the joke?"

"Well, there's a certain lack of trust all around. Especially since you lied about your real name. Did you think we couldn't find out who you really are? You're not that talented at covering your trail on the internet. Especially when we have people like Heinrich?"

He pointed to Heinrich, who looked like he wasn't out of his teen years, seated to Michael's right. Heinrich grinned and touched two fingers to his forehead in a salute.

Michael picked up his beer and checked his hands. No shaking. Good. "Do you want to see my passport?"

"Someone already saw your passport." Frederick took a bite of his hamburger and chewed slowly. Then he spoke again. "We have people everywhere. Why do you think I suggested you stay at the Paradise Hotel? The front desk clerk is one of us. Anyway, a passport means nothing, Nickolas. You can get good fake passports with the right connections."

He'd known that Frederick would probably penetrate the Michael identity, but he played it cool.

"You're not going to deny it?"

"Deny what?"

"That you're really Nickolas Kruger, not Michael Hall."

"Maybe."

Frederick continued as if reciting. "You are the grandson of Adolph Kruger, a member of the Waffen SS. Your father, Richard Kruger, died in a car accident when you were five, and your Ukrainian mother raised you in a Ukrainian community in the greater Chicago area. After you got out of high school, you joined the army and were good enough to become an Army Ranger until you were dishonorably discharged for killing civilians in Afghanistan five years ago."

Michael finished his beer. "So?"

"So—you don't have to hide with us. Most of us have family that had to hide. My grandfather was a concentration camp guard. Heinrich's great grandfather helped write the Nuremberg laws. Lisette's great grandfather was at Sobibor, Poland." Frederick nodded at Lisette.

Michael glanced at her. She smiled at him.

"That was two generations ago, and we're still being shamed. For something that didn't even happen." Frederick leaned over. "It's illegal to deny the Holocaust here. Shhhh." He pressed a finger to lips.

"In public," Lisette said.

"It's still illegal, even in private, to deny the Holocaust. And, yes, I just did, but who's going to tell on me?" Frederick said.

"It's not illegal in America." The server appeared with a new round of beers. Michael picked up his and drank.

Frederick laughed. "No, but killing people is."

"Killing people is illegal in most places."

"The point is—I know you're wanted for murder. That's why you were eager to get out of the country, correct?"

"It was self-defense. The son of a bitch attacked me."

"If you say so, Nick."

No one ever called him Nick. "Why don't we stick to Michael? It's what's on my passport—and better to be consistent." He was so tired that he was feeling dizzy. Or maybe it was the beer and the heavy meal.

"Very good." Frederick nodded. "Michael, then. You were worried that we could be working with American officials. We worry about the same. About you."

"You seem to know everything about me."

"We know a lot. It doesn't mean that we're not still cautious."

"I'm feeling really groggy." Exhaustion and the beer, no doubt.

Laughter around the table again.

"We're going to get you back to your hotel so you can get some sleep. Tomorrow, though, you're going to prove that you're one of us."

"Fine. What do you want me to do?"

Frederick leaned and spoke the words so quietly that no one else at the table, let alone the serving staff could have heard. "You're going to use that gun you're carrying and shoot Ben Rosenberg, the Jew director of the Equality Institute here in Berlin."

"What? You're kidding? What about the whole—we're a peaceful group—was that just bullshit?"

He had anticipated the possibility of being asked to commit a murder, but he'd hoped that it wouldn't happen.

Frederick took a long swig of beer. "No. It was not. We don't resort to violence, except in self-defense. We're pretty sure that the Equality Institute is responsible for the murders of six of our people. The police do nothing. We have to act."

"I'm already on the run. I don't want to do something stupid that'll get me on the radar of the German police."

"We scoped it all out, and it's safe. Ben Rosenberg keeps his car in a garage near the Institute, and he's had death threats from Syrian immigrants who hate Jews. That's who they'll look for."

Michael shook his head. "A garage. There'll be cameras."

"We'll take care of the cameras, a few hours before. They won't have time to get them fixed."

"And if I'm caught?"

"Did it worry you when you shot the Black activist in D.C.?" Frederick took a long drink of his beer.

"That was not planned. It just happened."

"So you're sorry you did it?"

"No. He was threatening me. And he deserved it."

"Is it the fact that we're planning ahead of time that's bothering you? Or that you'll be killing a Jew instead of a Black?" Frederick set his beer down. "Do you have moral qualms about killing?"

"I've killed a lot of people." That was certainly true. "I don't have any problem with killing a Jew. I just don't want the German police after me."

"We have people in the police. We have people in the intelligence service. And as I said, we've checked it out." Frederick looked hard at him. "We have to know that you're committed. You claim to be a supporter. I have to be sure. Are you in? Otherwise, you should just go back to the U.S."

There was an unspoken threat there—that Frederick would use his connections to the police to inform them of Michael's presence—if Michael didn't go along.

He wasn't happy about it. But he'd come too far to just back out.

Michael took a deep breath. "I'm in."

9

BERLIN, GERMANY

AFTER DINNER, HE WAS driven back to his hotel. Frederick and Lisette accompanied him. They followed him through the lobby, up to his room, and waited while Michael fished out his key.

"Are you planning to tell me a bedtime story?" He swung the door open.

"Until tomorrow night, I'm sticking close by. I have a room across the hall." Frederick gestured. "You're not to go anywhere or speak to anyone. And give me your phone."

"No. I have private shit on my phone."

"I'm not interested in your private life, although if you're with us, your life should be an open book. But I need to be sure you won't contact anyone. If you use the hotel phone, I'll know."

"I agreed to do what you asked."

"This is insurance."

He rolled his eyes but handed over the phone. "Fine."

"And your password?" Frederick held up a hand. "I'm not interested in your sex life."

"More insurance?"

"Of course."

Michael recited a series of numbers and letters. "I want my phone back tomorrow."

"After. Have a pleasant sleep."

"Goodnight." He shut the door and locked it. The exhaustion flooded his body. Not just exhaustion. Now that he was alone, no longer performing, the anxiety over what he'd been asked to do triggered the PTSD symptoms. Images of a cold dark room and a stocky man with a cigar in his hand popped into his mind, and he felt himself shaking. He did his breathing and his mantra—and he calmed. Then he was just tired. He looked longingly at the bed, but he had a few things to do before he could sleep.

He headed to the bathroom where he'd hidden the second cell phone.

* * * * *

"You're coming tomorrow." They were in bed. Frederick, after a particularly athletic sexual performance and an after-sex whiskey, was close to sleep.

"When Michael kills the Jew? You want me to come?"

"What I said. Do you have a problem with it?"

"No, of course not. But you've never asked me to come with you on any kind of operation before."

"If you're going to be my partner, I have to be sure."

"Sure?" She tried to keep her voice puzzled, not alarmed, although she was. "Sure about what?"

"Sure you're my partner. In every way. Now sleep."

He was snoring two minutes later. She waited another ten minutes before untangling herself from Frederick's arms and sliding out of bed. Why did he want her on a planned kill?

She thought about her father's murder and the six men she'd killed.

If Frederick knew, he'd kill her. She remembered his comment just a few days earlier, that there was a traitor in the group. A woman traitor. Was he starting to suspect her? Did he want to see what she'd do—how she'd react—to having an innocent man killed in front of her?

Maybe she should get out.

But she wouldn't. She was close. So very close. And maybe he didn't really suspect. Could she walk away when she was this close to finding her father's killer? Could she stop avenging the people murdered by neo-Nazis?

The answer was no.

Her life from the age of nine had been devoted to avenging her father. Nothing else had mattered to her.

The man who had shot her father had taken more than a beloved parent. He'd taken away hobbits and Santa Claus. He'd taken away her past with her father, but also her possibility of a normal life—a job, a family.

AUSTIN, TEXAS

It'd taken years of planning and plotting to get to where she was. She'd indeed spent twelve years in Austin, Texas, where her mother had fled after her father's death. Her mother remarried. Her stepfather, rich and generous, adopted her, and she took his surname.

"It's not healthy to dwell on bad things, Lisette," her mother would tell her.

Her father lived on only in her mind. And her father's memory was the only thing that offered her comfort and warmth.

Her mother couldn't offer her the same kind of warmth. After moving to Texas, her mother became involved in the country club and in the local church. She'd pushed Lisette to achieve in school, told Lisette not to associate with the children she designated as "socially undesirable"—Blacks, Latinos, Asians, Jews.

"What happened to your father could happen to you. I want you to make friends with the right people."

"I don't like your friends' kids." Even at ten, she knew they were spoiled brats who looked down on people who weren't rich. Or white.

Her mother could acknowledge some of the truth, but her priority was blending in. "I don't like all of them. But some aren't so bad. And it's safe."

By the time she was thirteen, Lisette was accustomed to feeling alone. She didn't fit in with the type of kids her mother wanted her to associate with, and she wasn't allowed friendship with the kids she might have liked.

She did learn to pretend.

Her mother never seemed to notice that Lisette wasn't happy, or if she noticed, didn't care. She did care that Lisette dressed well, ate well, did well in school.

Lisette loved her mother, liked her stepfather, and knew that her mother loved her. Still, it was a cold love, compared to what her father had offered her.

But life in Texas hadn't been completely terrible. With her mother's blessing, she'd learned to ride horses and developed a true passion for jumping and for the horse her stepfather bought her. She learned to shoot, and she studied martial arts. She acted in school plays. Without her mother's blessing, she secretly learned how to kill, watching videos about assassinations on the dark web. She studied poisons, reading volumes by a renowned Boston pathologist, Dr. Lily Robinson.

And she knew that she had to be a mystery. Fortunately, her mother had adopted an alias after her father's death and before leaving Germany. Remarriage had only solidified the new identity.

Lisette was careful in her use of social media, even as a teenager, revealing only the most mundane and boring pictures and facts. Pictures of animals. Pictures of clouds.

On her eighteenth birthday, her stepfather deposited one million dollars in a bank for her.

"If you don't spend it except for college expenses, when you're twenty-one, you'll get another five million."

She didn't spend it, knowing the money would be useful. But college was also useful. She took classes in chemistry and in forensic science. It was important to know not just how to kill, but how to avoid getting caught. She studied German literature and German history. She found she liked Goethe and Thomas Mann.

She had her first sexual experience as a freshman in college with Max, a boy she had a crush on. It was the first time she'd ever considered abandoning her quest. He told her that he loved her and that she was special. But then she walked into an off-campus bookstore and saw him kissing another woman.

She'd run from the bookstore, but he'd caught up with her.

"Hey. Did you think you were the only woman I was dating?"

"Go fuck yourself." She tore off a necklace that he'd given her and threw it at his feet.

A few days later, he came down with a serious stomach virus and was out of class for a week. It'd been a little tricky poisoning his coffee and in just the right amount to make him sick but not kill him. Being a jerk wasn't deserving of death.

She returned her focus to revenge.

She enjoyed sex, and she was good at it, but she never again allowed herself to become emotionally attached, choosing partners who only wanted a casual hookup.

The problem since she'd been nine was not that she didn't feel, but that she felt too intensely. First gut-wrenching sadness and guilt. Then the loneliness and the anger. A brief period of romantic attachment—only to be reminded that she was alone and could trust no one—which just intensified her anger.

She received the second infusion of cash after she graduated.

At twenty-two, she returned to Germany. Her mother remained in Austin with her stepfather. Lisette sent birthday and Christmas presents but rarely called.

She found a job and an apartment in Berlin, and slowly began to immerse herself in the anti-immigrant movement and the far right, creating a white supremacist online presence. Lisette also contacted her grandmother, discovered she needed a nurse and financial assistance, and gave both—along with a little psychological torture. It was the least her grandmother deserved for her lifelong devotion to Adolph Hitler and Nazism.

It took her months to work her way into the inner circle of Frederick Bauer's group, which publicly promised political action against the "enemy"—Muslim immigrants, Jews, liberal Germans—and secretly endorsed violence.

It was another few months before she went to bed with Frederick.

She quickly became more than just an occasional sex partner. All the while she gathered information and names.

BERLIN, GERMANY

Now she faced a crisis.

Not only was she worried that Frederick suspected her, but she knew what would happen the next day.

She'd never been in this position before—knowing that an innocent person was about to be murdered—in part because Frederick blamed the Jewish director of the Equality Institute for murders she had committed. That made her responsible, didn't it?

Did Ben Rosenberg also have children who would be devastated—who would never get over his murder?

She could stop it.

Kill Frederick now. If he were dead, the attack wouldn't go forward.

If she did kill him, her quest would be over. Even if she could tell a good enough story to convince both the police and the neo-Nazis that someone else, maybe a crazed Syrian, had broken in and murdered Frederick in the middle of the night, she'd never be trusted again. Never be this close to the inner circle. She'd have lost her chance to avenge her father.

Kill the American. Michael. Nickolas. Whatever his name was. He was already on her list after the conversation at dinner, when she'd learned he'd killed someone in America. Geography and jurisdiction might make a difference to the authorities, but not to her.

Still, killing Michael before the morning presented similar problems. She'd meticulously planned every other execution. Killing Michael without adequate planning increased the risk. She'd blow her cover and her chance for revenge.

Nothing mattered more than finding her father's murderer. And killing other murderers.

But she couldn't just let an innocent man die.

She came up with a solution, not a perfect solution, and it might not work. But it was something.

She carried her phone into the bathroom, and sitting on the toilet, she searched for the Equality Institute, locating the name of the director, Ben Rosenberg.

She typed an email stating that there was a threat against his life and warning him not to go into work the next day. She sent it and then deleted the message from her phone. Even if Frederick became suspicious and went through her emails, he wouldn't find it. Unless he was suspicious enough to put a tech expert on it, but by that point, she'd be dead.

She returned to the bedroom and slipped in next to Frederick, who slept on his back, but he turned his head and opened his eyes to stare at her.

"Everything okay?" Frederick looked more awake than she'd expected. Had he been watching her?

"Stomach a little upset. Maybe the burgers."

"I have just the right medicine." He pulled her over and pushed his hand between her legs.

Although despite her feelings towards him, she sometimes did enjoy the sex, at that moment, she had no interest, absorbed in thoughts of the next day and the planned assassination. Nevertheless, she did what she had to do. "That's good, baby." She pulled him down into her.

10

BERLIN, GERMANY

THE EQUALITY INSTITUTE OCCUPIED three floors of a modern building in Grunewald district of Berlin, an area that housed various embassies and bordered on Grunewald Forest, 3,000 acres of woods and lakes that had once been the preserve of the very wealthy and now was open to the general public. The Institute was one part museum, offering displays of injustice and hate, some from the Nazi era, some from the past twenty years in Germany, one part informational, keeping the public apprised of the threat of the new far right, and one part activism, tracking and exposing neo-Nazis.

The Director, Ben Rosenberg, was a British ex-pat who lived in Berlin with his wife Rachel and their two sons. His grandmother had been part of the Kinder transports in the 1930s, which took Jewish children from Nazi Germany to Britain and spared her the fate of her own parents. Ben's grandfather had survived Auschwitz. He told Ben stories about the camps and also of good non-Jews who'd risked their lives to help. The list of the Righteous Among Nations at Vad Yashem held the names of many Germans.

Ben was favorably impressed when he visited Berlin for a job interview at a museum. Germany had made huge efforts to move forward from the past. Memorials to the dead were everywhere. Not just the large memorials: plaques on the sidewalks memorialized Jewish people who had been murdered. Average Germans were friendly and became even more so when they realized he was Jewish and the grandson of Holocaust survivors. He decided to make the move.

While there were always neo-Nazis, there were not so many that it worried him. Not at first.

Then it began to grow. The hatred. The rhetoric.

The early targets were more likely to be immigrants from Turkey and the Middle East or people who helped them. After all, there weren't that many Jews left in Germany, not when he first arrived, although the influx of Jews from the former Soviet Union did raise the numbers. But it was the same ideology that had marked six million Jewish men, women, and children for death: the idea that non-white, non-Christian people somehow degraded the standard of living, made Germany less safe, stole jobs, changed the culture. While the adherents remained a vocal minority, opposed by most Germans, the rhetoric against Jews rose as well. Nevertheless, Germany continued to be a favored destination for Jews. In the years since his own arrival, more Jews returned to Germany, some from Israel, some from the former Soviet Union. Berlin now had almost 30,000 Jews.

Yet, the return of Jews also prompted the return of the old-style anti-Semitism.

In whispers, these new Nazis denied the Holocaust. More loudly, they spoke of global elites, code for Jews, bringing in brown and Muslim people to replace them. Nor did they consider Jews to be white.

After the murder of an African immigrant and street peddler ten years earlier, Ben was instrumental in helping found the Equality Institute. He and the other founders chose to set it in Grunewald because of the Track 17 Memorial at the Grunewald train station where tens of thousands of Jews had been sent to their deaths.

Both a museum and a force for social activism, the Institute tracked down and exposed neo-Nazis. One of those rare places where Jews and immigrants from Arab countries formed a partnership, the Institute had even been responsible for providing information that led to the United States expelling a ninety-seven-year-old former concentration camp guard and for the capture of various neo-Nazis inside Germany who had committed violent crimes. The death threats followed.

Ben took precautions. He parked in a garage with security, and he was careful not to take the same route home every night. He wore a baseball cap instead of a yarmulka outside the Institute, to avoid attacks both by neo-Nazis and by fanatical Muslims. He'd had death threats from members of Germany Now and from a Syrian group.

To enter the Institute required passing through a metal detector. And there were security guards.

So far the threats against him personally had just been empty air—which was why he didn't take seriously the warning in his email that morning— one of about a dozen death threats he received the same morning—and every morning. The majority were from neo-Nazis. A few were from Muslim extremists. His practice was to send threatening emails on to the police although he realized that they would do little or nothing.

That morning as usual, he forwarded the death threats to the police—as useless as it might be. The warning wasn't exactly a threat, so he didn't send it.

Sometime in the afternoon, his secretary knocked on the door and informed him that a young woman wanted to speak to him about volunteering. She ushered in a young and lovely Black woman who announced her name as Tehila. She didn't give her last name.

"Do you mind if we speak in English?" she asked. "I only know a few words in German."

"Of course." He gestured her to sit across from him. "Do you live in Berlin?"

"Visiting from the U.S."

"So—why do you want to volunteer?"

"I like the work you do. And I have some spare time. My partner is teaching a course here for a few weeks."

He tried to analyze her accent. It wasn't British. It didn't sound like any of the American accents he'd heard over the years. Nor did she sound African. It was something else, something vaguely familiar.

But he dismissed the thought. Americans were Americans. "We can always use volunteers. Would you like to help with tours? Or exhibits?"

She shook her head. "Those aren't exactly my area of expertise."

"Which is?"

"I'm offering you my services as a bodyguard. You're in danger."

He looked at her in surprise and, for the first time, noticed the necklace she wore—a silver chain with a mezuzah. What an idiot he was for assuming she wasn't Jewish. He mentally kicked himself, and then he placed her accent and her name. "Israeli? What's your surname, Tehila?" He switched to Hebrew, which he spoke fluently, to test her.

"I live in Washington now, but yes, I was born in Israel." She wore a bulky sweater that did little to hide her curves. She ignored the question of her last name and also switched to Hebrew, speaking with an Israeli accent.

"And how do you know I'm in danger?"

"It's not hard to figure out. And I have friends who know things."

"Friends?"

"Who know things. Not from the internet."

"And what exactly is your profession?"

"Let's just say I have had experience dealing with terrorists."

"You work in security?"

"You could say that."

"Police?"

"Not exactly."

"In America or in Israel?"

She tilted her head and didn't answer.

So, not police. Someone who knows people who know things. Was she in intelligence? He made a guess. "Mossad?"

"No, I don't work for Mossad."

"You're using present tense."

"Yes. I am." She met his gaze, and there was a long moment of silence during which he evaluated her calm self-assurance.

"I don't think it would help the Institute to have a Mossad agent protecting me." He remembered her qualification. "Even if she is a former Mossad agent." The Equality Institute promoted good relations in Germany between Muslims, Jews, and Germans, and there was a tacit agreement to disagree on—and not discuss—the topic of Israel. Outside, there were tensions between the Jewish and Muslim communities. The Institute managed a delicate balancing act. Having a Mossad agent for protection could destroy that balance.

"I never said that I formerly worked for Mossad."

"Correct. But you're not denying it."

"Also correct. However, it is true that I do possess certain... skills, as well as information. Skills which you are in imminent need of."

What did she know that he didn't?

"Imminent?"

"Yes." She emphatically pronounced the word.

"Are you carrying a gun?"

"I went through the metal detector."

"That's not an answer."

"It's an answer, maybe not the one you want."

"I don't think..." he started.

"It doesn't particularly matter what you think."

"Let me explain the mission of the Institute," he began.

"No need." She raised a hand to interrupt him. "I already know. That's why I'm here. No one needs to know where I was born or who you think I formerly worked for. It's irrelevant. Whether you like it or not—here's what will happen. I will hang around the Institute this afternoon. This evening I will walk you to your car, and then I will follow to your home in my car. In the morning, I will check your car, and then follow you here."

"That's ridiculous. I can't have you following me."

"Just for a few days. Until I get word that the risk is over."

He shook his head again. "Thank you, but no thank you."

"This isn't a choice. You can call the police and have them toss me out. But I'll just wait for you in the garage."

"You think the risk is that serious?"

"I know the risk is that serious."

He thought about his wife and his two sons. He deeply believed in

God, but then he knew that God worked in mysterious ways. Maybe it was God who had sent this woman. "Maybe for a few days, then."

"Good." She stood. "Do you have coffee?"

"I'll show you the lounge. And we have snacks."

"Kosher?"

"Of course."

11

BERLIN, GERMANY

MICHAEL SLEPT IN UNTIL ten, a sleep interrupted by only one nightmare, in which he was chained and lying on a cement floor. He woke, sweating, but a few minutes of his breathing exercises calmed him, and he returned to a dreamless sleep. When he finally blinked awake, it took him a moment to remember where he was. Then he did—a hotel in Berlin. And he remembered why he was in that hotel and what he had to do. For a moment, he regretted his decision, that he wasn't waking up in his own bed, next to the woman he loved, but the moment passed.

He pushed out of bed, stretched, did twenty pushups, and then showered and dressed, complete with a concealed weapon, a 9mm Ruger. A few calming breaths, a mental checklist, and then he was good to go. He picked up his key, left the room, and headed to the ground floor and the hotel's restaurant.

Frederick and Lisette nursed cups of coffee at a table with a view of the hotel's main exit. To slip out unnoticed, even if he wanted to, he'd have had to go through the kitchen.

He took a seat at their table and nodded a good morning.

The table was filled with plates of cheeses, fruit, vegetables, sausage, smoked fish, three different kinds of bread, honey, blackberry jam, and gooseberry jam. He raised eyebrows. "That's a lot of food for this time of day."

A young woman delivered him a cup of coffee. He dumped in two spoonfuls of sugar and then helped himself to a slice of a dark brown bread and a hunk of cheese.

"You should have a real German breakfast." Frederick pointed to the sausages. "Those are excellent."

He sipped his coffee. "If this is how you eat every day, I'm surprised you're not real fat Germans."

He half expected Frederick to be offended, but Frederick just laughed.

"We compensate by eating small dinners. And unlike Americans, we do a lot of walking."

"I exercise enough." He finished his bread and coffee. "Now what?"

"Now we'll show you the city."

"And our business?"

"Later this afternoon."

"Everything will be taken care of? Cameras? Security guards?"

"Timing will be tight, but we should be good."

He caught an eagerness in Frederick's expression. Frederick was looking forward to this. Lisette seemed to be as well, although he felt an odd vibe from her. She caught his gaze.

"You're quiet today, Michael."

"Need more coffee."

It was going to be an interesting day. Interesting and difficult.

* * * * *

It was a fairly pleasant day. If he hadn't known better, he'd have thought that Lisette and Frederick were professional tour guides. He saw the memorial to the Berlin Wall and Checkpoint Charlie. They also toured Gendarmenmarkt, twin churches flanking a graceful baroque square, and, at Lisette's insistence, Berlin's most famous chocolatier, Rausch, just off the square. They stood in front of the Reichstag, the seat of German government, and Lisette pointed out the glass dome of the remodeled building that had become one of Berlin's major tourist attractions. Going inside was out of the question, given that they would have to pass through security.

They didn't tour the Jewish Museum or any memorials to those murdered by the Third Reich. Frederick pointed out a few bricks on a sidewalk with names of murdered Jews without additional comment, but the three of them were in the open, with people walking by. Michael could tell from Frederick's tone that the bricks angered him.

Every now and then, Michael thought he caught a glimpse of one of Frederick's followers from the night before. But he wasn't sure. And no one ever approached.

Frederick did most of the talking, with Lisette hanging on his arm and laughing at every joke. By two o'clock, Michael suggested lunch. His leg still couldn't take unlimited walking and was starting to ache.

Frederick led the way to a street vendor, who offered currywurst, sausage topped by a ketchup curry sauce—a Berlin specialty. They found a nearby bench to sit and eat: Michael on one end, stretching out his right leg, Lisette next to him, and on her far side, Frederick.

"Nervous?" she asked.

"Not at all."

"Your hands are shaking."

"It happens periodically. It will stop." All true. He'd also hoped his demons would stay quiet for the day, but he never knew.

Still, it was manageable.

Until it wasn't. He could almost hear her voice.

"Do you have a physical problem?"

He took deep calming breaths, performed his mental exercise, and the shaking eased. "Not really. Souvenir of past bad times." He refrained from details, although he could have described Afghanistan, where he'd spent time, even if Afghanistan wasn't the reason his hands were shaking.

Frederick went with what he believed to be the reason for the tremors.

"I can't imagine what Afghanistan was like," Frederick said. "People like you shouldn't have been there."

"They did attack my country."

"Your country should have nuked the place."

"I didn't make the decision. I just obeyed orders." It was neutral and also true. "I'd like my phone back."

"Not yet," Frederick said. "Afterward. Anyway, no one has tried to reach you."

"Not the point. I'm tired of sightseeing." He decided not to mention his bad leg. "I'd just as soon sit here and read."

"We'll visit the lake in Grunewald Forest. Enjoy nature. And we'll be near our destination," Frederick said. "But I'm holding onto the phone—unless you want to back out."

Lisette turned intense green eyes on him.

"We've been over this. Not backing out," Michael said.

* * * * *

Frederick didn't tell either Lisette or Michael, but he also had a gun. Because the day was a test for both of them. If Michael wavered, Frederick would kill him. He hoped that he wouldn't have to. Michael would be a valuable addition to the group. He hoped even more that Lisette wouldn't try to interfere or indicate that she was less than committed to the cause. Maybe he loved her, but before committing to her, he had to be sure. If she were the vigilante who was killing Germany Now supporters, she was unlikely to just let a Jew be murdered in front of her. She'd do something. If she did, it would hurt him—but he'd kill her too.

12

BERLIN, GERMANY

BEN SPENT THE REST of the day on the phone, on the computer, or in meetings over the new extremist wing of the Germany Now party. He was also concerned about the warnings he'd received, both the anonymous warning he'd received in email and the warning delivered by Tehila. He called to the police to follow up on the emails he'd forwarded, and an officer had stopped by to question him. He took notes and left.

Tehila had made herself scarce while the officer was present. There was no point dragging her into it. She was not going to disclose sources. Her being a former Mossad agent, which he assumed despite her refusal to confirm it, would not go over well either.

Anyway, would the police take her warning any more seriously than they'd taken the email?

He doubted it.

As promised, Tehila stayed the entire day.

Sometimes, he saw her chatting with visitors to the museum section or helping staff with filing. He sat with her in the snack room for half an hour for a coffee break. He learned that her partner was female and a history professor, that Tehila liked her coffee with cream and sugar, and that she recited the correct *berakhah*—the Jewish blessing— before indulging in food or drink. He talked about his boys, his wife, and his work, and when he went back to his office, realized how little she had divulged about herself.

The staff liked her. His secretary Lena and Tehila exchanged recipes. Ernestina, his second in command, a young woman immigrant from Ghana, told Ben that she approved. The twins, Hasan and Ahmet, two college age German-Turkish men who worked part-time for the Institute tracking neo-Nazi activity online, seemed particularly interested in her. Ben decided not to mention to either that she had a partner or his belief that she had been Mossad.

Sometimes, Ben had no idea where Tehila was or what she was doing. She just disappeared.

At around seven, when he packed his briefcase and exchanged his yarmulka for a baseball cap, she reappeared.

"I thought you'd left," Ben said.

"Not yet."

Entering the elevator with her at his side, to get to the garage floor where his car was parked, he felt the weirdness of the situation. He envisioned telling his wife that a very attractive former Mossad agent had spent the day in the office following him. He decided not to describe Tehila in great detail. Tehila sensed what he was thinking.

"Your wife will just be happy that you're safe."

She hit the button for level two.

How did she know what floor his car was on?

* * * * *

Michael, Lisette, and Frederick left the lake at six. It had been a pretty setting if a little chilly, although there were still people swimming and one or two nude sunbathers. Getting close to nature, Michael supposed, although it seemed a little odd to be nude in a park. It was common and accepted in Germany. He imagined the response to spontaneous nudity in an American park. Lisette jokingly suggested that they all take off their clothes, or at least Michael assumed it had been a joke. He had no intention of letting either of them see his body. He had scars that required an explanation. But taking off their clothes might have exposed his gun, so it wasn't a serious suggestion.

By the time they left, the sunbathers and swimmers were gone. From a backpack, Frederick offered various identity-concealing items. Michael chose a hooded sweatshirt; Frederick, a cap and sunglasses; Lisette a scarf and a short black wig.

He was beginning to feel the familiar surge of adrenaline. Checked his hands. No shaking. Good. The earlier episode had been unnerving. He couldn't screw this up. One shot, and he had to be accurate. Calming breaths. He was in control.

Frederick was carrying a gun as well. Michael had recognized the bulge under Frederick's sweater sometime earlier in the day. He didn't know how good a shot Frederick might be, but he did know one thing. If he didn't take the shot, Frederick would. Or kill Michael. Or both.

Michael had to be the shooter. "Cameras are out?"

"I have a guy who works in the security office."

"No security to get into the garage?"

"Taken care of."

They walked the half mile to a modern building. No exterior signs for the Institute. A set of stairs that led to a door to the inside of the garage. Normally locked, the door opened easily.

"One floor up," Frederick said. "Then we wait."

"What if there are other people?"

"There shouldn't be. My guy inside says it's always empty at this hour."

"If there are witnesses, I'm calling it off."

"There shouldn't be. Just take the shot, and we head out. Heinrich stole a car, and he'll be waiting outside for us." Frederick paused. "Will one shot be enough?"

"All I need."

His heart pounded. He felt a tremor in his hands. *Not now.* This was so fucking dangerous. He could still back out.

No, he couldn't.

More calming breaths. He mentally recited his mantra, reminding him where he was—and where he was not, and it did the job. The tremors eased again. He'd just have to be careful—shoot with absolute precision. Aim for the middle of the chest and hope to hell that he didn't miss.

He noted that Lisette had that odd expression again. He wondered if she knew about Frederick's gun, but he had his mind on the task at hand. He wasn't about to try to decipher what might be going on in her head.

* * * * *

Lisette trailed Frederick, who led the way. Michael followed her. She had killed six people without any regrets or compunction, but now she felt sick to the stomach. For the first time in years, she questioned what she was doing. But maybe it would be okay. Maybe her message got through to Ben Rosenberg. Or would he have ignored her message? If he didn't show, if he'd gone home early, maybe the plan would be abandoned.

But that was unlikely. There would just be a new plan. Maybe a new victim.

She should've killed Frederick and Michael. The whole day had been one long horror show of pretending to be excited and thrilled to be participating in the murder of an innocent man. She was an expert at pretense, and she was experienced at killing. But all her victims had deserved it.

If she had killed Frederick and Michael, they wouldn't be here in this garage.

She wouldn't be responsible for the death of this man.

A father.

She'd looked it up. Rosenberg had two small children, younger than she'd been when her father had been shot. At least Rosenberg's children wouldn't watch it happen, but was she inflicting on them what had been done to her?

And Rosenberg was going to die for her actions. She wasn't sorry about anyone she'd killed, but she was very sorry that Frederick had seized on Rosenberg to blame.

She contemplated alternatives.

She could grab the gun from Michael, shoot him, and then shoot Frederick. Then run to the car that would be waiting for them and explain that Frederick and Michael had been ambushed.

But she dismissed the idea. Heinrich would be driving, and he wasn't stupid. Nor were the others. Even if she succeeded in killing both Michael and Frederick, her chance for revenge for her father would be gone. Years of planning for nothing.

But she also suspected that she'd never get that far. The neo-Nazis that she'd dispatched had been pretend soldiers, who'd killed unarmed, unsuspecting civilians. They'd been stupid and easy targets. Michael had the feel, despite his periodic bouts of trembling, of an experienced killer. He'd be more than capable of fending off an attempt to disarm him. And then, he'd shoot her.

If she wanted to kill him, she'd have to catch him off guard.

She'd caught him periodically gazing at her and not with the type of undisguised desire she often felt from men. More a questioning look than anything else. Why?

Then there was Frederick. He had a gun as well. Was he going to shoot the Director if Michael failed? Or was he going to shoot Michael if he didn't kill the Director?

They climbed a set of concrete stairs to the next floor and at Frederick's directions positioned themselves behind pillars, Michael behind a pillar close to the elevator. She was behind Michael, to his right. Also hidden, Frederick was behind both of them by about fifteen feet.

Why had Frederick brought her?

He hadn't taken her on other expeditions. He kept her in the dark about his bigger plans or his trips. But he'd wanted her to come today. Could he be waiting to see what she'd do—and preparing to kill her if she tried to stop Michael?

Of course he was.

Frederick was far enough from the elevator that he wouldn't have a good shot at the Director when he exited. Michael, though, was in his direct line of fire. As was she.

So this was a test for her as well as for Michael.

She wondered if Michael knew. If he did, he showed no sign. She was pretty sure he'd pass the test.

She'd pass it as well, but at a terrible cost.

If she weren't there, at least she wouldn't have to watch passively while Michael killed in cold blood. But would it be any less evil if she weren't watching? Would she be any less responsible?

Too late. She'd lost her chance.

She'd chosen her revenge over a human life. She'd chosen her own safety—so she could continue with her self-appointed mission.

The elevator doors opened. A man stepped out. To her surprise, a woman stepped out with him.

* * * * *

Everything happened very fast, so fast that Ben, when telling the story later, couldn't be sure exactly what had happened. To the best of his recollection, he and Tehila stepped out of the elevator and a man with a hood shadowing his face moved out from behind one of the concrete pillars. The hood fell back, revealing blond hair and a grim expression. The man raised a gun.

Tehila stepped in front of Ben, shoving him backwards, at the same time, pulling out what looked like a toy from her waistband. A plastic toy gun. Except that it wasn't a toy.

The man in the hoodie fired before she could get her arm up, and her blue oversized sweater exploded in a shower of blood. Ben caught her as she fell.

From a different direction, there was the sound of shouting. American voices shouting in English. "What the fuck! Son of a bitch."

Ben knelt on the ground, holding Tehila, as two men ran towards him. They continued to shout at the blond man, and then one of the men pulled out a gun and fired. The blond assassin hesitated and then turned and fled, his flight joined by two figures that had also been concealed behind pillars.

Everything moved in slow motion. Nothing felt real.

Tehila was still breathing, but the entire front of her sweater was turning red.

Tears rolled down his face. She'd stepped in front of him to save him, and now she was dying. What should he do? Lay her down and check the wound? He wasn't a doctor, and he couldn't bring himself to place her on the dirt and cold of the hard floor.

Instead he cradled her and mumbled words that had been said by the Jewish people for thousands of year when facing death. *Shema Yisrael*—Hear O Israel, the Lord is God, the Lord is One. Then he added a private prayer, hoping that *HaShem* would hear.

Please. Please. Not this lovely young woman.

The two Americans reached him. When asked later, he remembered little about their appearance. One man, well dressed, maybe in his thirties, followed by a younger man who might have been college age.

Ben just remembered pleading.

"Help me. Please. She's shot. Call an ambulance."

The first man scooped Tehila into his arms and stood. "No time. She needs to get to a hospital. Now."

"Yes. Yes. Of course." Ben could barely process what was happening. "Let's go." He stood and looked at his hands, covered in blood.

The younger man put a hand on Ben's arm as the first man carried Tehila towards a nearby car. "You need to wait here for the police. You have a phone?"

Shaking, Ben nodded.

"Call. We'll take care of her."

"But—"

"I promise we'll do everything we can. Call the police."

Ben pulled out his phone and dialed as the young man raced towards the car. He watched them drive off and only then realized that neither had given a name or mentioned where they were taking Tehila.

13

BERLIN, GERMANY

THEY DROVE THROUGH THE darkened Grunewald Forest, stopping at the end of the river, where they tossed Michael's gun, Lisette's wig, the hoodie, and Frederick's cap into the dark water. They heard the faint sounds of multiple sirens, but they were far enough to be safe. At least for now. They drove a mile from where they dumped the clothes and gun to switch from the stolen car into the van that had been parked near the river, wiping down all surfaces in the car. In case any CCTV had captured the vehicle and the police found it, there would be no traces of their presence.

Frederick rode in the front passenger seat, next to Heinrich, who drove carefully, observing all traffic laws. After dropping Michael, Frederick would return to his own apartment. No need to keep such a close eye on Michael.

Things hadn't gone as anticipated—the Jew director of the Equality Institute hadn't died—but Frederick wasn't disappointed. Michael had proven himself not only willing, but an excellent shot. It had been a direct hit in the middle of the woman's chest at maybe fifty feet. She would not survive.

Michael was one of them, a believer, a defender. He was worthy.

He was pleased that he didn't have to kill Michael. They needed people like Michael.

He was more than pleased that he didn't have to kill Lisette. She hadn't flinched, hadn't tried to stop Michael, had said nothing to indicate anything but support. He would look elsewhere for the killer of Germany Now supporters.

"That went well," Frederick said.

"You think so?"

He was surprised by the anger in Michael's voice.

"Relatively well. There's one less Black bitch in the world."

"Who was that woman with the gun? And the two men—Americans? The place was supposed to be empty. I thought you had a team on the ground."

"I did." Frederick felt a little defensive. "They took care of the cameras. They left the door to the garage open."

"And yet they didn't know that the target wouldn't be alone. Yet they didn't stay to provide backup."

"You did the job, and we got away."

"I didn't take out the target, and it was sheer luck that we got away. It was sheer luck that we weren't killed. I want to know that there's proper planning and backup for any mission that you ask me to undertake in the future. I don't want to be involved in something fucking stupid."

"It's not a ridiculous request," Heinrich said.

"Fine." Frederick was a little annoyed at the challenge, but Michael was right. The intelligence had failed. The fact that Michael had the balls to point out that the mission hadn't gone as anticipated increased his value. A good leader needed more than sycophants—he needed people whose judgment he could trust.

Lisette, seated directly behind Frederick, said nothing, but that was okay. She'd passed the test. She'd shown unwavering support. Of course, the violence would unsettle her. He found her irresistible in bed, and very smart and capable, but she still wasn't a man. Women were weak. That was why she was kept out of the loop in planning.

He switched gears.

"Michael, how would you feel about a trip north? Right now, given the stakes and the attacks on our people, I could use a bodyguard. You can start tomorrow here in Berlin, and we'll leave town the day after.

We'll be gone two or three days."

Now that he'd established his bona fides, Michael could work with men on weapons training. And they were going to need all the expert help they could get to pull off Day X. Frederick wasn't ready to trust Michael with the details of Day X—only the district leaders knew for now, but with Michael's knowledge of weapons, he'd be useful.

"I'd be honored. Now my phone please. And I'll need a new gun."

Frederick reached over the back seat and handed Michael the phone. "I can get a gun for you tomorrow." He could hand Michael the HK 9mm that he had under his shirt, but he didn't want Michael to know that he'd been armed.

"Fine." Michael clicked on his phone.

* * * * *

Lisette glanced over at Michael, who was absorbed in something he was reading online, and she pictured the woman he'd shot. She'd been beautiful. She'd still been beautiful as she fell, even with the blood flowing from her chest. Lisette's father had been shot in the face. They'd had to keep the coffin closed for the funeral.

Lisette wondered if the woman had been there because of the warning she'd sent. Had Lisette simply prompted Ben Rosenberg to hire a bodyguard? While the director had lived, a woman had died.

It wasn't her fault. She'd done what she could.

She'd keep telling herself that just as her nine-year-old self had kept trying to persuade away her guilt over her father's death. Maybe she'd believe it eventually. In the meantime, she would exact payment for this murder as well for as the murder of her father. She still had to locate her father's murderer. The killer of an innocent woman was seated next to her.

A killing that she had allowed to happen.

"Aren't we going to get dinner?" She tapped Frederick on the shoulder.

"Are you okay?" His voice showed concern.

Play the role. "I was a little scared, especially when those men started shooting at us. And," she threw in a demure hesitation, "I've never seen anyone shot before. It was a little unsettling."

He glanced back at her. "I'm proud of you. You were very strong."

"And I'm proud, too. Proud to be your woman. And now I'm hungry." Maybe after all of this, she'd become a real actor. She'd become accomplished at acting, and she had the kind of beauty Hollywood appreciated. Why not use her looks and skills after everything was over? Films, television. She could return to the States.

Who was she fooling? There would be no after.

"Me too." Heinrich, driving, was always hungry.

"Michael?"

He nodded without looking up.

"Then let's eat." Frederick said.

She would need Frederick until she'd found her father's murderer. Then she could kill both of them.

Michael, though, was another thing altogether. He wasn't necessary for her access to information. She didn't need to wait. She'd have to be careful, because he knew her, and it couldn't look like a murder, not after Karl, but she'd avenge the woman he'd just shot.

14

COLOGNE, GERMANY

THE FEDERAL OFFICE FOR the Protection of the Constitution, known generally by its initials in German, the BfV, was headquartered in Cologne in one of those nondescript buildings that were so typical of government offices everywhere. The BfV in Cologne employed some 2,500 intelligence professionals engaged in defending the German democracy against internal threats. In years past, the focus had been more on Islamic terrorism. In the current climate, far right extremists and neo-Nazis were of more concern.

Far right extremists and neo-Nazis were why Americans Jonathan Egan and Elizabeth Owen were paying a visit to the President of the BfV. Jonathan looked his diplomatic best in a bespoke suit that he could afford because of the trust fund that his grandfather had left him. But money wasn't everything. Elizabeth, whose parents had been inner city teachers in Detroit, looked every bit as good—to be honest, better—although Jonathan suspected that her very elegant white pants suit didn't cost a tenth of the ridiculous price for his outfit.

Which perhaps was as much a matter of intelligence as values—as Elizabeth had reminded him in the taxi ride from the hotel to the BfV headquarters.

He reminded her that he'd bought her the diamond earrings that she was wearing.

She pushed dark hair behind her ears and tilted her head to catch the sunlight. "Business expense."

It really hadn't been, although her shopping for jewelry in an exclusive shop had been necessary for surveillance on a recent operation, and her purchase with his credit card of diamond earrings had been useful in getting them out of a difficult situation by bribing corrupt Russian officials.

"Maybe for the original pair." He'd bought her replacements for the pair she'd handed over to the Russians. Celebrating a job well done, he'd told her.

She knew better—but she had accepted them.

"You can afford it." She eyed the bespoke suit. "What'd that cost, $5,000?"

"Maybe. But you can't make fun of the money I spend on clothes while wearing $2,000 earrings that I bought for you."

"Sure I can. I'm talented."

The taxi pulled up, and she opened her door and slid out. He followed her.

They paused before mounting the stairs to the door. "You know the drill."

"Yada, yada. Trust no one. Except Hannah Abt."

They had to show identification and go through two security scans—one to get into the building and one to enter the top floor where BfV President Hannah Abt had her office. It took longer than usual because the security personnel had to check and double-check that Elizabeth and Jonathan were allowed to carry weapons—which BfV personnel were not allowed to do. It was one of the conditions that Jonathan had insisted upon before their arrival.

They were escorted by Hannah Abt's personal aide to her office in a corner of the building, surprisingly small for the head of such a large agency and filled with functional white furniture that looked like it could have been purchased at an IKEA.

She rose to greet them, a small thin woman, with salt and pepper hair, whose age Jonathan guessed to be somewhere between fifty and sixty, since she and Jonathan's boss had attended Oxford together.

Her demeanor also reminded Jonathan of his boss: tough and no-nonsense.

"Mr. Egan? I met you in Washington several years ago. And you must be Ms. Owen." She extended her hand and solemnly shook hands with both. "Please thank Margaret again for sending you."

"I'm sure she'll figure a way for you to pay her back."

"No doubt."

They sat, her behind the desk, Jonathan and Elizabeth side by side in functional but slightly uncomfortable armchairs.

"Your office is secure?" Jonathan cast a look around the austere room.

"Of course." She smiled, indulgent. "It's swept every day and that," she nodded at a small device on her desk, "that would let me know if something had been missed."

"Still, probably best not to discuss anything of importance in here," Elizabeth said.

Hannah Abt turned her gaze on Elizabeth. "Agreed. And no need anyway. I assume that you've already been briefed on the essentials. I've informed Chancellor Jung of this arrangement."

Chancellor Christiana Jung had replaced the long-running previous Chancellor. As a member of the Social Democrats, Jung's policies were more to the left than those of her predecessor. But like her predecessor, she had little tolerance for those on the far right.

Jonathan nodded. "President Lewis is in the loop as well."

"Good. I have nothing to add to what Margaret already told you. Let me call in my vice presidents and introduce you. You'll be working with them. And then you can have lunch in our executive dining room."

A few minutes after she made the call, the two vice presidents filed in, Arnold Shafer, a friendly well-dressed man in his forties, and Reiner Muller, a tall grim man in a gray suit. Jonathan and Elizabeth stood. Hannah remained seated.

Arnold extended his hand. "Jonathan, right? We met several years ago when I visited your parents in Mystic, Connecticut. And Ms. Owen, a pleasure."

Reiner shook hands with a simple, "Welcome to Germany."

* * * * *

Lunch was potato salad and sausages, but a green salad was also offered, to appease the gods of healthy eating, Jonathan supposed. Polite and empty conversation. Arnold asked about Washington politics and Jonathan's father, a former Senator; Reiner spoke more rarely, his demeanor colder, throwing in a few comments about the upcoming American election with a disparaging tone about the quality of candidates. Then with the arrival of dessert, apple strudel and coffee, the conversation turned serious.

"The reason for your presence here?" Reiner asked. "All that we've been told is that American intelligence wants to coordinate with us on right-wing extremists."

"That's pretty much it." Jonathan forked a piece of apple strudel into his mouth.

Elizabeth shot him a look. "What Jonathan didn't say is that we have concerns about American neo-Nazi extremists communicating with their counterparts here in Germany, even exchanging skills and information."

Jonathan washed down the pastry with a sip of coffee. German pastries were the best thing about the local cuisine. "Essentially what I said only in more detail."

"Do you have names of Americans in Germany that you're concerned about?" Reiner checked his phone.

"A few." Jonathan took another sip of coffee. "You keep checking your phone. Do you have somewhere you need to be?"

"As a matter of fact, yes. Some legal opinions about surveillance on certain political groups need to be reviewed before we go to court."

Jonathan raised eyebrows. "Legal opinions?"

Arnold smiled. "Reiner is a lawyer, even though we Germans don't like lawyers much more than you Americans. Still we have a lot of lawyers in the BfV—because we're careful not to step over legal lines, in recognition of the past when secret police used their power for evil.

That's why the BfV doesn't have any power to arrest and we don't carry weapons. Don't you have lawyers in your agency?"

"Yes, the ECA does have a legal department although the lawyers mainly act as advisors so we don't stray too far from what is allowed." Not *too* far, although straying did occur.

"You are lucky, then." Reiner's eyes remained on the phone. "We spend too much time in court. It's necessary, but it's also inefficient."

"Go." Arnold waved him off. "I'll take good care of our American colleagues."

"A pleasure to meet you. I look forward to a good working relationship." Without further comment, Reiner rose and strode from the room, phone in hand.

They returned to coffee and dessert. Arnold helped himself to a second strudel. "So, Jonathan, what does your father think of your current president?"

"My father hates everyone. Including me."

Arnold laughed. "I remember that you and your father didn't get along."

"Something of an understatement."

Arnold turned to Elizabeth. "And have you met the former Senator? I imagine he'd enjoy meeting one of his son's colleagues, especially one who's both attractive and intelligent."

Elizabeth drank her coffee. "I imagine he wouldn't."

Arnold looked at her, assessing. "Because you're not white?"

"I'm sure that would be part of it."

"Perhaps he's not as intelligent as I thought he was."

"My father tends to not be as open as some in his racism," Jonathan said. "But it would be a part. The other part would have to do with class and money."

"We in Germany have learned from the past," Arnold said. "While the United States still struggles to admit that it ever did anything wrong. Did you know that the Nuremberg laws under Hitler were modeled after your Jim Crow laws?"

"Yes, I did know that," Elizabeth said. "And yet you have Nazis gaining influence in your country again."

"As do you. Which is why you're here, no?"

The conversation returned to more casual topics.

* * * * *

Later, in his office, a space with an austere and useful decor similar to that of the BfV president, Arnold described the current state of far-right extremism in Germany. "It's on the increase. Mostly young people, frustrated and concerned about their personal futures. There's an additional element here: a weariness from constant feelings of guilt over the actions of their grandparents or great grandparents."

"Hard to forget what the Nazis did."

"Especially with memorials on almost every street to the Jewish people who were murdered. But the young people now alive weren't responsible. And we here in Germany have the fastest growing Jewish community in Europe."

"Anti-Semitism?"

"It exists here as it exists everywhere, but the fact that Jews leave Israel to immigrate to Germany says a lot. We've had a few minor incidents. The more significant incidents have come not from neo-Nazis but from the Muslim community. Jihadists remain a significant threat, one I'm concerned that we're not taking seriously enough. Which I have mentioned to President Abt and to Reiner."

"I heard there was a minor incident just yesterday." Elizabeth crossed her arms. "A woman shot and killed in Berlin protecting the Director of the Equality Institute."

"We don't know the details of what happened." Arnold picked up a pencil and tapped it on his desk. "Do you?"

"We received a vague report from a friendly agency," Jonathan said.

"We got a report of the name the woman gave Ben Rosenberg. Tehila. Unknown last name. Rosenberg believed that she was Israeli. Did your friendly agency inform you what happened to the woman's body?"

"Nope. I did hear a rumor, though, that a private jet belonging to a private party associated with said friendly agency took off from

GlobeGround in Berlin a few hours after this minor incident."

"Mossad is not supposed to be operating in Germany."

"We tell them the same thing all the time about operating in the United States. They generally ignore us. I'm not saying that Mossad is the aforementioned friendly agency. Just that—generally speaking—they tend to be a little, shall we say, independent."

"It'd be unfortunate if Mossad was involved. That'd just stoke the anti-Semitism from people who oppose Israel's policies towards Palestinians."

"I'm aware." Jonathan said. "But whatever anyone feels about the policies of the State of Israel doesn't justify anti-Semitism."

"I agree. Have you heard any other rumors, like who was behind the attack or why?"

"The only thing I heard was what we've already said. Do you know?"

"I know less than you. Rosenberg stated that the attacker was a blond young man, and that there were two others. Two American men appeared, scared off the gunman, and carried the wounded woman off, ostensibly to a hospital." Arnold sighed. "That's all we have. We may never find out what happened."

"Well, except that someone tried to kill the Jewish director of an organization that opposes far-right extremism."

"As I mentioned earlier—some Syrian extremists, who arrived with the flood of immigration in 2016, target Jews. Some Palestinians attack Jews."

"In America as well," Elizabeth said. "Still, at the present time, the far right is more of a threat than the jihadists."

"You're farther from the Middle East than we are. Maybe that makes a difference."

"The world is very small these days," Elizabeth said. "So shall we return to the subject of neo-Nazi Americans operating in Germany?"

"You have names?"

Jonathan retrieved his phone. "We have some concerns that this man, Nickolas Kruger, might be in Germany. He's wanted for murder in the United States." He passed the phone to Arnold, who looked at the picture and nodded.

"Could you forward this to me? I will distribute it to everyone who deals with neo-Nazis. We'll watch for him." As Arnold spoke, he typed an email. Then he looked up from the computer and smiled. "Now let me show you to the offices you'll be using while you're here."

* * * * *

Later, in search of a restaurant in the Altstadt of Cologne, the compact and restored medieval center of the city, Elizabeth asked Jonathan, "You think he bought the story?"

"Seemed to." He looked up and down the street. It wasn't Berlin or Paris, but the area was attractive, if touristy, with the oldest cathedral in Germany and museums within short walking distance. They weren't there to see the sights, but it was always pleasant to check out a new place. One of the perks of the job. He took out his phone and searched. "How about *Sunner im Walfisch*? Traditional Cologne cuisine."

"I'd be fine with a salad. But whatever." They steered toward the restaurant. "If not too expensive."

"We're dining on the government."

"There's a budget, Jonathan. Not that you care." They halted in front of the seventeenth century inn with a black and white facade. "Looks nice. But salad tomorrow."

"If we can find one." Then he returned to the earlier topic. "I guess we'll get some indication tomorrow how things are going."

"If the story is passed on to the Nazis—doesn't that mean that Arnold's dirty?"

"Maybe, but not necessarily. Arnold sent an email out to the entire BfV on Nickolas Kruger. It could be anyone in the organization. Besides, I've known him for years."

"Yes, you have. He's very friendly, isn't he?"

"Which makes you suspicious?"

"Of course."

"He might just find you attractive."

"And you know, you might just be an asshole."

"There's that possibility." Jonathan glanced over at her. "You want to eat or not?"

She pulled open the door. "You might want to check out Reiner. Since you find unfriendly people suspicious."

"I intend to. And I'm not giving Arnold a pass, by the way."

15

BERLIN, GERMANY

MICHAEL WOKE AT MIDNIGHT. The nightmares were always worse after any stressful event. He performed his breathing and mental exercises with the usual calming effect, and then he returned to sleep, waking at eight, finally throwing off the last of his jet lag. It had been easier when he was in his twenties. Only in his mid-thirties and he was already finding the lack of sleep more difficult to overcome. He shaved, showered, dressed, and left to play bodyguard.

He spent the day trailing Frederick, remaining positioned outside doors during meetings. Lisette met them for dinner, as vivacious and friendly as she'd been on that first evening, and Frederick dismissed him for the night.

Michael returned to his hotel room, sent a text, and took a brief nap. When he woke, he checked whether she had responded. She had.

Hey back at you.

You buy a dress?

Yup. Low cut. You'll like it. Mom didn't.

Your mother pick out a place for our wedding yet?

She would if I'd let her. It's our wedding. We choose.

I'm leaving it up to you.

Like hell you are. Not getting out of it that easily. Anyway, we have time. The wedding's not until next summer.

He smiled at the response. *Okay. When I get back.*

K. Don't do anything stupid, goddamnit.

Too late.

??? You ok?

Fine.

Don't scare me.

Sorry. Bad joke.

It would be funny if I weren't worried, love. Just be careful.

Always. Love you and miss you.

Love you too. Miss you too.

It was true that he missed her. There was always the tension between wanting to be with her and wanting to do what he was now doing. As long as she was fine about his decision—it would work. If she changed her mind, he'd have to rethink.

After. He was already here.

The texts disappeared into the cyber void. He pulled on a jacket and left his hotel to wander the streets of Berlin. Like all cities, Berlin changed after dark. Sidewalks were crowded with hipsters out in search of a late dinner, late drinking, live music, a hook-up, or some combination of the four. Berlin was a favored city for young people, bustling with night activity. He liked the city, the undercurrent of excitement, the gathering of musicians and artists.

He was interested in the late drinking and live music, which meant a bar, although he had a specific bar in mind. However, he checked out several other establishments, going in for a few minutes and then leaving. He entered and left three different bars, finally settling on one about a mile from his hotel, with a piano in the corner, which no one was playing. The walls were wood-paneled with aged instruments, guitars, saxophones, hanging from hooks. There were few people inside: Two couples sat at tables distant from the piano, seemingly interested in each other and not their surroundings. A solitary man nursed a beer on a barstool.

Michael ordered a vodka and asked about playing the piano. The bartender nodded agreement and handed over a shot glass.

He carried the vodka to the piano, drank it in one swift motion, set the glass on a coaster, and seated himself on the piano bench. The bench was old, and the piano, an upright Yamaha, had seen better days, some of the keys yellow and stained. He played the C scale and an arpeggio. To his surprise, the piano was in tune, not a great instrument, but not terrible either, better than he would have expected in an establishment of this kind. He lightly rested his hand on top of the keys for a moment as he decided. Then he began to play Mozart's *Piano Sonata No. 16*, a piece he'd memorized when he was six years old—and more appropriate for a Nazi sympathizer than his favored genre of music.

Not that it mattered. If he'd recognized anyone as a member of Frederick Bauer's group, he would've left immediately. None of the few people in the bar were familiar from the meetings or gatherings he'd attended. But it didn't hurt to keep in character, and to keep in character, he played Mozart. He didn't play classical pieces often, except in honor of his mother, a concert pianist who'd loved Mozart and who had died when he was nine. And he did like Mozart—the elegance and balance. The melodies.

Just not quite as much as he liked jazz.

When he finished, the few patrons applauded. The bartender nodded approval. The man who had been at the bar—bald, muscular, a tattoo of a tiger on one arm and a dragon on the other—approached. He spoke English with a Brooklyn accent. "Nice. But kind of highbrow for this time of night. Buy you a drink if you play something a little more upbeat."

"Like what?"

"Know any Ellington?"

Well, the bar seemed safe enough. He didn't have to play Mozart all night. "I know *Satin Doll*." Along with every other Ellington song.

"That'll do. What're you drinking?"

He would've liked another vodka, but something weaker would be safer. "A beer will do." He swung into the piece as the bald man collected two beers and returned.

"You're clean." The bald man spoke quietly after setting the beer on the coaster on top of the piano. He pulled up a chair, watching the movement of hands on keys, as he drank his own beer. "I was behind you for the first twenty minutes after you left the hotel, then I headed here. Didn't spot a tail."

"I know. After you dropped off, I went in and out of bars for almost an hour to check as well. Wouldn't be here if I had company." He finished playing the melody and swung into an improvisation. "Is she okay?"

"A little bruised, but fine. She left the country, disappointed that she had to pull out of the operation so early. Even if she volunteered to play target. She was really excited at getting a crack at some Nazis."

"Understandable. Unfortunately, there are a lot of Nazis around these days. She'll have another opportunity. If she were spotted in Germany after I allegedly killed her…"

"Yeah, I know. So does she. Why she's off the team. Damn good thing you're such an expert shot. If you'd missed, you could have killed her or the Director."

"I was more worried about ricochets and whether the vest would hold up."

"You could have used blanks."

"Bauer might have tried out my gun beforehand. And if he'd discovered that my gun held blanks instead of live rounds, it would've blown the whole operation. Quite apart from getting me killed. Besides, I didn't have any blanks on me. No way to get them either."

"You could've just missed. Or not shot at all."

"Wouldn't have been as convincing. Anyway, Tehila had the deciding vote."

"I know. Still, dangerous game. The Bureau wouldn't have approved using live ammo against an agent, even if she was wearing a bulletproof vest."

"Yes, it is a fucking dangerous game. And do you really want to discuss the high moral standards of the fucking Bureau with me, *Frick?*" He paused, his hands resting on the keyboard, a little surprised at the level of his own anger.

"No, *Michael*," Frick put emphasis on the fake name. "I don't." He spoke in a lower voice. "And I'm sorry for my part in what happened to you. As I've said repeatedly. Is it going to be a problem for us working together, Kolya?"

He glanced around the room, again. He'd checked it before sitting at the piano, but better to be safe. No one was close enough to have heard, and then he resumed playing, choosing a different Ellington song, *Take the A Train.* "No, not a problem."

Frick drank his beer. "We good?"

"Good enough. Just don't use my real name. Not even here."

"Sorry."

He ran the events of the past year through his mind.

16

WASHINGTON, D.C.

HIS REAL NAME WAS Nikolai Ivanovich Petrov, although he never went by anything but Kolya. He was a Russian Jew who had immigrated to the United States at the age of fourteen, and he had spent ten years as an American intelligence agent for the Executive Covert Agency, "ECA," an organization not well known outside government circles

A year earlier, he had been unknowingly set up to be captured in an elaborate scheme devised by Margaret Bradford, his boss and the head of the ECA, to stop Mihai Cuza, a Romanian neo-Fascist terrorist, through tricking Cuza into accessing a fake ECA portal that would then upload a Trojan horse onto Cuza's computer. He had been shot, kidnapped, and flown to Romania for interrogation. Not knowing that his agency wanted him to give in, Kolya had resisted, despite days of excruciating torture, only capitulating after his fiancée Alex Feinstein was also abducted, her life threatened.

The FBI had been protecting Cuza, for various complicated reasons, and Frick had been a participant in kidnapping Kolya and Alex, although not a participant in the torture. Frick had a crisis of conscience, and subsequently defied his boss. With a small team of fellow ECA agents, including Jonathan Egan and Elizabeth Owen, Frick helped rescue Kolya and Alex, saving their lives.

Furious that he had been deceived and nearly killed by his own agency, Kolya resigned and took a job as an attorney. Like his fiancée Alex, he had a law degree, although unlike Alex, he had little appetite for the practice of law.

However, eight months after his resignation, while still struggling with the physical and psychological aftereffects of his ordeal, he was drawn back into the espionage game when his childhood best friend held the key to finding a deadly nerve agent in the United States. The successful conclusion of that mission led to a reconciliation of sorts with his former boss, Margaret Bradford, and the realization that he much preferred working as a secret agent to being an attorney. When he was offered the chance to take down neo-Nazis in Germany, he had found it irresistible. What Jewish operative wouldn't?

Still, Alex remained his top priority. Had Alex been unhappy at his accepting Bradford's offer, he wouldn't have agreed. But she'd told him to do it, saying that she preferred he not spend his life working at a job he hated. She wasn't shy about expressing her feelings. If at any point, she were unhappy at his rejoining the world of intelligence, she would let him know—and he would quit.

Or so he told himself.

* * * * *

One week before arriving in Germany, at seven in the morning, he'd met with the team: Jonathan Egan, Elizabeth Owen, Frick, Tehila Melaku, and Teo Lorenzo for breakfast at Jonathan's elegant and very expensive home in Chevy Chase, Maryland.

They gathered around Jonathan's overpriced dining room table in his oversized dining room under the crystal chandelier that probably cost more than Kolya made in a month. Other than the size, the house was tastefully—and expensively—decorated in modern whites, grays, and blacks. The trust fund set up for him by his industrialist grandfather allowed Jonathan to live a life of luxury while working for an intelligence agency that paid him what his grandfather would have considered pocket change.

Despite the early hour, Frick—real name David Fuller—was

drinking a beer. Everyone else drank coffee. Everyone except Teo and Tehila had a plate of scrambled eggs, sausage, and toast on the placemats in front of them, the food prepared by Jonathan—who liked to cook. Tehila, who kept kosher, had brought her own breakfast, an energy bar. Teo Lorenzo, the youngest at the table, fluent in fifteen languages, drank Diet Coke and toyed with a bowl of Lucky Charms cereal—a brand that Jonathan kept for the occasional visits of his nine-year-old son.

"We secure here?" Frick asked.

"More so than the office," Elizabeth said. "And this is bigger than the office conference room, too."

Someone in the ECA was selling information to a Russian mafiya head, and although the Russian mafiya would have little interest in the present mission, security was a concern. The search for the mole had narrowed to three people, none of whom were field agents or the technical staff, but until the culprit was arrested, field teams met outside the office. Jonathan's house was regularly swept for bugs and was protected electronically.

Elizabeth made another joke about the size of Jonathan's house, and then they got down to business.

"The plan," Jonathan said, "is for Kolya to assume the identity of a man who is hiding his real identity, which is that of the grandson of an SS officer who immigrated to the U.S. after the war. A legend within a legend. Pretty clever idea. If they have anyone who's any good on computers, they'll be able to dig beneath the first cover, Michael Hall, to find the second, hidden identity, Nickolas Kruger. They'll think how clever they are to have uncovered what they think is the truth. And stop looking. Meanwhile, Michael/Nickolas will offer his services to the group in Germany."

"Nickolas? Because it's close to Nikolai?" Teo asked.

"Bingo," Jonathan said. "Always better to keep a cover name close to your real name. When possible."

"And the team?" Tehila asked.

"We'll be in Germany to provide back-up should Kolya need it. Teo, Frick, Tehila, you'll stay in Berlin. I've met a few of the people in

83

the BfV—which is why I'm going with Elizabeth to Cologne instead of staying in Berlin."

"And you're doing what with the BfV, Jonathan?" Frick asked.

Jonathan cut up his sausage and took a bite. "Everyone eat. Your food'll get cold. We're going to co-ordinate with the BfV on finding American neo-Nazis in Germany."

"American neo-Nazis like me. Or rather like the man I'm pretending to be." Kolya finished his first cup of coffee and poured a second. He dumped in two teaspoons of sugar. "Identifying 'Michael Hall' aka Nickolas Kruger to the BfV as a person of interest to American intelligence is a nice touch."

"And we're doing this why?" Elizabeth asked. "How are American interests involved?"

"Well, I'm personally happy to kill Nazis anywhere," Tehila said.

"Neo-Nazis," Frick said.

"Not neo-Nazis. Nazis. You march around with swastikas, worship Hitler and hate Jews and immigrants—you're a Nazi." Tehila unwrapped her energy bar. "I always thought Mossad should kill more of them."

"Bad idea. We don't do assassinations," Teo said.

"Generally, I agree," Tehila said. "With exceptions. Like Nazis."

"We're gathering information," Kolya said. "As much as I personally agree that Nazis deserve to be killed, I don't agree with a policy of assassination. Causes more problems than it solves. Unless you're stopping an imminent attack."

"I hate those bastards as much as you do," Elizabeth said. "But still—what's the goal? It's a real question. We can't stop every right-wing crazy around the world."

Jonathan turned to Elizabeth. "We have several goals. Part of the mission is to help a fellow intelligence service. The President of the BfV believes that there are neo-Nazi sympathizers inside her organization on the highest levels, and she requested help from Margaret in uncovering them since she's not sure who to trust. Our cover story for everyone else in the BfV is that we're coordinating on white supremacist Americans in Germany. But getting information on neo-Nazi terrorists inside Germany working with American neo-Nazis, cover story or not, is definitely of value.

"There's also concern that neo-Nazis could be planning violence to destabilize the current German government, and that would certainly be against American interests," Kolya added. "It would be helpful to determine the extent and the threat."

"You speak German, Kolya?" Teo asked.

"Some. I understand better than I speak—but fluency in German isn't part of the cover." Kolya finished his second cup of coffee and started on the sausage. He felt Tehila's eyes on him, disapproving, and he tried not to smile. She'd been on a campaign for the past few months to get him—and Alex—to be more observant of Jewish law. An unsuccessful campaign —as far as obeying kosher rules went— although he was now baking challah for the occasional Shabbat dinner with Alex and friends.

"I'm fluent in German," Frick said. "My mother was German."

Everyone looked at him.

"Figures," Elizabeth said.

Frick took a swig of beer. "I know you've got this all worked out, but it should be me doing this. Not Kolya."

"The legend doesn't fit you, Frick. Unfortunately, the agency started building a neo-Nazi legend years ago in case we needed it, and it was designed for Kolya. Although your offer is appreciated," Jonathan said.

It took time to create an effective legend for deep cover. It required creating a fake identity, creating years of posts, the occasional photo—usually blurry, but it had to be close enough to the agent assuming the identity.

"I really don't give a shit if my offer's appreciated." Frick set the beer on the wood of the walnut table—then rethought, placed the beer on a coaster, and wiped off the damp spot on the wood with his sleeve. "This is too risky for Kolya. Can we start with the fact that he's still not completely recovered? Doing better, yeah, a lot better, but still, you're sending someone who's not one hundred percent into a possible shitstorm."

For the past year, Frick had been a loyal ECA agent, and Kolya appreciated that Frick had risked his life to save him. Without Frick's help, he and Alex would be dead. Still, had Frick not participated in the initial kidnappings, there would have been no need for a rescue. Had he not been abducted, Kolya wouldn't have had the injuries that continued to plague him.

Kolya kept his tone cool in response. "The PTSD is under control. I've been in physical therapy for my leg, and it's doing well."

"And he's really good." Teo picked damp marshmallows out of his bowl of Lucky Charms cereal and ate them with his fingers, one by one.

"Hell, I'm fucking filled with admiration for Kolya's abilities." Frick took another swig of his beer. "No, really, I mean it. Any of you ever try to take him down? I did. He'd been shot and drugged, and he still nearly killed me. But that's not the point. Besides the fact that he's not completely over his injuries, there's a little fact you *goyim* are just sweeping under the fucking rug. He's Jewish." He turned to Kolya. "What do you think some fucking Nazis would do to you, Kolya, if they realized that a Jew had penetrated their group? It would make what Cuza did to you look like a walk in the park. It's more dangerous for a Jew, even if you don't look Jewish."

Tehila leaned elbows on the table. "And what *do* we look like?" She smiled sweetly.

Kolya and Tehila were the only two Jews on the team, two of the only three Jews in the agency. Neither Kolya, blond and blue-eyed, nor Tehila, half Ethiopian and half Ashkenazi Jewish, fit the stereotypical physique that some people associated with Jews.

"No offense meant," Frick said. "Yeah, I know you come in all shapes and colors, although maybe Nazis don't. But Kolya, even though you look the poster child for a Third Reich stormtrooper—you're still Jewish. They find out, they'll fucking kill you—slowly—and they'll enjoy it."

Kolya felt the gaze of everyone at the table. Jonathan raised eyebrows—questioning. Time to respond.

"They'll fucking kill anyone slowly who they think is a spy, Jewish or not." Kolya appreciated the concern, but he wanted to do this.

He really wanted to do this. The prospect of taking down Nazis was one of the reasons he'd accepted the offer to return to his former profession. "And we don't have secret marks that identify us as Jews."

"It's not like Europe in World War II, when with rare exceptions, only Jewish men were circumcised so Nazis could identify them easily," Tehila weighed in. "The majority of American men are circumcised."

Kolya added, "And I'm not."

He had been born into the Soviet Union at a time when Jewish practices such as circumcision were illegal. Fear of being identified as Jewish had been part of Kolya's early life. Why his parents had named him Nikolai, a rare name for a Jew, after his father's non-Jewish father and a name that wouldn't mark him as Jewish. Why he knew so little about Judaism as a child.

It hadn't mattered. He'd still been identified as a Jew, still targeted at the boys' school where he'd spent five years after his mother's death until he'd learned how to fight back, a lesson that remained with him. Now in America, agnostic and secular, he was proud of his Jewish heritage, but he was not interested in elective surgery on that part of his anatomy.

"TMI, Petrov," Elizabeth said.

He glanced at her but said nothing. She already knew he wasn't circumcised. Prior to his getting together with Alex, he and Elizabeth had dated briefly.

Tehila's reaction was different. She shot him a reproving look. "I didn't realize, Kolya. A *bris* is important. I know a good doctor who's taken care of a lot of Russian Jewish men."

"Not important to me, but I'll keep it in mind if I ever become orthodox."

Frick wasn't giving up. "Okay, moving on from the fact we're sending a Jew, who is still fucked up from injuries—sorry Kolya but you are—undercover with Nazis—there's the fact that he has a Russian accent—and a bad habit of using rather rude but colorful Russian curses."

"Have you heard him use any Russian through this whole meeting?" Jonathan asked. "He's been working on eliminating the use of any

Russian for the past month."

"I thought you were being unusually polite, Kolya," Elizabeth said.

"I'm not being fucking polite." A third cup of coffee? Too much? He decided he didn't care and reached for the coffee pot. "I'm just cursing in fucking English. There's a fucking difference." He'd done this before when he had to go undercover for a prolonged time. It took about a month to work through old habits—but once the assignment ended, he could revert.

"You still have an accent. Slight, but it's there." Frick said. "I know you've spent a lot of time undercover, but weren't your previous legends someone of Eastern European background? You're taking the role of a native-born American this time."

"Not all my previous covers were Eastern European. Anyway, part of the legend is that Nickolas Kruger, who I will be playing, had a Ukrainian mother. He grew up in a Ukrainian neighborhood outside Chicago, and Ukrainian was his first language—which would explain my accent. The accent in English for Ukrainians is so close to that of Russians that no one, probably not even a native Russian speaker, would know." Ironic that his first language had been Russian, given that his Jewish grandparents had fled the Ukraine in front of Hitler.

"Unless you throw in some Russian words."

"As Jonathan said, I'm working on that."

Frick threw up his hands. "Okay. Fine. Your funeral."

"Hopefully not."

"Ok," Jonathan said briskly. "Anything else? We'll be going over assignments and getting necessary documents over the next few days. Otherwise, meeting's over. Kolya, mind staying for a few minutes?"

* * * * *

He lingered at the table, drinking yet another cup of coffee as the others filed out. His gaze wandered around the room as he waited, appreciating the original oil paintings on the walls, American scenes in a style reminiscent of Edward Hopper. Was it a Hopper? He looked closer. He couldn't tell. Maybe. Jonathan did like to support new artists, and he also had no qualms about expensive purchases. But did it matter? While Kolya enjoyed giving Jonathan a hard time about his wealth, Jonathan was generous with his friends and even with strangers.

Jonathan returned and helped himself to more coffee before seating himself across from Kolya. "I wanted to talk to you without the others present."

"Obviously." Kolya knew what the question would be, and it wasn't unexpected. Jonathan wasn't just team leader; he was a friend. "Did Frick raise concerns?"

"A little. I just wanted to double check, you know, that you're okay with doing this. Frick's right about what they'll do to you if you're blown. Being Jewish does raise the risks. If anything happens, no one will be able to get to you in time."

"I spent ten years as an operative. I understand the nature of the business."

"Yeah, I know. I was there along with you." Jonathan drank coffee. "Mostly. I wasn't there for all of it. Not for Romania. Are you sure you don't need more time to recover?"

"I may never completely recover, but I'm good enough to do the job. And bringing down neo-Nazis is enticing. Especially because I'm Jewish."

"Okay, your call. But you can bail at any point for any reason. Just so you know."

"I do know." He pushed back from the table. "You coming to dinner Friday night?" It would be his last weekend before he left for Germany. He and Alex would have alone time on Saturday and Sunday, but Friday night had become the night for dinner with friends. Their personal version of a non-religious Shabbat observance.

"As long as you're cooking." Jonathan grinned. "If Alex is cooking, I'm busy."

Alex was everything Kolya could ever want in a woman. He loved her deeply and completely, but she was a terrible cook. Which was fine with him. He preferred cooking to cleaning up.

"Me too."

17

BERLIN, GERMANY

KOLYA PULLED HIS THOUGHTS back from the last team meeting to the present. To the bar where Frick drank beer and he improvised on the rickety piano. And to the role he was playing. "And Teo?"

"He's in the coffee house across the street, keeping an eye on anyone entering the bar. You didn't see him?" Frick asked.

"I wouldn't have asked you if I had. He's gotten better at staying concealed."

"Yeah, the kid's tradecraft's half decent now. What a fucking surprise."

"Still annoyingly eager, though," Kolya said.

"He's a kid. Whaddaya want? By the way, he's also keeping an eye on the Director of the Equality Institute. Just in case your pals decide to take another crack."

"Tell Teo to be careful. I don't think my new *friends* caught more than a glimpse of him, but Ben Rosenberg saw Teo up close. If Rosenberg catches sight of him, he'll ask questions—maybe even call the police."

"Yeah, still, we owe it to Rosenberg to not let some fucking Nazis kill him. Tehila was especially insistent. You know, Rosenberg's pretty messed up, from what Teo says. Hasn't left his house since you *killed* Tehila. Teo said that he kept his kids home from school yesterday, too. Pretty fucking traumatic trick we played on him."

Kolya paused in the middle of an arpeggio. "I'm sorry he's traumatized."

"Yeah, fucking shame."

"It was the best of several bad options. At least he's alive." He thought about the deception used on him one year earlier, setting him up without his knowledge to be kidnapped and tortured. Still... that Rosenberg was physically unharmed didn't preclude his suffering psychological damage.

The team had come up with the plan to fake Kolya killing Tehila as the best way to avoid any actual harm to Rosenberg and yet solidify Kolya's position with Frederick Bauer. While they understood the possible toll on a civilian witnessing up close what he would think was a murder, the good to be achieved was worth the possible psychological trauma. But Kolya still felt bad for the man. Informing Rosenberg what had really happened might help—although Kolya wasn't about to risk the mission or his life. Maybe after it was all over.

"Rosenberg still in danger?" Frick asked.

He resumed playing. *Take the A Train.* "They don't tell me everything. Bauer thinks that Rosenberg had something to do with various neo-Nazis being murdered, but I don't get the impression he's planning another attempt."

"Tehila says Rosenberg's not involved."

"I tend to agree. I think there may be someone else infiltrating. I'm keeping my eyes open. And more importantly, something big is being planned."

"Any idea what?"

"Not yet. Hope to find out more before we meet again. Tomorrow, I'm traveling north as Bauer's bodyguard."

"Any lead on who infiltrated the BfV?"

"Not at this point. Bauer references someone he called the Leader as the person who gives the orders. Bauer claims to be second in command. I assume the Leader is the person of interest in the BfV." He finished the song and reached for his beer. The one remaining couple at the back of the bar applauded again. He raised the beer in salute.

"You get a crack at Bauer's computer?"

"No, but I'm not sure it'd be useful. Bauer has made comments about not trusting electronics. I suspect that's why we're personally visiting his district heads."

"So back here when?"

"A few days. Oh, and have someone check out Bauer's girlfriend. Lisette Vogel. She claims to have grown up in Austin, Texas. I'm getting a strange vibe from her."

"Will do. You okay? PTSD not kicking up?"

"I'm fine." It was something of a lie, but he'd been managing the PTSD, even if he continued to have symptoms. "I'll see you after I return to Berlin. Same signal. Same place."

"Any message to Alex?"

"Thanks, I texted her." He resumed playing, choosing a new song, *Moonlight in Vermont*. "But if I disappear, let her know."

"Someone will. Not me. She might fucking kill me."

18

COLOGNE, GERMANY

THE IMAGE CIRCULATED THROUGH the BfV. A man identified by an American intelligence organization as a far-right violent extremist was possibly in Germany. The Americans didn't have his current alias—just his real name—Nickolas Kruger.

The Leader'd been concerned about letting an American inside the movement. Security was too important. If the planning for Day X were discovered, it would fail. Still, the fact that Kruger was wanted by American intelligence, reinforced by his shooting the black bodyguard of a Jew, meant the American could be trusted. To a degree.

He waited until he got home, the two-bedroom apartment overlooking the Rhine River that he'd shared with his ex-wife, before she moved out. He changed from his suit into jeans and carried a glass of Riesling out onto the balcony.

He drank half the glass as the sun faded, and then left his apartment for a long walk. When he was a mile away, he used his burner phone to call Frederick and pass on the news.

"Extra confirmation is good. We'll need every man we can get," Frederick said.

"Don't tell him anything he doesn't need to know."

"Of course not. Still, I'm taking him on my tour of the northeast."

"Fine. And stay alert. There are American intelligence agents here in Cologne, looking into neo-Nazis, and that could be problematic.

Worse—there's the possibility that the woman Kruger shot was Mossad." The Leader worried about Mossad. They killed without compunction.

"Mossad? Are you kidding?"

"It's possible. Not clear."

"I thought Mossad stayed out of Germany," Frederick said.

"They're supposed to, but if anyone starts killing Jews, they get involved, whether they're supposed to stay out or not. Mossad does not follow rules set by anyone else."

"If she was Mossad, maybe that explains Karl's murder. And the others," Frederick said.

"It looked like Karl was killed by a woman he was fucking. Karl would have fucked a Black woman?" the Leader asked.

"She was very attractive, even if she was Black. Anyway, Karl would have fucked a female sheep, given half a chance. Did you find any video?"

"Not yet."

"What about other Mossad agents?" Frederick asked.

"I've heard nothing. Not that I necessarily would know. Don't go after Jews right now. That always gets their attention." The Leader disliked Jews as much as Frederick, but he had higher goals. Playing up the old hatred of the Jews, and linking them to the evils of the world, was a time-honored way to gain power. But best to avoid confrontations with a deadly agency. Once he gained power, Mossad wouldn't be a concern.

"Even if the Jew at the Equality Institute is the reason our people are being killed?" Frederick asked.

"Even if. Not right now."

"Fine. Not until Day X. Then he's on the list," Frederick said.

"Agreed."

"And the Americans? Who are they?"

"Two Americans. A rich boy playing spy. And a biracial woman who likes expensive jewelry. They're looking for Americans joining neo-Nazi groups in Germany—Americans like Kruger."

"We could give them Kruger so they'll go home. Although it would be a shame. He'd be useful," Frederick said.

"If necessary. But I don't think they're a threat. They're the usual product of the bastardization of America—stupid and gullible." The Leader thought about meeting the Americans. Nothing about them seemed remotely threatening. "They'll get some trivia to take back to Washington and go home. Hopefully, they'll leave before Day X."

"If they start looking too deep or causing problems…"

"Don't worry. If I have to, I'll kill them. But I don't want American intelligence swarming any more than I want Mossad. We're getting close, and I don't want anything to derail Day X. Speaking of which, there's a problem in one of the districts. A traitor contacted the BfV."

The Leader spoke quickly, and Frederick listened intently.

"Do you understand what you need to do?" the Leader asked.

"Yes."

"Good. I'm ditching this phone and getting a new one. Will text you the number. Then you do the same. But be very careful about calls and texts. From now on—phones only for an emergency."

"Got it," Frederick said.

19

NORTHEASTERN GERMANY

KOLYA PETROV DROVE FREDERICK'S Mercedes north, taking A11 out of Berlin to the federal state of Mecklenburg-Vorpommern. Frederick, next to him, was in tour guide mode, offering trivial information about the quaint small villages that they passed, waxing poetic on the history of Germany since the Middle Ages. Both Michael, the person Kolya was playing, and Kolya, in his real identity, tended to be on the introverted side and not particularly interested in non-stop chatter, although when the cover called for it, he could do a good imitation of an extrovert. He was just pleased when it wasn't necessary.

"And we're heading where?" Kolya asked.

"We're making stops in five towns."

"Which towns?"

"Most of them are small: you wouldn't have heard of them. First stop is a farmhouse on the other side of Anklam. And maybe you heard of Greifswald? We'll be there tomorrow. There's a wonderful open-air theater. Best in Germany."

"It's on the Baltic Sea, isn't it?"

"Yes. Very lovely."

"I look forward to seeing it."

"I spent a weekend there last summer with Lisette. She'll meet us in Greifswald tomorrow evening."

"Lisette's very pretty. You're lucky."

"Yes. She is lovely, and she is mine." Frederick's words and tone communicated both pleasure and a threat. "By the way, I looked through your phone. You had some texts from a woman—what was her name—Dara? They seem to have stopped two months ago. What happened with her?"

"I'd really prefer not to talk about it."

"We have no secrets among us. I need to know as much as possible about the people I surround myself with."

Kolya increased speed to pass a VW Golf. "I ended it a while ago. She was attractive but not for me." He'd have to compliment the department that had created his identity on the job compiling his legend, down to the details of creating a fake love life, using the image of a woman who was in fact an ECA agent and living in D.C.

"How so?"

"She looked good. Great legs and ass, big tits. But she was," he hesitated on the words, "more interested in my spending money on her than in pleasing me, sexually or otherwise."

"That is too bad. Too many women don't know their place in life. Maybe somewhere along the road I can find you a good German woman."

"I don't like to mix sex with work. It's distracting. And I really prefer not to talk about my sex life."

"What I said before about us being a unit."

"I've been a soldier. I know what it is to function as a member of a team. That doesn't mean I don't have a right to some privacy."

"I personally work better after a good fuck."

"I don't." He had never cheated on Alex, and he didn't intend to do so now.

"I guess everyone's different."

"True. How about some music?" Kolya turned on the radio and found a classical station. Wagner. *Tristan and Isolde.*

"I like Wagner. Turn it up."

Kolya increased the volume. Not his favorite, either the composer or the piece. Wagner was an anti-Semitic precursor to the Nazis, and apart from his politics, his music was almost unbearably romantic. Listening to *Tristan and Isolde* was like listening to the orchestration of a soap opera. Still, it was better than Frederick's misogynistic and anti-Semitic speeches.

20

BERLIN, GERMANY

THE DAY AFTER THE attack, Ben Rosenberg called every hospital in Berlin. He called the Israeli embassy. He called the American embassy. He called universities to locate a visiting American history professor, which was how Tehila had described her wife. No one had heard of Tehila—or at least no one admitted that they had heard of her.

Nothing.

Now, two days after the attack, he still hadn't returned to the office. Still couldn't bring himself to leave the house. He couldn't rid himself of the images playing in his mind: The man with the gun, Tehila blocking the bullet with her body, the blood, the Americans running up to help.

Where had they taken her? What had happened to her?

He was both horrified at what had happened and terrified at what could have happened to him.

He wasn't just afraid for himself. He was afraid for his wife Rachel and his two sons. Levi was only five and Natan, seven. What had he done, bringing a Jewish family to this country, the graveyard of so many Jews? He told Rachel to keep the children home from school. He also asked that Rachel, a talented painter who co-owned an art gallery, stay home. She'd agreed for the first day after the incident. The boys skipped school, and she didn't go into the gallery. But just staying home wasn't enough. When Rachel let the boys go outside to play in the yard, he ran after them and ordered them back inside. They looked at him oddly, but they obeyed. He put on a movie for them, closed window shades, and made popcorn.

The second day, Rachel'd had enough. She pulled back the shades on the windows to let the light flood in and told the boys to get dressed for school.

"It's not safe," Ben said.

"Not in front of them." She turned to the boys who had just finished a breakfast of challah with jelly and butter. "Go get your things for school."

They scooted up the stairs, and she spoke quietly. "They attend a Jewish school. There's security. There's no indication that the boys are in any danger."

He'd thought there was good security at his office. He'd been wrong. He told her that.

"You're overreacting. But if it'll make you feel better, I'll drive the boys to school."

It didn't make him feel better.

When she returned, he was sitting at the kitchen table. The plastic tablecloth with a polka dot pattern that covered the round wood table was sticky around the boys' plates that they'd failed to put in the sink. The challah and grape jelly were still on the table as well. The butter was starting to melt.

"You couldn't clear off the table?" Rachel offered a mild remonstration.

"I forgot." Normally, he did help, even if he didn't help as much he should. The truth was that he'd been so lost in his thoughts that he hadn't even noticed the food or the plates. He started to rise, but she motioned him to stay in his seat.

"I'll do it." She fixed a cup of tea, English Breakfast with milk, and set it in front of him. "Drink."

He said the blessing for tea—*Baruch atah A-donay, Elo-heinu Melech Ha'Olam shehakol nihiyah bed'varo*—and took a sip. He normally loved tea, but it tasted off, as if the milk were spoiled, but he knew it wasn't.

Still, it was probably a good idea to drink something. He nursed the cup as Rachel cleared the dishes and wiped the table with a damp cloth. She filled the sink with hot water and soap. "You're going to be late. And I'm going into the gallery today."

"I've already called in sick."

"How long are you planning to stay home?"

"I'm not planning anything."

"I see. Would you like me to make you something else to eat? Some eggs maybe? Or toast?"

He shook his head. He knew he was worrying her, but he didn't know how to stop.

It took her less than ten minutes to wash the plates from breakfast and wipe down the counter and sink. He knew that he should get up and dry the dishes, but he didn't. She made herself a cup of tea, sat down across from him, said the blessing, and then drank. "We could leave Germany, if you're that afraid. Sell everything. Go back to England."

"They hate us there, too."

"No, they don't. Some people—maybe. Some people everywhere hate Jews. A small number. Just like there's a small number here that hate us." She studied him. "You need to let go. It was two days ago. Maybe you need to talk to someone."

"You weren't there." He could still smell the blood. Feel Tehila's weight in his arms.

"We've lived here for years. Nothing has happened before. It was just one incident, one man, right? And the police are looking for him."

"They won't find him. All I could tell the police was that he was blond. A blond man maybe late twenties, early thirties—in Germany. How many blond men in that age group do you think there are in this country? I don't even know that I could identify him if they did find him. And I'm not even sure they're looking."

"Still—one man. It doesn't mean that everyone is out to kill you."

"There were at least two more, and they were all Nazis." He thought of the killer. Clearly a Nazi. "I got an email warning me that Nazis planned to kill me. I ignored it." And Tehila, a woman he'd known for

101

one day, had stepped into a bullet for him.

"I work with non-Jews. I have non-Jewish friends. So do you. And they're all appalled at these people."

"Some people were appalled in 1933. That stopped nothing."

"It's not 1933. Your office has security. Everyone there is a friend." She reached over to pat his hand. "It was terrible, but it's over. You need to go back to work. And we're in the hands of *HaShem*. What happens is what He wills."

"You can say that here, in Germany?"

"Yes, I can. Even here in Germany. Go back to work."

"Maybe tomorrow." But he never wanted to leave his house again.

21

ANKLAM, GERMANY

ANKLAM HAD SUFFERED HORRIFIC damage in the various European wars over the centuries. Kolya recognized the look of many buildings. After World War II, when Anklam was under the control of the East Germans, and the Soviets indirectly, it had been rebuilt in the functional but ugly Soviet style of so many areas in the Communist half of Germany. And in Russia, as Kolya remembered. But the town was small, so they quickly passed through it and out into the countryside. Five minutes later, they reached the farm.

The farm consisted of large fields flush with winter wheat, a pen for pigs, a farmhouse with a thatched roof, and a large barn, also with a thatched roof. "One of the few family farms not collectivized under the GDR," Frederick said.

Kolya parked the car directly in front of the farmhouse, and a middle-aged man, wearing a blue cap, stepped outside to welcome them. Frederick introduced Kolya as Michael and the man as Hans. "Hans is a district commander." He didn't give the man's last name, nor did Kolya ask it.

Hans stuck out his hand. "Welcome to my home."

Inside, Hans removed his cap, revealing thinning dark blond hair, and hung it on a peg near the door next to a weather-beaten jacket. Frederick and Kolya followed him into an expanded country kitchen painted a cheery yellow where the generations sat around a table, covered with a tablecloth embroidered with flowers, the age of each male in the family marked by varying amounts and shades of hair. Hans' teenage son Xavier had a full head of light blond hair. Hans' father, maybe sixty-five, had an impressive bald spot on top and a circle of white hair below, and a withered man who looked over a hundred, had a few wisps of white hair combed sideways across a pink scalp.

A flat screen television sat on a stand against one bright yellow wall.

The old man glared at Kolya with undisguised malice.

"My son, father, and grandfather." Hans gestured and motioned Frederick and Kolya to sit at the table. His wife, Gertrude, served hot bowls of dumpling beef stew.

"Eat," Hans said. "Everyone will be here in an hour." Gertrude, faded brown hair, overweight, seated herself next to him and vigorously dug into her bowl. "You will stay here tonight, of course. Frederick, you can have the extra bedroom upstairs. Michael, do you mind the couch?"

"The couch is fine," Kolya said.

"And the weapons?" Frederick asked.

"Barn." Hans shook salt onto his stew, ignoring his wife's reproachful look.

"Good." Frederick dipped his spoon into the bowl. "Michael, after dinner, we'll check out the weapons. Make sure they're in good condition."

"They're in good condition," Hans said.

"Not that I don't trust you, but we have to be sure. We're going to do some late-night training." Frederick nodded at Kolya. "He's a weapons expert. American Army Ranger. Correct, Michael?"

"Correct. What sort of training are we doing?"

"Self-defense." Frederick winked at Hans, who grinned. "You can teach self-defense?"

"Of course." Kolya assumed the weapons were for more than self-defense, but obviously, despite the show-killing of Tehila, he wasn't yet trusted enough to be told the truth. Not expected. He was a stranger and an American, even if of "German" blood.

"Speaking of self-defense, there's a matter to be taken care of tonight. Let's talk for a few minutes after dinner, Hans. Alone," Frederick said.

"Of course. Michael can entertain himself for a bit?"

"No problem." Kolya added pepper and took a bite of the stew. Not bad. "Thank you for dinner. It's delicious."

"Good traditional German food, Michael, not like the shit you get in Berlin," Hans said.

"This is the real Germany," Hans' father said. "Blood and soil. We are tied to the land, and the land is tied to us. We give our blood to the land, and the land nurtures us. That's what makes Germany. Has always made Germany. Land and purity."

The old man continued to glare. He loudly chewed a mouthful of stew, swallowed, and finally spoke. "What is *he* doing here?" He spat the words.

"You know, Frederick."

"I wasn't speaking of Frederick."

"*Grossvater*." Hans spoke a few sentences in German and then turned to Kolya. "My grandfather is a little paranoid, especially about Americans. He was always afraid they would come after him. But I told him that you are one of us."

Kolya looked at the old man and thought of the reason a German man of his age might fear Americans. "He was SS? So was my grandfather." To be precise, the fictional Nickolas Kruger's grandfather had been SS. The story within the story.

"Not just SS. Einsatzgruppen." Hans spoke with pride.

Hans' father nodded and smiled. "*Vater* was one tough guy. He saw a lot of action."

The teenager was laughing in approval.

Kolya took another spoonful of stew without a change of expression, although he felt the anger churn inside him. Einsatzgruppen had been execution squads—roaming units of SS that rounded up Jews in Eastern European villages and murdered them. Mostly by mass shooting. Men, women, children.

Kolya's grandmother had fled Kiev with her parents in front of the German invasion. She told him how her favorite cousin Simka, her uncle and aunt, her school friends, her own grandparents on her father's side, had been taken to a ravine north of the city, a ravine known as Babi Yar, where they were stripped naked, shot, and pushed into the pit. Simka had been ten. Her grandparents had been in their seventies. One of her neighbors who had escaped the massacre described what had happened. His own grandmother repeated it to him.

"My grandmother was loved. Anyone got sick—she was there with food. She was even friends with her non-Jewish neighbors. Not that it helped her. And Simka was smart and funny. We had such good times together."

Until they were both shot by the Einsatzgruppen for being Jewish.

Kolya's grandmother had wept every time she told the story. She would tell the story frequently, even though his own mother worried that Kolya was too young to hear about such things.

"He needs to know," his grandmother had said.

How young had he been? Young enough for it to be traumatizing, old enough to remember clearly. Maybe six. Maybe seven. His grandmother had died when he was eight, one year before his mother's death.

His mother had been secular, and she'd tried to shield him from the pervasive anti-Semitism in St. Petersburg. But even at a young age, he knew that people would kill him for no other reason than he'd been born Jewish.

People like this old man.

Over a million victims had been shot by the Einsatzgruppen before the SS had constructed the gas chambers and instituted factory-style death, because shooting thousands of people was too hard on the murderers. Over three thousand men had been members of the Einsatzgruppen. Fewer than two hundred ever faced consequences for mass murder.

How many had this old bastard killed?

Kolya didn't care that this wreck of a human being was nearing or over one hundred. He didn't care that it'd been more than seventy-five years. He wanted to shoot the old man and for good measure, shoot the three succeeding generations, the son, the grandson, and the great grandson, who were right now laughing, proud that their *Grossvater* had murdered children. But he couldn't—any more than he could show his hatred or disgust. He had a job to do—a job which could save lives, and that job required him to keep his cover.

Maybe later.

"My grandson is a liar. I am not afraid of Americans." The old man suddenly spoke and in English. "I am afraid of Jews. The Jews never forget, and they are strong again."

Then he raised a bony finger and pointed at Kolya. "Jew."

22

BERLIN, GERMANY

THE WOODS WERE LOVELY in the evening, and the tall blue flowers hidden under trees near the banks of the river were gorgeous. However, it was unwise to pick those flowers. The law forbade it. Parks existed for everyone, and allowing the casual picking of flowers would quickly decimate the vivid displays. Germans tended to follow rules, and this rule was generally followed. It was a good rule to obey. Not only was it illegal to pick the blue blooms in order to preserve the beauty of nature for the enjoyment of all, the flowers, monkshood, were deadly if consumed. Even touching the flower, especially the tuber, could have tragic results. However, the lethal possibilities of the flower were exactly why Lisette was there. She intended to do something much more illegal than merely picking a flower.

Lisette carried a basket and wore gloves. Inside the basket: newspaper, a trowel, and a knife. She picked out a batch of flowers for harvesting, but with the caution that had allowed her to remain undetected after six killings, she didn't immediately act. Instead she walked through the park, checking for lovers taking an evening stroll, dog walkers, or joggers. Only when she was satisfied that no one was near enough to observe did she circle back. She knelt on the ground and unfolded the newspaper. Then she began to dig with the trowel, careful not to let any part of the flower touch her bare skin. One by one, she laid flowers and roots onto the newspaper. Once she had harvested enough for a fatal dose, she wrapped the newspaper and placed her tools and the newspaper in the basket.

Another glance around to ensure she was still alone—and then she stood. She stripped off the gloves and dropped them in the basket as well.

Then she headed for the footpath where she almost collided with a teenage boy walking a small white dog.

Had he seen her digging up the flowers?

If he had, he showed no sign, his attention split between his phone and the dog. She breathed a sigh of relief and strode through the park to her car.

Back at her apartment, she pulled up an article by Dr. Lily Robinson, the toxicology expert from Boston whose volume on poisons she had read avidly years earlier. She'd left the book in Texas—having a book on poison in her apartment in Germany might be a tip-off to anyone who came across it—but fortunately, Dr. Robinson also had articles online.

What would Dr. Robinson think if she knew how her knowledge was being used?

The lovely thing about using this kind of poison was that it would look like a heart attack. Yes, Michael was young for heart issues, but he was an American—and Americans had terrible diets. At worst it would look like food poisoning.

She had more flowers than she needed to kill Michael. But she needed it in a form that she could slip into food or drink.

The tubers were the most toxic part of the plant. She'd initially thought of boiling the tubers into a clear liquid, but that was before she re-read Dr. Robinson's articles. Boiling monkshood could reduce the toxicity. People, especially in Asia, would boil it for an herbal tea to cure various ailments. Of course, there was a fine line between the medicinal dose and a fatal dose, but she didn't want to take the risk that the dose might sicken and not kill.

The monkshood had to be full-strength and kill quickly.

First, she dried the tubers in the oven. Then, donning a fresh pair of gloves, she cut the tubers into small pieces. With a mortar and pestle, she ground the bits of tuber into a fine gray powder. Using a plastic spoon, she carefully filled a large prescription bottle, layering it with sugar, and then she tightened the lid. For good measure, she wrapped the bottle in a clean piece of newspaper and taped it. She washed the knife, the trowel, and the mortar and pestle, letting the water run for a good half hour.

The remaining flowers and the plastic spoon were wrapped again in the newspaper. She wrapped both sets of gloves in a separate newspaper. For extra safety, she'd dump the bundles in public garbage cans that were at least several miles apart.

She'd bring the monkshood with her when she met up with Frederick and Michael in Greifswald and watch for an opportunity to slip the powder into Michael's food or drink. Then he would die painfully, which was what he deserved for killing the woman in the Equality Institute garage.

Although maybe she'd try it on someone else first to be sure of the lethality and the dose. Michael might be her primary target, but she had others on her list who also deserved to die. Frederick wasn't expecting her until the evening in Greifswald. A small detour to cross off another name wouldn't take that much time and would kill two birds with one tuber.

23

ANKLAM, GERMANY

THE WORD HUNG IN the air, and then the old man said it again, "Jew." He kept his finger pointed at Kolya. "Kill him before he kills you."

Kolya felt a flash of fear. His stomach clenched. And he heard the voice of the man who had tortured him a year earlier. *Fucking Jews are full of tricks.*

Stop it.

There was a tremor in his hands. He quietly did an exercise. Breath in. Count. Breath out. The tremor eased. He was in control.

The old man probably labeled every stranger a Jew, out of fear or repressed guilt. Still, Kolya's reaction had to be correct. Overreact and he'd raise suspicion.

He was carrying a gun, and he was a good shot. If it came to it, he could kill them before they could kill him. Possibly. Possibly not. But despite his desire to kill the old man for murdering innocents, Kolya hoped it wouldn't come to that. He'd have to kill everyone, including Hans' wife who, as far as he knew, was guilty of nothing except terrible taste in men. Not only could he be charged with murder by German authorities, but killing them, including Frederick, would blow the operation.

Still, it was ironic if Frick turned out to be right. Maybe being undercover with fucking Nazis was too dangerous for someone who was Jewish.

Defuse the situation. He considered his options: denial, indignation, anger —no, he'd sound defensive—before choosing what he thought would be the most effective response. He turned his head to look at Hans.

"It's sad, isn't it, when the old ones start to lose it. They deserve better in their final days. I saw it with my grandfather." His voice almost dripped sympathy. "He thought my mother was a Russian spy. Does he wander, too? My grandfather did. We had to have special locks."

"I haven't lost my mind, Jew!" The old man didn't back down. Then he turned to his grandson. "Don't listen to him. I'm not senile."

But Hans looked sheepish. "He does sometimes get a little confused, although this is the worst I've seen him. *Grossvater*, this is Michael. Look at him. Does he even look like a Jew?"

The old man didn't take his eyes off Kolya. "You think because he's blond and blue-eyed, he's not a Jew? I shot thousands of Jews. There were blond Jews. Some. Not a lot, but some. They intermarry, you know, so they can bring good gentiles into their race—and destroy their blood lines. But they can't fool me. I know their faces. He has a Jew face."

Kolya rolled his eyes.

"His face doesn't look Jewish," Frederick said. "And he's proven himself."

"I'm sorry." Hans looked genuinely embarrassed.

Kolya reached for a slice of bread. No trembling. Good. "Don't worry about it. Like I said, I saw it with my own grandfather. He was brave and a good man, but time and age do terrible things."

The old man turned his anger on his grandson. "You're a fool, Hans." And he looked at Frederick. "You as well. You've been fooled. You want to know if he's a Jew—pull down his pants. That's how you know."

"A lot of men who aren't Jewish are circumcised these days." Frederick buttered a piece of bread. "Doctors convinced parents that it was healthy for baby boys. Especially in America."

"Doctors." The old man sneered. "They're all Jews."

"Not all." Frederick took a large bite out of bread. "Although you're right, too many doctors are Jews. And this was bad medical advice. Still, being circumcised doesn't mean a man is Jewish."

"But not being circumcised does establish that a man isn't a Jew." Kolya turned to Gertrude, who had sat calmly eating and ignoring the fuss. "Excuse me, but would you mind leaving the room."

She checked with Hans, who nodded. She set down her spoon, pushed back her chair, and headed for the living room. "I'll put on coffee when I come back."

Kolya pushed his own chair back and stood. He glanced at Hans. "I'm doing this to calm things down, but it's ridiculous. Normally, I don't show my dick off to a group of men. You really need to get your grandfather on medication." He unzipped his jeans and pulled out his penis. There were barely visible scars from when he'd been burned with a cigar, but the foreskin was intact. "Take a good look, old man. Am I a Jew?"

The old man looked at Kolya's exposed member. There was a furrowing of his brow, his mouth moved for a full moment, and then he finally found his voice. "You fixed it. You had someone sew it back on."

"Enough. Do something about him." Kolya tucked back in, zipped his jeans, and sat down, feeling the absurdity of the situation despite the danger.

The old man looked directly at Kolya. "I don't care what my idiot grandson says. I know what you are."

"Oh for God's sake," Frederick said.

"*Grossvater*, be quiet," Hans said.

Hans' father finally spoke. "Shut up, old man, or I'll send you to that home for crazy old people."

The old man's mouth worked silently for a moment, then without another word, he picked up his spoon and began to eat. His gaze never wavered from Kolya, but he remained silent.

"I don't know what got into him today." Hans apologized again. "And I'm sorry you felt you had to do that."

"No need for you to apologize. As I said, my grandfather went crazy too. Now, can we eat? Perhaps Gertrude could come back and make that coffee." The adrenaline draining, he started on the stew again, hoping that the relief coursing through him didn't show.

It was the height of irony that the anti-Semitism of the old Soviet Union that had forbidden Jewish rituals allowed a Jew to keep his identity secret while infiltrating a Nazi organization. He made a mental note to tell Tehila.

24

ANKLAM, GERMANY

AFTER DINNER, FREDERICK AND Hans stepped outside and spoke quietly for a few minutes. Kolya remained at the table, drinking coffee, enduring the glares of the murderous old Nazi and answering questions about America from the teenage son. The PTSD that he'd managed to fight back earlier whispered in his mind, but he continued to count his breaths and remained in control, even as he chatted with people who would murder him if they knew who he was.

After a few minutes, Frederick returned and motioned to Kolya, and he trailed the two of them to the barn. It was a large unpainted weather-beaten structure, with a moss-covered roof that extended nearly to the ground. Inside, were empty stalls except for one occupied by a white horse, swaybacked and thin, but from age, not neglect. Hans paused to give the horse a pat and a biscuit that he kept in a barrel in front of the stall. "Thirty-two years old. That's ancient for a horse." The horse nuzzled Hans, and he stroked the animal's neck.

Then he led them past the stall to an open area and rows of wooden crates. Hans opened one and removed an HK-91. He offered the weapon to Kolya, who took it and examined it. It was a deadly effective weapon and in excellent condition.

Not what he wanted to see.

"Are you familiar with these?" Hans asked Kolya.

He nodded. "Nice weapon. How many do you have?"

"I have fifty, but we have thirty in our local group. I have a shooting range set up in the field behind the house. Perhaps Michael can help give pointers to some of the less experienced shooters in the group."

"Ammunition?" Kolya asked.

Hans swung open another crate. Enough ammunition for a small army, which was, it seemed, what he'd created.

What Kolya could surmise, given the kind and number of weapons, worried him. Thirty people with these weapons could mow down dozens, maybe hundreds. And he would be training them to shoot? He thought of the old man in the house, who had killed thousands of Jews. And his odious offspring applauding that fact.

What could he do?

For the moment—nothing.

* * * * *

They arrived an hour later. Mostly young, although a few were middle-aged. One man brought his twelve-year-old son, another brought a ten-year-old, both insisting that the boys were old enough to participate. All spoke at least a little English; a number were fluent. All of them white. Almost all men. Two young woman. Thirty-two people, not counting two boys.

He caught a disapproving glance from Frederick towards the young women. Frederick thought women's roles should be supportive. Equality between the genders was contrary to the Nazi philosophy.

Frederick ordered the women to stay in the barn with the boys. All four protested, but he was firm. "You have your place, and it isn't out there."

Then the guns were handed out to the men.

Kolya got some first names, but no last names. Men nodded at him as he helped hand out the weapons and demonstrate the proper way to hold the gun. Several in the group were familiar with weapons. Many were not.

They carried the guns out to the field behind the house, while Kolya carried paper targets. A chill wind swayed bushes and bent the tops of trees, and Kolya could feel the chill. He turned his jacket collar up.

He stapled five targets of human silhouettes to wood frames in a fenced area where he assumed the horse grazed at other times. The paper rustled with the gusts of wind.

Guns in hand, the group lined up to shoot. Five at a time, five at each target. Kolya answered questions and offered suggestions, hating that he was helping them learn to shoot. He took a gun from one young man who had laughingly pointed his gun at another man.

"Never point a gun at a person unless you intend to use it."

The young man apologized, and Kolya returned the gun.

Once he glanced back at the house. Silhouetted against a lit upstairs window was the old man. Kolya could feel the malevolent gaze.

He didn't look again.

After everyone had the chance to shoot, Frederick stepped to the front and faced them. He held up a hand. The chatter died down; weapons pointed towards the ground.

Kolya glanced around for Hans and saw him standing behind the group, his weapon raised and ready. His apprehension rose. Something bad was about to happen.

He had a gun, and he was not a prisoner. He fought down the fear.

Frederick cleared his throat. "It's one thing to shoot at paper. It's another to shoot at a person. Does everyone realize that?"

There were murmurs. Someone said something that expressed eagerness to kill.

Frederick waited for silence before speaking again. "Walter, will you come here and join me? Put your gun on the ground, please."

Walter, overweight, balding, with glasses, looked surprised at being called up. He shook his head and didn't move. Frederick motioned for him to approach. "Come on, Walter. Don't be shy. I have something special for you. A special honor."

The group began to applaud and chant his name. Hans took Walter's gun and placed it on the ground. Then he raised his own gun again. With men on either side pushing him, Walter shuffled forward until he reached Frederick, who laid a hand on his shoulder and turned him to face the crowd.

Kolya had a very bad feeling about what was about to happen.

"Walter," Frederick spoke loudly, "did you know that someone has been in touch with the BfV, offering to provide information on the plans of Germany Now?" Frederick spoke in German, but Kolya understood. So did everyone else.

The guns were no longer pointed at the ground. They were raised and pointed towards Frederick and Walter.

"*Nein. Nein.* I don't know. I never..."

"Oh come, Walter." Frederick's tone remained pleasant. "Of course, you do. The messages from your computer went straight to the BfV. And then to me. Did you think we didn't have people inside?"

Walter shook his head again, but his whole body quaked.

Kolya only had minutes, maybe seconds to act. He had the 9mm semi-automatic under his sweater. He could grab an HK-91 from the man nearest him. Then what? As good a marksman as he was, he'd be unable to shoot all twenty-nine of them—thirty-one, if he counted Frederick and Hans, before they shot him. It would be suicide. Just trying to eliminate Frederick would mean certain death.

Even if Kolya managed to shoot Frederick before he was shot, would that save Walter? Would it stop whatever plans were in the works? If Kolya managed to kill all of them, which was almost impossible, his cover would be blown. There were cells of Germany Now around the country, ready to carry out whatever plans Frederick had put into motion. And Frederick was the face of the organization, not the head. The head was someone unknown in the BfV.

Kolya couldn't save Walter. He would die with Walter, and with him, the chance of stopping whatever Germany Now might be planning.

He was in the same situation that he'd managed to avoid just days earlier, only then he could have walked away without shooting Ben Rosenberg. He couldn't walk away here.

But he had to try something, short of getting himself killed.

He held up a hand. "Frederick. Can I speak to you?" Without waiting to hear a response, he crossed the field in front of the men with guns, feeling the quiver in his body. But he didn't have the time to deal with it. Instead, he focused on the task.

He reached Frederick and the terrified Walter and spoke quietly in English. "Remember after the garage, I told you that I didn't want to be involved in anything fucking stupid. This is fucking stupid."

Frederick turned his gaze, keeping his grip on Walter. "Traitors have to be punished. This is not up for debate."

"You will have twenty-nine witnesses to a murder. Any one of them could have a crisis of conscience and go to the cops. Or tell their wives. You'll have a body to get rid of. And people—maybe his family, maybe the people he's in touch with—will know he came here tonight. Someone will come here looking for him."

"Get back to the line, Michael. This is a leadership decision. And if I don't follow through, there will be no discipline. You are either one of us or you're not. Are you one of us?" Frederick's voice was hard and cold. Any hint of his gregarious, friendly veneer had disappeared.

Kolya could almost feel the raised guns behind him, the old Nazi peering down at him from the house. The chant, *Jew*. He had only two choices. Make a futile gesture that would result in his own death or retreat and leave Walter to his fate. He took three breaths to still the tremors and nodded, "I am one of you," before retreating, hating himself and the role he was forced to play.

Walter begged again. "Please. Please. I didn't betray the cause. I have children."

Frederick's demeanor turned friendly again. He patted Walter on the shoulder. "Here's what I'm going to do. I'm going to let the other men here decide what to do. Talk to them." He released Walter's shoulder and took his place in the line of men.

Walter faced the line and tried again. "I didn't do anything."

"Blood traitor." The words were shouted by one man.

"Spy." Another shout.

"*Nein. Nein.* I am a true German." Walter raised his hands in supplication, and Kolya's heart thudded.

Then one of the men in the line shouted. "Run!"

Walter turned and began to run, an awkward overweight man forcing his legs to move. It was a shambling uneven imitation of a run. But even if he'd been a world-class sprinter, he wouldn't have made it. Twenty-nine men opened fire with the assault rifles, and Walter went down, his body almost torn in half.

Kolya tried to fight down his revulsion and his anger—at the men firing—and at himself.

"Michael."

Kolya almost didn't respond to the name, too absorbed in hatred. Then he remembered who he was pretending to be and turned to Frederick. "Yes?"

"You have a pistol. You have the honor of administering the coup de grace."

He felt the eyes on him, the eyes of the men who'd just committed murder, the eyes of the old Nazi watching from the upstairs window.

He removed his gun from the holster on his belt. He hesitated, wanting to shoot Frederick and as many of the others as he could—but instead he crossed the field. The wind shifted, and he could smell the blood.

When he reached Walter, Kolya stooped and placed his fingers against the pulse spot in the neck. Nothing. Walter was out of pain. But he reported otherwise. "Still alive." Then he stood and fired a round into the side of Walter's head—to the cheers of the group behind him.

The fact that he didn't actually kill Walter didn't absolve Kolya of responsibility for failing to stop a murder. But he'd maintained his cover. That was what fucking mattered. Not a man's life.

* * * * *

Four men dragged Walter's body to the pig pen in front of the barn. Hans, Frederick, and then the rest of the men followed. The body was rolled into the pen.

"It's supposed to storm early tomorrow morning. That should take care of any blood." Hans slung his gun over his shoulder. "The pigs will take care of the body. By tomorrow, there will be nothing much left. My family and I will dispose of anything that the pigs leave."

The men returned to the barn, where the two boys fed biscuits to the old white horse, and the two young women, looking very disgruntled, perched on top of haystacks.

"Stop." Hans took a biscuit from the hand of one of the boys. "You can overfeed a horse. It's not kind to overfeed an animal. You," he looked at the two women, "were supposed to watch the boys."

One woman yawned. The other shook her head. "We came to be fighters, not babysitters."

"You will do what you're told to do in Germany Now." Frederick's voice contained just the hint of a threat. "Did any of you go outside?"

Both young women shook their heads. "We stayed here."

"Fine. Now we are all going to clean the guns. Even you can learn. You should know how to do it. Michael?"

Emotions and PTSD barely under control, Kolya demonstrated how to clean a gun. Then the group began the process of cleaning the weapons. Supplies were adequate, and it took another fifteen minutes. Then one by one, the men handed over their HK-91s, and Kolya started packing the guns back in the cases.

All the while, he weighed options. Walter's murder had underscored the deadly nature of Germany Now.

He had to prevent any more deaths—and to atone for the death he'd failed to prevent.

Disable the guns? He could sneak out in the middle of the night. Remove all the firing pins, but doing so with fifty guns would take a lot of time.

He thought of the old man peering out from the second story of the house, the old man who had shot thousands of Jews. His mind flashed to the image of Walter's terror, and his own failure. His hands started to shake again. *Breathing exercise. Focus on the sensory details of the barn.* Then he was back.

"Are you having more practice sessions?" he asked Frederick.

"It's up to Hans. Hans—how many sessions have you planned?"

"Two or three." Hans was also busily packing weapons.

So disabling the firing pins wouldn't work. Anything he did, short of destroying the guns, could be reversed if found in time. And if they found that the guns had been sabotaged, they'd look for the culprit.

He would be the prime suspect. It didn't matter whether they thought he was Jewish—although the old bastard screaming that he was a Jew had been more than a little unnerving. If something happened to the guns right after he'd appeared on the scene, it would be reasonable to blame it on him. His feeble attempt to save Walter would be additional evidence that he was the saboteur. And he could be discovered before he'd obtained—and passed on—information about just what Frederick planned.

So not the best alternative.

How many more groups like this existed? They were going to four more towns. In how many more towns were there armed groups training for whatever the fuck Frederick had in mind?

Was he going to have to watch again while more people were murdered?

He might.

While he played alternatives out in his mind, he continued to check and pack weapons.

One of the young women approached and smiled at him. "Where are you from in America?" She wore a halter top and low-cut jeans. He suspected she was under twenty, maybe even under eighteen.

"I've lived all over. Why?"

"I always wanted to go. I like Americans." She leaned, giving him a view of her breasts. "Do you like German women?" She tossed her head and her hair in a way that she probably thought was alluring.

"I like German women. I just like them a little older." And—not Nazis.

She pouted. "German women mature early."

"Check with me in five years." He didn't look at her again, but he could feel her anger at the rejection.

Still, she left him alone and joined the group gathering in a circle.

He packed the HK-91s, as the excitement of the waiting followers grew. The room buzzed with conversation.

Frederick and Hans spoke to each other, close enough for Kolya to overhear a few words.

"Where?" Frederick's other words were muffled.

"Safe. Below." Hans said more, but Kolya couldn't hear.

What was safe and where was below?

Then they moved on.

Shifting crates to stack them more efficiently, Kolya noticed a hollow sound under the straw. With his foot, he scrapped the straw aside and saw a metal handle in the floor. A trapdoor. What was underneath? Was whatever Hans had referred to hidden underneath?

Take a look—after everyone goes to sleep.

Frederick held up his hand for silence. A hush fell on the crowd.

Then Frederick gave his standard speech, the speech Kolya had already heard his first day in Germany. But it ended differently. He informed the group that they were all on call, to respond to their district commandant without hesitation—when they received the order. The order would be coming soon. Then they, the pure of blood, would cleanse the soil.

There was applause and raised fists.

25

BERLIN, GERMANY

BEN ROSENBERG TUCKED THE boys into their beds in the room they shared and read them a chapter from a book about magicians and golems. Levi, the youngest, fell asleep while Ben read, but Natan stayed awake through the chapter, sometimes interrupting to ask questions.

"Are golems real?"

"Of course not."

"Monsters?" Natan at seven thought he was very grown up, but he wasn't quite as brave as he pretended.

Ben hesitated. Monsters were real; he'd seen one just a few days earlier, but Natan wasn't thinking of human monsters, of the monsters that killed a million Jewish children or their modern counterparts, who carried on the bloody traditions. He was thinking of imaginary and magical monsters, and Ben couldn't burden Natan with the knowledge of the real evils of the world, not yet. "No, Natan, monsters are make-believe."

After finishing the chapter, he gave the sleeping Levi and the almost asleep Natan goodnight kisses and then lingered upstairs for a few minutes until Natan also dropped off. Normally, he performed the bedtime rituals with Rachel, but tonight, she'd had a phone call just as they started up the stairs. She'd waved at him to go without her, and he had. It happened from time to time, but now any deviation from the normal left him uneasy. He knew it was irrational. It didn't mean he could stop.

She was off the phone by the time he returned to the kitchen, where she'd left his dessert, a slice of apple cake, on the table. He picked it up and returned it to the cake dish. Then, mindful that he needed to contribute, he washed the plate.

"You barely ate," she said.

"I'm just not hungry."

She gave him a look somewhere between concern and exasperation.

They moved from the kitchen to the living room, where they settled into their usual spots on the couch where they watched a show in the evenings, but neither made a move to turn on the television. She read something on her phone. He took out his phone but couldn't focus enough to read.

"Why don't we go to bed," he said.

"At eight o'clock?"

"So no?"

"No."

The outside light illuminated the porch. Normally, it would be off. They both tried their best to be good stewards of the earth and conserve energy. But tonight he wanted it on, and, for some reason, she didn't argue.

He understood why fifteen minutes later when the doorbell rang, and she welcomed in four people from the Equality Institute: the German-Turkish twins, Hasan and Ahmet, his secretary Lena, and his second-in-command, Ernestina.

"We're here for an intervention," announced Hasan, the twin majoring in chemistry. He was identical to Ahmet except for a scar over one eyebrow.

Ben glanced at Rachel, who offered an apologetic smile.

"So that's why you were on the phone."

"This has got to stop, Ben," Rachel said.

"I know. I'm just scared. For you and the boys as well as myself."

"We understand," Ahmet, the second twin said. "After we heard what happened, we were all scared. It's terrible what happened. But if you let the bastards get to you, they win."

The twins seated themselves on the spotless floor. Lena took a wing chair. Ernestina sank into the other wing chair. Rachel, ever the hostess, bustled from the room and returned with springerle, anise-flavored biscuits, and cups of rosehip tea. The twins dug into the biscuits.

"We need you back." Ernestina picked up a cup of tea but declined the biscuits. "We're seeing a lot of neo-Nazi activity on various dark sites. We think something is up. You always took the lead on tracking them down."

"Maybe that's why they tried to kill me," Ben said.

"Or scare you," Lena said.

"They shot Tehila. If she hadn't been there, it would have been me. And I'm not just scared for myself." Ben glanced over at his wife. "As I told you. I'm scared for you. And for the boys sleeping upstairs."

"I know," she said gently. "That doesn't mean it's healthy."

"We all understand. That's why we recruited some friends from college," Hasan said. "To take turns watching your house."

Ben rose from the couch and crossed to the window. He peered out. He saw an unfamiliar car parked four houses down, but he couldn't see anyone in it.

"You won't even know they're there," Ahmet said.

"He knows they're there because we just told him," Hasan said.

"Other than that," Ahmet said.

"And we're going to take turns driving you to the Institute. All of us," Ernestina said.

Ben remained at the window, not because he saw Hasan's friends, but because he didn't want his co-workers—his friends—to see his tears. Yes, there were terrible people out in the world, violent neo-Nazis. But he wasn't alone. He hadn't appreciated that fact.

Maybe he would take the risk and rejoin the world. It was worth it. Not just for himself—for Hasan and Ahmet. For Ernestina and Lena. For Rachel. And for his sons sleeping upstairs.

26

HEAVY CURTAINS BLOCKED THE windows of the living room, the furniture was old and shabby, and the air was heavy with the odors of onions, garlic, and meat, left from dinner. Still, the couch was comfortable, and Gertrude made it up with sheets, pillows, and a blanket. Kolya was exhausted and despite his guilt and anger at the murder he'd been unable to stop, he had to fight down the impulse to let go. But if he were going to check out whatever was under the trapdoor in the barn, he'd have to do it when everyone else was asleep—which meant staying awake. Maybe it would shed light on Frederick's plans. It wasn't much, but it was all he could do.

He'd kept an eye on Frederick's use of electronics as another possible source of information, but that didn't look like it would pan out. Frederick kept his phone on him and rarely used it. Kolya had not seen a laptop among Frederick's possessions. Whatever computer Frederick owned was probably still in Berlin. If Hans had a computer, he kept it somewhere other than the kitchen, the living room, or the barn.

Kolya was an accomplished hacker but hacking into a computer required a computer. Searching the house would be even riskier than checking the barn.

Frederick and Hans, upstairs, had not yet gone to bed—or at least so he assumed from the footsteps on the wood floors. To be safe,

127

Kolya would wait at least an hour after the noise ceased. Maybe two. If he fell asleep, he might not wake up until the morning. If he set an alarm to wake him in two hours, someone upstairs might hear it. The phone on vibrate might not do the job. Best to stay up.

He slid off his shoes, and then, fully clothed, he settled onto the couch with his phone. He had to tamp down a surge of hatred. He wanted to take his gun upstairs and shoot them all, everyone from the hundred-year-old Nazi down to the teenager, including the passive housewife. But he couldn't do it. And he couldn't let anyone see his anger, either. *Calm down.* He'd killed people before. He had been in worse situations.

But had he ever just stood by while an innocent person was shot?

A memory surfaced. A year earlier, Eric—a fellow agent—had been murdered in front of Kolya's eyes when Kolya had been taken prisoner. But that was different. Then he'd been a prisoner—helpless, held down by four men while a thug placed a gun against Eric's head and pulled the trigger.

And he'd been helpless tonight.

No, not helpless. He'd had a gun. He hadn't had men holding him down. He could have tried to save Walter, even if he would have failed and died himself. But he'd been held back by his responsibility to the mission—a mission which would've ended with his death.

He did try to intervene. It just didn't work.

But his emotions were familiar. As a prisoner, he'd felt anger, fear, and helplessness, and now he was feeling it again, as he flashed between the present and the memories from a year ago.

The breathing exercises weren't sufficient. He tried a grounding technique, focusing on the sensual details of the room, the feel of the couch under him, the smells from the kitchen. Then he went a step further—he dredged up the memories of his captivity, let himself feel the rage and the terror, and then he shifted his thoughts to what had happened earlier. Some of the feelings were the same, and some were not. He mentally compared the two situations. He'd had no control then; he had control now.

The panic and the fury began to ease. Then he was back in the present, with a job to do.

Think of something else. Something pleasant.

Alex.

He let his thoughts drift in her direction, remembering their last evening together.

GEORGETOWN, WASHINGTON, D.C.

He sat at the piano, improvising on a Bill Evans tune while the salmon with maple syrup that he'd prepared for dinner baked in the oven. While he improvised, she climbed stairs to their bedroom. When she returned, she wore her sapphire engagement ring—and nothing else. She slid next to him on the piano bench.

He stopped playing. "You could have asked me upstairs."

"I thought—something different for your last night in town."

"I should go turn down the salmon."

"Maybe you should." She leaned in, placing his hands on her nipples.

He kissed her long and deep, enjoying the softness of her breasts, and then he slid his hands downward. "Fuck the salmon."

"The salmon's not what I want to fuck," she breathed into his ear.

"Me neither. Although the bench is a little small. And a little hard."

"Is it?" She slipped a hand down the front of his jeans. "Not the only hard thing here. We could do it on top of the piano."

"I love this piano, but it's not exactly comfortable." He always mocked television shows where a couple had sex on a desk, a table, or the floor, but he had to admit that this was exciting. "I don't want it collapsing under us. We could move to the couch. Or the bed."

"You're surprisingly conventional for a guy who regularly risks his life." She kissed his chest, her tongue tracing over his burn scars as she unbuttoned his shirt.

"And you're surprisingly adventurous for a top attorney." He unbuckled his belt and unzipped his jeans.

"You think attorneys are boring?"

"Some are."

"But not me."

"Never."

She positioned herself on his lap. Then there was no more talking. The piano bench was awkward, but not too small after all.

The salmon was a little overdone but still edible. She put on a robe for dinner and then they headed upstairs for a second, more traditional round in the bedroom. They didn't talk about his trip or her worry for him after what had happened a year earlier. That conversation was saved for the morning. Her tears in the car. Then her parting words at the airport: "If you die, I'm going to be really pissed."

ANKLAM, GERMANY

He woke with a start. Despite his resolve, he'd drifted off. *Stupid. Stupid.* Thinking about Alex, about sex had calmed him—a little too much. Farmers rose at the break of dawn to start on the daily chores, and if it was close to daybreak, he risked running into Hans.

He checked his phone. Three a.m. Still enough time.

The house was dark. He sat on the edge of the couch and slid his shoes on, grateful he'd worn running shoes, and listened for any sound of movement as he tightened the laces. Nothing. Just in case, he arranged the pillows and blankets so his absence wouldn't be immediately obvious. It wouldn't fool a close inspection, but anyone casually glancing at the couch on the way to the kitchen for a snack might not notice.

He picked up the phone and cautiously crossed the room, pausing at the bottom of the stairs. He heard a few muffled snores but no other sounds.

He headed through the kitchen and out the back door.

* * * * *

Once his eyes adjusted to the darkness, he followed the path towards the barn, dimly illuminated by a three quarters moon, although he saw increasing clouds moving across the face. The rain would start in an hour or two. He paused at the pig pen. Even in the dim light, he saw the pigs working on what was left of Walter, a horrific sight. Equally horrible—Walter's family wouldn't know what had happened. Walter would've just disappeared. There would just be an emptiness, and no finality.

If Kolya survived his assignment, he'd find Walter's family.

He reached the barn, slid the door open, and waited until he closed the door behind him to turn on his phone flashlight. The old horse gave out a soft whinny at the sight of a human. Kolya reached into the treat barrel and offered the horse a biscuit with the flat of his hand, feeling the velvet of the animal's muzzle against his palm.

The horse, apparently satisfied, returned to doing whatever horses did in the middle of the night, and Kolya moved on.

The trapdoor was blocked by the crates containing guns, and they needed to be carefully moved. He switched off the light to save the phone battery as he repositioned the crates while listening for any possible threat. But he heard nothing except the wind in the trees outside, the creaking of the wooden boards, and the old horse shifting in its stall. Five minutes to move the crates, and then he pulled open the trapdoor.

He aimed his flashlight into the darkness. It illuminated a wooden ladder, but the beam wasn't powerful enough to reach the floor below. The ladder was old, with graying wood and blackened patches.

The state of the ladder worried him. If the ladder broke and he fell, he'd be trapped—an easy target when found. Or he could be injured, almost as bad. Quite apart from the fact that his leg wasn't completely back to normal and reinjuring it would hamper his ability to operate, it was doubtful that Frederick would accept an explanation on how Kolya'd managed to injure his leg in the middle of the night.

Still… Hans weighed more than Kolya, and he would have used this ladder.

Unless the teenager had been the one to climb down. Unless there was another entrance. Unless the room below wasn't even used, and Kolya was risking exposure and death for no good reason.

He tested the top of the ladder. Firmly planted.

If you die, I'm going to be really pissed.

So would he.

He turned off the flashlight, plunging the barn back into total darkness. After pocketing the phone, he turned around and, grasping the top of the ladder, carefully eased his left, stronger leg onto a rung. The rung creaked but held. He put his right foot on the next rung, gripping the sides of the ladder—just in case. More creaking. Step by step, rung by rung, he proceeded in the blackness.

The next rung gave way as soon as he put his weight on it, and the entire ladder shook as the wood broke off and fell. He clung to the sides of the ladder and pulled himself up, breathing deeply.

Abort?

No, he had to be at least halfway down. He'd come this far.

It couldn't be much further. Could it? *Just keep going.*

He waited for his breathing to calm and then he lowered himself past the broken rung to find a firm foothold. Then he continued his descent.

A few tense minutes, and then his right foot felt the solidity of the floor. Both feet on the ground, he let go of the ladder, retrieved his phone, and switched on the light. He shone it upward to judge the distance. Maybe twenty feet, the height of a house. The broken rung was maybe ten feet off the ground. He'd have no problem getting back up, but would the broken rung signal to Hans that there had been an intruder?

Maybe. In any case, there was nothing he could do.

Then he shone the light around the room. It was big, maybe twenty feet by twenty feet, concrete walls, concrete floor. Cold and damp. It reminded him of the underground room in Romania where he'd been held captive and tortured. The light of the flashlight wavered as his hands shook.

I'm not a prisoner. It's not Romania.

The trembling eased, and the feeling passed.

He checked the time. Three thirty. The sun rose between six and seven in Germany in September. He had time.

He noticed what looked like a wooden door on a section of the wall to the far left. An easier way out? The door, cracked and dirty, looked ancient. He turned the knob and pulled. The door slowly creaked open, and he ran the flashlight over the small space behind the door. If there had ever been an exit, it was long gone. Two feet of open space dead-ended in a wall of dirt. He thought of the history of the region, of the hundreds of years of wars. Had someone wanted a hiding place —or an easy exit? If so, it had been filled in long ago.

He stepped back into the main room and shut the door. Then he began to explore.

There was a pile of something on the far right of the room. He ran the flashlight over the pile of dark shapes. Body bags. Dozens of them.

He moved to several white sacks stacked next to the body bags. Quicklime. Perpetrators of genocide often used quicklime at mass grave sites to conceal the odor of decay and the acidification of soil from so many bodies. Some killers also held the incorrect belief that quicklime destroyed bodies. That quicklime was more likely to preserve bodies than destroy them didn't change the unnerving fact that there was only one reason to accumulate and hide body bags and quicklime. Frederick—and Hans—intended to kill a lot of people.

Who? And when?

27

HAMBURG, GERMANY

LISETTE HAD RARELY VISITED Hamburg since her return to Germany. The last time had been six months earlier for recon before approaching a target. But that target hadn't panned out, and she hadn't returned. She'd expected the visit to her former hometown to be more emotional, but she barely remembered any of the city, except the house in Blankenese where she'd lived as a child and where her father had been murdered.

She was a little tired. Not surprising. Not only had she been up late, preparing the monkshood, she'd woken at 4:30 a.m. It was almost a three-hour drive from Berlin to Hamburg, and she needed to be there by breakfast.

On reaching the city, she parked her car three blocks away from her destination. Best not to have her means of escape too close. She walked to the coffee shop where her target normally ate breakfast, and before going in, looked through the window. And he was there, right on time.

Christian was in his sixties, overweight, out of shape, one of the children of Hitler's followers in the Third Reich, but one who'd regretted that his parents hadn't done more to rid Germany of undesirables.

Christian would have made the architects of the Third Reich proud. He'd participated in the riots of Hoyerswerda in September

1991, where German neo-Nazis firebombed a dormitory filled with immigrants. He'd moved on to Chemnitz, where a flourishing far-right underground killed people of African or Middle Eastern origin. Lisette knew of at least three people he'd killed. She'd had him on her list since she'd heard Heinrich describe how Christian had bludgeoned to death a family of African immigrants: a mother, father, and infant son.

Heinrich had laughed, describing it.

Christian moved to Hamburg in the mid-'90s with his wife and two children, and mostly stayed off the radar of law enforcement in the years that followed. Frederick knew of him from far-right recruits in both Chemnitz and Hoyerswerda and had sent Heinrich to Hamburg to invite Christian to join the group. Christian had rejected the gesture, stating that he was too old to join any group, and he wasn't going to take orders from someone who could be his grandson.

Lisette had overheard Heinrich and Frederick discussing Christian—and then independently confirmed the information.

There were police records—officers who suspected Christian and who'd spoken to him. He was on the Equality Institute's list of violent neo-Nazis. But charges had never been brought, and he'd never paid any price for what he'd done.

As far as Lisette knew, Christian had stopped killing people in the twentieth century, and he was too old to have been one of the men who killed her father. Nevertheless, what he'd done thirty years earlier still required justice.

Lisette wore a black wig and large tinted glasses for the occasion, dressed in a biking outfit, spandex pants, close fitting T-shirt, and biking gloves. This time, she didn't have a bike nearby. But in September, there were few reasons to wear gloves. Biking was one of them. She hoped that the death would be written off as natural, but just in case, best not to leave fingerprints.

Christian was seated alone at a small table in the crowded café, reading a newspaper and drinking his cappuccino.

She had worked out several possible scenarios, and now, she made a decision.

She took out her phone, holding it in front of her face as if her attention were on it, much like almost everyone else in the restaurant. And walked forward. Paused and waited until Christian lifted his cappuccino for a sip. Then she clumsily collided with his chair, knocking his arm and his coffee.

"You idiot." He rose, furious, his shirt stained, the rest of the coffee in a puddle on the table. "You goddamn little idiot."

She grabbed napkins and began to sop up the mess. "I'm so sorry."

"You should be sorry."

"Let me buy you another coffee. What were you drinking?"

He wasn't mollified. "You ruined my shirt too." He wore a T-shirt that looked ten years old.

"And I can give you five Euros to have your shirt cleaned. I'm so very sorry."

The offer calmed him. "Just the coffee will do." He mopped the chair with a wad of napkins. "And another cinnamon roll."

A cappuccino and a cinnamon roll probably cost more than his shirt was worth, but it was still a small price to pay. And at least she didn't have to perform a strip tease for this one. "Sugar in your cappuccino?"

"A lot of sugar," he growled.

She stood in line, patiently waiting her order. After ordering, the scent of the roll, cinnamon, and butter, was heady, and she considered buying one for herself, but in an act of caution—and self-denial—decided against it. She did fill her travel mug with coffee as well as purchasing the items for Christian. She carried the small plate with the cinnamon roll and the beautifully prepared cappuccino over to a wooden counter where sugar and various additions to coffee were laid out and then waited patiently while a young man doctored his coffee with milk and chocolate. After he finished and joined a group of friends, she checked that no one was near before slipping the bottle with the sugar and ground monkshood out of her purse and dumping two tablespoons into the cup. She added another three teaspoons of pure sugar to counter any bitterness in the taste and mixed the sugar and the poison with a plastic stirrer.

Then she carried the cup and the pastry over to the table where Christian sat, finishing the first cinnamon roll. Ironic. Given his girth, his diet, and his age, he was likely to keel over at any time without her help. Of course, that also suited her purposes. No one would be surprised at Christian suddenly dying of a heart attack.

She set the plate and cup in front of him. "We okay now?"

"Okay." Then he seemed to see her for the first time. He smiled at her and patted the seat next to him. "You look like my granddaughter. Sit down. Keep an old man company."

She didn't like the comparison to his granddaughter. She didn't like to think of him as a father or a grandfather. He'd killed people, so he had to pay. His family didn't matter. The men who'd thrown children into gas chambers had had families. The man who'd killed her own father probably had a family.

Then she reconsidered.

He had lived in Hamburg for twenty years. He was a neo-Nazi going back thirty years. Maybe he knew the man who'd killed her father.

She sat down, took off her glasses, and smiled at him. "I'll stay for a few minutes. I never knew my grandfather." She kept the gloves on.

"That's a shame." Christian started on the new cup of coffee. He didn't notice the taste.

"Wait." She acted surprised. "Do I know you?"

He looked uneasy. "I don't know. Do you?"

"Yes, yes. I think I do. My boyfriend told me about you. Showed me your picture." She smiled, a smile that had never failed to work with men. "Frederick Bauer."

Christian relaxed. "Yeah, I remember him. Wanted me to follow him. Like I would follow some kid."

"But you believe in the cause." She leaned on an elbow. "Don't you?"

"It's a lost cause. Not worth bothering with. Not at my age." He drank more of the coffee, and then he started on the fresh cinnamon roll. "I believe in the principles, but I'm not risking my neck, not anymore."

He was halfway through the coffee. How fast did monkshood

work? She wasn't sure. But she needed to move things along.

"I used to live in Hamburg. I remember back around 2006 there was a big fuss over some lawyer—a race traitor—who was shot on his porch. Was that you?"

"Nah, wasn't me, but I was glad when it happened. Bastard was helping those immigrants." He drank more coffee.

Any sympathy she might have felt for the old man evaporated. Not that she showed it.

"Do you know who did the shooting? Frederick's always looking for new people."

"Good luck." He looked a little ill. "They left Hamburg, all of them."

"Do you know any of their names?"

"One guy—Wolf—he was the leader. I think he's in the government somewhere. High up. Don't know where."

His color was definitely changing, but he finished the coffee. It was time to get out, before Christian collapsed.

She checked her watch. "Oh, damn, I'm late. I have to go. It's been nice chatting with you." She gave him a last smile and left the café.

She lingered in a bookstore next door, skimming book titles in English and in German until she heard the ambulance siren. Mingling with curious bystanders who dotted the sidewalk in front of the café, she watched through the window as paramedics worked on Christian before loading him onto a stretcher, covering his body with a sheet, and carrying him out.

The crowd outside the café began to disperse, and she causally strolled back to her car, grateful for the coffee in her travel mug. Now that the adrenaline was ebbing, she was feeling the lack of sleep. She glanced at her watch. Six hours to kill before meeting up with Frederick and Michael.

Two tablespoons had done it for Christian. Michael, much younger and in good physical shape, might need a stronger dose—but the monkshood should work on him as well. She just needed the opportunity.

28

KOLYA FOUND IT HARD to sleep when he finally returned to his spot on the couch, and his usual technique of running musical pieces through his mind was ineffective. He managed to drift off a little after five but was awakened too soon by the flood of morning light, the scent of freshly brewed coffee, and the old man pointing a shotgun at his chest.

Kolya's own gun was in his holster, on his belt, near his right hand. By the time he pulled it out, he'd be dead.

It would be the height of irony to be shot by a crazy former SS officer who in the thralls of dementia had correctly concluded that Kolya was Jewish.

"Tell me who you are, and what you're doing here." The old man kept the gun pointed at Kolya's chest.

"You met me last night." Was it possible the old monster didn't remember? "I'm a friend of Hans."

"A friend of Hans?" He almost sounded puzzled. "Hans?"

"Your grandson." Kolya pushed the sheet off, sat up slowly, and swung his legs off the couch. Almost close enough. The barrel of the gun was two feet away. If he lunged, he could grab it.

But the old man's finger was on the trigger.

There was no way Kolya could make it without being shot. He needed a distraction.

The old man's eyes focused, as if he remembered who Hans was. "Hans isn't friends with Jews."

"For fucks sake. We did this last night. I'm not Jewish."

The old man's grip on the gun tightened. "I remember. You also said I was crazy."

"I meant no disrespect."

"I saw you. Last night. You were outside."

This wasn't good. If Hans knew Kolya'd gone to the barn, he might check the cellar. He might find the broken rung on the ladder and realize that Kolya had been poking around. *Don't even acknowledge what the bastard said.* "If you shoot me, your grandson is going to put you away."

"I know that." The old man kept the shotgun pointed at Kolya's chest. "But I'm protecting him. Some Jew isn't going to stop Day X."

Day X? The body bags, the guns? *What did the old man know? Keep him talking.* "I'm working with Frederick."

"Old man, put the gun down." Frederick spoke from the stairs.

Startled, the old man glanced in the direction of Frederick's voice. Kolya lunged, grabbed the gun barrel, and aimed it towards the wall. The old man fought back, surprisingly strong even if he was no match for Kolya. Then he pulled the trigger. The pellets shattered a window, a lamp, and peppered the plaster wall with small holes. Kolya wrestled the gun free, stood, and pointed the shotgun at the old man. "Sit down, motherfucker."

"Fuck." Frederick reached the bottom of the stairs. "Are you okay, Michael?"

"Don't shoot him." Hans hurried down the stairs after Frederick, alarm on his face.

"He could have killed me." Kolya felt the adrenaline draining, his body shaking. "The demented old fool."

Gertrude, in a blue and white plaid apron, ran into the room. She pointed a finger at the old man, rigid on an armchair, his expression still defiant.

"You horrible little man. My lamp. My window." Then she rounded on Hans. "Do something about him."

"Hans, you're an idiot. He's a Jew, and he was outside last night, while you were sleeping. I saw him." The old man looked at Gertrude. "Shut up, woman."

Hans looked at Kolya. "You were outside?"

"So?" Kolya didn't lower the gun. "Easier than climbing the stairs to take a piss." Good thing the house only had one bathroom. "He's fucking crazy, Hans. He didn't even remember your name. I had to tell him you were his grandson. Then he started raving about something he called Day X."

"He mentioned Day X?" Frederick asked.

"Did he say what it was?" Hans was alarmed.

"No. But whatever it is, do you want him talking about it?"

"Michael's right." Frederick put out a hand for the shotgun, and Kolya gave it to him. "Hans, you have to do something, before he talks to the wrong person."

"I'll lock him in his room when anyone's here," Hans said.

"That's not good enough," Frederick said. "He's had a good life, Hans. A long life."

There was a long pause as Hans realized what Frederick was saying. Hans shook his head. "He's my grandfather."

"Michael can do it if it's too hard for you. It'll be fast and painless."

Hans and Frederick faced each other. Hans' father and teenage son at the top of stairs, heard the words. Hans' father began his own descent, limping, shouting. The teenager raced down the stairs. Three generations of Nazis gathered, raising voices in protest.

"*Nein, nein.*" The teenager's voice was the loudest.

Even Gertrude began to wail. The old man remained stoically silent.

The old Nazi deserved a violent death—even if he was a hundred years old. Some crimes were unforgivable, no matter how long since the commission, and the old man had shown not the slightest remorse for what he'd done. Kolya thought of the terror of the hundreds of thousands of men, women, and children mowed down by the Einsatzgruppen. He could deliver a little justice.

Still—ingratiating himself with Hans could pay off down the road.

Justice had waited eighty years. A few more days wouldn't make a difference.

"I don't want to shoot the old man, Frederick. He didn't hurt me, and he thought he was protecting Day X, whatever it is. Hans can keep him locked up. For God's sake, just don't let him near a gun."

"See, Frederick, Michael agrees. He's the one who has reason to be angry." Hans shot Kolya a grateful look.

"You're sure?" Frederick asked Kolya.

"He was a hero of the Third Reich, and we should honor that. I'm sure."

"Okay. Fine. Last warning, Hans." Frederick unloaded the shotgun and handed it to Hans.

"Medication, Hans. I've told you. He needs medication." Gertrude wiped nervous hands on her apron. "Now, I have hot food ready on the table. I know you two have to get going, Frederick."

As Kolya and Frederick followed her toward the kitchen, the old man remained in his chair. The look he gave Kolya was neither apologetic nor grateful.

29

COLOGNE, GERMANY

ELIZABETH GLANCED UP FROM the files she'd been perusing online. She was working in a small office inside the BfV, much smaller than her office in D.C. and very white. White desk, white walls, white bookshelf, white lamp. The computer was the usual color, metallic silver, although she suspected that was only because it didn't come in white.

More annoying than the size or the glaring whiteness of the decor, she had to share the space with Jonathan—who'd been gone most of the morning and who now sank into the seat at the desk next to her. He'd been doing what he was good at—chatting up the lower level BfV agents, especially the ones who identified as female. "Talk to Reiner?"

"I tried. He wasn't in. And his secretary wouldn't let me through the door."

"Anything interesting?" she asked.

"I have several possible dates for tonight if I want them—but otherwise, no. Nothing much on the Americans we're trying to locate." Jonathan stuck to the cover story, at least in the office. Just in case someone was listening, which was likely. They were in a spy agency, after all. "You?"

"Nothing on the computer on any of the Americans either, but I have a definite dinner date tonight."

"Arnold?"

"Yup. Jealous?"

He shrugged. "Always."

She and Jonathan had had one sexual encounter a year ago. Since then, they'd teased back and forth from time to time, but it never progressed beyond words. He'd be interested if she were, and she did like him, even if she wasn't interested in a committed relationship. Although Jonathan might be safe for occasional sex. Still, sex with a fellow agent did complicate life.

"I hate to see you get hurt." Jonathan leaned forward to tap on the computer keyboard on his desk.

"I'm a big girl. And I don't hurt easy."

She knew he wasn't referring to emotional bruises, but he didn't need to worry. She wasn't a swallow—an agent who used sexual entrapment to gain intelligence. That could end badly; they both remembered a young woman who'd been murdered by her target a year earlier. Anyway, it wasn't a role she wanted to play. Going out for dinner and drinks, though, would be tame enough. And it would keep Arnold out of his apartment for a designated period of time.

"Anything in the BfV files on Nickolas Kruger?" Jonathan changed the subject. "I checked with ECA technical, and they've got nothing."

"Nope. No idea where he is or what he's doing." Elizabeth played the game, in case they'd missed a listening device, so that no one would suspect Nickolas Kruger, a.k.a. Michael Hall, was really an American agent. Outside the BfV, they'd received a briefing from Frick on his latest meeting with Kolya. The fact that Kolya wasn't on the BfV radar was probably a good thing. It meant his cover was intact.

Or he was dead.

Jonathan leaned back in his chair. "I'm putting in a late evening myself. Maybe stay here until seven. Put in a call to the home office."

And sneak into Reiner's office when the secretary was gone.

"I'm not a workaholic." She tossed her head, knowing that the movement would allow light to catch on the diamond earrings.

"Me neither. I just don't have a dinner date. Yet. What time you meeting up?"

"Around seven. We'll probably hit the bars after. Probably get back to the hotel around midnight. Don't call early tomorrow."

She met his eyes, and he nodded. After Reiner's office, he could pay a visit to Arnold's apartment.

30

GREIFSWALD, GERMANY

LIKE SO MANY TOWNS in what was formerly East Germany, Greifswald had its share of non-descript Soviet style buildings. However, the area near the town square remained much as it had for hundreds of years. Quaint. Charming. Or at least that's how the guidebooks would describe it. If it hadn't been Germany, a country that held so many ghosts, Kolya might have found it charming as well.

"You should've just put a bullet in the old man's head." Frederick offered the commentary as Kolya searched for a place to park on a street in the heart of Greifswald. "You'd have been doing him a favor. The crazy old goat should be out of his misery."

It was the first time Frederick had mentioned the old man since leaving the farm.

"I doubt that Hans would have seen it that way. Or his father."

"Someone gets to that age, they're just a burden."

"True. But people are funny about family." Kolya spotted a parking spot and deftly began to maneuver into the space. "I assume you need Hans. You shoot his grandfather, and you may lose his loyalty."

"You're right. People do tend to act irrationally when it comes to family. Although I don't want you to publicly contradict me again. As you did about Walter."

"You agreed not to do something stupid." Kolya's tone remained neutral, with no trace of anger at even the mention of the incident. He glanced out the car mirrors. Too far from the curb. He pulled the car out and tried again. "I thought it was stupid. I still do."

"Killing Walter wasn't stupid. It sent a message. No one will betray us if they know the price. Still, don't do that again. A private challenge is one thing. Publicly, you obey my orders."

"And I did. I finished him." Kolya turned so he had a better view as he backed into the parking spot. "Are you angry I didn't shoot Hans' grandfather?"

"That was different. We weren't in front of a crowd. And the old goat was demented, not a traitor. Maybe you were right about keeping Hans happy. In the future, though…"

"Message received."

"You're not going to ask me about Day X?"

Kolya turned the ignition off. "I figure you'll tell me when you're ready—if I need to know." Better not to seem too interested.

"Discreet. I approve of discreet." Frederick opened his door. "I'll fill you in soon. For this stop, your job is bodyguard."

Kolya joined Frederick on the sidewalk. "Fine. Where we going?"

Frederick nodded at a building that dated back centuries—two stories high—a bookstore on the street level. "Second floor. The guy we're meeting here owns the building."

"No target practice?"

"Not on this stop. We have two stops tomorrow, and at least one will involve some training. This is just a meeting."

"And after?"

"We take the evening off. I told you Lisette will be meeting me."

*   *   *   *   *

The flight of stairs led to an apartment where Gunter, who owned the building, waited. He looked younger than Kolya had expected, even younger than Frederick. In his early twenties, light blond hair, blue eyes, Gunter had inherited the building from his grandfather, a high-ranking member of the Communist party during the reign of the

Deutsche Demokratische Republik. Before that, the great grandfather had been a high-ranking member of the Nazi party, despite East Germany's insistence of moral superiority over West Germany for purging all Nazis from the government and the country.

The entrance was guarded by a German shepherd who stood in the doorway growling lightly. At Gunter's command, the dog allowed them to enter. Gunter's living room, furnished with stained older furniture and a wood-frame sofa with chewed armrests, looked more like a generation Z drug hang-out than the headquarters of a violent neo-Nazi gang. But looks could be deceiving.

The dog sat, waiting for Gunter's signal.

"Well trained." Kolya wasn't a dog person, but he did respect their capabilities.

"He should be. I work with Turk every day. You are an American?"

Kolya nodded. Frederick introduced him and described his role.

Gunter raised an eyebrow. "Bodyguard?"

"Karl was murdered. We think maybe Mossad. To be on the safe side, I have a bodyguard, especially for travel." Frederick crossed to the dog and bent over to scratch behind its ears. "And Michael's helpful with weapons training."

"Everyone on my list is already trained." Gunter raised eyebrows.

Frederick anticipated the question. "I'll fill him in closer to the day. Your office?"

Gunter indicated the couch. "Make yourself at home, Michael." They disappeared into the office, shutting the door.

Listening at the door was tempting, but not worth the risk. He didn't know who else might be in the apartment or who might walk in. Besides, what he needed to know was unlikely to be discussed. He needed the date, the targets, and the participants. There had to be lists. But where?

Kolya seated himself on the sofa, despite the springs poking through the cushions and the felt material covered with dog hair.

The German shepherd approached. Kolya assumed that he was sitting on the dog's preferred bed. He held out a hand but made no further move. "*Guten tag*, Turk."

Turk gave a sniff, and the tail wagged. Satisfied that Kolya did not represent a threat, the dog returned to his position by the door.

Kolya's gaze roved around the room. No computer visible. Nothing that might offer information. At the far end of the living room, a doorway led to what looked like a small kitchen. The most likely location for a computer or a list would be the office currently occupied by Frederick and Gunter.

Hurried footsteps on the stairs, and then a series of loud knocks. Kolya glanced at Turk. The dog's ears perked up, but he didn't growl. Someone the dog knew.

Kolya kept a hand on his gun as he cracked the door. Not that he wanted to kill anyone to protect Frederick and Gunter, but he didn't want to be killed either. Anyone targeting Germany Now might attack Kolya on the assumption that he was the Nazi he was pretending to be.

His caution was unnecessary. A young man, short brown hair, looked at him startled. "*Wo ist* Gunter?"

"Meeting." Kolya answered in English.

He responded in kind. "Who are you?"

"Michael." Kolya kept the door partially closed, but Turk stuck a nose through the crack. "And you?"

"Peter. I am Gunter's friend. I need to speak to Gunter." The young man's manner was agitated.

"As I said, he's in a meeting." Kolya took his hand off his gun and swung the door open. "If you want to wait."

They sat together on either end of the sofa. Turk positioned himself in front of Peter. Peter fished in a pocket and came out with a small treat. The dog snapped it up and then lay down in front of Peter. Peter patted Turk on his head.

Another ten minutes, and the door to the office remained firmly closed. Peter rose and paced the length of the room and then back to the sofa. He glanced at Kolya and then paced again.

The dog, stretched on the floor, didn't seem to care.

"Is there a problem?" Kolya asked.

"No." Peter sat again. Then he rose and paced to the office door.

"Do you know what he's doing?"

"Like I said, meeting. I'm just the bodyguard."

"Bodyguard?" Peter looked taken aback. "For who?"

"Frederick Bauer."

"Bauer? Oh shit. He's here. They are planning it, aren't they?"

Don't show interest. But he was interested. Maybe Peter had information. Kolya shrugged. "I assume so."

Peter rose and paced again. He returned and stood over Kolya, his manner agitated but not threatening. "We talked about calling it off. He said he'd consider it."

"Gunter?"

"Yes, Gunter. We've been friends for a long time."

"You want to sit down?"

"I can't sit." Peter paced again, this time to the window looking down at the street. "This is just crazy. Too many are going to die."

What the fuck were they planning? But Kolya kept his voice neutral. "Sometimes sacrifices have to be made."

Peter wasn't listening. He leaned closer to the window and then ducked back. Something in the street had alarmed him. "Fuck. I think it's them. They followed me."

"Who?"

"I have to leave." Peter sounded terrified.

"If you leave, you'll be seen."

"There's a back door. Tell Gunter I need to talk to him."

"He has your number?"

"No. I changed my phone. They called me on the old one after the last time I talked to Gunter."

Who was stalking Peter?

"Give me the number, I'll pass it on." Kolya had no intention of doing so, but he did want Peter's number.

Peter recited the numbers, and Kolya tapped them into his phone. Then Peter rushed out the door and down the stairs. The dog lifted his head to watch Peter's exit before relaxing back onto the floor.

Kolya crossed to the window to check the street below. Two men looked up at him and then, as if on a prearranged signal, strode off in synchronized motion. They were a type he recognized. He didn't need to see uniforms to know that they were military. The haircuts. Their general bearing. The not-so concealed weapons that both men were wore on their hips.

On which side were they?

Behind him, he heard the click of the office door opening. He turned as Frederick and Gunter emerged.

"Was someone here? I thought I heard voices," Frederick asked.

"Peter. He said he was a friend." Kolya nodded at Turk. "And the dog knew him."

"I do know him," Gunter said. "He didn't want to wait?"

"He waited for a bit and then rushed off. Said some men were following him. I looked—there were two men below." Kolya glanced out the window again. "Should I be concerned?"

"No. They're mine. They're watching Peter. He say anything?"

Gunter and Frederick had recruited members of the military? Kolya had been concerned about accidently being targeted, but this was worse. At least the crowd at Hans' farm was comprised of amateurs. Soldiers would know how to kill. And soldiers would be the ones called in to help stop any attack by Frederick's group. If they were a part of the group…

He had to find out how many had been recruited—and who they were.

Peter might be a starting place. Part of Kolya's job as an intelligence operative was to recruit potential informers close to a target, and to do so meant looking for the disaffected. Peter fit the bill. But right now, Kolya needed to deal with Gunter.

Kolya chose words carefully. "He said he wanted to talk to you. He seemed upset. Then rushed off." It was close enough to the truth that if Gunter did speak to Peter, it wouldn't be obvious that Kolya had concealed information.

Except maybe the phone number.

"What's going on with Peter?" Frederick asked Gunter.

"Nothing you need to worry about."

"I am worried. Why is he upset?"

"He's having second thoughts. About," Gunter glanced at Kolya, "you know."

"Second thoughts?"

"He won't say anything."

"I don't care," Frederick said. "We can't have loose ends. Too much is at stake. I know he's your friend, but he's unreliable. We had to take care of a traitor yesterday."

"I know what I have to do. I've been putting it off. Don't worry. I'll have my men take care of him."

"When?"

"Tonight," Gunter said. "Late. When there will be fewer people to see or hear."

"Good," Frederick said. "Do it."

Another murder. Maybe this time, Kolya could prevent it.

31

ELDENA, GERMANY

AFTER CHRISTIAN'S DEPARTURE, LISETTE drove by her former house. She knew the address although she'd never been there as an adult. But it was time. She pulled her car over in front of the house and sat, gazing at the porch where her father had died. She could almost hear her father describe it as a hobbit hole. Now, fifteen years later, it was smaller than she remembered. Not magical either. Not a place for hobbits. Just for ghosts.

She lingered for ten minutes, until a woman walked out onto the porch, and then she put the car into gear and headed in the direction of Berlin. Long before Berlin, she cut a diagonal and then drove north towards Greifswald. Backtracking was probably unnecessary. Unlikely that Frederick or Michael would spot her car coming from the wrong direction. But just in case, better to come from the expected direction.

From Greifswald, Lisette drove to the hotel, within walking distance of Strand Eldena beach, on the outskirts of the town. The front of the hotel offered a spectacular view of the Baltic, and the salt air blew from the north. Quite a lovely spot. Too bad she was here to meet two men she despised—one of whom, if all went well—would be dead by morning.

Behind the desk in the lobby, an efficient and polite young woman checked that Lisette had reservations, scanned her credit card, and presented cardboard keys. She'd reserved two rooms: One for herself and Frederick, and the second for Michael. Lisette checked both rooms. They were clean, comfortable, and spacious: studio apartments with a small kitchen, a desk, and a queen size bed.

She examined the refrigerator in Michael's room, hoping there might be a complimentary bottle of wine that could conceal the monkshood. But there was nothing. Not even a bottle of water. Not that water would do it. The taste would be too bitter. He wouldn't drink enough to kill him.

She thought about buying a bottle of wine, doctoring it, and leaving it in his room, as if it were a gift from the management. But what if he offered to share it with Frederick and herself?

Risky.

No, she'd find some other way.

* * * * *

She waited for them in the lobby. They arrived two hours after she did, both looking tired, although Frederick had a glow of exuberance, Michael as unreadable as when she first met him. She embraced Frederick with the passion of a new bride.

"All going well?"

"Perfectly." He kissed her in what seemed to her to be something of a show for Michael. Michael was checking his phone and not paying attention. "We have dinner reservations?"

"Yes. That seafood place we went to last time. For all three of us." It would be tricky poisoning Michael at dinner, especially with Frederick there, but it'd be doable. A drink would be best. Wine. Beer. Maybe in his after-dinner coffee? Michael liked sweet coffee. She'd noticed that during the breakfast before the murder, and she could put extra sugar in the coffee to mask the taste, as she had for Christian. Whether she'd get the chance to put anything in his coffee with both Frederick and Michael present was a different question.

And whether Frederick would be suspicious if Michael keeled over right after dinner with them was an additional complication. Well, she could poison Frederick as well—but all the reasons she didn't want to kill Frederick remained in play. She still needed him. He might know the real name of the man that Christian had called Wolf.

She thought back to the garage: the beautiful woman falling, blood gushing from her chest. Lisette should and could have stopped Michael before he killed an innocent woman. That she hadn't was on her. She bore that guilt.

The guilt she'd felt over her father's death when she was a child was irrational. The guilt at the death of the unknown woman was not. She'd had a chance to prevent the murder. She'd done nothing.

It hadn't been personal with any of the other men she'd killed. She'd just been an impartial instrument of justice. With Michael— she bore responsibility for what he'd done. That responsibility made it personal—just as killing her father's murderer would be personal— once she found him.

To do either, she was willing to take risks.

But being willing to take the risk and having the opportunity were separate matters. The opportunity depended on Michael accompanying them to dinner and then her finding a moment to doctor one of his drinks.

She turned to him. "You're coming, right?"

Michael shook his head. "I'm going to beg off. I'd be intruding on your private time. And I'd like to take a walk. Unless—Frederick— you want my services as bodyguard?"

"I'm safe enough. No one knows I'm here except the three of us. Have a good evening."

Lisette intervened. "Frederick, Michael doesn't know anyone in Greifswald. We can have alone time later in our room."

"He's a grown man. He'll be fine."

"I don't want to be inhospitable."

"Maybe he can find a woman, since he's not on duty. His own woman. I thought you drove here to be with me, not Michael."

She identified an odd thing in Frederick's voice. Jealousy. Did he think she was attracted to Michael? That was almost funny. Objectively speaking, Michael was an attractive man, but that he could kill so coldly made those good looks repulsive.

"Of course, I'm only concerned about Michael for your sake, to be polite to a man who's working for you."

Michael weighed in again. "I appreciate the gesture, but it's unnecessary. I'm going to take my walk, grab a quick bite, and go to bed. Do you have the key to my room?"

She forced herself to smile and handed Michael one of the cards that unlocked his room. So, no chance to kill him at dinner. She'd figure something else out. Maybe after Frederick went to sleep, she'd pay a visit to Michael's hotel room. If she couldn't get him to drink the monkshood, there were always her usual methods. Even if that made it obvious that he'd been murdered.

* * * * *

Relieved that Frederick had not insisted on his presence, Kolya dumped his bag in his room and then walked the quarter mile to the beach. He felt the release of adrenaline, the physical relief from being on his own, temporarily not playing the role of Michael the Nazi. And for the moment, his unwanted shadows had left him in peace. If he could save Peter, it would be a partial atonement for not saving Walter—and that thought was calming.

The evening was clear but cool. Wind stirred whitecaps on the surface of the sea, and the sunset, although not directly over the water, turned the sky and a few lingering clouds into shades of orange and red. There were a few late beach walkers, like him, although now in September, only one or two brave souls ventured out into the water. It was a pretty scene. Even if Kolya wasn't particularly fond of beaches or water sports, he did have a strong aesthetic appreciation of natural beauty. But he was not there purely for aesthetic reasons. A beach was a perfect place to make a phone call without any risk of being overheard. No listening devices, and no one could get close without his knowing it.

He dialed the number that Peter had given him earlier in the day. The phone rang and clicked off. He tried again with the same result. Not surprising. Few people answered unknown phone calls anymore, and someone as justly fearful as Peter would be less inclined to do so.

He considered texting Peter, but he'd have no idea who might be reading it on the other end. Peter could already be dead, and one of Gunter's people could have his phone.

New plan.

He dialed a number that he hadn't called since leaving Washington. It was risky. If anyone was tracking phone calls originating in Germany and going to the United States, they could pinpoint the call coming from Eldena beach. Still, it was an emergency. It was very early morning in D.C. Kolya expected to get someone from the night shift. He got the second in command, Mark Leslie.

"Everything okay? I thought you were incommunicado for the duration."

The voice that answered his call was guarded, and not just out of concern for his breaking cover. Mark had been a player in the deception that had resulted in Kolya's being captured and tortured. A reluctant player, but still a player. While they had reached detente since Kolya's return to the ECA, Mark remained a bit embarrassed and Kolya a bit angry. Still, Mark was good at his job, and so was Kolya.

"I need to locate someone asap. All I have is his phone number."

"Gotcha. And that would be?"

Kolya recited Peter's number.

"May take a few."

"I'll stay on the line. Speed would be appreciated."

"Do my best."

Mark was gone. Kolya strolled the beach, careful to keep his distance from any and all. It wasn't hard. There were a few couples holding hands as they walked. A family picnicking. And the two swimmers. One of the late swimmers emerged from the water and grabbed a towel from the sand. Attractive. Good body and a pretty face. With the sun setting behind her, she was a striking image. Not anywhere near as lovely as Alex, but he was in love, not dead. He could appreciate the beauty of other women without acting on it.

Kolya's mind drifted to the conversation with Alex on the drive to the airport. Maybe a weekend in Miami when he returned? He didn't like the beach, but she did. He'd like to see her in that new bathing suit, and he'd like to do something that would make her happy. Besides, Miami had great Cuban jazz.

He typed a quick text. *You up?*

She responded immediately. *Yes. Brief due tomorrow.*

All okay here. Love you and miss you.

Same. You free?

"Kolya?" Mark's voice.

"Yes."

He typed: *Just touching base. Later.*

K. Stay safe.

The messages disappeared.

"Okay, I'm sending you an address. One problem—it's an apartment building—and the data can't tell me which apartment. You're going to have to knock on doors. Hope it's good enough."

"It'll have to be. If he leaves, let me know."

Kolya tapped the address into Google maps. It was almost an hour walk. He could take an Uber, but it would be traceable. He also had no idea who might be driving an Uber, how many people in this small town were Nazis, and who might know that he was accompanying Frederick.

He thought of the two men with military bearing who were following Peter. They were going to take care of Peter later that night. Did he have time to make it?

32

GREIFSWALD, GERMANY

KOLYA DECIDED AGAINST THE Uber and started off on a slow jog. Before Romania, he'd regularly run five miles a day. Now, after a course of physical therapy and continued exercise, on a good day, he could jog maybe a mile before the pain in his leg started to build.

He pushed through it, jogging through the city for at least twenty minutes. He slowed down when he felt the beginning of pain. If he overdid it, he'd wind up back on crutches. And that would mean the end of his undercover role.

By the time Kolya arrived at the address, the sky was dark. Streetlights illuminated trim cut lawns and a row of well-kept buildings on Shiller Strasse, a few blocks beyond the university.

Peter's apartment building had a plain box-like appearance, reminding Kolya of the Stalin-era architecture of his native city of St. Petersburg. A bicycle leaned against the wall near the front door. Trimmed low bushes on either side. He checked his phone for any change in Peter's location. Seeing none, he deleted the address and the directions.

It only took him a minute to pick the lock to the door of the building.

The door to the lobby creaked, which meant that anyone listening would know he was entering. But that also meant that he would know if anyone entered behind him. He quietly closed the door and checked the mailboxes. Three floors. Nine apartments. Only last names on the labels. All of the ground floor apartments had two names. Peter had said nothing about a wife or a girlfriend, a partner, or a roommate, not that that was definitive, since they'd only exchanged a few words.

He'd try apartments with single occupants first.

Two of the three apartments on the second floor had only one name listed on the corresponding mailbox. One name looked Polish, the other, German.

The German would be a better bet.

He climbed the two flights and knocked heavily on the door. Leaning against the frame, he waited. A young woman, college age, short brown hair, cracked the door.

"*Peter, bitte.*" He slurred his words and swayed.

She frowned at him. "Peter Neumann?"

As good a guess as any. "*Ja. Ja. Mein freund.*" He gestured broadly and nearly fell over.

Even with his imitation of drunkenness, his accent gave him away. She switched to English. "You are drunk."

She wasn't close enough to notice the lack of alcohol odor on him. He continued the lie.

"No, no, not drunk. Just feeling good. Peter invited me here."

"He lives upstairs. Apartment nine. We don't want noisy drunks in this building."

He put a finger to his lips, signaling his agreement, and staggered towards the stairs. She sniffed her disapproval and closed the door.

Kolya climbed the next flight, ignoring his increasing leg pain, and tried the doorknob for the apartment marked with the number Nine. As expected, locked. He considered jimmying the lock, but Peter—afraid and with good reason to be afraid—would be unpredictable if he just broke in. Kolya didn't want to have to fend off an attack, risking an injury to either of them.

He rapped the back of his hand softly against the wood. "Peter?"

He heard movement but no response. He tapped again. "Peter, it's Michael. We met earlier today. At Gunter's."

Still no response.

Kolya glanced at the other apartments. No one was checking on Peter's visitor, but the hall wasn't safe. Someone could emerge at any point. Or Gunter's men could show up.

He tried again. "Peter, it's urgent that I speak to you."

The knob turned, and the door creaked half open. Peter stood in the gap, his right hand clutching a kitchen knife. He looked even younger than Kolya had remembered.

"What do you want?"

Kolya held up both hands. "Just to talk."

"Go ahead."

"Not out here." He nodded at the apartment. "Inside."

"Okay." Peter backed up two feet. Kolya pushed the door open. Peter backed another five feet. "I'm keeping the knife."

"Fine." If he wanted to, Kolya could easily take the knife from Peter. But that wasn't a way to earn trust. He advanced into the apartment and shut the door behind him.

"What is so urgent?"

"You're in danger."

"I know that!" Peter's voice rose. "Those men were following me. That's why I wanted to see Gunter. He'll stop them."

"Those men take orders from Gunter. And Gunter ordered them to kill you. Tonight."

Peter shook his head. "No. No, no. Gunter and I have been friends since we were children. He would never hurt me."

Kolya restrained the impulse to roll his eyes. "Being a childhood friend only gets you so far. Gunter sees you as a danger to the cause. To Day X."

"Day X is a mistake."

"You're not even supposed to know about it."

"Gunter told me about Day X. He wanted me as his lieutenant." Peter sank into an armchair and dropped the knife on the floor.

"What did Gunter tell you about Day X?" Kolya sat on a faded red couch, facing him.

"Don't you know?"

"I know about Day X. I don't know what Gunter told you about

Day X."

"That we were going to take back the country by killing those who've betrayed the German people. Then the Leader will take control."

"The Leader?" Kolya asked.

"You don't know about the Leader?"

Kolya shook his head. "Frederick doesn't tell me much."

"Frederick answers to the Leader. None of the rest of us know who he is, but he'll reveal himself on Day X."

They were back to Day X. "And you think Day X is a mistake."

"I was a little dubious when he first told me, but Gunter's my friend. So I said yes. Then I thought about it, and it scared the shit out of me."

Kolya thought about what might make a man as young as Peter change his mind about involvement in a possible Nazi coup. "Did you discuss Day X with anyone?"

"I might have said something to someone."

"Someone important to you?"

"Kristin is a good friend and really smart." Peter flushed. "She said it was crazy, and I should stop it. She," he looked down at the floor, "she doesn't like the far right."

Kolya had wondered about Peter's change of heart. But if Peter had fallen for a woman who disapproved of Nazis and Day X—that made Peter's conversion believable.

That Peter had been willing to join a group of neo-Nazis at all was not a mark of good character. That he'd been willing to leave for a young woman improved Kolya's opinion of him. Peter might not be a strong-minded person, but at least he wasn't strongly committed to white supremacy either.

Peter continued to talk. "Even if we have some of the police and the military with us, it'll be a bloodbath. On both sides. I told Gunter to call it off three days ago. Since then, those men keep showing up when I go outside. That's why I got rid of my phone."

"You no longer believe in the cause?"

"I don't like the immigrants coming into Germany. I don't like that they've changed the country. But Kristin is right. Hate isn't the way.

And I don't want to kill people." Peter looked at Kolya quizzically. "Wait. You're Frederick's bodyguard. Why are you here?"

"Maybe I don't want to kill people either." Walter's image flashed into his mind.

"Frederick is following the Leader's orders on organizing Day X. You work for Frederick. I don't understand."

"You don't have to understand." This was taking too long. He dimly heard the creaking of the lobby door two flights down. If it were the killers sent by Gunter, they were earlier than he'd anticipated. He crossed to the window and looked out. Unfortunately, he only had a view of the green lawn behind the building. No view of the street. On the other hand, while he couldn't see anyone at the front of the building, any watchers at the front couldn't see them either. "Do you have a fire escape? A rope ladder?"

"No," Peter said. "Neither. Why?"

"I think it would be prudent to leave immediately. And not by the stairs."

Footsteps on the stairs. More than one person. Peter turned a terrified face towards Kolya, who pulled the window open and leaned out. They were only on the second floor but high enough that a fall could still maim or kill. He leaned farther. A ledge ran along the side of the building, about a foot in width, and ten feet from the window, a drainpipe extended from the roof to the ground.

The ledge was wide enough, and the drainpipe offered a safe descent. It was an alternative to a violent confrontation with possible killers.

The second time in two days he'd have to push his leg. Only unlike the expedition into the barn, his leg was already acting up.

"Out the window, Peter, quickly."

Peter joined him at the window, and Kolya pointed out the escape route.

"I can't."

"Sure you can." The footsteps were closer. "Just hug the wall. It's not far to the drain. And the drain has footholds and handholds. It's practically a ladder."

Peter hesitated. "I'm afraid of heights."

"The only other choice is to kill Gunter's men before they kill you. And me. There's at least two men coming up the stairs. I have a gun. It's possible I could kill them before they get off a shot. More probable that I couldn't. Escape has better odds. Your choice."

Peter took a deep breath and swung one leg out the window, turning to face Kolya as he felt for a foothold. "It's too narrow."

"It's wide enough. Keep your weight on the ball of your foot."

Peter clutched the windowsill, and then the second leg followed the first. He froze on the ledge, hands gripping the windowsill, blocking Kolya's exit. Peter crab-stepped sideways but continued to clench the sill.

"Let go of the sill and move," Kolya said. "I need room to get out."

They both heard the knock at the front door.

"Go." Kolya resisted the urge to physically shove him out of the way. Peter took a few reluctant steps, and finally released the windowsill, his arms outstretched as if hugging the concrete, his body flattened against the wall. Kolya swung out onto the ledge and lowered the window behind him. They'd search the apartment for Peter, but they might not look out the window. Unless it was open.

Kolya wasn't particularly afraid of heights, although he did respect anything that could kill him. A fall from a second floor had that potential. Of greater concern—the leg that had started to ache on his trip to Peter's apartment and the PTSD that surfaced at inconvenient times.

Of greatest concern: Peter's painfully slow inching towards the drainpipe.

Balanced on the ledge, he was still framed in the window, visible to anyone entering the apartment. They'd be inside any second. Unless Peter moved, he had nowhere to go.

"Move, Peter." He hissed the words.

Peter shuffled one step. Another step.

"Keep going."

"I hate heights," Peter whispered.

"How do you feel about bullets?"

"I understand." Peter shuffled two more steps.

It was just enough room for Kolya to squeeze next to him and out of sight of anyone glancing out the window from the living room. They were still vulnerable if one of the killers opened the window and leaned out. Kolya's gun was holstered so he could use both hands for balance. If the killers spotted the two of them, he'd have to pull his gun, shoot, and keep his balance—all before they could shoot him.

"How much farther?" Peter's face was pressed against the wall.

"A couple feet. You're almost there." Kolya heard a crashing sound coming from inside the apartment. The intruders had made it in.

Peter heard it, too, and the fear of the men hunting him outweighed his fear of heights. He shuffled faster, finally reaching the corner where the drainpipe descended from the roof. He leaned sideways to grab the pipe and lost his balance, teetering backwards. Kolya grabbed Peter's arm, yanking him back against the wall.

They both stood immobile, breathing heavily. While keeping his grip on Peter's arm, Kolya felt the sweat running down the back of his shirt. The ache in his leg was getting worse. He needed to get off it as soon as possible.

"Try again." Kolya spoke a few inches from Peter's ear.

"I'll fall." Peter was shaking.

"You won't fucking fall. I have your arm."

Peter reached and this time he managed to grasp the pipe with his left hand.

"Now swing your leg over the pipe and feel for the joint." Kolya shifted his own position, so he could maintain his grip and his balance. He held on until Peter had both hands and both legs on the pipe.

Peter froze in position on the pipe.

"You could almost just slide down."

Peter shook his head again.

"Can't." He gasped.

"You damn well can." Kolya wanted to place a hand on Peter's head and shove downward, but that might make the kid fall. Annoyed as he was, Kolya didn't want Peter hurt. He controlled his impatience. "One foot at a time."

Peter began his descent. A painfully slow descent. Inch by inch.

Kolya cast an eye back at the window of Peter's apartment. From this angle, he could see nothing. So far, their escape path had gone unnoticed.

Peter's foot slipped, and he froze again.

Kolya gritted his teeth. "You're okay. Keep going."

"I can't," Peter repeated. The he looked up and caught Kolya's expression. "Okay, I'll try." He slid down another two feet.

There was enough room for Kolya to fit. He maneuvered into position on the pipe directly above Peter's head and waited.

When Peter was halfway down, his speed increased. Kolya followed, reaching the ground a minute after Peter. "We go that way?" Peter pointed towards the building directly behind his apartment and an expanse of green stretching between the two structures.

That direction would be in the line of sight of the windows of Peter's apartment.

Kolya shook his head. He unholstered his gun, holding it straight down by his side, and peered around the corner of the building. He beckoned Peter to follow and cut across the side lawn to the next building. They jogged through the back yards of three more buildings before heading diagonally across a lawn, around an apartment building, finally reaching the next street. They halted out of sight, on the side of yet another concrete structure.

Kolya's leg ached, but at least it wasn't collapsing on him. How much longer he could keep going, though, was uncertain. And he'd barely slept the previous night. "Do you have a car?"

"No. Don't you?"

"No."

"You and Frederick drove in from Berlin."

"He has the car. I walked here from the hotel. You need to get out of town. Preferably out of Germany, at least for a while."

"How do you suggest I do that without a car? Do you know how to steal a car?"

"With a computer." He could hotwire an older car, but those were not prevalent in Germany. The new keyless cars could be hacked, and

Kolya had the technical expertise to do so—but not with a burner phone.

Kolya's leg signaled increasing displeasure with the evening activities. He leaned against the concrete wall to rest.

"I could call an Uber," Peter said.

"No. Too dangerous. What about your girlfriend? Did you ever mention her to Gunter?"

"No. I never mentioned her. And she's not my girlfriend. She's just a friend."

"Whatever she is, does she have a car?" At the barely visible nod from Peter, Koyla said, "Call her. Have her pick us up."

"I don't want her involved."

"Picking us up won't involve her any more than she is already. I don't know if it's occurred to you, but if Gunter's people have been watching you, they probably know about her. If he's ordered men to kill you, he's probably ordered them to kill her as well. They may be on their way to her place now." Kolya considered calling Frick or Teo, but they were three hours away: a dangerously long time to be lingering in the streets. Anyway, he was concerned that Peter's girlfriend—friend—could be a target. *Get both of them to safety.*

"Jesus." Peter pulled out his phone.

33

COLOGNE, GERMANY

ELIZABETH LEFT THE BFV building sometime after six to prepare for her dinner date, offering only a few sarcastic remarks as to what she would be doing and Jonathan's interest therein, a continuation of whatever the hell was going on between them. After her departure, he remained at his desk pretending to read through files while the clock ticked down.

At quarter to seven, Jonathan strolled to the water cooler. The other offices on the floor were dark. He found a clean glass—no paper cups, that would be unecological—and poured himself water. Carrying the glass, he meandered towards Reiner's office.

It was also dark, the secretary gone.

He set the glass on a desk and picked the lock. Then he entered the office and flipped on the light. The room was furnished with the simple white desk, credenza, and bookcase that he'd come to expect in the BfV offices, even those of the higher officials. No papers on the desk. No disorder. Everything in its proper place.

Very German.

The desktop computer appeared new. He seated himself at the desk, pulled the keyboard toward him, and tapped the space bar. Of course, it was password protected.

Kolya might've been able to get in—he was an accomplished hacker. Jonathan was not. But secretaries often kept the passwords to their boss's computer, even in top secret agencies.

He returned to the hall and rooted through the secretary's desk and filing cabinet.

It took him three minutes to find a file labeled "passwords."

He carried the file back to Reiner's desk, flipped through, and typed in the combination of letters and numbers. Then he took out his phone and called the ECA technical office. Mark Leslie answered.

"Sorry to keep you there so late," Jonathan said. It was seven in Germany; one o'clock in Washington, D.C.

There was a muffled yawn on the other end. "No problem. Just as well that I was here. Kolya needed some assist a little while ago."

That Kolya broke cover was worrisome. "He okay?"

"Yeah, just needed to locate someone. Didn't tell me anything more. You ready?"

"Ready."

Jonathan typed the necessary codes to allow Mark to access Reiner's computer, thereby enabling a more thorough search than Jonathan could do on his own. "Got it?"

"Yup. Will take a few to upload on this end—longer to do a search."

"Can I turn off the computer?"

Mark took five minutes to respond. "Yeah, go ahead. I'll call you with what I find. It'll be a few. I'll delete any images of you breaking in from the surveillance cameras."

"That'd be helpful." Jonathan clicked off the phone and turned off the computer. He returned the keyboard and the chair to their previous positions. He'd replace the file on his way back to his own office. The less time exposed, the better. Now to pay a visit to Arnold's apartment.

* * * * *

Arnold had chosen Cologne's best French restaurant for their dinner date. Elizabeth was pleased, if a little surprised. She liked French food better than German food, not as heavy, not quite as caloric, possibly because one sometimes needed a microscope to see what was on the plate. Still, it was tasty. And he was paying—which was okay with her, even though she could have expensed the meal.

They did the chitchat thing during the oyster hors d'oeuvres, Arnold telling her about his college years in Berlin, Elizabeth telling him about Georgetown University, where she'd majored in international studies.

He wasn't bad looking, and he was friendly and even charming, which just made Elizabeth more suspicious. Not that she wasn't damn attractive and worth a man being friendly and charming, but men who were friendly and charming tended to want something. Usually, it was sex. Sometimes, it was something else.

She wasn't sure which it was with Arnold.

Over the main course—a beef dish with raspberries and raspberry sauce for Arnold, and a turbot with a cream-based sauce for Elizabeth—the conversation took a turn towards business.

"So what are you and Jonathan really doing here in Germany?" Arnold cut his meat into small precise slices.

"We already told you." Elizabeth picked up her wine glass. She took an experimental sip. Not bad.

"Looking for American far-right radicals in Germany?"

"Yup."

"It wasn't far-right radicals who attacked your country on 9/11. I think you're losing sight of the real enemy."

She shrugged. "We watch them too. All possible threats are of interest." She replaced the wine glass on the table, picked up a fork, and took a bite of her turbot.

"True. But some are more urgent than others."

"That's why we have so many intelligence agencies and officers, so we can investigate various threats. My job is to follow up on American neo-Nazis. If I get information about a jihadist threat, I won't ignore it."

"Fair enough. Another question—you and Jonathan…"

She ate more of the turbot, trying to decide about the flavor. Mushrooms, onion, cream. But what was the spice? Anise? Maybe. But definitely good. "What about Jonathan and me?" She knew what he was asking, but she liked making him be specific.

"You know what I'm asking." He smiled, a warm, friendly smile.

He'd probably be good in bed. Elizabeth liked sex, although she had no intention of having sex with a target. The last ECA female agent who'd gone to bed with a target had wound up with a stake shoved through her body.

But keeping him interested with a bit of a tease should be safe enough.

"Yeah, I do know what you're asking." She picked up her wine again. French food should be savored. A bite at a time, with wine to compliment the flavors, knowledge she owed to dinners with Jonathan. She sipped the wine and let it linger on her tongue. "You want to know if we're fucking."

"Jesus, Elizabeth."

She cocked her head to one side. "Not what you're asking? Or are you expressing shock at the use of the word, 'fucking'?"

"The latter. Most of the women I know aren't quite so direct."

"Then you've led a sheltered life."

"Possibly. So are you?"

"That's actually none of your business, is it?"

"Maybe not." He returned to his beef. "But I guess that answers whether you'd be interested in coming by my place for dessert."

Maybe the charm and friendliness were about sex. Maybe. But she was also experienced in the spy game. Charm and friendliness were tools.

She heard the tone signaling that she had a text. She removed her phone from her bag. Jonathan. *Interesting stuff from Mark about our friend R.*

Did that mean that Reiner was the Nazi and that Arnold was clear? Too soon to judge.

"Anything of importance?"

"Not really." She clicked her phone off and replaced it in her purse. "It can wait. We were discussing dessert?"

"I was, at least."

"I like French desserts. And I don't like to rush through dinner." Elizabeth needed to give Jonathan time to check out Arnold's apartment. She may have had no intention of sleeping with him, but she knew how to use sex appeal.

34

GREIFSWALD, GERMANY

THEY WAITED IN A small park several blocks from Peter's apartment building, on a bench in the shadow of trees, where they could glimpse the road, but where they were, for all practical purposes, invisible. On Kolya's instructions, Peter had given Kristin the name of the two streets that intersected along the edges of the park as the meeting place. When she arrived, she'd park, and they'd approach—after confirming that she was alone. Kolya assumed that having failed to find Peter at home, the killers would crisscross the streets of the small town, scanning for any sign of their intended victim. But unless they came into the park, the killers would be out of luck. The streetlights didn't penetrate the darkness, and there were no lights on the paths that wound past beds of flowers.

It was a pleasant enough place to hide. A flower bed near their bench scented the cool air. While he couldn't make out colors, Kolya could see the shapes of petals and leaves.

He massaged his leg, hoping that a little rest would do the trick, although he was engaging in wishful thinking. He'd pushed it too hard for the past two days, first at Hans' farm, and now helping Peter. It would take a day or two of rest before it would be back to what currently passed as normal. He could use a decent night's sleep as well to fight down the PTSD, which kept threatening to surface.

Maybe Frick had been right. Going undercover when he wasn't

completely recovered, when he might never be completely recovered, was stupid.

Peter had only said a few words since calling his girlfriend. Was Peter appreciating the magnitude of his own folly in joining a neo-Nazi group, or was he just in shock at the realization of how close he'd come to dying?

Or both.

But this wasn't a bad time to pry out some information.

"Peter, tell me everything you know about Day X."

Peter examined the scrapes on his hands and arms. "First, tell me who you really are, Michael. You only saved me because you want to know about Day X."

"I would have saved you regardless. But yes, I do want to know about Day X."

"Then tell me who you work for?"

"I don't work for anyone. I just don't like what I'm finding out about this Day X shit." Regardless of whether there was any risk to telling Peter the truth, it was information Peter didn't need. Peter had already demonstrated that his loyalties fluctuated depending on circumstances and the girlfriend of the moment. "What can you tell me?"

Peter leaned over and plucked a blade of grass from the lawn in front of the bench. He rolled it between his palms. "I don't know much more than I told you in the apartment. When the Leader signals, Day X will commence. Gunter and the other district commanders will activate their supporters and assign lists of politicians and officials to kill. I think," Peter hesitated, "that Frederick will lead an attack on the Reichstag and officials in every state are also targeted, but I'm not sure. Gunter said he'd tell me the targets on the day of. Then the Leader will take over. I don't know how."

Kolya absorbed the horror of the plan. "When?"

"In a couple weeks, I think. We'll be activated the day before. Frederick has people—police, military—on the inside as well."

That would give Kolya time to brief Frick in person. He preferred not to take another risk with the phone.

"Gunter knows the targets?"

"Just for the district, although he probably knows the master plan. I think all the higher ups know it. The Leader drew it up."

"Who is the Leader?"

"Don't know his name." Peter shrugged. "Someone in the intelligence services who's supposed to be stopping terrorist threats inside Germany. That's all I know. I don't think Gunter knows his name. Frederick knows. The Leader will reveal himself to everyone after Day X. Until then, he has to hide so he can destroy the government from within. That's all we've been told."

The head of the BfV had been convinced that some of her people were secretly working for a Nazi takeover of the German government. This would seem to confirm that not only had the BfV been compromised, but that it was someone high in the ranks. But confirming the existence of a traitor was only a first step. Kolya needed a name.

Frederick knew the identity of the Leader as well as the information about Day X. How to get that information? Frederick didn't trust computers. He'd already told Kolya that much. He could have been lying, but Kolya believed him, at least on this. Which meant that getting the information might be more complicated than breaking into a computer. Would Frederick have shared information with anyone close to him?

Hans probably knew everything. But the idea of returning to that farm was less than appealing.

What about Lisette? Would Frederick have shared anything with her?

Kolya checked his watch. Fifteen minutes since Peter had called his girlfriend. She should show up any moment. He watched headlights pass by the park. Not her—yet.

"What kind of car does your girlfriend drive?"

"I told you," Peter's voice had a whinny quality, "she's not a girlfriend. Just a friend."

"Fine. What kind of car does your friend drive?"

"VW Golf."

A car that could possibly be a VW Golf drove the length of the street, passed the park, did a U-turn, and returned.

"Silver?"

"Yes." The silver VW Golf pulled to the curb almost directly across from them, near the intersection of the two streets, but out of the illumination of any of the streetlights. Peter stood up. "It's her."

Kolya could see only one shape inside the car. From what little he could see, the shape appeared female. "Wait. You told her to get out of the car, didn't you?"

"I did."

But she wasn't getting out.

Peter's new phone buzzed with an incoming text. He retrieved the phone from his pocket and showed Kolya the text. *I'm here.*

The occupant of the driver's seat rolled down the window, and the driver was a woman, shoulder length brown hair, slim. No other cars around. No one near the car. Someone could be hiding in the back seat. Staying alive in his business meant to always assume a trap.

"Tell her to get out of the car and cross the street."

If the killers were in the car, they wouldn't allow her to step out.

But Peter had already texted. *Coming.*

"Not yet Peter. Tell her to get out and cross the street."

Peter hesitated and then sent the text.

She didn't. There was a long pause, then a text back. *Why? Where are you?*

"She thinks this is weird."

"Tell her that you'll explain later," Kolya said. "The killers could be hiding in the car."

Another text.

If you're not here in a minute, I'm leaving.

"There's no one else there, Michael. I'm going. She came here for me, and I'm not going to let her leave."

"No, Peter. Wait."

Peter didn't listen. He dashed forward, out of the park and towards the car. Kolya cursed to himself in Russian—falling back on lifelong habit despite his resolve and the months of work—drew his gun and followed. But between the bad leg and Peter's head start, Kolya lagged about twenty feet behind.

The woman in the driver's seat turned to look in their direction, and the face was terrified.

"Peter. Stop!" he called.

The back car door swung open, and a man, half crouched behind the driver's seat, leveled an automatic pistol and fired. Peter collapsed in the middle of the street.

Kolya fired back. The killer fell, his body halfway onto the street. A second man, concealed behind the first, raised himself to shoot. Kolya's round hit him between the eyes.

The young woman in the car screamed.

She opened her car door and ran to Peter, who lay face down, blood pooling in the street around him. Kolya started to shake as the adrenaline drained and in the aftermath of the gun fight, memories stirred. Then he forced himself back into the present, crossed the road, and knelt next to Peter. The young woman was sobbing uncontrollably, as Kolya gently turned Peter onto his back. The front of his T-shirt was soaked in blood. He'd been hit in the upper left chest, in the heart. He had died instantly.

Another person he'd failed to protect. Two dead in two days.

"They were waiting downstairs," she sobbed. "When I left my apartment. They told me they just wanted to talk to him."

"It's not your fault." He stood wearily, feeling the range of emotions, from rage to sorrow to guilt. Peter had just been a kid, who'd stupidly blundered into a dangerous and deadly game. "We have to get out of here."

The young woman gently stroked Peter's hair. "We have to call the police."

"They'll be here any minute." Kolya indicated the nearby buildings. "Someone undoubtedly reported the shots. You don't want to talk to the police. There could be Nazi supporters among them."

She looked at him, horrified. "We can't just leave him."

"I'm sorry, but we have to. It's not safe." He held out a hand, and she reluctantly took it and stood. She was still crying.

"But…"

"Listen to me. The people who ordered Peter's murder are still out there, and they'll kill both of us if they find us."

Still crying, she helped Kolya pull the bodies of the assassins from the back of her car and dump them in the street. She turned for a last look at Peter. "I'm so sorry, Peter." She turned her gaze to Kolya. "I didn't know him that well. We weren't in love or anything, but I liked him."

Peter had loved this woman enough to make a decision that cost him his life. Sad that she didn't feel the same. "The car. Now." Kolya circled and slid into the front passenger seat.

She closed the door behind her.

* * * * *

Fifteen minutes later, she dropped him five blocks from the hotel where he and Frederick were staying. It was probably safe to get closer, but there was the risk of being seen, and Kolya didn't trust her enough to tell her where he was staying. He was exhausted, and in the aftermath of action, his personal demons were stirring. Still, he lingered in the car for a moment. "Are you okay?"

She was no longer sobbing, but tears still streaked down her face. She nodded. "I feel bad about leaving Peter."

Peter deserved to have someone mourn him. As useless as that might be.

"He'd want you to be safe. And you're leaving Germany immediately, correct?" It was for both their protection. If Frederick's playmates caught her, she could tell them about the man who'd shot Peter's murderers. Even if she didn't know Kolya's cover name, he'd be blown. The description of a blond American with a gun in Greifswald would be enough. And he had no doubt, given that she'd brought killers to Peter, even though it was under duress, that she would tell Frederick or his friends everything they wanted to know.

She nodded again. "I packed a bag after Peter called, and it's in the trunk. I have friends in Denmark…"

"Don't tell me where you're going." He interrupted her before she could finish the sentence. Unlike her, he wouldn't give her away, even to save his own life, but he didn't want to have to protect her information as well as his own.

"Understood." She reached for a tissue from a box on the back seat. She wiped her face and blew her nose. "You were limping. Are you going to be okay?"

"I generally am." But not always. And it wasn't just his leg acting up. Still, not this young woman's concern.

"How long do I need to stay away?"

"Watch the news. You'll know." He opened the car door. "And thank you for the ride."

He wanted a shower and maybe some vodka. Normally he was careful about drinking while on assignment, but this had been a difficult two days, starting with Walter's murder, continuing with the old Nazi shoving a shotgun in his face, and ending with Peter's death. He assumed Frederick and Lisette would either be asleep or engaged in activities that did not involve him, which would free him to have a few drinks safely before he went to sleep. Earlier he'd spotted a store where he could pick up a bottle.

35

ELDENA, GERMANY

THE MEAL HAD BEEN excellent. Frederick had been in a good mood, and Lisette preferred to have him in a good mood, even if the mood had to do with his organizing work. He didn't discuss what he'd done on the trip—instead he discussed music, food, and the history of the town as they shared oysters and shrimp. He could be amusing. He was intelligent, and he appreciated the good things in life. If she hadn't known who and what he was, she might've enjoyed his company. Since she did know, every charming or funny comment was tainted and made her angry. But she was skilled in concealing and channeling her anger.

That anger did make the sex with Frederick more exciting. She practically tore his clothes off when they got back to the hotel, pulling him into her as she braced against the wall, one leg around his ass, arching towards him.

He, of course, had no idea that anger and hate drove her heightened performance and brought her to orgasm. He probably thought that she was delirious with desire out of love. It was pretty funny.

Afterwards, they sipped glasses of peppermint schnapps as they lolled on the bed. Lisette went light on the alcohol for the first round. She needed Frederick to go to sleep, and to sleep soundly. The best way to ensure that he did so, was to tire him out before he drank too much.

After finishing her drink, she straddled him. This time took a little longer, and this time, she faked it, her mind on what she planned to do. Frederick didn't know the difference.

Afterward, he lay in bed, caressing her breast. "You're going to be a proud woman." His voice sounded sleepy.

"I'm proud now."

He leaned over and kissed her. "I know. But you'll be prouder soon. The day is almost here."

"What day is that?" She had been so focused on killing murderers that she hadn't focused on his vague talk of a big day—assuming it was all just bravado. Maybe she should have paid more attention. Maybe there was a real risk.

"The day we take back Germany, when the Leader guides Germany in a new path."

"The Leader?" She knew that there was someone above Frederick, but he'd never spoken directly of the man.

"Yes." Frederick was speaking a little more freely than usual. "I'll be second in command when he takes over."

"Have I met him?" Could the Leader be the man described by Christian, the man known as Wolf?

"No, not yet. You will soon. He's been busy in the government."

"How exciting." And Lisette was excited. In ways that Frederick couldn't know.

But Frederick was finished talking about the Leader. "What do you think of Michael?"

"I think he's a good shot." Which made Michael dangerous and even more important for her to take out.

"Yes, he's good with guns. He's been useful so far. That woman in the garage. And he gave the coup de grace to a traitor yesterday." Then he described Michael shooting a man in the head.

If she'd needed any additional motivation to kill Michael, she now had it.

Frederick kept talking. "Weird thing this morning. One of the old guard, an ancient SS officer, shoved a shotgun in Michael's face. Hans' grandfather. You've met Hans."

"Yes, I've met Hans. Why?"

"The old man got it into his head that Michael was a Jew."

She laughed. "What is he, senile?"

"Probably. He must be a thousand years old. I thought we should put the old man out of his misery, but Michael talked me out it. He was right. It would have alienated Hans, and Hans is important for Day X." He reached for his glass of schnapps. She poured liberally. Frederick didn't notice that she was barely sipping her own drink. She could poison him easily when the time came.

The information from Christian—that the man with the wolf tattoo was someone in the German government—coupled with the information about the Leader was interesting. Had she wasted all this time killing nobodies—murderous nobodies but nobodies—while the man she wanted was at the top of the organization?

She felt stupid.

Frederick drained another glass of schnapps and pulled her down to lie on his chest.

While he drifted towards sleep, Lisette contemplated her next move. If the man with the wolf tattoo was the Leader, all the more reason to stay close to Frederick. But Michael—would she be risking it all to kill him?

The two stories—that Michael had killed a traitor—and that he'd refused to kill Hans' grandfather—were odd. Equally odd that the old Nazi had thought Michael was a Jew.

It didn't mean that he had a conscience, and it didn't make up for the other murders. Michael needed to die for what he'd done, and that he was training other people to kill increased the urgency. She couldn't kill Frederick yet, but if Michael's death appeared to be from natural causes, it shouldn't affect her position with Frederick.

Frederick was snoring when she slid out of bed. In the bathroom, she took a long shower, scrubbing all the places Frederick had touched her. When she emerged, Frederick lay on his back, not stirring when she said his name. The alcohol and the sex had done the job. He'd sleep through the night.

She dressed quietly, sexy underwear, jeans, and shirt, combed out her hair, found the bottle of ground monkshood in her purse, and picked up the bottle with the remaining liquor from the night table. The peppermint flavor would help conceal the bitter taste of the poison. The sugar should do the rest. She carried the monkshood and the peppermint schnapps into the bathroom, poured in the powder over the sink, and then rinsed both bottles and the counter, just in case any poison had spilled.

Two minutes later, she tapped on the door to Michael's room. There was no response. She tapped again.

Was he there? If not, where had he gone?

She had kept the extra electronic key that would open the door to Michael's room. She fished it out of her back pocket and pressed it against the electronic lock. The door clicked open.

Inside, she heard running water and realized why Michael hadn't responded when she knocked. He was in the shower.

Perfect.

She poured a glass of the schnapps, placing it on the bedside table. She'd pretend to imbibe from the bottle, to encourage him, but she expected that his attention wouldn't be on her drinking or lack thereof. To ensure his distraction, she stripped down to the black lace underwear and bra. Then she stretched out on the bed, bottle on her side of the bed, glass on his, and waited.

36

ELDENA, GERMANY

KOLYA LINGERED IN THE shower, as if the warm water could wash off the remnants of the past two days. He leaned his hands against the tile wall as the stream poured over his head and his back, balancing his weight on his good leg. With the water beating down on him, he mentally recited the mantra that his former therapist had suggested and that usually worked. *This is not Romania. I am in control.* Of course, it wasn't Romania: he wasn't a prisoner undergoing torture, but events were not completely under his control. He'd killed two men, and he'd failed to prevent two murders. He could very easily be exposed and killed. Yet he'd willingly, even eagerly, put himself in this situation. Alex—at the airport: *If you die, I'm going to be really pissed.* He'd be pretty pissed himself if he died—except, that he'd be dead and wouldn't know it.

He'd sent a quick text to Alex after returning to his room, a simple *I love you, I'm fine. Later.* He didn't expect a response. That was okay. It wasn't as if he had anything more to say. He couldn't tell her about Walter, Peter, the old Nazi, or that he'd been lucky not to be killed. Even after a mission ended, he had to keep details of an operation secret. Still, he knew she worried when he was in the field. Periodic messages reaffirming his love mattered in case something did happen.

The warmth, the water, the mantra, and breathing exercises finally did the job, relaxing him and calming the trembling. He stepped out of the shower and toweled himself dry. His leg still ached, but the hot water had helped.

He picked up the bottle of vodka that he'd carried into the bathroom and took a swig. He'd already downed the equivalent of two shots, and maybe he'd have another after he got in bed. But even if alone, he knew not to get drunk while undercover.

Not bothering with a towel, he swung the bathroom door open— and saw Lisette lying on his bed in her underwear.

* * * * *

When Michael opened the bathroom door, Lisette reclined alluringly on the pillows, striking a pose that emphasized her breasts and legs, and she contemplated the full-frontal nude view of the man. Michael had a better body than Frederick.

She raised the bottle of poisoned schnapps in greeting and smiled in the way that always drew men to her.

His reaction was not what she expected.

"What the fuck?" He stepped back into the bathroom and slammed the door.

Surprised, she sat up. "Michael? It's just me. Lisette."

"I know who you are." A minute later when he emerged, he had a towel wrapped around his waist. He also carried a bottle of vodka, which he placed on the dresser. He was more polite, but not any friendlier. "Please leave. Now."

"I thought you might be lonely." She indicated the peppermint schnapps. "I brought a bottle to share."

"I have something to drink, and I'm not lonely."

"I am. Frederick is sleeping, and I'm bored." The display of herself in her underwear was not having the desired effect. She thought of what might be a point of resistance. "Frederick wouldn't care. He's very open minded about sex."

"I'm not. Even if Frederick is, which I doubt."

Had she miscalculated? Her sexual appeal had worked reliably to get her close to all the men she'd killed. With the exception of

Christian, of course. But Michael wasn't buying. Was she losing her touch?

Regroup.

"Just talk then? Over a drink." She faked a pout. "Like I said, I'd like some company. I'm not ready to sleep."

"If you want to talk, put on some clothes." He grabbed a pair of jeans and a shirt from one of two chairs in the room. "And please relocate into a chair. I'll be right back." As he turned to re-enter the bathroom, she caught a glimpse of his back, crisscrossed with long scars. It looked like he'd been whipped, repeatedly and brutally.

What'd happened to him?

But she didn't ask, and he disappeared, shutting the door. The scars made her feel something close to sympathy. But not enough to change her mind. Whatever abuse he might have suffered that had twisted him, he was still a killer who deserved justice. To deliver it, she had to entice him to drink the schnapps.

It might not be as easy as she'd anticipated.

She slipped into her clothes with a sigh. As she zipped her pants, she heard the buzzing sound that signaled a text from Michael's phone on the nightstand. She picked it up and saw the message.

Love you, too. Stay safe.

He emerged from the bathroom dressed and saw her with his phone. She handed it to him. He glanced down and then deleted the text.

"Girlfriend?" she asked.

"There's that possibility."

That explained why he'd rejected her. He was faithful to a girlfriend. Charming, if old fashioned. It didn't change her mind.

"And you're monogamous. That explains it." She gestured towards the bed.

"It's one of the reasons." Then he smiled, but it seemed a little forced. "Not that I don't think you're attractive. You are very much so. And you know it, too, don't you?"

"I do." She sauntered over to the dresser, picked up the bottle of vodka, and carried it with her to a chair on the far side of the room.

If she had the vodka, maybe he'd drink the schnapps. She took a sip from the bottle, just for effect. She had to remain in control.

"I believe the vodka's mine. You brought your own drink, didn't you?" Michael's tone was mild.

"Don't you like to share?" She sprawled in the chair and waved a hand casually at the glass still on the nightstand. "I intended to share with you. One of Germany's finest."

He picked up the glass of schnapps and carried it with him to the chair that had previously held his clothes. He sat, but he didn't drink. "How much have you already had?"

"I'm not drunk." She tilted the bottle to her mouth, as if drinking, but this time she kept her lips pressed together, not even taking a sip. But if Michael thought she was drinking, he might keep her company.

Infuriatingly, he didn't. He set the glass on the dresser. "I suspect that you've had enough."

She pretended to drink again. "I'm just relaxing. Don't you ever relax, Michael?" She held up the vodka and looked questioningly.

"Sometimes. Alone. I wasn't planning on company. Not that your company is unwelcome. Just a little surprising."

He was trying to charm her. Were they both playing games?

"If my company's not unwelcome," she tilted her head towards the bed, "care to change your mind?"

Sex and alcohol went together. If she could lure him into bed, she could get him to drink the schnapps. Especially if she kept the vodka away from him.

But he wasn't buying.

"I can enjoy your company without having sex with you."

"Your girlfriend's jealous?"

"Not the point." He picked up the glass, and she held her breath. But he just held the glass. "Still, enough about me. Let's talk about you. You must be excited about the big day."

She noted the change in direction. "A little."

"Just a little?"

"Frederick doesn't tell me that much about what's going on. Women, you know. We're weak."

"I would never describe you as weak. You really don't know anything?"

She actually did feel a little stupid that she'd been so intent on taking revenge on individual actors that she hadn't dug deeper into Frederick's greater plans. But then again, she'd always assumed that while the neo-Nazis were monstrous, they weren't smart enough or organized enough to pull off anything big. "Not much. Frederick told me that I'd be proud after."

"Do you know when it's happening?"

The turn in the conversation was almost as if he were grilling her. Was he really trying to get information from her? She didn't understand it, but she decided to probe him in turn. "I don't. What do you know?" She took another pretend drink from the bottle of vodka.

He turned the glass in his hands but didn't drink. "I just know the name. Day X."

"From Frederick?"

"No. From two people who probably shouldn't have said anything."

"One of them the crazy old man who tried to shoot you?"

"Frederick told you about that?" He still didn't drink. Infuriating.

"How else would I know? Why didn't you shoot him?"

He shrugged. "Didn't seem like the best way to promote group harmony."

"That's what Frederick said. More or less."

"I thought Frederick didn't tell you everything."

"He tells me some things."

"Just not about Day X."

"I hadn't even heard the term. Until just now. I knew he was anticipating something big, but I don't know any details."

He turned the glass in his hands. "Have you met the Leader?"

"No. Very few have."

"That must be disappointing. Wouldn't you like to?"

"I will. In time." She felt as if she were in a duel, a game whose rules she didn't understand. She knew her own goals—get whatever information Michael might have about Day X and entice him to drink. But he seemed to be as interested in information from her as she was in information from him. She'd play along. Besides she had now had an interest in the Leader and in Day X. "Why are you asking?"

He smiled again. He did have a nice smile. Probably knew it too, the bastard, and was trying to use it. "Just curious. I just thought—you and Frederick are close—and I hate to bother Frederick with questions."

That he didn't have any more information than she did about whatever Frederick was up to or about the Leader meant that she could kill him now. *Get him to drink.* "You should try the schnapps. It's one of Germany's best brands."

He brought it up to his face, and she waited, on edge. But instead of drinking, he took a sniff.

"Peppermint?"

"Try it with vodka." She pushed up from the chair and crossed the room, vodka in hand. Anything to get him to drink.

He held up a hand. "Don't waste good vodka. I don't like sweet drinks."

She heard something now that she hadn't noticed before. A slight accent. Then she remembered his history: Ukrainian had been his first language.

She inched closer, so that her breasts were inches from his face. "Oh come on. Stop being so stiff. Try it."

He made no move to touch her. "No, thank you."

She bent over and kissed him. His mouth tasted of vodka. Then he pushed her back with one hand.

"Sorry. You're a lovely woman, but I'm not interested."

She glanced down at his jeans. Did he have an erection? Maybe. "You're lying. Your body says that you're definitely interested." She poured some vodka into the glass he held. "Try the drink. And then let's see just how uninterested you are."

"I've already told you that I find you attractive. And, yes, I have a physical response. That doesn't mean I'll go to bed with you." He set the glass on the dresser and stood, pushing her even farther back. "I also said that I don't like sweet drinks."

She made one last try. "You put a lot of sugar in your coffee."

"That's coffee. Not alcohol. It's time to call it a night, Lisette. I want to go to bed. Alone."

She felt frustration and disappointment. She'd never failed to make a kill once she zeroed in on a target. She thought of the ways she'd killed other men, but Michael wasn't drunk, and he wasn't asleep. She doubted that he'd be easy to kill with a sword or a knife if he were in full possession of his faculties, which he clearly was. He also had a gun—somewhere. In any event, she'd wanted to make his death appear to be a simple heart attack. Killing him violently would defeat her other goals, even if she could manage to pull it off.

Give up for the night.

She yawned. "Okay, I get it. It's been nice talking to you." She set the bottle of vodka on the dresser.

"Yes, but next time, consider knocking instead of barging in with a spare key. Speaking of which…" He held out his hand. She dug it out of her pocket and handed it to him.

"Sorry."

"No need to apologize."

"Sure you don't want the schnapps?"

"I'm sure."

She crossed to the nightstand and picked up the poisoned bottle. If he wasn't going to drink it, she needed to wash away any evidence. "Glass?" she asked him. That was also evidence, and it needed to be cleaned.

He handed it to her. "You want to finish it?"

"You were right—I've had enough. But maybe later. By the way, it might be best if neither of us tells Frederick about this." She glanced back at the room.

"I was thinking the same thing." He opened the door to the hall for her.

She'd failed this time, but she'd find another way.

37

COLOGNE, GERMANY

AT SEVEN O'CLOCK THE next morning, Jonathan texted Elizabeth, hoping he wouldn't be waking her. Sort of. Just as she sometimes liked to give him a hard time, he liked to reciprocate. If she'd gone to Arnold's apartment, she deserved an early morning call. But she returned the text within minutes, and her return text showed no indication of irritation.

Five minutes later, she met him in the hotel lobby, where he handed her a soy cappuccino, her usual morning drink. Then they strolled outside, arm in arm, to all appearances, a loving couple seeing the sights. Outside was a safer place to exchange information. In the heyday of the Cold War, when Germany was Spy Central, the sidewalks of the cities, especially Berlin, resembled a track meet with the dozens of intelligence officers practically running each other over.

Now, not so much. Especially in Cologne.

"What did you find?" Elizabeth removed the plastic lid from her cup.

"I didn't find anything in Arnold's apartment, but then I wasn't there too long. Nice place. No Nazi paraphernalia. No swastika decorations. How long were you at the restaurant?"

"Maybe ten o'clock."

"Any conclusions?"

"You and he have similar taste in food. As to any indication of his being a secret neo-Nazi—no. But I remain suspicious of anyone trying that hard to charm me."

"You know you're attractive, Elizabeth. Men generally try to charm women they want to screw."

"Except for you."

"Yeah, except for me. So did you go to bed with him?"

She tossed her hair back, the diamond earrings flashing. "How is that any of your business?"

"Team leader," he said. "Arnold is a suspect, and sleeping with him could be dangerous. I don't want you taking that risk. Has nothing to do with the two of us."

"Doesn't it?" But she shrugged. "In any event, I didn't screw him. You said Mark found something interesting about Reiner?"

They changed their pace, stopping and starting, checked store windows and the faces of people passing. No one appeared interested. No one lingered.

"Reiner had a bunch of neo-Nazi propaganda on his computer."

"So you think Reiner's a Nazi?"

"Maybe. No indication that he's called or emailed Frederick Bauer, or any other known far-right activist. The propaganda could be for research. There was also some stuff about the Islamic State, more deeply buried, jihadist sites he's visited."

"You don't think he's a jihadist, do you?" Elizabeth asked.

"I don't. But Arnold tried pretty hard to convince us that the Islamic State and sympathizers were the real problem," Jonathan said.

"That topic continued at dinner last night while he was trying to seduce me."

"It's possibly a real concern. Jihadists remain a problem." Jonathan sipped his coffee. "Or it could be camouflage."

"Or that. Any word from Petrov on neo-Nazis inside the BfV?"

"Nothing from his meeting with Frick. He apparently called in to Mark but to get information, not to pass it on. Don't expect to hear anything until he returns to Berlin." Jonathan didn't voice his concern. What if Frick was right about Kolya operating in the field?

"Well, damn. I guess I'll just have to go out with Arnold again—and eat more French food." Elizabeth drained the rest of her coffee, crumpled the cup, and tossed it. "The things I do for my country."

38

ELDENA, GERMANY

IN THE DREAM, KOLYA sat on the bench of the used upright piano. Curled in a comfortable armchair, his cousin Rifka, who had brought him to the United States and adopted him at the age of fourteen, listened as he played Mozart. Rifka, like his mother, had loved Mozart. Kolya was both in the dream and watching the dream, aware that in the dream, he was seventeen, about to start college, and aware that Rifka had less than ten years before breast cancer would kill her. The dream shifted to Russia, to when he was seven or eight, his mother playing the same piece as he listened. Then both Rifka and his mother were gone, and a stocky man with dark blond hair entered the cell where he lay on the floor, chained, his leg broken. Someone pounded on the wall.

No, not Romania.

Someone was pounding on the door, calling a name that was not his name. Another minute before he fully woke and remembered where he was and who he was pretending to be.

"Michael." The voice that accompanied the pounding belonged to Frederick, and it sounded alarmed.

"Coming." He rolled out of bed, wondering if the early morning intrusion had anything to do with Lisette's strange visit the previous night.

Probably not. Most likely, Frederick had learned about Peter—and the two soldiers that Kolya had shot.

He pulled on jeans and a shirt, not wanting Frederick to see the scars on his body, although it was probably an unnecessary precaution. Lisette had had a full view of everything, and she hadn't asked any questions.

He swung the door open. "What? It's early."

"Pack up. We're heading back to Berlin." Frederick looked panicked. Lisette, fully dressed, clung to Frederick's arm, giving no sign that she'd ever been in Kolya's room or had a sexual thought about another man.

"What's going on?"

"They struck again. The assassins. Gunter called. I don't think we should talk here."

Frederick had previously expressed concern about his people being murdered. Maybe he thought that the same person had shot Peter's killers. Kolya hoped so.

"What happened? Want to come in?" He gestured towards the room.

"Not secure," Frederick said. "We have to get going."

"Lisette coming with us?" Kolya asked.

"She's driving with me. You'll follow in her car."

"I don't want to be separated from Frederick," she said.

A good actress.

"Coffee first." He was barely awake. Two night's poor sleep in a row, and he wasn't a kid anymore.

A lot of coffee.

"I'll get a couple cups to go while you pack up," Lisette said. "Maybe a breakfast roll for the road. And two sugars, correct?"

"Yes, two sugars. Thank you." He had a bottled Starbucks in his refrigerator that he'd purchased with the vodka, but as tired as he was, the more coffee the better.

"Will do. And while I'm getting coffee, you can take a walk on the beach," Lisette said.

"Good idea," Frederick said. "Beaches are a good place to talk."

"Fine." Kolya backed into his room, leaving the door open. "Two minutes."

"See you in a bit." She smiled at him, a friendly smile but with a message. *Do not mention last night.* He had no intention of doing so.

But his instincts signaled an alert. She *was* a good actress, but something was off. He'd sensed something wrong that first day, before and especially after he'd faked shooting Tehila. He felt it even stronger after last night's attempted seduction, and now with her innocent and seemingly helpful act. His instincts were generally right, which was how he'd managed to stay alive for ten years in a very dangerous business.

Once he got back to Berlin, he'd set up a meeting with Frick. He had information to pass on, and maybe Frick had something for him.

* * * * *

With a squeeze of Frederick's arm and a wave at Michael, Lisette headed for the small restaurant next door to the hotel. Outside the hotel, the wind blew the scent of the sea, and gulls cawed overhead. The restaurant was simple, offering cheap meals for beachgoers. She put in the order and leaned on the counter, waiting.

She couldn't believe her luck. After the previous night's failed attempt to kill Michael, she'd assumed that justice would have to wait. But the phone call from Gunter had given her another chance.

It wouldn't need to be a lethal dose to do the job. Not that she wouldn't put enough in to kill him, but if Michael, driving her car at high speeds, became ill and lost control, the crash would kill him if the poison didn't.

Michael would be driving her car, but it was insured. Besides, she had plenty of money thanks to her stepfather.

And it was fortuitous how the opportunity had presented. Frederick had woken her in a panic after a call from Gunter. Two of Gunter's men had been killed, good job whoever did it, and Frederick, on edge since her execution of Karl, had assumed the same assassin had struck again.

She wouldn't be suspected of any involvement in Michael's death, since she'd be with Frederick.

Still, it was a risk. If Michael crashed, she'd be unable to dispose of the coffee cup with any remaining trace of monkshood. A risk, but a small risk and one worth taking. Had she eliminated Michael that first night, two people would still be alive. How many more people would he kill?

It was unlikely that any toxicology studies would be run on Michael, other than to establish whether he'd been drinking alcohol or taking drugs. No one would be likely to check his body or his coffee cup for aconite, the poison in monkshood.

She was more worried about Frederick becoming suspicious than the authorities, but the fact that she'd be with him when Michael died should allay any doubts. Whoever had killed Gunter's men the previous night had also done her a favor. Lisette and Frederick had been eating dinner together when the shooting took place. She wouldn't be suspected.

The order arrived, a small brown paper bag with the food and napkins, and a holder with three cups of coffee. She carried the bag and the container to a nearby table, where she poured sugar and cream into her and Frederick's coffees and two tablespoons of crushed monkshood and five teaspoons of sugar into Michael's, the extra sugar to conceal the bitterness.

She considered doctoring his wrapped egg and cheese roll but discarded the idea. There would be nothing sweet in the sandwich to counter the bitter taste.

The coffee would be enough.

She pulled a pen from her purse and marked the cup lids with initials. Then she carried the brown paper bag with sandwiches and the cardboard drink container with the three coffees back to the parking lot for the hotel, where Michael leaned against her car as Frederick talked, animatedly, gesturing. Michael glanced at her.

"Keys?"

She noted the bottle of Starbuck's cold brew that he held in his hand.

She handed over her car key along with his breakfast sandwich and cup of coffee. "I didn't realize you already had coffee."

"More is always better." He unlocked her car, leaned in, and placed the poisoned coffee in a cupholder, the sandwich on the empty seat. "For the road."

She wasn't hearing his accent quite as distinctly this morning. Had she imagined it? Or had last night been a slip on his part, out of tiredness.

It didn't matter. All that mattered was that he drank the coffee.

39

BUNDESAUTOBAUN A-20, GERMANY

KOLYA PUT LISETTE'S CAR into gear and pulled out behind Frederick. They wound back through the heart of Greifswald, driving at reasonable speeds until they reached the A20. Then Frederick, ahead, accelerated to over 160 kpm, over 100 mph. Kolya, a little more conservative, kept the speed at around 120 kpm or around 75 mph. Frederick zoomed out of sight.

Kolya was adept at high-speed driving but did it for function, not fun. Unlike his friend Jonathan, he didn't subscribe to the American love affair with automobiles, maybe because he'd spent his childhood and then his teenage years without a car, first in Russia and then in Brooklyn, and hadn't learned to drive until he was in his twenties.

Kolya was driving fast enough, especially considering how tired he was.

He picked up the bottle of Starbucks cold brew and drank, grateful for the caffeine and grateful he had more coffee when he finished off the bottle.

As he drove, he weighed whether to call Frick. Or Jonathan. Even though he lacked details, he had to alert the ECA about Day X. But Kolya had already taken one risk to phone Mark the previous night. Cell phone tracking would only show that someone on the beach had called the United States. One call—from the phone that Frederick didn't know he possessed—would not be suspicious.

Multiple calls—and always from a location where Kolya could be placed—more problematic.

And more dangerous, if he called a number inside Germany—dangerous because Peter had confirmed that the Leader was in fact high up in the BfV. National intelligence agencies monitored phone calls and texts. Whoever the Leader was might have access to that data.

He'd texted Alex earlier, but that shouldn't be a problem. As usual, he had just sent his love, and she'd returned it, indicating nothing except that he had a girlfriend in the U.S.

Irritating that Lisette knew—but not dangerous.

Get back to Berlin, signal for a meeting. Nothing should happen for at least a few days, and he didn't need to break cover to brief Frick. There was time for secure communication. More critical that he not be suspected—and not break security unless he had no choice.

He'd had no choice but to make the call to Mark the previous night. As it was, he'd been late, barely getting Peter out of the apartment before the killers arrived, but ultimately failing to save Peter's life.

If he'd been faster, could things have ended differently? If he'd been able to run, as he had in the past, and had arrived half an hour earlier? Or if he'd taken the risk to grab a cab.

Despite any lingering guilt, he knew it wasn't his fault. Just as Walter's death hadn't been his fault.

A car passed him, going maybe 180 kph. Way too fast.

Kolya increased his speed to pass a Volkswagen. He glanced at the driver as he passed. An old woman. Probably not old enough to have been alive during the years of the Reich, but the question was ever present in his mind on this mission. Just as being Jewish was.

Odd. He had so little knowledge of Jewish customs or laws. His parents had given him his one non-Jewish grandfather's name, as if that might protect him from the anti-Semitism of the then Soviet Union. For the fourteen years that he'd lived in St. Petersburg, first with his mother and then in the *dyskeii dom*—the abusive boys' home after his mother's death—he'd observed no Jewish holidays or Jewish customs. As an adult, he was agnostic and not fond of rituals or ceremonies. Yet, he'd wanted this assignment because he was Jewish.

And he'd never felt more Jewish than he did now, when he had to conceal anything that might even hint that he was a Jew.

He pulled his egg and cheese roll onto his lap and ate, holding the sandwich with his right hand and steering with his left. Then he crumbled the paper wrapping and tossed it to the floor on the passenger's side. He'd pick it up when he got to Berlin. No reason to leave trash in Lisette's car. She, unlike Alex, kept her car neat.

The thought took his mind back to the events of the previous night.

Lisette hadn't provided any information, but her presence and her repeated attempts to get into his bed raised questions.

Even before his involvement with Alex, he hadn't approved of seduction as an intelligence tool, although admittedly it worked under the right circumstances. So did torture. He didn't approve of that either.

His colleagues in the ECA followed the international rules on torture but had fewer qualms than he did on the use of honey traps. Sex was a powerful motivator and could induce people to act irrationally—to give up secrets on either the promise of a secret love affair or the threat of revealing it. But, doing so put agents in danger of losing not just their lives, but whatever might pass as a soul. If agents had souls. If anyone had a soul.

All of this brought him back to Lisette. What was going on? She had wanted something, and it wasn't a good fuck.

The previous night had seemed almost orchestrated, an elaborate game where the rules were vague and the goals uncertain. He had wanted information from her. What had she wanted?

Could she be an intelligence operative? The U.S. wasn't the only country interested in neo-Nazis. No other agency, American or other, would know that he had infiltrated. Nor would he know if another agency had done the same. As far as the other intelligence services knew—he was Nickolas Kruger posing as Michael Hall.

Could Lisette be playing the same role he was?

Or maybe Frederick had sent her as a test.

Or perhaps Lisette was exactly what she seemed to be—a bored young woman who took up with neo-Nazis to fill an emptiness in her life and who liked casual sex. Occam's razor—the simplest explanation is usually correct.

Another car sped by him, a silver BMW. He glanced at the speedometer. He was going 140 kpm. The BMW had passed as if he were standing still. Why did people with expensive cars drive so recklessly?

He remembered a line from *The Great Gatsby* about rich people: "they smashed up things and creatures and then retreated back into their money or their vast carelessness." Funny how some people thought that *The Great Gatsby* celebrated wealth.

Funny how he still remembered the book years after he'd read it in college—that his life had taken him in such a different direction.

He could almost hear Alex's voice when they'd finally starting dating, years after they had met in law school, years after he'd first fallen in love with her.

"You majored in English, went to law school, all to become a spy?"

He'd teased her back. "You majored in English, with a focus on novels of the late 19th and early 20th century—all to become a lawyer?"

"Studying novels of that period helps me write briefs containing long, boring descriptions and archaic language. How is it useful to you?"

"It's not. I just like being a well-read spy."

He made the turn from the Autobahn A20 onto the Autobahn A11. Traffic picked up.

Grateful not to have Frederick as a traveling companion, he flipped on the radio and found a jazz station. While hip hop and rap were also big in Europe, jazz had never gone out of style as it had in much of America.

He picked up the Starbucks cold brew and finished it. Ten minutes later, he picked up the cup of hot coffee.

40

BERLIN, GERMANY

FREDERICK PARKED THE CAR in the garage attached to his apartment building. He accompanied Lisette upstairs, asked her to make coffee, then took his phone into his office and shut the door. Things were coming apart.

He dialed the number he had for the Leader, even though he'd been instructed not to use it except for emergencies. But this was an emergency, wasn't it? Two rings and then the Leader's voice.

"I'm in the office." There was irritation in his voice.

The office was a dangerous place for the Leader to talk. Frederick knew that. Still, it couldn't wait.

"It's urgent."

"I'll talk a walk and call you back."

"When?"

"Half an hour. Are you at home?"

"Yes."

"You shouldn't be. Half an hour."

The Leader hung up, and Frederick clicked the phone off. He heard a tap on the door, and Lisette opened it. She carried two cups of coffee—depositing one in front of Frederick.

"Are you okay?"

"No." He was realizing now what needed to be done. "I am very much not okay."

She sat on the chair next to his and placed her hand on his knee. "I'm here for you."

"I know. It's just I've worked for this for the past ten years. We were on the edge of success, and now I don't know what's happening."

She cocked her head. "I know that two men got killed yesterday. That's what's upset you, isn't it?"

"It's not just that they were killed." Should he explain what was happening? Maybe. "It's what it means for the movement."

"As upsetting as it is—it's only two men."

"I'm worried that someone has penetrated Germany Now. Someone who wants to destroy us. I don't know who Peter talked to. If Peter talked to anyone. But someone was protecting him."

"And you think this could stop your plans?"

"That's my concern." He checked his phone. No calls yet. He could feel the tension boiling up inside, as if he were a kettle about to explode. "If there's a traitor, we could fail." He picked up his phone and his keys. "We'll talk later. I'm going for a walk." Then he headed out of the apartment.

* * * * *

Lisette poured herself another cup of coffee and considered following Frederick. Since her conversation with Michael, she started to wonder about Frederick's plans. What was Day X—and how could she stop it?

Search his office? Maybe. But if anything was out of place, he'd notice. Given how suspicious and on edge he now was, she couldn't take the risk.

She'd find another way. She always did.

She glanced down at the street. No sign of Michael. It could mean nothing. It could mean that he was a more cautious driver than Frederick. She hoped that it meant he'd drunk the coffee and that either the monkshood or a car crash had done the job.

A horrible thought occurred to her. What if Michael had crashed into another car? She could be responsible for another innocent death.

What was wrong with her that she hadn't thought through the

possible consequences of poisoning someone driving at high speeds? She'd considered that a crash could kill Michael, but not that more than one car could be involved.

Why was it only now occurring to her?

She crossed to the sink and the gleaming stainless-steel counter and picked up the coffee pot. After pouring another cup of coffee, she opened the refrigerator, took out the milk, and spilled some on the floor, realizing too late that her hands were shaking. She wiped the spot with a damp paper towel and then carried her coffee to the table.

She took a sip of the coffee, the bitter taste reminding her of the monkshood. Not that she knew what monkshood tasted like—she was not stupid enough to sample it—even though a small amount wouldn't kill. Why *had* she poisoned Michael's coffee without considering all the alternatives?

Couldn't she have eliminated him in a way that didn't put other people at risk?

Why was taking Michael out so important that she'd focused on killing him and on nothing else? Every other killing had been carefully weighed and considered, the possible risks and the consequences. With Michael, though, she'd been reckless.

Was it because she'd witnessed him commit a murder—a murder that she could've prevented? Was it out of frustration for his evading her attempt to poison him with the peppermint schnapps?

Or was it because, despite knowing what he was, she found him attractive—and she didn't like that she found a killer attractive? She had a sudden flash of the image of his body when he stepped from the bathroom.

Okay, she could be honest. He was good looking. So what? He was a murderer, and he was helping Frederick prepare for whatever Day X might be. Her body responded to stimuli, even if her mind disagreed. So what if she'd liked the look of Michael's body? It meant nothing.

She hoped for two things—that Michael had died and that he hadn't taken anyone else with him.

COLOGNE, GERMANY

The Leader walked several blocks to a small park where children played tag and old men played chess. There were empty benches, but he didn't sit. He found a trail that he liked, with flower beds on either side of the walk. As he walked, he took out his latest burner phone.

"So?"

Frederick's voice on the other end sounded strained. "We need to meet. Immediately."

This was a nuisance. Frederick was supposed to handle things—that was why the Leader made him second in command. "I'm busy today." And even if they met half-way, it would be an almost four-hour drive. Eight hours round trip. "It's safe talking here. Briefly."

"That was before. Now I'm not sure. I think we need to move things up."

"Because of what happened in Greifswald?"

"You know about that?"

The Leader made a snorting noise. "Of course, I do. I also know you're panicking."

"I'm not panicking. I'm worried that we're being targeted. We need to make adjustments. And if we're being watched, we shouldn't discuss details on the phone."

The Leader thought about the long drive and his plans for the evening. He wouldn't be back until close to midnight. Still, there was something to be said for taking extra precautions, this close to success. "Okay. Meet you at six. Hanover. Usual spot."

41

BUNDESAUTOBAUN A-11, GERMANY

THE COFFEE WAS VERY hot and almost unbearably sweet. Kolya liked some sugar in his coffee but not this much. And he preferred lukewarm or cold liquids to boiling hot. He took a small sip and then replaced the cup in the holder, removing the lid so the coffee would cool down.

He was driving through miles of forests on either side of the road with light traffic, Thelonious Monk playing a piece that he didn't recognize. He tapped fingers on the steering wheel, appreciating the artistry. *Bluehawk*. How had he missed it? He listened carefully, memorizing the melody. Maybe he'd try playing it next time he had access to a piano.

Maybe two more weeks on this assignment. If he managed to survive Day X, he'd be due time off. Would Alex prefer Paris to Miami? He would, but a vacation was wherever Alex might be.

About ten miles farther down the road, the nausea hit.

He tried to ignore it. *The egg and cheese sandwich, probably*. But ignoring it didn't work. The nausea continued to grow, and he felt sweaty, his heart racing.

He slowed, not wanting to lose control of the car. A Mercedes driver behind him leaned on the horn. He waved the car around, slowed further, and then he realized that slowing was not enough. He pulled the car onto the highway shoulder, opened the door, and stumbled out, hoping that fresh air would help.

He felt worse.

He made it to the edge of the woods before he started to vomit. He vomited up the sandwich, the Starbucks cold brew, continuing to retch, even after there was nothing left to bring up.

He heard cars passing on the A11. No one pulled over.

Feeling wobbly, he sat heavily on the ground, leaned against a tree, and closed his eyes.

Food poisoning would be a ridiculous way to go, wouldn't it? All the risks he'd taken in his professional life, as close as he'd come to death so many times—it would be deeply ironic to die of food poisoning. Done in by an egg and cheese breakfast roll.

If it was the egg and cheese. If it was food poisoning. He thought of the overly sweetened coffee that Lisette had given him and the reasons why she might've added so much sugar. Then his mind flashed back to the previous night. He remembered the glass of alcohol left on his bed table, how she'd appropriated his vodka, leaving him with a drink that she'd poured. Everything she did during that visit to his room—all the sexual moves, all the chit chat—had been focused on trying to get him to drink the peppermint schnapps. Another sweet drink, where the sugar could conceal the taste of something else.

Not food poisoning. Intentional poisoning. If he was right.

Maybe he wasn't.

But he usually was.

He was a fucking idiot not to have put it together. "*Yob tvoyu mat.*" He let his mind retrieve the Russian curse. There was no one to hear, and after all, concealing his identity didn't matter right now, not if he'd been poisoned.

Why would she poison him?

Did she suspect he wasn't the Nazi he was pretending to be? Or did she think he was?

If she suspected his true identity not to be that of Michael Hall/ Nickolas Kruger, wouldn't she have said something to Frederick? Why try to kill him herself?

Maybe she just liked to kill.

Then again, maybe Lisette was the anti-Nazi vigilante that Frederick feared, and she had put poison in his coffee because she believed the role he was playing. That would be ironic.

It was immaterial. If whatever poison he had drunk didn't kill him—assuming he was right about that as well—he'd figure it out later. Right now, he was more worried that the information about Day X, meager though it may be, wouldn't get to the ECA.

He felt in his pocket, but he'd left his phone in the car. Could he drag himself to the car to call Frick? Calling Frick might not be secure, but security wouldn't matter if he died.

He tried to stand but felt too sick to move.

He'd rest for a few minutes and then give it a try.

BERLIN, GERMANY

Frederick returned to the apartment even before Lisette had finished washing the coffee cups and fixing lunch. Her decision not to search his office had been the correct one. He could have walked in on her.

"I'm making Kaesespaetzle." She knew he liked the dish, small pasta layered with grated cheese and topped with fried onion.

"No time." He glanced at the table, decorated with flowered china plates. "I'm sorry. I have a long drive. But I appreciate the effort. I'll be back late tonight."

"You're meeting the Leader?"

He hesitated, and she worried whether asking the question had been too much. But when he answered, his voice showed no concern. "Yes. We have decisions to make."

"Do you want me to come with you?" She wanted more than ever to meet the Leader. The face of the man who'd shot her father remained a vivid memory. Even if he'd aged, she should recognize him. And if he had still had the tattoo—that would be the final proof.

But he shook his head. "Not yet. You'll meet him soon enough." He pulled her in for a long and passionate kiss.

She kissed him back and then pulled away with a small laugh. "I thought you were in a hurry."

"I am. But after Day X, when we've taken the country, I want to make it official. I love you, Lisette."

"And I love you." *When had lying become so easy?*

"You can go home if you'd like, but I'd prefer you to wait for me. And Michael should be here any time with your car." He picked up his keys. "I have no idea why he's taking so long."

"Maybe he stopped somewhere. Or maybe he got lost." She glanced at the clock. More than two hours since they'd arrived home. Even if Michael drove slowly, he should have been back. She ticked him off her mental to-do list.

"Maybe. Whenever he gets here, tell him I'll need him first thing in the morning." And he headed out.

She wondered what he'd think when he learned that Michael was dead. Probably that the unknown anti-Fascist vigilante had struck again. Which she had.

With Frederick gone for hours, she'd have the time to search his office.

BUNDESAUTOBAUN A-11, GERMANY

Kolya closed his eyes, still leaning against the tree. His mother, blonde hair disheveled, dressed in the clothes she'd worn to the hospital where she'd died, hovered over him. *"I'm proud of you."*

"Are you? For me stupidly drinking poisoned coffee?"

"Don't be so hard on yourself."

His mother smiled at him.

Was he dying?

Maybe, but at least he knew she wasn't real. He was in that half-awake, half-asleep state where he knew that he was dreaming even as he continued to dream. He preferred this dream to the nightmares he had so often, where he was imprisoned and tortured.

She frowned at him. "Why haven't you been practicing?"

"Busy. And no piano where I'm staying. Anyway, I mainly play jazz now. You wouldn't approve."

"Just keeping playing. Whatever the style. Even if it's jazz."

Odd, he didn't remember her ever saying anything of the kind. She'd given him love and taught him to play piano, read books to him and with him. But she'd expected him to be a classical pianist. She'd been annoyed that he preferred jazz to classical.

He was about to ask if she meant it, but she disappeared. Alex took her place. He liked seeing her even if he knew she was a hallucination. *She regarded him, a worried expression on her face.*

"You look terrible. How are you feeling?"

"Not so good. You're not pissed?"

"A little, but you're not dying."

"Hopefully not." The nausea seemed to be receding. Maybe he hadn't drunk enough of the coffee to kill him. He'd only had a small sip. With some poisons, the sip would have been enough. Maybe he'd lucked out.

"About last night… were you tempted?"

"By Lisette?"

"Has there been any other person in a state of undress in your bedroom?"

"Not recently."

"So were you?"

"Maybe a little."

"A little?" Alex raised eyebrows. *"You had an erection."*

"She's an attractive woman, even if she did try to kill me. My body will do what male bodies do. But she's nothing compared to you, and you're always on my mind."

"Good thing too, or she would have gotten you last night."

"Also good that I prefer lukewarm coffee."

"That too."

She smiled at him, and then she was gone.

42

BEN HAD FINALLY MADE it to the Equality Institute, although parking his car and walking to the elevator was more than a little terrifying. But he was back, reviewing research of internet posts on various Nazi and white supremacist sites. Most of the posters had disguised their identities, but his people had ferreted out some names. He had a master list of every one of them.

The twins weren't in yet. They'd promised to follow his children to school, and his wife to her gallery.

It gave him some comfort, but he still knew how badly things could go and how quickly it could happen.

He remained tense until he saw them walk through the door and past the armed security. A few minutes later, Hasan, accompanied by Ahmet, tapped on Ben's door, and then cracked it open. He waved them in, and they seated themselves in front of his desk.

"Your family's fine." Ahmet anticipated Ben's question.

"You know, your wife is annoyed that we're following her," Hasan said.

"Very annoyed." Ahmet seemed to think it was amusing.

"She wants us to tell you that we're following her, but not do it," Hasan said.

"She's not the one who pays your salary." Ben found himself also amused, despite his worry for his family.

"She makes good cinnamon rolls," Hasan said.

"And coffee," Ahmet said. "She fed us breakfast before she left for school."

"You're getting free breakfasts for guarding my family?"

"We'd do it anyway," Hasan said. "But it's a nice bonus."

"You're going to follow her home, too, right?"

"Of course," Ahmet said. "She'll call us when she's ready to leave her gallery for the school. I went inside. Your wife does nice paintings. And what's the name of the young woman who works there, by the way."

The young woman, and not the paintings, was more likely to be the subject of Ahmet's interest.

"I'm not a dating service. If you want a woman's name, ask her. Or my wife. Anything else?" Ben returned his attention to the emails on his computer, but the silence after his question drew his attention.

He saw Hasan and Ahmet exchange glances.

"What?"

"Someone was watching your house this morning." Ahmet said. "We think. He was there when we arrived. Then he was gone. But he didn't follow you to work, and he didn't follow your family."

"Are you sure he was watching my house?"

"He was there last night," Hasan said. "Someone was there anyway. Young guy. White. Our friend was watching the house yesterday morning. He said something about some young white guy yesterday morning, and then we saw him last night and this morning. Doesn't seem to live in the neighborhood, from what any of us could tell."

Ben felt fear rising again. "Blond?"

"No, not blond. Looked maybe Italian, but hard to say. He was in a car."

"You didn't get a picture of him, did you?"

"I did. It's not the best picture, but you can make out his face." Ahmet pulled out his phone and thumbed through it. Then he handed it to Ben. "You ever see him before?"

Ben stared and then nodded slowly.

The image was blurred and shadowy. But Ben stared in recognition at the features. He'd only seen the man once, but he'd never forget him. The young American from the garage, who'd helped chase away the killers and carry Tehila off after she'd been shot.

What was he doing in front of Ben's house?

Ben handed Ahmet his phone. "Okay, tell your friends. Anyone sees him again—follow him. And then call me."

"You think he's one of the Nazis?" Hasan looked worried. "We don't want to risk a confrontation."

"I don't think he's a Nazi, but I don't know who he is. I need to find out."

43

BERLIN, GERMANY

LISETTE METHODICALLY SEARCHED FREDERICK'S desk—wearing gloves and photographing the contents before she started her search, so she could put everything back in the same place, after lifting each item carefully to examine it. She started with the center drawer. Inside he kept bills and receipts, not in any organized fashion, but each item was photographed before being touched.

It took a lot of time.

The receipts and bills told her nothing.

Using the photos, she replaced each piece of paper, each paper clip exactly as she had found it.

It took her an hour to carefully search the top drawer and uncover— nothing. She was about to start the top drawer on the right side of the desk when she heard a knock at the front door.

She ignored it, opening the top right drawer.

Another knock on the door, followed by a ring of the bell.

Probably one of Frederick's people—Heinrich maybe—checking in. Not answering could raise questions. She closed the top drawer in case whoever it was insisted on entering the apartment and glanced over the desk. Satisfied that nothing looked disturbed, she stood, shoved the chair under the desk, and headed for the front hall.

Frederick had a security system, but she checked the old-fashioned way, peering through the peep hole. Whoever had rung the bell was standing to the side of the door where she couldn't see a face.

She was more than capable of dealing with any of the idiots who worked with Frederick. They knew her and trusted her.

She swung the door open. Michael leaned against the wall, face pale and tired, but very much alive.

She tried to control her shock. She should've anticipated the possibility that he might not drink the coffee. "Michael. Where have you been? Frederick was concerned."

"A problem on the road."

"Nothing serious, I hope."

"Didn't seem to be." He held out her key. "I cleaned out your car, by the way."

What did that mean? Had he thrown away the cup of poisoned coffee? Where? It would have her fingerprints on it. She hadn't worn gloves.

She examined him closer. He clearly wasn't feeling well, but not to the level that he should have if he'd ingested much of the poison. Maybe he had drunk some of the coffee, not enough to kill, just enough to make him sick. Another try? No, not in Frederick's apartment and not immediately. She didn't want him dropping dead here, and she was already worried that he might have figured out what she'd done.

She accepted the key. "Do you want to come in? Frederick's not here."

He shook his head. "No thanks, I'm tired. Going back to my hotel and catch a nap. I'm assuming Frederick doesn't need me tonight."

She was relieved. She didn't really want him coming in, and she needed to think. "Not tonight. I'm sure he'll want you in the morning. He's very nervous about the shooting in Greifswald."

"I know."

"Do you have any idea who might've done it?" She'd do what she could to save or protect whoever had killed the two Nazis in Greifswald if she knew the identity of the shooter. But she didn't.

"Not really." He shrugged. "I'm sure Gunter is investigating. He'll tell Frederick if he finds anything."

Frederick wouldn't necessarily tell her. But that was a concern for a later time. Right now, she had to act hospitable.

"Are you sure you don't want to come in? I can make you something to eat. Maybe coffee?"

"Thanks, but it's too late for coffee. Anyway, I'm not hungry."

Given what had happened in his hotel room the previous night, he'd have to be stupid not to suspect her of poisoning his coffee, and Michael didn't strike her as stupid. If he suspected, she'd have to do something before he exposed her.

But right now, try to dispel suspicion. "Thanks for not mentioning my visit last night to Frederick. And I'm sorry. I drank too much, and I acted inappropriately."

"No problem. I've had too much to drink on occasion myself."

"Can I give you a ride to your hotel?"

"No need." He pushed off from the wall. "A walk will clear my head. See you tomorrow morning."

She watched him disappear down the stairs.

44

COLOGNE, GERMANY

IN HER STARTLING WHITE office at the BfV, Elizabeth was bored. There was still no concrete evidence against either Reiner or Arnold. She'd casually chatted up staff; she and Jonathan had surreptitiously scanned all available files, which offered nothing. All she had to do now was sit and twiddle her thumbs and wait for a screw up. She almost envied Petrov's role, despite the risks. The phone buzzed that a text was coming in. Elizabeth thumbed it on. Arnold.

Sorry, have to postpone dinner. Tomorrow?

She replied—*No problem. Tomorrow's fine*—and handed the phone to Jonathan.

"He doesn't say what he's doing." Jonathan clicked the phone off and handed it back to her. "Disappointed?"

"Always like a good dinner out." She tucked the phone in her purse. "You've been hanging with Reiner?"

"Some. He's not as friendly as Arnold. I stopped by his office earlier. He's out. In court, his secretary said. Not expected in until tomorrow."

"We have to entertain ourselves then." Elizabeth knew the drill. Say nothing of consequence in the office. "And I'm bored."

"We could take a ride to see something of Germany. Maybe Berlin?"

"It's a six-hour drive."

"It's only two o'clock. We'll make it by eight." Jonathan glanced at his watch.

She narrowed her eyes. "You want to see the sights?" What he really wanted was to check up on Petrov, who was a perfectly competent agent and didn't need his hand held. But if something happened to Petrov, Jonathan would feel responsible. Needlessly. Petrov knew the risks.

"It's supposed to be an interesting city with great night life."

BERLIN, GERMANY

On his way back to his hotel room, Kolya stopped at a coffee kiosk near the Brandenburg Gate. It was small, run by an older man of Turkish ancestry, who faced the world with low expectations and an expression to match. Kolya picked up a copy of *Die Welt*, a Berlin daily newspaper, tucked it under his right arm, and ordered his usual coffee with two sugars.

Not that he had the stomach to drink it.

He caught a barely perceptible nod from the owner of the kiosk as he rang up the purchases.

Kolya walked the short distance back to his hotel. His leg, which had been painful the previous night, only protested mildly. The gentle exercise was probably good for it. Or at least it was a good story to tell himself.

Back in his room, he locked the door before beginning his inspection. His bag was where he'd left it before returning Lisette's car, and nothing appeared to have been disturbed. He checked the bathroom, the bed, the closet, and the dresser for any signs of entry or search and saw nothing.

He deposited the newspaper in the trash bin and placed the coffee on the bedside table. Maybe he'd drink it later. Then again, maybe not. He still felt the aftereffects of whatever poison he'd drunk, and just the thought of coffee made him queasy.

Lissette had been calm when he appeared at the door, no visible sign of surprise that he was alive.

He'd hoped for more, although, given how smoothly she'd made the attempts, he hadn't expected her to give away the game. Did she realize that he was suspicious?

Probably.

Intelligence often depended on turning people against their previous friends or colleagues. But to do so required understanding the person and what motivated them.

He had no clue about Lisette.

He considered calling Alex, wanting to hear her voice, but it wasn't secure, and anyway, he didn't want to deal with the conversation that he knew would follow. Alex had an uncanny ability to know when something was wrong, and, quite apart from the details being classified, he didn't want her to know anything about the last few days. Not any of it. Not the killings or Lisette's attempted seduction, or his nearly being poisoned.

Not nearly. Poisoned. Just not a fatal dose.

Easier not to call.

After setting the alarm on his phone, he stretched out on the bed, waves of tiredness and the remaining effects from the poison making him feel as if he were floating on an air mattress on a choppy sea. He thought about the Thelonious Monk piece, *BlueHawk*, that he'd heard on the radio just before the nausea had first kicked in. He pulled the melody from his memory, then from the melody, he built the notes and chords.

Then his phone beeped with an incoming text, and he started, not even aware that he'd been asleep. It was Frederick with the message that "Michael" would be needed in the morning.

"Michael" would be there.

But he first had to do his real job.

He splashed water on his face and drank part of the cold coffee. The nausea had subsided enough that he could keep it down.

He slipped on his jacket, picked up the cardboard room key, and headed out. He didn't pause in the hotel lobby, but he checked it before walking out into the Berlin night.

45

HANOVER, GERMANY

EILENRIEDE PARK IN THE heart of Hanover, one of the largest urban parks in Europe, with miles of hiking trails winding through forests, with fifty wooden bridges over waterways, ten playgrounds, miniature golf courses, and lawns, was a favored meeting ground. Frederick, tired after the rushed exit from Greifswald and the long drive to Hanover, trudged down a forested path that he would have normally enjoyed to one of the ten playgrounds.

The Leader, wearing sunglasses and a cap that shaded his face, stood on the edge of the grass, watching the few children playing despite the hour. Half a dozen children. Three boys chased each other, one blond, two light brown hair, but unmistakably German. Two small girls on swings appeared to be immigrants, a conclusion reinforced by their mother in a headscarf.

When Frederick joined the Leader, he gestured at the boys.

"That is what we are fighting for." And with a glance at the girls. "And what we're fighting against. Let's walk."

Frederick fell into step next to him.

"Is there anything else that you've found out about the killings?" Frederick asked.

"Whoever did it was very good." The Leader took out a cigar and lit it. "Precision shooting. You think it's the same person as the one who beheaded Karl. I think it's possible that there are at least two people involved."

"Based on what?"

"This is the first time the vigilante shot anyone. The vigilante tends to go after one person at a time. She—or he—has stabbed, beheaded, or garroted her victims. This was different."

"Two people." Frederick felt a cold fear. "That would be bad."

The Leader tapped ash onto the path. "Yes. Makes it look organized, doesn't it?"

The prospect of an organized effort against Germany Now was chilling. "Could the Americans embedded in the BfV have anything to do with any of this?"

"I don't know. They seem clueless, but I'm beginning to suspect that they may not be as stupid as I had assumed."

"Are you going to do anything about them?"

"It's under control. But your new American bodyguard—interesting that he's an excellent shot."

Frederick shook his head. "It's not him. I saw him shoot that Black bitch protecting the Jew from the Equality Institute. On my orders, he finished off the traitor. And he was asleep in a hotel room next to mine when our people were shot."

"Maybe." The Leader took a puff on his cigar. "But interesting that the first time any of our people were shot was after he joined. And he was in Greifswald. Not saying he's not loyal. Just that it's worth checking."

"I'll check." Frederick did have a tinge of doubt after the Leader's words. Still, Michael would be an asset on Day X. Every man counted.

Assuming that Michael wasn't playing a double game.

"What about moving up Day X?" Frederick asked.

They were walking at a brisk pace. The longer they stayed in one place, the greater chance they'd be noticed.

"I think you may be right. How much time do you need to activate our people?"

"Three days. Maybe two."

"Make it two. The Reichstag is in session in two days."

Frederick frowned. "Notifying everyone that quickly will be tricky unless I call them."

"Minimal phone calls. Direct contact is best."

"I change phones every week."

"Just reiterating the procedure. Personal contacts. Phone calls are routinely intercepted by intelligence. We're too close."

"Of course." Frederick would visit as many district leaders as he could and send others to those he couldn't. The district leaders would notify their members.

Michael would be useful for that. If he wasn't a traitor. Was there a way to check whether Michael could be the shooter?

Frederick had suspected Lisette—but she had proven herself. Besides, she'd been with him when Gunter's men were killed. He remembered how she'd arched against him, and the thought almost made him dizzy.

He did love her.

But his thoughts of love and Lisette were interrupted by a middle-aged male jogger in a tight-fitting red and white running outfit who instead of passing them paused and peered inquisitively at the Leader's face. "Hey. Don't I know you?" He walked forward, hand outstretched. "We met at a conference. Last year."

"I don't remember your name." The Leader took the offered hand and glanced at Frederick.

Frederick understood.

He looked both ways on the wooded path. No one else in sight. Then as the jogger shook the Leader's hand, Frederick stepped behind him, grabbed his chin and before the man could even register surprise, broke his neck.

46

BERLIN, GERMANY

BEN FOLLOWED HASAN AND Ahmet into a trendy coffee shop that offered pastries and Italian coffees and was located directly across from a bar. At this hour of the evening, there was still a smattering of people seated on wrought iron chairs at glass tables, sipping coffee and listening to American rock. "At the table next to the window." Hasan indicated with his head a young man seated alone at a table for four in front of the window, a man whom Ben had last seen in a garage, helping to carry away the prone figure of the woman he'd known as Tehila.

Flanked by the twins, Ben approached the American. The young man glanced up, and his expression changed to alarm.

"Mind if I sit?" Ben pulled a chair out and seated himself.

"I was just leaving." The young man spoke in German. Flawless German. He started to stand, but the twins pushed him back into his chair.

"I don't think so," Ahmet said.

The young man glanced around the café, almost as if he worried more about being noticed than about Ben's presence.

"Who are you?" Ben asked. "And why have you been watching my house?"

The young man swallowed. "You're mistaken. I haven't been watching your house."

"Of course you have," Ahmet said.

"You were in the garage." Ben watched the young man's face. "I want to know what happened to Tehila."

"I don't know what you're talking about." The young man recovered his composure. "I've never seen you before."

"Are you waiting for someone?" Ben asked.

"My girlfriend. But it seems she's not coming." He glanced out the window in an almost involuntary movement, and then quickly refocused on Ben's face. "I'm sorry. I'm not the person you think I am. Now if you'll excuse me." This time he pushed back from the table, despite the presence of the twins. "If you have a problem, let's take it out back. We're disturbing the other patrons."

They weren't. No one was looking at them. But the young man pointed towards the back of the café. Almost as if he wanted to keep Ben's attention from the street in front of the café—which had the opposite effect. Ben glanced out the window. What he saw was the face of a man he would know anywhere, a face from his nightmares ever since he'd held a dying woman in his arms.

The man with blond hair who had shot Tehila was entering the bar on the opposite side of the road.

* * * * *

It was the same bar as the last time. Wood panel walls. Musical instruments as decorations. Fewer than five people at the tables: one group of three on the verge of leaving, and a couple, heads close together, seated at a second table. Frick, residing on a barstool, engrossed in his phone and his ale, didn't look up as Kolya ordered a beer that he had no desire to drink. Kolya ignored Frick, paid for the beer, and carried it to the piano.

He placed the beer on a nearby table and seated himself in front of the instrument, playing a quick arpeggio and a series of chords. The piano was still reasonably in tune.

The group of three pushed back their chairs and left the bar. The hand holding couple remained.

Kolya didn't bother playing Mozart. Instead, he played the Monk piece that had been running through his head since he'd heard it on the radio. He played the melody as he remembered it and then moved on to improvisation, his focus only on the music.

Minutes later, Frick approached, but this time he wasn't alone. The couple also moved towards the piano. Kolya continued to play

"Not bad. What's the piece?" A male voice behind him.

"Thelonious Monk. *BlueHawk*. And don't you hate jazz, Jonathan?" Kolya had spotted Jonathan and Elizabeth on his entrance to the bar, which was one of the reasons he'd had no concerns about his musical selection.

A muffled laugh. "Generally speaking, yeah I do. Finish, grab your beer and join us."

Kolya played another chord before sliding off the bench and picking up the beer. He followed Jonathan, Elizabeth, and Frick to a table in a corner, where he seated himself with his back to the wall.

"You look like shit, *Michael*. Rough night?" Elizabeth's voice had the tone of a disinterested observer.

"You could say that." But before he could explain what had happened, the door to the bar opened to reveal Teo, who was assigned to watch the bar from the coffee shop across the street, flanked by two athletic young men and followed by a fourth man in a baseball cap. Kolya couldn't see the fourth man's face until all of them were inside. But when they reached the table, the man's features were clearly visible.

Ben Rosenberg.

"Fuck, Teo," Kolya said.

"Oh shit." Jonathan also recognized the man in the cap.

Teo shook off the two men who'd been holding his arms. "Not my fault. They," he nodded at one of the men, "followed me. And then *he*," Teo indicated Ben Rosenberg, "saw you go into the bar."

"I've spent the last week terrified to go outside and guilty that a woman died to save me. And now I find her 'killer' having drinks with one of the men who carried her from the scene. And the other 'rescuer' was watching from across the street." Rosenberg pulled a

225

chair from a neighboring table and seated himself. "Who the hell are you, and what the hell is going on?"

Well, at least Rosenberg hadn't pulled a gun. Bad enough one person had tried to kill him today. Kolya glanced at Jonathan, who shrugged.

"You're team leader," Kolya said.

"Your neck, your call."

Rosenberg and the two young men now knew enough to endanger the mission. Would it be any riskier to bring them into the circle? It might be more dangerous to hold the information back—Rosenberg and company might not keep quiet unless they knew what was actually happening.

And, the Equality Institute, Rosenberg's organization, *was* fighting against the far right in Germany. Rosenberg would be an ally.

Annoying that Teo had allowed himself to be followed—but irrelevant. They had to deal with the situation.

Given what Kolya now knew about Day X—the more allies, the better.

"You really need to work on your tradecraft, Teo." Kolya gestured. "Sit." He looked at the two young men, clearly twins, still flanking Teo. "You too." Eight chairs crowded the table, and then he turned to Ben. "I'm sure you can make an educated guess as to who we are."

"American intelligence? CIA?"

"Not CIA. Otherwise, I can neither confirm nor deny." Which was, in fact, a confirmation.

47

BERLIN, GERMANY

KOLYA TILTED HIS CHAIR back against the wall, balancing it on two legs, and let Jonathan explain, which Jonathan did succinctly, describing the effort to penetrate Frederick Bauer's group and the decision to fake the shooting. He left out some of the more sensitive details, but he progressed to giving the first names of the team.

"So she's okay? Tehila. She's okay? I was sure she was dead," Ben said.

Ben was drinking a dark malt beer, which he claimed was kosher. Kolya—whose knowledge of the kosher rules was sketchy—took his word for it.

"Tehila is fine." Jonathan said. "Out of the country and disappointed that she's not working the op with us. But if Bauer caught sight of her after Kolya 'killed' her…"

"It felt so real." Ben's voice still registered disbelief. Kolya couldn't blame him.

"Fake blood. Exploding squid. Bulletproof vest. And she's very good. So is he." Jonathan nodded in Kolya's direction.

"Still fucking crazy if you ask, but no one did." Frick finished his beer and then looked at Kolya's untouched glass. "Not drinking tonight?"

"No. Help yourself."

"So why did you have him," Ben waved at Teo, "watching my house?"

"We were worried that Bauer might send someone else after you."

Teo overcame his embarrassment enough to speak.

"He blames you for the murders of some of his group," Kolya said. "Apparently, six men have been killed over the past two years— and Bauer wants the person responsible. And so far, Bauer has only given me limited information about his plans. If he sent someone else to kill you, I might not know in time."

"We couldn't say anything to the police either," Teo said. "Which was why I was periodically checking your house."

"Seemed like the least we could do after traumatizing you," Jonathan said.

"I get why you faked the shooting. But couldn't you have let me know that it wasn't real—after it happened, if not before? We're on the same side. It was a pretty nasty thing to do to me. To my family."

"I understand how you feel." Kolya pushed his chair off the wall to sit up straight. "More than you'll ever know. But telling you could have risked the operation. I'm undercover. The more people who know, the more likely a leak."

"You think we're going to fucking tell a fucking Nazi anything?" One of the twins. Hasan. "Any of us?"

"Not directly. Not intentionally."

"Not any way," Assad said.

"You might say something to someone who then says something to someone else. And one of Bauer's supporters hears it and passes it to him. My position is precarious. Do you know what Bauer would do to me if he uncovered that I'm an American agent?"

"And Jewish." Teo, of course, would blurt it out.

"You're a Jew?" Ben turned his surprised face towards Kolya, and Kolya knew what he was thinking. *You don't look like a Jew.*

"So my mother informed me."

"*Mispocheh.*" Ben spoke the Yiddish word for family and raised his glass in a salute.

"Jesus Christ, boy wonder. I thought you were over blurting out secrets," Elizabeth said.

"Fuck you, Elizabeth. They should know," Teo said. "They should know what Kolya's risking."

"My being Jewish isn't a state secret, Elizabeth," Kolya said. "At least not any more than the fact that I'm an American agent. Which they already know."

"It must be hard for you to pretend to be a Nazi." Assad chimed in.

"No, actually, I think it's easier. At least in terms of incentive."

Frick cleared his throat. "Now shall we all hug, sing Hava Nagila, and have our new buddies leave so can we fucking get down to business?"

Jonathan nodded. "I agree. It's time for you and your friends to leave, Ben. We've answered your questions about what happened. If any of you tell anyone—your wife, your best friend, your mother— anyone—who Kolya really is and what he's doing—he could be killed. But you don't need to know anything further."

"We already agreed to keep this among us," Ben said. "And maybe we can help. The Equality Institute has a lot of support, and a lot of information on members of the far right."

"You're civilians," Elizabeth said. "You're not trained to deal with these people."

"All we do is deal with these people, as you call them."

"We might need the help," Kolya said.

Jonathan turned to him, surprised. "It's not protocol. And it's not secure."

"Fuck protocol and security. You don't know what's going on." Quietly, Kolya outlined the past two days, including the murder of Walter, the escape with Peter, Peter's death at the hands of two members of the German military, and the information about Day X.

Ben's expression hardened. "This time you did kill someone?"

"No. Walter was already dead when I fired a shot into his head. Yes, I regret that I did even that, but I wasn't going to throw away my own life in a futile gesture. Although I did shoot two killers—but I assume that's not what you meant."

"Sorry," Ben said. "I can't imagine being in that situation."

Kolya waved a hand.

"No wonder you looked tired," Jonathan said. "You've had a rough few days."

"I'm not just tired. I'm pretty sure that I was poisoned. Earlier today."

"What the hell?" Jonathan spoke the words, but the shock was reflected in the faces around the table. "Are you sure?"

"Reasonably." He described Lisette's visit to his room, her attempts to get him to drink the schnapps, followed by her handing him the coffee, and his illness shortly after.

"No wonder you're not drinking. You should get checked out." Jonathan continued to look concerned.

Kolya shook his head. "I'm okay, although I suspect that if I'd drunk the whole cup, I'd be dead." He reached into a pocket and pulled out a crumpled paper cup inside a plastic bag, which he handed to Frick. "It would be nice to know whether I'm right. And what it was."

"Yeah, no problem, but it may not come back in time to stop another try at you. Just be really fucking careful about what you eat and drink." Frick pocketed the bag. "And where you put your dick."

"I generally am."

"Any idea why she might have tried to kill you?" Teo asked.

"All sorts of ideas, from her being a secret anti-Nazi to her suspecting my real identity and killing me for not being a Nazi, to her being a serial killer, but nothing definitive. Bauer is worried about someone on the inside killing his people. I'm wondering if there's any chance that she's the anti-Nazi vigilante. If she is—the attempt on me makes sense."

"It would also make sense if she's a psychopath," Jonathan said. "Many Nazis are."

"That too. Any word from Mark on her?"

"According to Mark, she and her mother immigrated to Texas when she was around ten," Frick said. "No idea why they left Germany. Nothing on them before that. Rich stepdaddy. She returned to Germany a few years ago and became involved with Germany Now. Only stuff on social media is pro-white supremacy, going back to teen years. Nothing from her time in Texas. We could send someone out to snoop in more detail, but it could get back to her."

"No connection with any other intelligence service?"

"Not that the tech department could find."

"Father?"

"Nothing on file. Mark thinks that the name her mother used to get into the States was fake, and that they were running from something. There were several murders in Germany by far-right groups around the time Lisette and her mother immigrated. Maybe the dad was one of the killers."

"She sounds like a true believer. You could return the favor, Kolya," Elizabeth said. "Take her out. Before she tries again."

"I'll think about it." But unless he was sure that she wasn't the anti-Nazi vigilante, he would do nothing. "On your end—what's happening?"

With a glance at Ben and the twins, Jonathan spoke. "Two guys pretty high up—we think one of them is in cahoots with Bauer's group—which would fit with what've you've learned about the Leader. We're checking both of them."

"Bauer is out of town tonight, right after running back to Berlin. He was pretty badly spooked this morning," Kolya said. "I suspect he's meeting with The Leader."

"Kind of figured that too," Jonathan said. "We'll check it out."

"Do it quickly. My shooting two Germany Now soldiers may prompt them to move up Day X. And we have no idea how many are in the group or who might be embedded in the police or the military."

"Targets?" Frick asked.

"Peter said the Reichstag was one target. Local politicians who support immigration or oppose the far-right agenda are also on the list—although I don't have names." Then he looked at Ben. "I assume you're on the list as well."

"Probably am. Not surprising. We can help," Ben said. "We'll start going through every posting by every known member of Germany Now."

"That could be helpful. Maybe you could share your database with our technical department," Jonathan said.

"If you agree to share what you find out about Day X."

"Deal," Jonathan said. "Teo and Frick will facilitate communications.

Kolya, the guy at the newsstand—he's still how you signal for a meeting."

"That's all fine and good," Kolya said. "But plans for Day X are in flux, and I might not have time to pick up a latte."

"You've got the phone for an emergency," Jonathan said.

"If I can manage to call. If I'm not dead."

"As always, you're just full of light and happiness, Kolya," Elizabeth said.

They ignored her.

"We can all watch *Michael's* social media accounts," Frick said. "Post something every night. If nothing changed, write the usual white supremacy bullshit. If the date for Day X has moved up, say something about the weather."

"Not the weather," Kolya said. "I'll post music." He listed the pieces and what they'd mean. It wasn't perfect, but it was a plan. "If I can't post at night, I'll post the following morning. If nothing…"

"If no post for twenty-four hours, we'll know you're in trouble."

Or no longer breathing.

48

BERLIN, GERMANY

LISETTE HAD PAINSTAKINGLY GONE through every drawer in Frederick's desk. It'd taken her hours to pull everything apart and then put it back together. She'd also checked his computer, but she knew him. He didn't trust electronics. So, no information on Day X. No information on the Leader.

By midnight, she finished both her search and her clean-up. She hadn't really expected to find anything—Frederick was too careful, except, perhaps in whom he chose as a bed partner.

But the search had been something to do—to divert her mind from the various unpleasant thoughts that kept surfacing.

How could she have not suspected that Frederick might be meeting with the man who'd killed her father? How could she have not wondered more about where he went and who he was talking to?

Then again, Christian had just described "Wolf" as being someone in the government. Maybe "Wolf" wasn't the Leader.

If she saw him, would she know? She remembered the face of the man fifteen years earlier—but people's appearances can change. Maybe she wouldn't recognize him, but regardless, taking out the "Leader" would still be in line with her mission.

Michael was the more pressing problem.

She'd made two tries to kill him and failed. Quite apart from the personal humiliation, her attempts had put her at risk. He was smart enough to suspect that her midnight visit to his room wasn't because she found him irresistible—especially if he'd become sick after drinking some of the coffee.

Despite herself, her mind drifted to his appearance the previous night—the full-frontal nudity, following by the glimpse of his scarred back. What had happened to him?

And what would it be like to sleep with him?

She angrily shook off the thought.

It wasn't as if she couldn't get as much sex as she wanted. Most likely she was having that perverse reaction—where a man's lack of interest made him more interesting.

But that was irrelevant. Her failed attempt to seduce him—and two attempts to poison him—made her vulnerable. If Michael said anything about suspecting her or even described her midnight visit, she'd be killed. She couldn't be exposed. Not this close to finding her father's murderer.

She'd had motive to kill Michael before. He was a Nazi killer, and she hunted people like him. Her failure to act immediately had allowed him to murder two people. Now to add to the mix: he could destroy her.

She had to destroy him first.

But her usual techniques weren't going to work.

Try something else. Quickly. Before he could say anything to Frederick. She now had a clear path to her end game. If the Leader was the Wolf, killing him and Frederick would finally avenge her father. And with both the Leader and Frederick dead, whatever Day X might be didn't matter. Without them, it wouldn't go forward.

She needed to stay alive. She needed Frederick to trust her and get her close to the Leader.

Thinking about Day X gave her an idea.

She rehearsed it, step-by-step, exactly what she would say and do, and then she curled up in an armchair in Frederick's living room to wait for him.

49

BERLIN, GERMANY

WHEN FREDERICK UNLOCKED THE door to his apartment at one a.m., he saw Lisette waiting for him. *She was so lovely.* This was why he was fighting so hard, so that men like him could come home to a loyal and beautiful German woman. He felt a little guilty for ever having suspected her, but she'd never know.

He crossed the room and bent to kiss her forehead. She stirred and pulled him down for a deeper kiss. Normally, that would be a prelude to something better, but now, he was too tired. And he had too much on his mind.

"I need a drink." He moved towards the kitchen, and she followed him. She found cognac and poured two glasses, handing him one and keeping one for herself. He smiled, enjoying the service. "Thank you. But you should have gone to bed." He liked that she hadn't, that she'd waited up for him. But he also felt a warmth and a concern for her.

"I missed you."

"You won't be missing me much in the future. You'll be by my side." He took a sip of the liquor. Just what he needed. "Did Michael ever show up?"

"He did." But she hesitated as if something were bothering her.

"What?"

She looked down at the liquor in her glass. "Are you sure about him, Frederick?"

"What do you mean?"

"Are you sure you can trust him?"

Frederick reached for the bottle and poured another shot. "If he weren't one of us, would he have killed people on my orders?"

"I know. That's why I'm puzzled." She set her glass on the kitchen counter, and he poured more into her glass as well. "Why did he take so long to get here from Greifswald? And then, after he got here…"

Frederick tensed. "What after he got here?"

But she didn't answer immediately. He could see that she was uncomfortable.

"Lisette. Tell me."

A long silence. Then she picked up her glass. "He made moves on me."

"Did he touch you?" Frederick was angry, but if Michael hadn't touched her, it was a lapse rather than something more severe. After all, Lisette was a temptation. Beautiful women were, and even some of Frederick's most trusted subordinates had made appreciative comments about Lisette. An appreciative comment was acceptable. Touching was not.

"Not really." She shook her head. "My hand. He told me that a beautiful woman like me should be worshipped, and that he'd love to pray at my altar. I told him that I was your woman, and he said that I was too special to restrict myself to one man."

"That bastard."

"Some of the other men have made some comments, too. I don't take it seriously. And he didn't step over the line. He was trying to seduce me, not force me. But—I don't think he just wanted to go to bed with me. He was asking me questions."

"Questions?"

"About Day X. About someone named the Wolf. You've mentioned Day X—but nothing about a wolf. Do you know what he's talking about?"

Frederick did know. But Lisette didn't need to know. "Never heard the name. What was he asking about Day X?"

"Nothing I could answer. When it was happening. What was happening."

Just as well he'd never trusted Michael with too much information. "What did he say exactly?"

She frowned, turning the glass in her hand. "I don't remember his exact words. Just the general drift of the conversation. There's something else, Frederick. Last night, I went out of the room to look at the sea in the moonlight. Remember? You woke up as I was leaving."

His memory of the previous night was clouded, thanks to the alcohol and the sex. "I don't remember."

"While I was outside," she hesitated, "Michael came back. I'm not sure of the time. Maybe midnight. He looked—strange. And he asked me not to mention that I saw him returning."

Gunter's two men had been shot around eleven o'clock. By an expert marksman. Oh God, could Frederick have been this stupid? This blind?

"Why didn't you tell me this earlier?"

"It didn't seem important. If he wanted to go out, why shouldn't he? And I wasn't suspicious of him, not until last evening, when he was asking questions."

Frederick thought about the last few days. He'd known Michael less than a week. He'd accepted that Michael was Nickolas Kruger on the strength of Heinrich's research, and Michael had proven himself with the killing of the black bodyguard in the Equality Institute garage and by finishing off Walter. But could the shooting have been faked? Or could he have been willing to sacrifice people on his own side to solidify his position? He remembered Michael trying to save Walter and only shooting him when Walter could have already been dead.

Someone had warned Peter. Someone had tried to get Peter to safety and then shot the men that Gunter had sent to kill Peter. Michael knew men were being sent to kill Peter, and Michael was an excellent shot.

According to the Leader, no one had confirmed the Black woman's death. No body had been discovered. She hadn't been taken to a hospital. The Americans visiting the BfV had suggested that she might be Mossad and that she'd been flown out of the country. Maybe

Michael was Mossad as well. Maybe they'd been working together.

Or maybe Michael was American intelligence.

The Leader thought there were two people involved in killing members of his group. Maybe the Black woman had been the one to kill Karl and the others and maybe she and Michael had staged her "death" to entrench Michael in Germany Now.

The old man at the farm had labeled Michael as a Jew. Could he have been right? That was the problem with Jews. Some of them could blend in. Whether Michael was a Jew or not, the old man's instincts had been right in one respect. Michael wasn't one of them.

But Frederick had to be careful, especially if Michael was working with the Americans in the BfV. A dead American agent in Berlin could bring unwanted scrutiny. Best if Michael just disappeared.

Frederick downed the rest of his drink in a single gulp. "Don't worry, Lisette. All will be well. But I'm going to need your help."

50

COLOGNE, GERMANY

JONATHAN AND ELIZABETH MADE it back to Cologne by six in the morning, into the BfV by eight a.m., and were waiting outside her office to greet Hannah Abt, wearing a trim blue pants suit, when she arrived at quarter to nine.

Elizabeth and Jonathan followed her inside. Jonathan seated himself on one of the hard chairs in front of her desk and outlined what they had learned without any mention of Kolya or his role.

"You have no idea the targets or date for this Day X?" Hannah asked after Jonathan finished.

Jonathan shook his head. "The Reichstag and political officials in the various states were mentioned but no specifics."

"That's it? How do you expect me to stop an attack when you don't even know when it's going to happen or the targets? I can't put out a general alert, can I?"

"Not unless you want to tip off the Leader that you have inside information."

"And you have no idea who he might be either?" She looked at Elizabeth.

"Jonathan thinks it's Reiner. I think it's Arnold," Elizabeth said. "Arnold has been very insistent that we're wasting our time on neo-Nazis. He keeps talking about jihadists as the real threat. Which is a very neo-Nazi thing to do."

Hannah Abt sighed. "Unfortunately, Chancellor Jung has expressed similar concerns about hidden Islamic State terrorists. And Arnold is a personal friend of hers, even if he is a suspect. You need to bring me something concrete. Besides, just because the far-right targets Muslim immigrants doesn't mean there isn't still a threat from Islamic extremists. Last year, they killed five people at a Christmas market. They've targeted synagogues and Jews as well."

"As soon as we have anything, you'll know." Jonathan hoped Kolya would be able to uncover the plot.

BERLIN, GERMANY

As requested, Kolya rang the bell to Frederick's apartment at nine o'clock. He'd had a decent night, only briefly interrupted by nightmares, so he felt reasonably good. The effects of whatever poison he'd consumed had worn off.

Time to play the game again.

Lisette opened the door, all smiles and friendliness. Nothing to hint that she'd tried to seduce or kill him. "Hi Michael. Frederick's having coffee. Would you like some?"

"I've already had three cups." He didn't know if she'd slip something into his coffee in front of Frederick, but he preferred not to take the chance.

He followed her into the kitchen, where Frederick, seated at the table, read a paper edition of *Jung Freiheit*, the right-wing weekly newspaper, while finishing off a plate of sausage, eggs, cheese, and bread. "Michael." He gestured to the chair at the table. "Sit. How about some eggs? Isn't that what Americans eat for breakfast? Lisette's an excellent cook."

Kolya seated himself. "I already ate, thanks. What's the schedule for today?"

Frederick chewed a large bite of sausage and wiped his mouth. "I need you and Lisette to return to Anklam today. Pick up some things from Hans."

"We were just there. And I thought you wanted me as your

bodyguard." He had no desire to return to Hans' farm. He thought of the old Nazi. Of Walter's remains, by now thoroughly digested by the pigs. Well, he did want to go back, after he was done with the assignment. He would very much like to shoot Hans and his entire miserable family. But he wouldn't. Probably wouldn't. In any event, that wasn't a decision that he had to make now.

"Yes, of course, but things have changed. I think the danger is minimal here in Berlin, and I will be in a safe location for all of today." Frederick took a sip of his coffee. "Is that a problem?"

Kolya affected nonchalance. "Not at all. What do you need me to pick up?"

"A few of the things he's storing in his barn." Frederick sliced a piece of cheese and placed it on a slab of bread. Then he made a gun with his fingers.

Hans had twenty—no twenty-one—HK-91s more than he needed.

Kolya's role was not to ask questions. But he assumed this meant that the date for Day X had been pushed up. If the guns needed to be collected, something was imminent. The exact date was important. Did Hans know? Or his grandfather? Frederick certainly knew. "Is something going on?"

"Nothing you need to know until you get back."

"Okay." Kolya would post on social media to indicate that Day X had been moved up. He'd inform the team of the precise date when he knew it. The monstrous former SS officer might be useful. The old bastard did have trouble keeping his mouth shut. "You want me to take Lisette's car?"

"No, mine's bigger. You'll need the space. We're switching for the day."

"Why is Lisette coming?"

"Because I asked her." Frederick chewed his cheese and bread. "I trust you can control yourself, even if she is beautiful."

There was a slight undercurrent that Kolya didn't like. He glanced over at Lisette. Had she mentioned her late night visit, manufacturing a story that blamed "Michael" in case he told Frederick of her attempted seduction? But if Frederick thought that

"Michael" had stepped over the line with Lisette, why send the two of them off together?

Or was something else going on?

But the game required that he not question Frederick's authority. Or show any nervousness.

"Of course. She's your woman. I was just wondering why she's necessary."

"Cover," Lisette said. "A couple is less suspicious than one man on the road. In case someone stops us. We know that there are American intelligence agents in Germany looking for you."

"Fuck. Why didn't you tell me?" What Nickolas Kruger would say in this situation. "Maybe I should leave Germany."

"Before Day X?" Frederick raised eyebrows. "And miss everything? Isn't the cause worth it?"

"Don't worry, Michael," Lisette said. "We've got people watching the Americans. The risk will be minimal. This is just a precaution, especially given what we're bringing back. We don't want to give any unfriendly police reason to search the car. Isn't that right, darling?" She looked at Frederick.

"Exactly."

"Okay. I'm willing to take the chance," Kolya said.

"As are we all." Lisette leaned over Frederick's chair and circled his neck with her arms, a gesture of affection that looked vaguely sinister, as if she couldn't decide whether to hug him or strangle him. Kolya remained undecided about her. Was she a true believer or was it an act?

"You can be the first to congratulate us, Michael." She smiled at him. "It's official. We're engaged."

"Congratulations." A surprising turn. "Have you set a day?"

She released Frederick's neck, bent over to kiss him, before heading to the kitchen sink and the dishes. Frederick returned to his breakfast.

"Not yet," Frederick said. "After we change Germany for the better. Which is why Lisette is so anxious that we succeed."

"I want what you want, Frederick." She dried her hands and picked up her purse. "I'm running to the bathroom, then I'll be ready to go."

"Fine," Kolya said. There might be an upside to a long drive with Lisette. She and Frederick seemed closer than ever. Maybe she now knew the date for Day X or the name of the Leader.

51

BERLIN, GERMANY

FREDERICK LEFT THE APARTMENT a few minutes after Lisette and Michael. He'd alerted Heinrich and the others and sent them off to various districts to spread the word. One more day. Tomorrow morning, Germany Now supporters would take back the country. But until then, nothing by phone. Nothing by computer. Except for an absolute emergency.

He was also going to spread the word. He'd drive to Leipzig and then to Nuremberg and stop at Dresden on his return.

How could he have been so stupid about Michael?

Heinrich, who was traveling to alert district commanders in the northwest, should have already delivered the message to Hans. Kill Michael but not too quickly. His suggestion: after Michael helped load the weapons and the body bags—pigs would eat a restrained living person thrown into the pen as well as a dead person. Being eaten alive would be a fitting death.

He checked his route. Bayreuth lay between Leipzig and Nuremberg. Didn't Lisette's grandmother live there? Wouldn't it be a nice surprise for Lisette if he stopped to meet her grandmother, maybe took the old lady some chocolates?

After all, Lisette was going to be his wife. Her grandmother would be his family.

BUNDESAUTOBAUN A-11, GERMANY

Lisette drove. As she steered onto the autobahn, she glanced sideways at Michael, on his phone, in the passenger seat. She liked the irony of her plan: Michael, a Nazi killer, would be executed by other Nazis because they thought he'd betrayed the cause. Nazis killing Nazis. It was such a fitting end. And, she wouldn't have to do anything. Frederick had given the order. Hans and his family would carry it out.

She wanted to laugh out loud from the pure beauty of it all.

But she didn't. If Michael suspected, he could still get away. He could even kill her. So—pretend to be cordial, friendly. She glanced again at Michael, tapping something on his phone. "Girlfriend?"

"Excuse me?" He didn't look up.

"I know you have a girlfriend in the States. I was asking if you were texting her." The girlfriend would never know what had happened to him. He would just be gone. Lisette would feel sorry for this unknown woman never knowing if the man she loved was alive or dead except that the girlfriend probably shared his ideology. She thought about the man Michael had killed at Hans' farm. Did *he* have a family?

"No." He tapped something else. "I was just posting on social media."

"You want to tell me about her?"

"Not particularly. Why don't you tell me about your engagement?" He flashed a smile.

"Frederick just got carried away, and so did I."

"No ring?"

"He hasn't had a chance to go shopping." Her long-term intention towards Frederick was to kill him, not marry him, but not having a ring made her less credible.

"I don't see Frederick as someone who enjoys shopping."

"Do you? Enjoy shopping?"

"Depends on what I'm shopping for. And for who." He answered as if she'd never tried to seduce him—as if he'd never suspected her of trying to poison him. Maybe he wasn't as smart as she'd feared. "I guess moving Day X up prompted this?"

"I guess." It probably *had* prompted Frederick's proposal. Hopefully when she returned from delivering Michael to his fate, she'd meet the Leader. Then she'd take care of both. "Frederick's excited about Day X."

"You're not?"

"My role is secondary."

"You're not going to be on the front lines?"

"Frederick hasn't said one way or the other, but I suspect not. I'm a woman."

"You seem like a very tough and capable woman. Don't you want to see history being made?"

She smiled at the compliment. "Maybe."

"Did he tell you when it was happening?"

"Soon, I assume."

She noted the questions. The kind of information she wanted as well. Why? Was he just curious?

Or was he something else? Could she be wrong about him? Could he be like her—infiltrating Germany Now to destroy it? What if she'd missed who Michael really was and had betrayed a fellow anti-Nazi to be killed by Hans and his creepy kin?

She'd checked Michael out, as she'd checked out every other target, but she hadn't had the American sources to confirm the information. Could his background have been faked? Was it possible? Of course—if he was working with an intelligence organization—with people who could realistically fake a shooting.

That was what Frederick assumed. That Michael was working with the Nazi hunter who had killed six Germany Now members over the past eighteen months. Frederick had leapt to that conclusion with her help. Except that she knew Michael wasn't working with the vigilante.

Still, if he was playing a role, like she was, it would make sense that he hadn't told Frederick about her late-night visit. On the other hand, the failure to say anything to Frederick wasn't evidence, was it? He might not want to anger Frederick, who might assume that Michael had encouraged her.

But what if she was wrong?

It wasn't too late to stop this. She didn't have to deliver him to his death.

Stupid! This was stupid. She had never doubted herself before, not with any of the previous killings. Michael was a murderer, and she eliminated murderers. He'd killed more than once. Three murders that she knew of. The activist in the States. The woman in the garage. The unnamed person that Frederick had described, shot at Hans farm.

She'd never looked back after any of the killings. Never felt any guilt, never felt anything but satisfaction in a job well done. She'd worried about being caught, more worried about Frederick than the police, but she had never regretted anything she'd done.

Watching Michael die wouldn't be any different.

And Hans had been alerted. Frederick had sent the message ahead. She didn't know how Hans would kill Michael, but it would be gruesome. Still, the manner of Michael's death didn't bother her—if he were a killer.

What were the odds that Michael was not the killer he appeared to be? One percent? Two percent? There was absolutely no indication that he was anything other than a Nazi thug.

And delivering Michael to Hans was also essential for her purposes.

Frederick would know if she decided to save Michael's life, and that would be the end of her.

It didn't have to be. She could save Michael and leave. Head back to the States. But after all these years? All this effort? Just when she might finally have a shot at the man with the wolf tattoo. Was it worth blowing it all on the slight possibility that Michael wasn't who he appeared to be?

She wasn't making a mistake.

"What kind of music do you like? We have another two hours in the car." Michael's voice drew her out of her thoughts. "I found a good classical station."

"Classical? You mean like opera? You're kidding."

"Country western? Pop? Jazz?"

"I'm really not into music."

"How can anyone not be into music? Fine. Then I'll choose." He found something that had a lot of violins. Classical. He'd chosen classical.

"You like classical?" Not what she'd have expected of him. But then, she'd read about the SS during the war, how some had loved music and would listen to Mozart after a day of murdering Jewish children.

"I enjoy it, but it's not my favorite."

"Your favorite is?"

He ignored the question. "If you don't like music, what do you like?"

"Excuse me?"

"Movies. Books. Hobbies. I don't know much about you."

"I don't read a lot." In her teen years, she'd read *The Lord of the Rings* maybe a dozen times, trying to recapture the magic she'd found in it as a child. But she didn't want to share that with Michael.

"You must have something you like to do. Yoga? Stamp collecting?" He adjusted the volume. "This is Mahler's Fifth. He wrote this after he nearly died, as both a contemplation of death and as a celebration of life. Listen. The trumpet calls in the other instruments, then the strings set the somber theme of the first movement. Then discordant tones change the mood again."

Despite herself, she was impressed. "You know a lot about music."

"My mother loved music. We'd listen to orchestral pieces while she taught me music theory."

She heard the orchestra changing the mood as the piece progressed. "It's not bad." The explanation of the piece made it more interesting. "Do you play an instrument?"

"Piano. From time to time. There must be something you like."

What *did* she like? She thought of something. "I like horses."

"Do you ride?"

"I used to." Riding had been one of her pleasures as a teenager. She had loved the horse her stepfather had bought her on her sixteenth birthday, a gray Danish warmblood that she'd named Shadowfax, the one thing she'd regretted leaving behind in Texas. "Did a little jumping. A few shows." She thought of the feel of the horse under her, of the moment the two of them left the ground to soar over a fence. The softness of Shadowfax's muzzle when he greeted her. Funny. For the past few years, she'd been so focused on her goal that she hadn't thought about Shadowfax or riding. After everything was over, if she were still alive, maybe instead of acting, she'd raise and train horses. "You ride?"

"No," he sounded regretful. "Lived in cities my whole life."

"You learned how to shoot."

He glanced sideways at her. "They have guns in cities in America. Haven't you heard?"

"There are stables close to cities, too. Not that far a drive—if it matters to you. It's a wonderful feeling, being on a horse."

"I should try it sometime."

"You should."

But she knew he'd never have the chance. That wasn't something she wanted to think about, not right now, any more than she wanted to think about Michael as having had a mother who'd taught him about music.

52

ANKLAM, GERMANY

THEY STOPPED IN THE town of Anklam at a pub for a heavy lunch. Kolya would have preferred something light, but the offerings were lunch platters, laden with meat, a carbohydrate component, and vegetables. Kolya was careful not to let Lisette within reach of his potato salad with meatballs or his coffee. She chose fish sticks with mashed potatoes and stayed on her side of the table. Conversation was minimal, both of them on their phones—which was fine with Kolya. He'd tried to draw her out during the ride to Anklam, but she had disclosed little—except that she liked horses and wasn't that interested in music—nothing about why she'd poisoned him the day before. No hint of whether she might be the anti-Nazi vigilante—a potential ally—or just a psychopathic killer. No details about what was planned for Day X.

Still, the ride had been pleasant enough. She was intelligent and, on occasion, witty. Unlike Frederick, she didn't give long monologues about the purity of the German race—as if it were a race, which it wasn't. She was curious about his relationship with Alex but didn't push too hard. If he had just met Lisette—and didn't know anything else about her—he would have found her likeable as well as attractive.

But she remained a mystery.

Was that the reason for his growing unease? As they got back into the car, he could feel the shadows whispering at him and a slight tremor in his hands as he fastened the seat belt.

The PTSD could be inconvenient, but it could also be a warning. But of what?

Was it just his nervousness being with a woman he knew had tried to kill him? Or nervousness at their imminent arrival on the farm that had been the scene of Walter's murder? Where a hundred-year-old SS officer who had murdered thousands of Jews had correctly labeled him as Jewish?

The image of Walter's body being consumed by pigs flashed through his mind.

Did Frederick possibly suspect the truth? If so, then the reason to send him to Anklam—was to dispose of him.

It was possible. Still, nothing in Frederick's manner—or Lisette's for that matter—had indicated suspicion or distrust, which could only mean that they were both good actors.

He already knew that about Lisette.

He could tell Lisette to stop the car. If she refused, he could draw his gun on her or just open the door and jump. He'd survive the fall. And then what? Assuming he could evade Hans and his monstrous family, he'd be out. Even if police picked up the people he could identify as part of the conspiracy, he had no idea how many others were out there. Or of the identity of the Leader. Then there was the question of who in the police or intelligence services were in on the plot. Would they even act?

Frederick, the Leader, and their merry little band of neo-Nazis could still launch Day X.

His social media post had alerted the team in Berlin that plans had changed, but that wasn't specific enough. If Lisette knew anything, she wasn't sharing. He needed four pieces of information: the timing for Day X, any targets besides the Reichstag, the detailed plans, and the identity of the Leader.

Hans would know. Maybe the old Nazi would know.

It was a gamble. Maybe he was panicking for nothing. Maybe this was exactly what Frederick had said it was—a run to get guns. In which case, Kolya still had a job to do.

But the alternative was just as possible.

The tremor in his hands was more obvious. Lisette glanced over at him. "Is something wrong?"

They reached the outskirts of Anklam and were within a mile of Hans farm.

"Nothing." He began the breathing exercises.

* * * * *

A light rain was falling. Hans and his son emerged from the barn as Lisette parked next to Hans' Ford Ranger pick-up truck, Hans with an HK-91 slung across his shoulder. Kolya stepped out of the car. He zipped his jacket and turned up the collar against the chill and the damp, glancing towards the house. Hans' father strode down the path towards them, also with an HK-91 over his shoulder.

Framed in the farmhouse doorway, the grandfather radiated hatred.

That both Hans and his father were armed was a clear signal that they were planning to kill him.

Lisette introduced herself to Hans, and he shook her hand. Then he glanced over at Kolya. "Ready to work, Michael?" The voice tone was cordial, and Hans' expression gave nothing away.

"What do you need me to do?" *Play the game. Wait for the right moment.*

"Before we load up Frederick's car, I'd like you to help me to put the other crates in the back of the truck and then get some things out of the barn cellar."

The things in the cellar were the body bags and the quicklime.

But he pretended ignorance. "Cellar?"

"There's a trapdoor. Under the guns. You didn't notice it?"

"No."

"It's heavy stuff, best carried by young men. Xavier can help." He laid a heavy hand on the teenager's shoulder. Xavier's expression mirrored that of his grandfather. Hostility. Hans turned to Lisette. "My wife has cakes and tea in the house. Why don't you keep her company?"

"Certainly." She headed towards the house without the slightest hesitation.

"I've got something stronger for us later," Hans said. "Schnapps to toast to the future."

"Sounds good." Kolya knew he wouldn't be drinking schnapps, but this wasn't the moment to act. Hans and his father were far enough apart that he wouldn't be able to eliminate both. By the time he could draw his gun and shoot one of them, the other would kill him.

He followed the teenager into the barn. The inside of the barn was the same as it had been three days earlier except that the old white horse was not in his stall.

"What happened to your horse?"

"Nothing," Xavier said.

"He's in the pasture." Hans stood directly behind Kolya. Behind him was his father. Both armed with assault rifles. Not pointed at Kolya, but in position to be swung around and fired quickly. "Right beyond where we had target practice."

"In the rain?"

"Horses don't care."

Kolya had no knowledge of whether they did or not. But Hans was fond of the horse. Safer for the horse to be out of the barn.

For now, wait. He might be wrong.

At the far end of the barn, the HK-91s were packed in crates. The teenager took one end of a crate. He took the other. Together they carried it from the barn to the truck.

* * * * *

Lisette sipped tea and ate a square of butter cake. She was seated at the table covered with a cloth embroidered with red and golden flowers while Gertrude, Hans' wife, told her the recipe. Eggs. Flour. Two sticks of butter. Two cups of sugar. Lisette made a show of repeating the ingredients, as if she were interested, which she was not. But she fooled Gertrude.

"I hear you're marrying Frederick. I'm so pleased he's going to settle down. He loves my cakes." Gertrude leaned forward conspiratorially. "Good food and sex. That's what keeps a man. You have to give him what he likes when he wants it."

Lisette ate her cake in silence, wondering if Gertrude had been transported from another century. But Gertrude was a believer in the same repulsive ideology as Frederick. Hatred of Jews and non-white people. A belief that women's only roles were those of wife, lover, and mother. Still, as much as she hated the beliefs, Lisette didn't kill people for holding them but for being murderers. Did Gertrude deserve to die for being a member of this family?

She'd think about it.

The old man wandered into the kitchen and snapped on a television placed on a stand against a wall. Gertrude turned if off again.

"When can I go out there?" the old man asked.

"Not yet." Gertrude cut a square of cake, placed it on a plate, and the plate along with a fork on the table in front of an empty chair. "Sit. Eat."

But he restlessly paced back to the door. "I don't want to miss it."

"Miss what?" Lisette decided to play dumb.

"Before they feed him to the hogs, Hans will come get you. You won't miss it." Gertrude forked a bite of the cake into her mouth and spoke while still chewing. "But he does have a gun. If he resists, they may have to shoot him first. And you'd be in the way, old man."

"I won't be in the way. And that's too easy a death."

"It's not Hans' preference. He'll try to get the bastard alive."

"Good. I want to be the one to cut off the Jew's dick."

"Cut off his dick?" Lisette kept her tone curious and indifferent.

"Once he's tied up." Gertrude sipped her tea. "The plan is cut off his clothes and then cut off his dick and his balls to feed to the pigs. The blood will get the pigs interested, and they weren't fed this morning. He should still be conscious and aware when the pigs start on him. But Hans doesn't want anyone hurt. If Michael goes for his gun, Hans will do what's necessary. After he finishes loading the truck. After all, may as well have him do the work."

The old man nodded. "It's what we did. Made the Jews dig their own graves before we killed them."

"That's the idea."

"I told them he was a Jew. Fools. I killed enough Jews to know one when I see one."

"He's Jewish?" Lisette asked.

Gertrude answered. "Hans isn't sure, but Grandfather is convinced. Whether he is or not, he's a traitor. That's what matters."

"He's a Jew." The old man insisted. "Hans should have believed me when Michael tried to stop the men from killing Walter."

Lisette tried not to look interested. "Who's Walter?"

"A traitor that the men shot when Michael was here last time. Michael tried to talk Frederick out of killing Walter, which we didn't think much about at the time. Now—it's clear why. Sit down, old man." She turned to Lisette. "Eat up. Don't you like my cake?"

"It's delicious." But the image of Michael castrated and then eaten alive by hogs had left her with little appetite. "Large lunch, though. I'm not very hungry."

It was a terrible way to die, but why did she care? He was a Nazi and a killer.

But if he was, why would he try to stop the murder of someone who had betrayed the cause?

53

BAYREUTH, GERMANY

FREDERICK HAD STOPPED AT the homes of leaders of units of Germany Now in Leipzig, Gera, and Hof to spread the word and precise day and time. It had to be coordinated. The attacks would take place simultaneously around the country, which would keep the opposing forces divided, while the main attack would happen in Berlin.

He met with the men in charge of local groups who would send one of their people to personally alert the other members. And since he couldn't get to every group, not in the allotted time, he designated who would send word to other districts. It reminded him of the tale of the American Revolution and the rider Paul Revere, calling forth patriotic men to fight. Too bad the effort had been wasted, and America had become so decadent.

America wasn't his concern. The American agents, even if they knew something, wouldn't know enough, and he'd ensured that Michael would never pass on critical information.

One more day.

Now that it was almost here, he could barely contain his excitement.

Just before noon, he reached Bayreuth, a town where Wagner had lived and built his magnificent Festspielhaus where his operas were staged and where Hitler had been an appreciative fan. Frederick had tried to get tickets to the summer Wagner opera festival only to be told that there was an eight-year waiting list.

He found Lisette's grandmother's house on the outskirts of town, a two-story house, painted white with blue trim, flowers lining the walk. He rang the doorbell and introduced himself as Lisette's fiancée to the middle-aged woman who opened the door.

"I'm so pleased to meet you. She's such a lovely girl, and so devoted to her grandmother. I'm Helen, the caregiver."

He followed Helen through the house to the backyard, where the flowers that decorated the beds surrounding the patio were beginning to lose their petals with the approach of cooler weather. Lisette's grandmother, wrapped in a blanket, sat in the sun in front of a wrought iron table and regarded him with dark suspicious eyes.

Helen offered to get coffee and scones and bustled off.

"Hello. I'm Frederick."

The old woman didn't respond.

"Has Lisette told you about me?" He pulled out a chair and seated himself.

"She doesn't talk." Helen reappeared with a cup of coffee and chocolate scones on white china. Setting the cup and the plate in front of him on the table, she gave him a smile. "I'm not sure if she just doesn't want to talk—or if she can't. The doctor says she can't speak, but maybe she just doesn't have anything to say."

The old woman glared at Helen.

"I'll leave you two alone," Helen said. "I have to make lunch. Would you care to stay?"

"Thank you, no. I have meetings in Nuremberg. But I couldn't be so close without saying hello." Frederick didn't really care for old people or for disabled people, but he did care for Lisette. For her sake, he could spend a few uncomfortable moments. He waited until Helen left them alone and then he leaned forward. "I know that your father was a hero of the Third Reich. I wanted to let you know that we're taking back Germany. Lisette and me. We're going to rid the country of immigrants and Jewish influence."

He didn't expect a reaction. He assumed the old lady had dementia of top of everything else, which added to the fact that she was the daughter of a hero, made it safe to tell her in vague terms what was about to happen. He was totally unprepared when she snaked a shaking hand out from under the blanket to grab his wrist.

The mouth worked soundlessly, spit dripping from one corner. Then, she gathered herself for a supreme effort and uttered a word. It was barely audible. "No."

He was both revolted and surprised. "No?" No to what? The engagement? The taking back of Germany?

The old woman licked her lips and tried again. "Lisette. Evil."

He removed the bony hand that gripped his wrist. "What are you trying to say?"

"She… hates me. You. She… she…"

Frederick shook his head in disbelief. Crazy old woman.

"My son… her father…" the old woman stopped, mouth working, eyes darting sideways and then back to Frederick. "Was… killed."

"Someone killed Lisette's father?" Why had she never said anything. "Damn Muslims."

"NO!" She was speaking more distinctly now. "He liked them. Turks. Muslims. Immigration lawyer—killed—Hamburg. She hates her heritage…" the mouth moved for a moment without sound and then the words came out "wants revenge."

54

ANKLAM, GERMANY

THE OLD MAN SAT down at the table while Gertrude busied herself with dishes. From the kitchen window, Lisette watched Michael and the teenager place crates into the back of the pick-up truck with Hans and his father standing nearby. *What if she was wrong about Michael?* Which would be worse—helping a killer survive or allowing the brutal murder of a man who might be on her side?

She'd already made up her mind about him. She'd delivered him to be killed.

But the fact that Michael had tried to stop the murder of a "traitor" changed the equation. Why would Michael do that? Unless—maybe—he wasn't a Nazi any more than she was. What if the story she'd come up with—that Michael had shot Gunter's men in Greifswald—was true? When she'd entered his room at midnight, Michael had been showering. Why so late—unless he'd been out. Gunter's men *had* been shot at around eleven o'clock by someone using the same caliber gun as the one Michael carried.

What had she done?

She glanced out the window. The group had returned to the barn. They'd be done soon, and then Michael would be killed.

Michael's mother had loved music and had taught him to love it in turn. And he'd asked her about her love of horses. Both conversations had made her uncomfortable because she didn't want to see him as human, even when she believed him to be a Nazi. But he *was* human. And she'd delivered him to be mutilated and fed alive to hogs.

She could see the edge of the pigpen. How long would he live after the pigs started on him? Long enough to suffer horribly. Would he deserve that brutal a death even if he were a Nazi killer?

And what if he wasn't?

The story about Walter had changed the odds on who Michael really was.

But what could she do? If she intervened to save him now, she'd lose her chance to kill The Leader, who might be the man who'd murdered her father. If she intervened, they would kill her as well as him. Her mission—and her life. If she'd realized earlier, she could have saved Michael. But now? It was too late.

Maybe it wasn't. Maybe if she warned him.

No, too risky.

She'd killed seven men. What was one more death on her conscience, even a gruesome death?

But she'd only killed men who deserved to die.

If she did nothing—given that she now believed it strongly possible that he wasn't a Nazi—how was she any better than Gertrude or the monstrous old man?

If Michael was Jewish, as the old Nazi kept insisting, and she did nothing because doing something could be risky for her personally—how was she any different from the people in World War II who'd known that their Jewish neighbors were being murdered and had done nothing?

She made up her mind.

"I almost forgot. I promised Frederick, I'd text him when I got here." She pulled her purse off the chair and fumbled through it. "Damn. My phone. It's not here."

Gertrude turned to her with a solicitous expression. "In the car, perhaps?"

"Maybe. Oh no. Damn. Damn! I forgot. Michael borrowed my phone on the drive here. He must still have it."

"You let him borrow your phone?"

"His phone died, and he wanted to post on a few websites. I didn't want him to become suspicious." She pushed back from the table. "I'm going to go get it."

"Just tell Hans. He'll take it from Michael when they tie him up."

"And if Michael starts shooting? Hans will have to shoot him, and my phone could be destroyed." She grabbed her purse and stood. "It'll be okay. I'll just ask him for it and leave. He doesn't suspect anything, does he?"

"He doesn't seem to," Gertrude agreed.

"Good." She opened the door.

Gertrude called after her. "Be quick."

She intended to be.

* * * * *

The guns were loaded in the pick-up truck and in the back of Frederick's car. Next, the body bags and the quicklime. Kolya had concluded that his objective now was to get out alive—and that it was very unlikely he would do so. Lisette had delivered him to be murdered.

He thought of Alex and was glad that he'd sent her his love in a text. If he were killed, Jonathan would tell her. Even if his body was never found.

He knew what would happen to his body, but he'd be dead, so what would it matter?

In the barn, Hans pulled up the trapdoor leading to the cellar. "There's some things in the corner. Some black bags and some sacks. Be careful on the ladder. It's kind of shaky. And there's a broken step."

Kolya had been watching for any opportunity, but he'd seen little chance of his killing them before they could shoot him. Maybe grab the kid, use him as a shield, and then shoot the two men, who might hesitate to shoot at Xavier. A small chance of success.

Still, it would be something.

Then, he considered the cellar. A large room, lined with concrete. Once he was down there, and if he stayed far enough away from the opening in the barn floor, they wouldn't be able to shoot him without climbing down the ladder. And he could shoot them as they descended.

They would know it, too. They wouldn't try.

They could drop in explosives—but that could undermine the foundation of the barn. Poison gas? It would be an ironic end to die from being gassed by Nazis in Germany. But he doubted that Hans had poison gas on hand.

Most likely, they could simply lock the trapdoor and pile weight on it. He'd be trapped. In a cellar that reminded him of being held prisoner and tortured and where he would eventually die of thirst or hunger.

But eventually was preferable to immediately.

And he remembered his previous visit to the cellar. Locked in the cellar, he would still have a chance. A small chance, but better than nothing.

Xavier picked up an electric lantern, switched it on, and preceded Kolya down the ladder. Kolya proceeded carefully but a little faster than on his previous visit. His leg was not yet back to normal, and he still didn't want to injure it further.

After reaching the cellar floor, the teen placed the lantern on the ground, lighting the area around the bottom of the ladder, the far side of the room—where the body bags and sacks of quicklime were stacked—only dimly visible. Xavier headed toward the body bags. Kolya followed but seated himself on a sack of quicklime.

"My leg's bothering me. We've been working nonstop. Cigarette break." Kolya disliked smoking, but he always carried a pack. Smoking was an excuse to linger. And it could be a way to make a connection.

"A break sounds good. And I'd like a cigarette." Xavier's sullen expression lightened.

Kolya pulled out a pack of Marlboros and offered one. He struck a match, lit his own cigarette, and then held out the flame.

Xavier inhaled. Then he seated himself on a sack next to Kolya. "My mother doesn't like me to smoke. She says I'm too young, but I'm fifteen. Not a child anymore."

No, Xavier wasn't a child, but he wasn't an adult, either. "Mothers tend not to like a lot of things. I won't tell her."

"Thanks. I figured you wouldn't." Xavier's features were illuminated by the glow of the cigarette. In that light, he looked very young, and his previous expression of hostility had diminished. "You're the only American I've ever met. Have you been to New York?"

"A few times." Kolya had been raised in Brooklyn, spent his early adulthood in Manhattan, and retained a fondness for the city, but "Michael" grew up in Michigan and then moved to the D.C. area. "It's an amazing place. Expensive though."

"I want to go sometime. Even if it's filled with degenerates."

"No more than anywhere else. Lots of good music. Great restaurants. You should go."

"Someday," Xavier said.

It was an eerie conversation. Xavier appeared almost friendly. Kolya wondered if the teen knew what his father was planning to do. The night that Walter was murdered, Xavier hadn't participated. On the other hand, here he was. Maybe this was going to be his induction into killing.

"Xavier, Michael—what are you doing?" Hans shouted down.

"Taking a break, Papa." Xavier shouted back and then tapped ashes onto the concrete floor. "He's always pushing me."

"What's the hurry?" Kolya exhaled smoke, feeling the rush of nicotine. "It's not today, is it? Day X."

"No, but we have a lot to do before tomorrow, and it takes a few hours to get to Berlin. Have to leave early." Xavier tossed the cigarette on the ground and stepped on it. "We should get to work."

"In a minute." He indicated his cigarette.

Keep the teen with him as a hostage? One way to ensure that Hans wouldn't use poison gas or explosives. On the other hand, Xavier would not take kindly to being held, and Kolya would have to subdue him. Kolya didn't want to kill the kid if he didn't have to. Moreover, dealing with Xavier could complicate the only chance Kolya had to remain alive.

Let him leave.

Kolya picked up a stack of body bags and followed Xavier to the ladder. Waiting until Xavier was halfway up the ladder, Kolya retreated to the far corner, dumped the bags, took his gun out of the holster, and from various pockets retrieved two extra magazines. More than enough ammunition, given the situation. The lantern remained on the cellar floor, the light dimly illuminating Kolya's location but brightly lighting the ladder.

He placed one of the body bags against the wall to cut down on the cold emanating from the concrete and leaned back. Adjusting his position so his back was supported, he had a good view of the top of the ladder. He rested one arm on a bent knee and aimed at the light shining through the trapdoor. With his arm supported, he could stay in position indefinitely.

Hans would have to either descend the ladder or insert his head and shoulders through the opening to fire. In either case, Kolya'd have the first shot.

He heard a commotion in the barn overhead. Lisette's voice called his name.

"I told you to stay with Gertrude and my grandfather." Hans' voice.

"Michael has my cell phone. Is he down there? Michael? I need my phone."

What game was she was playing? He didn't have her cell phone. But he went with it. "Yes, I have it."

"Michael will be up in a minute." Hans again.

But Lisette was already climbing down the ladder. Kolya weighed whether to shoot her. After all, she'd tried to poison him, and she'd delivered him to be murdered. But she was not doing what Hans expected or wanted her to do. Curious. Take the chance that she'd try to kill him, or risk killing a possible ally?

His whole life was taking chances.

Holding his fire, Kolya watched her descend. She almost lost her footing on the broken step, took a second to regroup and then continued, reaching the bottom, where she was caught by the circle of light cast by the lantern. He could tell nothing from her appearance.

Lisette approached and looked at his gun, now aimed squarely at her chest. She held up her hands so he could see she was unarmed. "I loaned you my phone," she spoke loudly, almost shouting, so Hans could hear. "I need it back."

"What are you doing? I don't have your phone." In contrast to her, he spoke quietly, his voice just above a whisper.

"I had to come up with something." Now she too was whispering. "They're planning to kill you."

"I know."

55

FREDERICK STARED AT THE old woman's twisted face. He remembered his suspicions about Lisette, suspicions he'd set aside after Michael had "shot" the woman in the garage. But that shooting had been a test for Michael and Lisette, which they both had passed. Now, he was convinced that the shooting had been faked. So Lisette hadn't proven herself any more than Michael had.

No, wait. Was he too quick to accept the word of a crazy old woman—who'd had a stroke?

There was *something* he could check.

"What was your son's name?" Maybe he could look up the son online—whether he'd been a pro-immigration lawyer who'd been killed.

The old woman moistened her lips. "Dieter... Frank."

He didn't need to look it up. He knew the name, and he knew who had killed Dieter Frank. The Wolf. The name that the Leader had used when he lived in Hamburg. Just last night, Lisette had talked about the Wolf but put the mention of the name on Michael.

Then he noticed the book on the table. He picked it up. *The Diary of Anne Frank.* "This?"

"They make me listen. She... chose it. M... m... my granddaughter. Because the name."

It was enough.

Lisette's father had been shot, rightly so, by the Wolf, a fact that Lisette had never mentioned. The killings of Germany Now members had begun soon after Lisette had become his lover.

The level of betrayal was almost unbearable. He'd loved Lisette. He'd wanted to make her his wife, and all the time she'd been using him. How could he have been this stupid? This gullible?

He should have known—or at least suspected. But he did suspect. He remembered the dinner when he first became suspicious. He should have killed her then.

Love and sex—they were weaknesses. Michael was right about that, at least.

Had she lied about Michael as well?

He didn't know, and he didn't care. Two military members shot by an expert marksman, by someone protecting Peter, when Michael was in town and one of the few people to know that Peter was scheduled for elimination. It was too much of a coincidence. Better to be safe.

Get rid of both.

The old woman looked at him with large eyes. She might have been beautiful in her day, but now, she was a crippled shell, unable to walk, barely able to speak. He appreciated that she had warned him about Lisette, but that didn't take away his disgust at her physical condition.

He wondered how Lisette really felt about her grandmother. Lisette had cared enough about her grandmother to pay for her upkeep. But was it out of love? Maybe Lisette was just prolonging her grandmother's misery. On the other hand, he remembered something else Michael had said: people are funny about families.

He knew the right thing to do. The old lady deserved to be out of her misery, and Lisette deserved to be punished.

"Don't worry. I'll take care of everything." He spoke reassuring words and patted her arm even as he reached into his waistband for the gun. Still smiling at her, he pulled it and shot her between the eyes. Then he carried his plate and teacup inside, placed them in the sink, walked into the living room and shot Helen. He returned to the kitchen, ran the water over the dishes, and then wiped down everything he'd touched.

Next, call Hans. Use of phones was risky, and the Leader had said not to communicate except in person until after Day X, unless there was an emergency. He considered this an emergency. At least, he had a new burner.

There was no other way to get the message to Hans so that Lisette would die with Michael. Given the depth of Lisette's betrayal, Frederick was a little sorry he wouldn't be there to watch it—but there wasn't time. Securing the success of Day X mattered more.

56

ANKLAM, GERMANY

KOLYA COULD HEAR ARGUING above even if he couldn't make out the words. Maybe Hans had realized that "Michael" wasn't coming back up. Maybe something else related to Lisette's decision to warn him.

"You're a little late." In the dim light, he could see her outline but not her features. "I assume you knew what they intended when you drove me here."

"It's not too late. You're still alive."

"For now." He distinguished a new voice overhead. Gertrude—screeching. Hans yelling back at her. Why had Gertrude emerged from the kitchen and why was she screaming? Then he made out a few words. *Kill her.* Lisette was now a target as well?

"If that's your attitude—I'll just go back up," Lisette said.

"If you do, they'll kill you. Don't you hear Gertrude?"

Hans called down. "Michael, what's taking so long?"

Hans should have figured out by now that "Michael" was no longer playing the game. Kolya chose not to answer.

"Michael?"

"Go fuck yourself." Kolya called back. The role-playing was over. "I'm staying here."

More excited and angry voices shouted over each other.

He turned to Lisette. "Not that I'm not grateful that you changed your mind—but maybe grabbing one of the HK-91s would have been useful."

Lisette sighed and seated herself on a sack next to him. "I thought about it. But Hans' father was by the truck, and I couldn't grab a gun without his shooting me first. Shame. If you knew that Hans planned to kill you, why did you come with me? Why did you get back in the car after lunch?"

"I wasn't sure. After we arrived, I picked up on the signals, but it was too late. I've been playing for time."

"You're really just going to stay down here?"

"Better than being shot."

"Not what they were planning."

"What were they planning?"

"It was horrific."

He thought of what kind of death would be horrific compared to being shot. "The pigs?"

She nodded.

"Alive?"

"After castrating you."

They'd planned to restrain him, cut off his genitals, and dump him into the pen while he was conscious but unable to move while pigs consumed him. A gruesome death, but Hans and company would've had to take him alive—and he would've made that difficult. He flashed back to a year earlier—images of being whipped unconscious, of being chained to the floor where they'd broken his leg with a golf club, of hanging from a chain while his torturer ground a lit cigar against his penis. His hands trembled. He took long breaths, counting, focusing on the light of the lantern, repeating the mantra. Then he was back in control—or at least in control of the space he currently occupied. He turned his attention back to Lisette.

"Was that what changed your mind—the way they planned to kill me?"

"One of the reasons." She gave a visible shudder. "The repellent old man said that you tried to save a man that they shot. That raised questions in my mind. Then there's the fact that he's convinced you're Jewish."

Kolya gave a quiet laugh. "He's a piece of shit, isn't he?"

"So, are you?"

"Am I what?"

"Jewish."

"Why? Does it matter?"

"It matters to me. Because of what Germany did to Jewish people. It makes my betraying you worse."

Interesting, but he wasn't sure enough of her to tell her anything personal.

Hans called again, this time his voice was harsh. "Michael, if you don't come up, we'll come down after you. You don't want that, do you?"

"Feel free." The lantern at the bottom of the ladder illuminated a circle about three feet in circumference. It would take Hans' eyes a few minutes to adjust to the dim light, but Kolya, who'd been in the cellar for fifteen minutes, could see well enough to put a bullet through Hans or any of his family who were so stupid as to try climbing down. "I'll shoot anyone who tries."

More muttered conversation above.

He glanced over at Lisette. "Any other reason you decided to help me?"

"Should we take the ladder down? Give us the chance to climb out later?" Then she answered her own question. "No. If we tried, we'd be within gunshot range, wouldn't we?"

"Yes. Although the ladder would be useful." He turned his attention to the ladder, which was disappearing as it was slowly drawn up into the barn. "They've figured out their move."

The small circle of light on the ceiling disappeared as the trapdoor was closed. There was the banging of a hammer on wood—probably nailing boards across the door. He heard a motor start and then felt a vibration. The small tractor? Probably on top of the door now.

"They're going to let us die of hunger and thirst," she said.

"Unless they decide to blow us up—which I think unlikely. Hans is proud of his barn."

Lisette stood, crossed to the lantern, and carried it back. "How long will the batteries last?"

"A few hours if we keep it on." Kolya holstered his weapon.

"How long will we last?"

"Somewhat longer than the lantern. There is sufficient air filtering through the floorboards to ensure that we'll die of thirst and hunger and not from lack of oxygen." He stood and stretched, taking care to flex the bad leg. "You didn't finish telling me why you changed your mind. Given that you tried to poison me. Twice."

He picked up the lantern and one of the body bags and returned to the area where the ladder had been positioned. Searching the ground, he found a shaft of wood from the broken step. It wasn't much, but it was what he'd bet on when he made the decision to remain in the cellar.

"You think I tried to poison you?" She followed him.

"Let's not play games, please." He picked up the wood. It was about a foot long, with a jagged end. He tested the end. Sharp enough. "I kept the cup, by the way. It's being analyzed. But you could just tell me what you put in it."

"Monkshood. I put monkshood in it."

"Good thing I prefer lukewarm coffee. I barely tasted it, and it still made me sick as a dog. Aconite in the peppermint schnapps as well?"

"Yes. Who's analyzing the cup?"

"A friend. Are you going to tell me why you changed your mind?"

She took a deep breath. "I started to have doubts about whether you were a true believer. Because if you were, you probably would've told Frederick that I'd tried to poison you, which I assumed you suspected. It was only a small doubt. Then I heard that you'd tried to save a man—and also realized that you could have been the shooter in Greifswald. So, who are you really? Michael Hall? Nickolas Kruger? Or someone else."

"First, tell me why you tried to kill me." He wanted her to confirm his guess.

"You shot that woman. In the garage. I blamed myself for not stopping you and Frederick. I thought I should have killed you both before that."

Lisette *was* the anti-Nazi vigilante that Frederick feared.

"If it makes you feel any better—she's not dead."

57

FRICK WAS HALFWAY THROUGH a beer at his second favorite bar in Berlin when Teo appeared and seated himself at his table, which was fucking annoying since Frick already knew the news. He took another swig of his beer and set it down. Not that he didn't like Teo, but he had a feeling his afternoon plans—which consisted of finishing his beer and drinking another two or three—were about to be shot to hell. "Before you say anything, I saw Petrov's post. I know the timing's changed."

"I was contacted by Ben. He wants to know if we have anything more specific."

"Petrov will get in touch when he has anything."

The waitress approached. In perfect German, Teo ordered a beer and currywurst. The waitress disappeared, and Teo turned back to Frick. "You think he's okay?"

"As far as I know." Frick had lingering concerns over Petrov's playing a Nazi, but he'd pulled it off so far.

Except for nearly getting himself poisoned.

"Maybe we could get Mark to locate his phone?"

"We could. But why? Petrov posted this morning, so he was okay a few hours ago. He's not scheduled to post again until tomorrow morning." Frick leaned back in his chair and watched Teo consume a currywurst in five bites. "Your mother ever tell you to chew your food?"

"Very funny. Why wait until we know he's in trouble to track him?"

"Resource allocation. And fucking security. The more closely we have anyone tracking Petrov, the greater the chance of a leak. Don't forget, the agency is still chasing down moles. And the BfV has access to some information from our side. Anyway, what's the point? Wherever Petrov is now might not be where he is tomorrow. If he misses a check-in, that would be different."

"I guess." Teo drank more of his beer. "I thought German beer was supposed to be so great. It's really bitter."

"You're drinking it."

"Blending in."

As if Teo, with his fresh-faced American eagerness, could blend in.

"Look. I wasn't crazy about Petrov taking this on—for all the reasons I've previously stated. But everyone disagreed, and he wanted to do it. He's doing it. Now let him do his goddamn job." Frick picked up his own beer and drank steadily. Finishing the pint, he set it down heavily. "Damn good beer. Anything comes up, you know where to find me."

COLOGNE, GERMANY

The Leader liked to take the same walk every lunch hour, unless he had meetings to attend. Sometimes he took a sandwich, sometimes he ate at his desk and then walked. But he liked the park. And he liked his routine.

Walking kept him focused, reduced tension—and now, one day before he either succeeded in changing the country or failed miserably—he could use the relief.

Except that on this walk, the relief was transitory, interrupted by a phone call. Frederick was violating security and ignoring the order to stay off phones.

The Leader listened to the recitation. It was succinct—that Frederick's lover and the American were both traitors. He interrupted before Frederick finished. "Are they dead?"

"Not yet."

"Why not?"

"Hans was an idiot. He let them both go into the cellar under the barn, and then they refused to come back up."

"What the hell was he thinking?"

"He wanted Michael to bring up the quicklime and body bags. He didn't think Michael suspected anything. Then before I called with the news about Lisette, she'd joined him in the cellar."

"Hans didn't go down to finish them?"

"Michael has a gun, and he's a very good shot. He'd kill Hans if he as much as poked his head through."

"No chance they can get out?"

"The door is nailed shut, and there's a tractor on top."

The Leader thought about the Americans who'd been wasting time inside the BfV. He had been puzzled about just what they were really doing. Now he understood. It made sense if they were backup for a team infiltrating Germany Now. "Not good enough. They need to die. Tell Hans to blow up the barn. Or burn it down."

"Hans isn't going to like it. The barn's over two hundred years old."

"We all have to sacrifice. Tell him to do it tonight. When it's late enough that no one is likely to be driving by to see the fire, but before the Americans figure out Michael is missing and go looking for him. Just in case Michael or your girlfriend knows anything about Day X. We can't have Michael alive to counter the story that jihadists attacked the country. Call Hans, even if it is breaking security. By the time anyone processes the phone records, we'll be in control."

The Leader clicked off the phone and took a deep breath. Time to lay the groundwork for the next day. He clicked on his phone to call.

58

ANKLAM, GERMANY

HE WAS HEADING TOWARDS the far end of the cellar directly from the stacks of body bags and quicklime, carrying the piece of wood and a body bag. She trailed him, amused at the illusion, relieved that the woman's death wasn't on her conscience and that her attempts to kill "Michael" had failed. She hadn't exactly succeeded in saving him—or herself for that matter—but at least she had tried.

"She had exploding capsules under the sweater?" Now that she knew it'd been a trick, the details interested her.

"And a Kevlar vest. Tehila's a good actress as well."

"But you did shoot the man you tried to save."

"By the time I put a round into his head, he was already dead. The group used him for target practice. Still, even if he'd been alive, I would've done it. I couldn't have saved him. If I'd tried, I would've died with him. I made the decision that stopping Germany Now was more important than throwing my life away on a futile gesture. Nevertheless, I do bear some guilt for not making the effort." Then he turned his gaze on her. "So I do understand how you felt when you thought I had shot Tehila."

They reached the far wall. The lantern illuminated a decrepit dark wood door in the wall, and she had a sudden surge of hope. So that's why he'd appeared calm when Hans nailed the trapdoor shut. Then he opened the door.

Two feet past the door was a wall of heavily packed dirt.

"You're planning to dig out of here? With that?" She indicated the piece of wood. "Are you kidding?"

"I'm open to other suggestions. In the meantime." He unzipped the body bag. Stepping into the opening, he placed the body bag against the wall of dirt and began to scrape with the sharp end of the stick. A few chunks of dirt landed inside the bag.

"We're twenty feet down."

"I know. I'm not an engineer, but it seems feasible to make a hole about waist high and then go straight up. We'll need an area large enough to fit inside but small enough that we can brace legs and back against the shaft as we dig. Since we don't have a ladder."

"It'll take forever."

"Do you have an alternative?"

She didn't. She watched him scrape a handful of dirt at a time and then searched through her own purse for a possible tool. She found a pocketknife. It wasn't much, but it was something. "Move."

He did, and together they began to scrape at the wall of earth with the only tools they had.

It was slow and painful. Handful after handful. Each handful was dumped into the body bag. After an hour, they'd hollowed out a two-foot space. Loose dirt filled her lungs and she started to cough.

"Take a break." He continued to dig, but the shaking in his hands had come back.

"I will if you will."

He hesitated and then nodded agreement. "Five minutes."

They sat on the dirt floor, backs against the concrete wall. He turned the lantern off to save the battery. The cellar was completely black. She could almost feel the heaviness of the dark and the damp.

"This bothers you, doesn't it?"

He was taking deep breaths and letting each one out slowly, a technique he seemed to employ frequently. "Some. Doesn't bother you?"

"I used to be afraid of the dark. Before I realized what there really was to fear. People like Hans. Or Frederick." Or the man with the wolf tattoo.

"You don't strike me as someone who's afraid of much."

"I'm afraid periodically. But I sometimes think I like the sensation."

"Is that why you hunt Nazis?"

"No." She told him then, what she'd never told anyone—about the house in Hamburg, about her father and hobbits, about the man who killed him and her childhood. She told him about fleeing to Austin under another name. She described her mother, her stepfather and her grandmother, and her decision at a young age to devote her life to revenge.

He was silent for a long moment after she finished her story. "I'm sorry about your father. But dedicating your life to killing—from what you've said of your father—do you think that's the path he would've wanted you to take?"

"You know nothing about my father." She was angry in turn. "You don't think that Nazis deserve to die?"

"Whether they do or not, don't you deserve more than this?"

"You're doing the same thing I am."

"Not exactly. I want to stop people like Frederick, but I try not to kill unnecessarily, even if they do deserve it, although it is tempting to make an exception for Hans and his family. And this is my job, not my life."

"Who are you to judge?"

"Sorry. Something about being trapped twenty feet underground."

They sat in the silence and the dark for a few minutes. She heard his breathing exercises. "I would have been a different person if my father had lived. I was only nine."

"My mother died when I was nine."

"Your father raise you?"

"No." There was a brief hesitation as if he were reluctant to share even this much. "He was already dead."

"What happened? To your father? To you afterward?"

"It doesn't matter."

Clearly there was more to the story of his childhood than the loss of his mother, but he didn't seem interested in sharing. She kept pushing anyway.

"Did your mother really teach you about music?"

"She was a concert pianist. I learned to play when I was three. I prefer jazz though."

He'd given up something personal. That was a start. What else did she know about him? He was intelligent, capable. He, like her, was tracking down Nazis—which was his job—although he hadn't explained what that job was. And he was fighting personal demons. But she knew almost nothing else. Not even his name. "You don't seem like the kind of person who would be bothered by the dark. What happened to you?"

"I just don't like cellars."

"Have anything to do with the scars on your back?" She could feel his discomfort even though she couldn't see his expression.

"It's related. Something that happened a year ago. I still have periodic... difficulties."

"That's vague."

"Intentionally so."

"Oh come on. I just told you everything about myself—and I know almost nothing about you. You're not Nickolas Kruger, are you?"

"There's that possibility."

She waited for more, but nothing was forthcoming. "You could at least give me a first name. If I need to get your attention, it would be nice to say something besides—hey, you."

"Is there anyone else here?" His voice was amused. "But you can call me Kolya."

"Kolya. For Nikolai? That's a Russian name. Not a Jewish name." She returned to the earlier question, which he'd avoided.

"I'm named after my father's father. Who wasn't Jewish."

Was the phrasing the answer? One of his grandparents wasn't Jewish—and by implication, the others were? In her zeal to kill Nazis, had she come close to doing the work of Nazis by murdering a Jewish undercover agent?

"And you work for American intelligence?"

"I can neither confirm nor deny." He turned the lantern back on. "Back to work. We have to get out of here before morning. Xavier confirmed that Day X is tomorrow. I already knew that the Reichstag was one target. We need to pass that on before a lot of people are killed. And, if possible, get more details."

* * * * *

Another hour and they had scraped out enough dirt for one person to squeeze into the opening. They agreed to alternate digging since only one would fit, Kolya taking the first turn tunneling upwards.

Tunneling seemed an overly optimistic word for it.

Working with gravity helped, but it was still painfully slow. A handful of dirt at a time. When he could work the shaft of wood deep into the dirt, he could bring down larger chunks.

Dirt showered down onto his head. He kept his mouth firmly closed, and tried to protect his eyes, by closing them when the dirt began to fall or by shielding them with his left hand, but he couldn't protect against the dust.

He breathed dust through his nose. He could taste the grit. His eyes watered, and he continually blinked to clear the dust and his resulting tears. Periodically, he'd cough.

It would help to have something to drink. To be able to wash off his face. But there was no water. No food.

His phone and his gun were below, wrapped inside one of the body bags. He'd need both if they managed to make it out—and dirt wasn't good for either.

At his suggestion, Lisette turned the lantern off after he got into position to dig. Stretch the batteries out as long as possible, even though the dark could be problematic for him. He didn't need the light when he was digging, but when they changed shifts, the light was useful. They both had phones, but he didn't want the battery on his phone to die. He would need the phone to alert the team to what he knew about Day X—if they could make it out, and he had a signal.

Digging in the dark was an almost out-of-body experience. He had to employ the breathing exercises more than once. He had moments when his mind flashed back to the cellar in Romania where he'd been held prisoner and tortured. There were moments when he hallucinated Alex sitting next to him, her head on his shoulder.

"You know—there are better ways to get out of planning a wedding." *He could see the amusement in the dark eyes turned on him.*

"Not my intention. Even if I hate big family gatherings."

"Just come home to me." She touched his face and brushed dirt from his hair. And then she was gone.

The opening inched upward. From that initial hole, three feet by two feet by three feet, he had expanded upward another few feet, not enough yet that he needed to stand—just enough to crouch awkwardly.

It would get tricky when he had to be suspended inside the shaft ten feet or more above the floor level—while trying to dig. He had a way to go. He concentrated and managed to push all other thoughts out of his head. It worked for at least five minutes. Then the thoughts and images were back.

A large chunk of dirt showered down on him, and he had an attack of coughing.

"Kolya." Lisette turned the lantern back on. "You've been digging for two hours. My turn."

He crawled out of the hole, shaking the dirt from his clothes, before sinking onto the floor. His entire body shook, but he focused on the breathing, on the flickering light of the lantern, and he calmed again.

Lisette swept the small pile of dirt from the bottom of the shaft into the body bag, and then dragged the bag to the nearest corner where she had dumped previous loads.

"Are you okay?" She sounded genuinely concerned.

"I'm fine. It's just hard going." He tried unsuccessfully to moisten his mouth by swallowing. "We don't have to do equal shifts. Take it for half an hour, and then I can take over again."

"I'm stronger than I look." She held out her hand for the wooden stick. "How do you think I killed six—no seven—men?"

"Different skill set, but okay." He handed her the wood. "Be careful not to break it."

"I'll try. If need be, we've got my knife. How far do you think we have to go?"

The hole was waist high, maybe three feet off the ground, and he estimated that he had dug upward around four feet. "Thirteen feet. Maybe more."

"Almost half-way there. Turn the lantern off. Rest."

He would, but just long enough to recoup his strength.

59

ANKLAM, GERMANY

AS DIFFICULT AS THE digging had been previously, it was harder now. He was maybe ten feet up the shaft, his back planted against the dirt on one side, pressure from his legs keeping him in place as he continued to scrape the dirt overhead. He had ripped the lining from his jacket to wrap around his hands and keep them from blistering. Maybe five feet left to go. Maybe seven.

Another shower of dirt. Along with fighting the PTSD, his bad leg ached from the effort to hold his position. He shifted to try to ease the leg and lost the pressure he needed to keep himself stationary. He slid five feet down the shaft before he could brace himself enough to stop his descent.

"*Yob tvoyu mat.*" He spoke the Russian words that had been his go-to curse for most his life and that he'd suppressed during his time as Michael the Nazi. But his cover was blown—so what did it matter?

"Switch again?" Lisette's voice below.

"What time is it?"

A flash of light from her phone. "One a.m."

"Did you sleep at all?"

"Not much. But some." She'd created a bed of sorts from the body bags. Not particularly comfortable, but better than the dirt floor.

"Try and sleep a little more. Maybe another hour, and we'll switch."

"You're so tired, you almost fell."

"I'm okay."

"Sure you are."

That was the kind of comment Alex would've made. He'd already noted similarities—both strong, intelligent, determined women. Unlike Alex in other ways though. The single-minded focus on revenge—in some ways admirable—and in other ways off-putting. Still, he liked Lisette. Not enough to let his guard down, but she was proving herself to be a good partner.

He wondered what Alex would think of Lisette—Alex who tried to find the good in most people. Would she approve of Lisette's vendetta? She would definitely not approve of the attempts to kill him, but she might understand Lisette's motivation.

And he briefly acknowledged that but for his love for Alex, he would be very interested in Lisette, assuming they got out alive.

"We've got another five hours until dawn. We should make it unless you injure yourself."

"Point."

She switched on the lantern. Using his legs and his arms, he lowered himself to where he could stand, and then he slid out of the hole. He unwound the cloths around his hands. "It'll help with blistering." He offered the cloths and the wooden stick. Then he set his phone. "Two hours. If you get too tired before that, wake me."

"I won't get tired." She twisted the pieces of cloth around each hand, picked up the stick, and headed up the shaft.

He waited until she was positioned before taking a trip to the far corner to try to relieve himself, although as dehydrated as he was, there wasn't much to pee out. Then he turned the lantern off and stretched out on the makeshift bed. It took a few minutes for the mental exercises to calm him, and then he was asleep.

* * * * *

She dug with determination, even though her arms ached, and the dirt obscured her vision and clogged her lungs. It wasn't just her desire to survive, or to prevent Day X—both of which mattered but were not her prime focus, although they were what primarily motivated the man who she had to remember was Kolya, not Michael. She'd spent most of her life seeking vengeance against the man who'd murdered her father. The man with the wolf tattoo. She finally might have found him, ironically—or not so ironically—the man in charge of whatever Frederick had been planning. If she could get to the Reichstag in time, she'd have a shot at him. Maybe she'd finally know. And if they couldn't dig themselves out, she would've failed.

She didn't like failure.

But she was very glad for one failure. She had tried to kill Michael—no, Kolya—three times, twice with poison, once by betraying him to Frederick, and she was very happy that she hadn't succeeded.

In the long hours without food or water that they had spent trying to dig out of the cellar, she'd respected his dedication.

And she liked him. A lot, but not *too* much. Yes, he was attractive, and under other circumstances, she might have been interested, although she hadn't had a real boyfriend since she'd dated that bastard her first year in college.

He did have a good body, and whatever ghosts were haunting him did make him even more intriguing.

But she wasn't going to go there.

She didn't steal other women's men.

Still, she'd been alone for so long, without even a friend. To have the sympathetic ear of someone opposed to Germany Now was a pleasant experience. For the first time in a very long time, possibly since the death of her father, she felt understood.

She had a new thought. He was an American intelligence operative even if he'd refused to officially confirm the fact. He and his agency had constructed the Michael Hall/Nickolas Kruger identity in order to penetrate Germany Now. Was it possible that the text she'd seen from someone she assumed was a girlfriend was another deception, part of his cover identity?

She was a little disconcerted to realize that she hoped so.

* * * * *

He took over again at three o'clock and worked steadily. He didn't have any way to measure the distance, although he knew that he was high enough that a fall could result in serious injury.

He had to keep focus. Keep in position. Tired, hungry, and thirsty, it was hard to do so, but he mustered all his reserves and kept going. He'd been in worse situations. He could manage.

At five, when she called up to him for a shift change, he refused to stop. "I'm almost through." A few more passes with the wooden stake, and he could feel the roots of vegetation.

Between digging and pulling on the roots, he managed to make a small hole—and through it he could see a starlit sky.

He breathed in the fresh air with relief. They had made it. But they still had to crawl out without Hans or any of his family noticing. He slowly widened the hole enough to cautiously poke out his head.

The hole was in the field behind the barn. They'd be out of sight of the house.

It took time to enlarge the hole enough to fit through. Periodically, he'd check the field outside for any danger. The sky was still dark, but he could see the first glimmer of dawn.

As he finished opening the exit hole, he caught sight of a light brightening the path from the house to the barn. A flashlight.

He couldn't risk calling to Lisette. Instead, he used tired arms and legs to descend to the bottom of the shaft. The lantern batteries had finally given out.

"We're through." He couldn't see her in the dark.

"Someone's up there." Lisette's voice was a whisper.

He listened. Footsteps on the floor overhead. What were they doing? Whatever it was, he didn't care. If Hans and company were busy in the barn, they wouldn't be watching the field.

"It doesn't matter. You go first. Be careful. It's a long way up. When you get out, lay flat on the grass until I'm out as well." He felt for his gun and phone, located them both, and secured them.

Then he followed her back up the shaft.

60

ANKLAM, GERMANY

THEY LAY FLAT ON the ground, both covered in dirt, which was convenient camouflage. Kolya saw the old white horse in a fenced field several hundred yards away, and beyond the horse, the fields of wheat and the trees that surrounded the farm and hid it from view. Why was the horse still outside?

Light filtered through the wooden siding of the ancient barn, and two people were moving inside. Was Hans planning to destroy his own barn, believing that Kolya and Lisette were still trapped in the cellar? He'd figure it out after he contacted the team. He checked for a signal and then sent a text: *Day X today. Reichstag is a target. More later.*

Lisette on the ground next to him lifted her head. "I'm going to get a gun. From the car or the truck."

"Good idea." An HK-91 would have a lot more firepower than the HK 9mm gun tucked into his waist. He also wanted to check what Hans was doing in the barn and to keep the guns in the pick-up truck out of the hands of Germany Now.

They kept low as they circled the barn. His leg ached but not enough to hinder movement. The PTSD symptoms, so troublesome in the cellar, had receded. The requirements of action kept his focus on the present.

The Ford pick-up truck had been moved back from the barn, as had the pigs. It must have taken them most of the night to build new fences and move the pigs to a safe distance. Frederick's car remained where Lisette had parked it. Both were shrouded in darkness.

Quietly, Kolya extracted two assault rifles from the back of the pick-up and loaded them from a box of ammunition conveniently stored nearby, handing one rifle to Lisette, slinging the other over his shoulder. Then he moved to the truck cabin and checked. Keys were in the ignition.

He had a view of the inside of the barn, where Hans and his father, guns slung over their shoulders, stacked bales of hay against the walls. The most likely explanation: They weren't going to explode the barn. They were going to burn it down. Less dangerous for any nearby structure, like the house. But equally likely to kill anyone trapped in the cellar. The wood floor would burn and fall, and if he and Lisette didn't die from falling debris or fire, they'd die from smoke inhalation. Somewhat better than being eaten alive by pigs—but still terrible.

The time needed to move the pen and the pigs had saved Kolya and Lisette. Had Hans set a fire earlier, even an hour earlier, both of them would've died.

In Latvia during the war, the Einsatzgruppen had locked thousands of Jewish men, women, and children in synagogues, and set the synagogues on fire. In Poland, Jewish people were locked in barns and burned to death. Men, Women. Children. Babies. Burned. The odious old man in the house had probably burned children alive as well as shot them. Hans and his father were so proud of the old man's war record.

The open barn door was old, on a rusty track. If Kolya slid the barn door closed, Hans might hear and shoot. Rounds from an HK-91 would tear right through the ancient wood. On the other hand, maybe Kolya could take care of both the guns in the pick-up and Hans at the same time.

The narrow barn door was just a little wider than the pick-up truck. If he wedged the front of the truck into the opening, it would block Hans and his father unless they squeezed through on either side or scrambled over the hood. Either option would allow Kolya and Lisette to pick them off.

Hans was an integral part of Day X. Hans and his family had to be stopped. That Kolya would feel some personal satisfaction in killing Hans and his father was irrelevant.

Then he reconsidered.

Hans was in on the planning for Day X. If Hans surrendered, he could provide information. There was still much about Day X that Kolya didn't know, and his job was to stop it.

Offer to let Hans and his father out alive if they threw out their weapons. Even if Kolya half hoped that they'd refuse.

He motioned Lisette closer and then whispered. "If you see either of them near the door, shoot." After sliding into the driver's seat of the pick-up, he turned on the ignition and put it into drive, tensed for any reaction from the barn.

A flicker of flame inside the barn, and Kolya moved his foot from the brake to the gas, accelerating and ramming the front of the truck into the barn opening. He hit the brake, shifted into park, and turned off the engine. Then he opened the truck door and rolled out onto the ground.

Gunfire erupted from inside the barn. He crawled out of range as Lisette returned fire.

The firing stopped. There was shouting as the two trapped men tried to put out the fire. But they were too late. The fire roared higher, catching the thatched roof.

Hans and his father tried to scramble over the hood of the truck. Kolya raised his gun and fired in union with Lisette. The two men retreated, firing.

He shouted, offering them the chance at life they wouldn't have given him. "Throw out your weapons and come out with your hands up!"

Hans' father peered over the roof of the truck, pointed his gun in Kolya's direction, and pulled the trigger. He missed by inches. Kolya aimed and fired twice. The man collapsed. Hans tried to squeeze around the far side of the truck, firing randomly until Lisette shot him. He fell backwards into the inferno.

"For someone who's so moralistic about killing, you're pretty expert," Lisette said.

"Not the point."

The fire continued to accelerate, debris falling into the truck's cargo bed and onto the stacks of assault rifles.

Kolya watched until the one side of the barn collapsed. Then he started up the walk to the house, Lisette next to him.

61

ANKLAM, GERMANY

GERTRUDE STOOD AT THE stove in the kitchen, cooking bacon and eggs. The old man sat at the table nursing a cup of coffee, his back to the door. The television in the kitchen was on at high volume, a war movie with guns blazing—which would explain why neither had been alerted to the sound of gunfire. Although the burning barn could be viewed from the kitchen window, neither Gertrude nor the old man gave it a glance. Kolya noted the casual acceptance of what was intended to be his own murder.

He also noted the smell of the bacon. He hadn't eaten since lunch the previous day, and the allure of the sizzling bacon was almost dizzying. But the thirst was worse.

"Bacon and eggs, Hans." Gertrude didn't turn around. "You should have a good breakfast before you drive to Berlin. And get the boy up."

The truck wedged into the barn opening exploded, a sound heard over the roar of the television. She startled then, turning from the stove to the window.

"Hans won't be going to Berlin." Kolya kept his gun on the old man—Lisette trained her gun on Gertrude.

They swung around almost in unison. Gertrude glanced out the kitchen window at the burning barn. "Hans?"

"In the barn," Kolya said.

"No." She let out a wail of anguish.

Lisette motioned with the gun. "Shut up. Sit down."

The old man's mouth worked but nothing came out.

Gertrude continued to wail. Then the wailing took the form of words. "Monstrous. You're monstrous."

"We were kinder to Hans than he would've been to us. Sit," Kolya said.

Gertrude flopped into a chair. Tears streamed down her face. She stared at Lisette. "And yesterday you ate my cake. At my table. Hans should've killed you then. If only Frederick had called a little earlier."

"Frederick called?" Lisette asked.

"I ran to the barn as fast as I could. To tell Hans to kill you too." Gertrude was rocking back and forth. "I should've known. I should've known."

"Traitor. Whore," the old man burst out.

Had Lisette not decided to try to save Kolya, she would have been in the kitchen when Frederick called. Her moment of conscience hadn't made much difference to him—Kolya had already guessed that he was marked for death and planned to stay in the cellar—but it saved her. He stole a glance at her. Judging from her expression, she realized the same thing. But that wasn't important right now.

Lisette backed to the sink and poured two glasses of water. She handed one to Kolya.

"Day X. What are the targets?" Lisette gulped down liquid and then aimed her gun at Gertrude's face.

"You might want to answer her question. She really does like to kill people." Kolya drained the glass of water. He could drink another and still be thirsty.

Gertrude gripped the arms of her chair. "I don't know." Her voice trailed off in a wail.

"But you do." Kolya addressed the old man.

The old man picked up his coffee and drank without speaking.

This was going to take too much time. "Keep them here," he said to Lisette. "Xavier knows. He's probably upstairs in his room. If he doesn't give me the information, I'll shoot him."

He had no intention of shooting Xavier unless the kid tried to shoot him. But he assumed Gertrude would take the threat seriously.

Gertrude screamed. "Not my boy. No."

"Then talk." Lisette stepped closer to the stove and fished a piece of bacon from the pan. While keeping her grip on the gun, she ate greedily and then scooped out another slice.

"Tell them, old man." Gertrude spat out the words. "I don't know anything. But he," she pointed to the old man, "he knows."

The old man pressed lips together.

"Just shoot him," Lisette said. "I'd do it, but it would be more appropriate if you did."

It'd be appropriate. Kolya thought of his grandmother weeping for her cousin Simka, shot in a pit at Babi Yar. It would be not just appropriate—it would be just.

"Jew." The old man spoke softly but distinctly. "At least admit the truth. Or are you ashamed?"

"Do you really think provoking me is the most intelligent move right now?" As much he loathed the old Nazi and wanted to avenge the people slaughtered by the Einsatzgruppen, his objective was preventing a terror attack. Unlike the piece of garbage sitting at the table, he wasn't a cold-blooded killer. But using threats to get the information to stop a neo-Nazi assault was perfectly acceptable.

"Day X. Where? Who? Or I shoot. Her first." He indicated Gertrude. "Then you."

"Stop!! Don't." A new voice, Xavier, stood in the doorway, barefoot and in his pajamas. He carried a laptop under his arm. "Not mama. Not great grandfather. Papa's computer. It will have everything you want."

"I thought Frederick told your father not to put information online." Kolya trained his gun on Xavier. He didn't see any weapons—just the computer. But he wasn't taking chances. After a word to Lisette, he crossed the room and patted the boy down. Then he took possession of the laptop.

"My father didn't put anything online. But he also didn't do everything Frederick told him to do. He was writing the story of Germany Now. For history. He said he wanted my grandchildren to know what we did. He wanted me to know his part—if something happened to him."

"Sit down, Xavier." Kolya carried the laptop to the other side of the table, set it down, and opened it. "Password."

"Don't give the Jew anything." The old man's anger was directed at his great grandson.

"If the old bastard moves, shoot him." Kolya told Lisette. "Password, Xavier."

Xavier stuttered out a series of letters and numbers.

Kolya typed in the password and found the document quickly. *Blut und Erde.* Blood and Soil. *Funny. Hans couldn't even come up with an original title.* He'd written almost ninety pages, detailing his time in Germany Now, with a lot of ramblings about race, immigrants, and Jews. Kolya skimmed to the end where, as anticipated, Hans had detailed the plans for Day X, and then he read with closer attention. It was a list of horrors. First—various "acts of terror" by people pretending to be Muslim against government figures in Bonn and in Cologne. Local pro-immigrant leaders in towns around Germany would be assassinated, and their bodies removed. *That explained the body bags.* The Leader would travel to Berlin to declare a state of emergency in front of the Bundestag and in the company of the Chancellor.

Once the Leader was inside the hall, Germany Now would converge at the Brandenburg Gate, march to the Reichstag, overwhelm the small security force that would be on duty, push into the legislative chamber, and force a vote of no confidence in the Chancellor, simultaneously voting in the Leader as the new Chancellor. The Leader would then appoint Frederick Vice Chancellor.

After the vote, opponents of Germany Now would be shot.

The head of the police force that protected the Bundestag would ensure that reinforcements weren't sent. All security cameras in and around the Reichstag would be shut down. Attacks on the Berlin city police and the military headquarters in Bonn would ensure no other interference.

It was the planning for a coup, and it had the possibility of succeeding. Whether the Leader could maintain control or not, a lot of people were going to die.

Kolya pulled up an email account that he used for emergencies and quickly typed a message summarizing what he'd read before attaching the manuscript and sending it to the team. For good measure, he also sent it to the head of the ECA, Margaret Bradford. Maybe if the right people could be alerted in time, they could stop Day X. Maybe. If the right people weren't sympathizers.

There was another solution. Cut off the head, and the snake dies. Two snakes to kill. The Leader and Frederick.

He closed the laptop and turned his attention back to Xavier.

"You were meeting at the Brandenburg Gate today? What time?"

"Ten thirty." His tone had gone from frightened to somber.

Kolya would need to leave soon to make it to Berlin in time. "And the identity of the Leader?"

"If Papa knew, he didn't tell me." The teen swallowed hard. "I didn't want to kill you, you know. I thought you were okay. I tried to talk to Papa—talk him out of killing you. He might have listened to me. But you killed him and my grandfather."

"I gave them a chance to surrender and live, which is more than they offered me." Kolya shifted his gaze to the old Nazi, who was glowering at the boy.

"Do you think there's more to learn here?" Lisette asked.

"Not really. Now, I need to get back to Berlin."

"I'm coming, too."

"Of course."

"And them?" She indicated the three: Gertrude rocking and sobbing, the old man glaring, and Xavier sitting quietly, hands folded. "They could contact Frederick. If Frederick knows that we know, and that we're alive..."

"Maybe he'll call it off. Not the worst thing," Kolya said.

"Frederick won't call it off. He'll just be waiting for us." She touched his arm. "I know you don't want to do what has to be done. But they're a danger."

Kolya wasn't the only one who understood what she was saying.

Xavier and Gertrude stared at him in terror. Only the old man's expression remained unchanged.

"No." Kolya shook his head. "There's a basement where Hans kept his beer. We can lock them in."

"Don't be stupid. How many people," she pointed to the old Nazi, "did he kill?"

If it'd only been the old man, Kolya would've had a hard time resisting the argument. But it wasn't.

"Xavier is fifteen."

"He was going to help tie you up and then feed you alive to hogs. He was going to help his father kill more people. Gertrude told Hans to kill me."

They locked gazes.

"It's not necessary," Kolya said softly. "And I don't murder children."

"You think any of them deserve mercy?"

"It's not about them."

* * * * *

The entrance to the cellar was at the far end of the living room. They filed from the kitchen to the living room, Gertrude in front, the old man next, and then the teen, with Kolya and Lisette following.

Once inside the living room, the old man darted to the side, surprisingly fast given his age. He grabbed a shotgun leaning against the wall in the corner, and swung around, aiming at Kolya.

Feeling something close to gratitude, Kolya shot the old man in the chest. He collapsed, but he didn't die immediately. Kolya crossed the room, whispered in German, "For the Jewish children," and finished him with a shot to the forehead.

Xavier and Gertrude had dropped to the floor, and Lisette stood with her HK-91 pointed down at them. Lisette motioned with her gun. "Cellar."

62

COLOGNE, GERMANY

THEY ARRIVED AT THE BfV early, 7:00 a.m., before most of the German personnel. Jonathan didn't particularly enjoy early hours, but the first text from Kolya—at around 6:00 a.m.—stating that Day X was commencing made it necessary. He alerted Hannah Abt, who stated that she'd be in her office and waiting to hear from him when he had more details.

They waited in their office: Jonathan, nervous, Elizabeth less so.

"He broke cover to text us," Jonathan said. "He could be in trouble."

"I'm not one of Petrov's biggest fans, but he's competent." Elizabeth yawned.

"Even competent people get killed." Jonathan checked his watch. Almost an hour since the text.

"Yeah, but worrying does nothing." Elizabeth yawned again. "While we're waiting, I'm going to go pick up some coffee from the cafeteria. You want?"

"Fine. Get me one too."

Two minutes after she left, the email came in. Kolya's summary of the plan and the attached manuscript. He called Hannah Abt's office.

"I have details. I'm coming up. Five minutes."

"My vice presidents are here now," Hannah's voice was careful. "I can meet with you in half an hour."

If the information that Kolya had sent was accurate, the Leader would be before the Bundestag in a few hours, proclaiming a national emergency.

"You could be a target, Hannah."

"You and Ms. Owen should stop by to say goodbye. I'm pleased that you're wrapping everything up."

She was being coy. Was she in danger—or did she think she could uncover which one of her vice presidents was the Leader?

Maybe, but it was a dangerous game. He decided against waiting for Elizabeth to return. He strode down the hall, texting Elizabeth to meet him at Hannah's office. She replied instantly. *Coming. Wait for me.*

But seconds could make the difference between life and death.

I'm going in. Just get there as fast as you can.

He had to pass through security to get onto the third floor, and that took precious minutes. But once through security, the hallway was empty.

Hannah's door was shut. Jonathan stepped to the side of the door, listened, and heard nothing. He then rapped sharply, drawing his gun.

The door swung open, and Arnold stood in the doorway, his face stricken, but his right hand was not visible.

"It was Reiner." The words were choked out. "I warned Hannah that we weren't paying enough attention to jihadists. I called the Chancellor last night about the possibility of an imminent attack by Muslim radicals. This morning, I called Hannah. She asked Reiner and me to meet here. When I arrived…" His right hand was still obscured. "Reiner killed her and tried to kill me. I knew he had connections in the Muslim community. I didn't realize he'd been radicalized. I've called for help."

"Reiner's dead?"

"Yes. And Hannah. Help will be here any second."

But Jonathan neither saw nor heard any help arriving. No rush of emergency personnel. Which meant that Arnold had called no one.

"Put your hands up, Arnold." He aimed his gun at Arnold's chest.

"For God's sake, Jonathan. You know me. I've visited your home. Is this because I've been dating Elizabeth? I'm the good guy here. I have a meeting with Chancellor Jung in two hours in Berlin to brief her on the threat."

"Fine. We can sort it all out when security gets here. Meanwhile, put your hands up." Jonathan caught a glimpse of Arnold's right hand. "And drop the gun."

Arnold darted to the side and fired.

Jonathan fired at the same time.

BERLIN, GERMANY

In his office, Ben Rosenberg read the email and skimmed the pages of the manuscript. His first thought was to grab his wife and their children, get in the car, and drive. *Get out of Germany.* A flood of terror similar to what he'd experienced in the aftermath of the playacting of Tehila's murder almost paralyzed him. But then, he remembered what had pulled him back: his wife, his friends, and the people he worked with at the Institute. He pushed the fear down and summoned his staff: Ernestina, Lena, and the twins. There were also a few volunteers in the building. He called them in as well.

He was still frightened for himself and for his family. But he was frightened for more than himself and his own loved ones; he was frightened for all the people who'd envisioned a different kind of future. For the people who were his friends. For the country that had become his adopted home.

Once everyone assembled, he explained what he had in mind: A flash mob to counter Germany Now. They had almost a hundred thousand subscribers and supporters. Send out an alert. If enough people showed up, they could stop Germany Now from accessing the Reichstag. "We'll call it the White Rose Mob."

White Rose had been the revered resistance movement to the Nazis formed by German college students during World War II, an effort that cost the organizers their lives. Honoring the resistance of ordinary Germans to hate fascism seemed appropriate for an effort by contemporary Germans opposed to the odious ideology of a new generation of Nazis.

"Are you asking us to stand in front of neo-Nazis armed with weapons? We'll just be mowed down," Lena said.

"Not standing there, no. Pacifism doesn't stop Nazis. We're going to fight. With whatever weapons we have." Ben understood her fear. "But not in front. Not the best tactic."

"It's dangerous," Ahmet said. "Frederick Bauer and his followers are killers."

"So is doing nothing dangerous," Ben said. "If the Nazis could have been stopped in 1931, think how many people wouldn't have died."

He was a little surprised at his own words, given his paralysis following the show assassination attempt. But he was already fighting Nazis, just not physically. It was time for something more active. He'd never considered himself a person of action. He worked for change through words and persuasion. Sometimes it wasn't enough.

He thought of the nearby train station where Jews had been deported to killing centers. He thought of the Memorial to the Murdered Jews of Europe, the silent concrete blocks testifying to the six million victims who'd died so horribly.

He owed it to all of them.

"You should call your wife," Hasan said.

"I have a lot of calls to make. She'll be one of the first. But you need to send out texts to our supporters. We'll go over the wording."

"Ernestina and I will make calls." Lena sent him a frown of worry. "To people we know personally. To organizations that'd be on board."

"Get going. We have a few hours. That's it." He'd call Teo and lay out the plan.

* * * * *

At a crowded restaurant in the heart of Berlin, Frick and Teo ate breakfast, which for Frick consisted of sausages and cheese on bread and for Teo, apple pancakes. The noise from adjoining tables was almost deafening, which made it a less risky place to talk as well as to fill up with good German food. Frick knew it'd be a long day, and sugar wasn't going to do it for him. He needed real food.

But Teo was still young enough to burn through sugar.

"Email from Kolya." Teo had his phone on the table in front of him.

"Open it." Frick preferred to finish his food, but he figured Teo would let him know if Petrov had come up with anything.

And he did.

"Shit."

"What?"

"All hell's breaking loose today."

"Yeah?" Frick chewed his mouthful of sausage and bread, then swallowed. "Tell."

"Read it yourself."

Frick wiped the grease off his hands and clicked his email open. Then he repeated the curse. "Shit. Double shit."

"What do we do?" Teo asked.

Frick was already on his phone. "Egan's team leader. He makes the call." If Frick knew anything from his twenty years in various government services, it was to follow the hierarchy. Egan, as team leader of the operation, would be making the call on the next move.

But Egan didn't pick up. Frick tried Elizabeth Owen. She didn't pick up either.

"Call Bradford." Teo referred to the head of the agency, their boss, whom Frick had met only a few times.

Egan was the one who talked to Bradford. It was the team leader's responsibility to report to the head of the agency. But Frick couldn't reach Egan. Maybe let protocol go. He put in the call to Margaret Bradford.

Her voice was brisk. "I have Mr. Petrov's email in front of me. I'm trying to get hold of the President, but there's a crisis with North Korea moving troops to the DMZ. He's unavailable."

"Can't you call your German counterparts?"

"Something happened to Hannah Abt. I can't get through. I've been trying the head of the Federal Intelligence Service and the Military Security Service, but no luck there so far. I've also put in a call to Chancellor Jung, but I fear it'll take someone on a higher level than me to get through to her."

"Things are going down in a few hours."

"I'm aware. But the call needs to come from someone higher in the American government than I am, and they're all focused on the prospect of a war with North Korea."

"Jesus."

"I suspect Jesus won't be of much help. The Reichstag police and the Berlin police will be on the scene. They'll handle it."

"Not according to Petrov," Frick said.

"I'm doing what I can on my end. You do what you can on yours."

They were fucked. The operation, democracy in Germany. Everything was fucked. *Get another beer and ride it out.* Frick turned to Teo, but Teo was on a call.

Teo clicked his phone off. "That was Ben Rosenberg. He has a plan."

63

WHEN ELIZABETH STEPPED OFF the elevator on the top floor, she saw no one at the security post that had to be passed to get to Hannah Abt's office. She saw personnel running in the direction of the President's office. She broke into a run.

More people were exiting the elevator behind her.

Two security officers knelt on the floor in front of Hannah's office, administering first aid to someone lying prone. With a jolt, she saw that it was Jonathan.

She dropped to the floor next to him.

"Jesus Christ. Jonathan."

One of the men applied pressure to a wound in Jonathan's chest. Recognizing her, he spoke in English. "He is still alive. Ambulance is coming."

She placed her hand over his. It was warm. Jonathan's chest rose and fell. And the blood was everywhere.

Just a few minutes ago, she'd been making fun of him—as usual.

"What happened?" She could barely choke out the question.

"It was Reiner Muller," the second man said. "He shot President Abt and your friend. We are lucky that Vice President Shafer was here to stop him."

"Stop him? Muller is in custody?"

"No, dead."

"He'd become a jihadist," the medic pressing on Jonathan chest added. "Vice President Shafer wrestled the gun away."

Elizabeth's head was spinning. None of this made sense. "And Shafer is where?"

"On his way to meet with Chancellor Jung. She requested that he join her."

"In Berlin?" She'd only skimmed the email sent by Kolya, but this would fit the pattern that was described. An artificial emergency blamed on Muslim extremists followed by a neo-Nazi takeover of the government. "No one stopped him?"

"No reason to," the medic said.

She felt a pressure on her hand and turned her attention back to Jonathan. His eyes were open and fixed on her. He was conscious. She leaned closer, her ear to his mouth.

"Arnold. Shot. Vest." His voice was barely audible.

"He shot you, and he's wearing a vest?" she asked him.

"Yes." His voice was barely audible.

She squeezed his hand. "I'll get the word to Frick. Just don't fucking die, Jonathan. Do you hear me?"

The depth of her own fear surprised her a little. Jonathan could be so annoying. The ease with which he moved through his privileged, rich, white world, taking for granted what so many people like her had struggled to attain and might never be able to do so. And yet, she knew that if he died, she'd feel an emptiness.

He didn't answer, but he pressed her fingers.

* * * * *

Arnold boarded the Gulfstream at Cologne-Bonn airport, approximately eighteen minutes north of the city. He'd considered stopping at his apartment to change shirts—the round fired by Jonathan Egan had ripped a hole in the cloth that was above his heart—but he'd decided that he liked the look. It showed that he'd barely escaped with his life, which was true. Had he not decided to wear a Kevlar vest for the day's events, he would've been killed.

Fortunately, Jonathan wouldn't be alive to contradict the version that he'd told the security people and Chancellor Jung.

He'd known Christina Jung for years and had prepared her for the event for months. After speaking to Frederick the previous night, he called her to express his deep concern about Reiner—and to say that Hannah had dismissed his warnings. When he called after the shootings, Christina had accepted his explanation and his request to inform the Bundestag of the grave threat that faced them all.

He'd arrive in Berlin in style, after a fifty-minute chartered flight as opposed to a six-hour drive. It cost a lot of money, but he had it to burn from his secret donors around the world.

He seated himself on a deep leather chair in the middle of the plane and accepted a glass of champagne from the flight attendant. She looked like she had Arab ancestry—pretty, brown hair swept into a bun, large dark eyes, and a slender figure. He wanted to preserve the beauty of native German women, but that didn't mean he couldn't appreciate women who didn't fit the type.

He felt a slight tinge of regret that he'd had to shoot Jonathan. In some ways, he liked him—and Jonathan's father, the former Senator, could be an influence in the States. He also was a little sorry that he hadn't managed to sleep with Elizabeth Owen. Good-looking woman, a lot of spirit. Sex with her would have been enjoyable, even if it was somewhat offensive to his ideas of racial purity. Although he was less rigid than his followers, who needed a strong hand and a strong leader. Maybe—after he was Chancellor —he'd invite Elizabeth for a visit.

But probably not. She wasn't completely stupid. If she suspected that he, and not Reiner, was the one who'd killed Jonathan, she might act on her own, even if not endorsed by the United States.

He expected the United States to do nothing once everything was finished and he was in office.

He was more worried about the Germany military. The plan was to take out the Minister of Defense and the Chief of Defense, who were in control of the military forces. The Vice Chief of Defense was a supporter. If all went well, Germany Now would control the military.

With control of the military, Arnold would control Germany.

Not that it mattered. Once the Bundestag voted him Chancellor, he'd be Chancellor. There was no mechanism to remove him except another vote by the Bundestag. And that wouldn't happen. Every politician who'd vote against him would be dead.

He checked his phone as the plane taxied. Nothing in the news yet about the shooting at the BfV. It would break soon, though, and the first news story, the one that his people would plant, would be picked up by every other media outlet.

Nothing from Frederick either. That was good. Frederick knew to keep off the phones and the internet now that things were moving. But he and his followers would be there outside the Reichstag.

Arnold would give a rousing speech about the dangers from Middle Eastern immigrants before Germany Now made its move.

64

BUNDESAUTOBAUN A11

LISETTE DROVE WITH A sandwich of bacon and eggs on her lap and coffee in the cup holder. After locking Gertrude and Xavier in the basement, they'd both washed the dirt from their hands and faces and helped themselves to the food and cups of coffee. Kolya, next to her, was finishing his own egg sandwich. He'd given her a glance before taking a sip of the coffee.

Did he still have reservations about her? "It's not poisoned."

"Thought never crossed my mind."

"You hesitated before drinking."

"I like my coffee lukewarm." He took another tentative sip and then drank half the cup.

The coffee, as much as the food, was essential. Neither of them had slept more than a few hours, and she felt exhausted with the aftermath of the adrenaline rush. Still, she was pleased that Kolya had killed the former SS officer.

"Tell me you didn't enjoy killing that old Nazi."

"I'm not sure enjoyment is the right word. I'll admit to a feeling of satisfaction that I killed him on behalf of the Jewish people he murdered."

He'd been moralistic about her killing, and she liked that she got even this much of a concession. And that he was opening up a little. "I hope you appreciate that I didn't shoot Xavier or Gertrude."

"I do. I hope your restraint wasn't just for my approval."

It was at least in part. If she'd been alone, she probably would have killed them too. "I don't kill innocents." Although neither Xavier nor Gertrude was innocent. "You're the only mistake I've made. Almost made. Did you ever kill the wrong person by mistake?"

"Not as far as I know. I don't do targeted killings. Generally. I do make some exceptions. The old Nazi was one, although arguably it was self-defense. I'll also make exceptions for the Leader and Frederick."

"You don't have to worry about taking out the Leader. He's mine." She had spent her entire life seeking to avenge her father, and she deserved the kill, especially if he were the man she'd been hunting. "Don't rob me of this."

"Do you have a speech prepared?"

"What?"

"Something like—'Hello. My name is Lisette. You killed my father. Prepare to die.'"

He had quoted from *The Princess Bride*. "Are you making fun of me?"

"A little. Not that I don't understand why you'd want to avenge your father. But this is about more than revenge. It's about stopping a coup and mass killings. If I have a shot at either the Leader or Frederick, I'll take it." He was on his phone, texting.

"But you won't stop me from taking the shot if I'm there first."

"Why would I? Just don't miss."

"I never have. Except for what happened with you." She hesitated on the next question but decided to ask. "What does your girlfriend think about your job?"

"Fiancée. She's not crazy about it, but she tolerates it." He was sending a second text as he answered.

"You're engaged?" She hadn't realized just how much she'd been hoping he wasn't really involved with someone. But he was. The text she'd read the night she'd tried to lure him into drinking the monkshood-laced peppermint schnapps hadn't been cover; it had been real. Oddly the fact that he was engaged made him more attractive—as did his fidelity to the unknown woman—while eliminating any possibility of her sleeping with him.

What had intrigued her about Kolya—she still didn't know his last name—was not just that he, like her, was a capable killer, but that he nevertheless adhered to a moral code. That added to the bond that she'd felt over the last twenty-four hours, and the fact that he had a hot body had raised her interest. But his being engaged ruled that out. She wasn't interested in a quick fuck. She'd had more than enough of those.

Moreover, if he cheated on his fiancée, it would mean he wasn't the person she thought he was. He would be just another jerk, like so many others she'd slept with. What she liked about Kolya was that he seemed… different.

With a little effort, she let go of the fantasy. "I guess that's why it was easy for you to resist when I tried to fuck you."

"It wasn't *that* easy. You're a very attractive woman. If I wasn't in love with someone else… I'd probably be dead now."

She had to laugh. "I would be too, I guess." Since, if she had succeeded in poisoning him, she wouldn't have been with him in the cellar when Gertrude took Frederick's phone call, ordering her murder. "We both owe your fiancée thanks."

"If we survive today, I'll tell her."

"You think we won't?"

"Good chance we won't. It's going to be bloody."

His phone buzzed. "Updates?" He listened for a minute before responding. "Okay, we're headed back to Berlin. Okay. We'll meet you. Where?" A silence. "Did Jonathan call Bradford?" A pause then words that she didn't understand—presumably Russian—the same words she'd heard him use several times while digging out of the barn cellar. Then he switched back to English, his voice strained. "How bad?" Another long pause. "Where is he?" A deep breath. "Elizabeth's with him?" Another pause. "And Bradford?" Another long silence. "Okay. Okay. Understood."

He clicked off his phone.

"What?" she asked.

"It's begun."

"What's happened?"

"The Leader is Arnold Shafer, a vice president at the BfV, who just assassinated the president of the BfV and blamed it on a second vice president, whom he also murdered. He also shot my closest friend."

"He wasn't arrested?"

"Apparently, the security personnel and the Chancellor believed his story. And my friend wasn't able to counter it."

"Where is Shafer now?"

"Either in the air or in Berlin. My boss has been trying to get word of what's happening to the BND or to Chancellor Jung."

"We'll stop it." They'd be there in an hour, and she might finally have a chance at the man she'd been hunting her entire life. She glanced sideways at Kolya. "I'm going to kill him."

"One of us will."

65

BERLIN, GERMANY

FREDERICK AND THE MEMBERS of the Berlin group were waiting at the Brandenburg Gate by ten o'clock. It was a glorious September morning, endless blue sky with only a random cloud. Within his sight, trees were turning gold and crimson.

He took the beauty of the day as an omen.

He hadn't slept, but sleep was a luxury he could indulge in later. After killing Lisette's grandmother, he'd driven on, stopping at the homes of group leaders in smaller towns, alerting them to the change in schedule. Then he'd driven back to Berlin. After spending most of the previous day and night in the car, he'd showered, dressed, placed an HK-91 in a gym bag, and headed to Brandenburg Gate to wait for the troops to assemble.

They started to trickle in at a little after ten, in groups of twenty or thirty. Some had driven six hours, some only two.

By eleven o'clock, there should be somewhere between three and five thousand.

The other actions were critical. The Leader had taken the first step, but Germany Now had to take the next. Across the country, dedicated men who were willing to die for the cause would be rounding up and executing traitors.

His anger and pain at Lisette's betrayal was still there, simmering below the surface, but she was dead. He hoped it'd been a painful death. He would think about her later—how he had fucked up by allowing her to get so close to him—after he had installed the Leader as Germany's new Chancellor.

* * * * *

There were five vans and two cars. Five in each van. Everyone carrying an HK-91. Some of them were military. Everyone else was well trained. All of them had fake identification with names of Syrians or Germans of Turkish descent. Hair and skin had been darkened to give the appearance of Middle Easterners.

Gunter was in the front car. He'd intended for Peter to lead this assault while Gunter joined Frederick for the honor of ushering in the new era with the Leader as Chancellor. But Peter didn't have the courage or the stomach for what had to be done—so Peter had had to die. Gunter regretted it—he'd known Peter all his life, and they'd been friends—but it'd been necessary.

What he was doing now was also critical to a new and better Germany. He was willing to make the sacrifice—of his men—of himself. If he died, he'd be remembered as a hero.

He hoped he wouldn't, but he was willing.

The first van pulled into the *Platz der Luftbrücke*—a transportation circle around a green space—dominated by a three-pronged memorial to the Berlin Airlift, the operation after the end of World War II in which American and British pilots saved West Berlin from starvation after a Soviet blockade cut off all deliveries on land. The *Platz der Luftbrücke* had once been an international airport and now buildings around the circle were mostly government offices and, the reason the site had been chosen, the headquarters of the Berlin Police Department.

The next four vans and two cars pulled into the *Platz* after the first, all stopping directly in front of police headquarters and blocking traffic.

Gunter took a deep breath. He was the leader—which meant he was first. He steeled himself and then swung out of the van, his HK-91 lowered and ready, followed by his men. The drivers remained in place for the possible escape of any who survived the action.

Almost in unison, they shouted *Allah Akbar* and opened fire on police officers standing outside. Then they surged towards the building.

BONN, GERMANY

The Federal Minister of Defense had her office in the Hardthohe section of Bonn where the headquarters of the Federal Ministry of Defense was located. She was the official Commander in Chief of the Bundeswehr, the armed forces of Germany. That afternoon, she was scheduled to meet with the Chief of Defense in her office.

The entrance to the headquarters was guarded. Metal gates denied admission to those without authorization. But those authorized—including members of the armed forces—were allowed inside the gates even with their weapons. Three of the Germany Now members who were also soldiers stationed in Bonn had access to the Federal Ministry of Defense and were tasked with the assassination of both the minister of defense and the chief of defense.

The vice chief of defense would take over the military, and the vice chief supported the Leader.

They wrote statements to be published online after the fact should they not survive, claiming to have converted to Islam and to being members of a Syrian jihadist group. It was all part of the plan, coordinated with the attack on the Berlin police headquarters, and timed to coincide with Arnold's arrival at the Reichstag. It was critical that the military be in friendly hands and ordered to support the new Chancellor.

* * * * *

In Hamburg, in Leipzig, in Frankfort, in Munich, in towns all around Germany, small bands of armed men readied themselves to storm private homes and offices. The targets were local political officials who'd either supported immigration rights or those who'd most loudly opposed Germany Now. Each team had body bags in their possession: as planned, they would not commit the killings where the public could see either the act or the corpses. They would remove the targets, kill them, place bodies in bags, and bury the bodies in forested areas with quicklime.

It was a lesson learned from the Einsatzgruppen. If mass killings were hidden, the perpetrators could claim innocence and even attack as delusional any who dared to expose the truth.

66

BERLIN, GERMANY

AT TEN O'CLOCK, BEN Rosenberg unlocked the door to his house. *Rachel and the boys should be home.* He'd warned her to pick up the children and go home, but he wanted to see Levi and Natan just in case. Stepping into the living room, he saw the boys sprawled on the couch, watching a video. Sitting next to them was Claire, an artist in her late seventies whose work had been featured in Rachel's gallery, and who sometimes babysat for them.

Claire was chatting with the boys about the video, something animated that Ben didn't recognize. Then she turned to Ben. "Rachel is in the kitchen. She'll be out in a minute."

"And you're here—why?"

"You should ask your wife."

"I will." He hugged each of the boys, telling them how much he loved them. Levi was still young enough to hug back, even though he was focused on the video. Natan squirmed out of the embrace, obviously embarrassed. Ben released his grip and kissed Natan on the cheek, which embarrassed him further.

Rachel emerged from the kitchen followed by five people, her partner at the studio and four more artists, all German, all under thirty. Rachel, uncharacteristically, was dressed in jeans and a sweatshirt. She wore a white baseball cap and carried a small backpack.

"What's going on?" he asked.

She indicated the others. "We're coming with you."

He shook his head. "It's too dangerous. I can't let you."

She placed hands on her hips. "You can't *let* me?"

He glanced over at their children. "The boys."

"Claire is here."

"That's not what I meant." He stepped closer to her and lowered his voice. "They need at least one parent to survive."

"If something happens to us, Claire has my parents' number. I've already called them."

"You told them what was happening?"

"Of course not. I just said that they may have to help out with Levi and Natan, and they were more than willing. I'm coming, whether you like it or not. This is my fight, too. For the boys. For their future."

"That's why I'm doing it—for our children. And for all the murdered. We can't let it happen again. But that doesn't mean we both have to risk our lives."

She indicated the five people near her. "My friends are. You are too. From what you said, you need as many people as you can get." Then she lowered her voice. "I wrote a letter to the boys. If the worst happens, they should know why. What we stood for. What we thought worth dying for."

"Do you understand that we're going to be attacking them? We won't be just passively blocking their way."

"Yes, I do understand that. I spoke to Ahmet. Are you trying to protect me from being killed or from committing violence? Or from seeing you?"

"All of it." The idea of his gentle wife fighting Nazis was bad enough. That she might see him striking people, even possibly killing them, was worse.

"Don't be ridiculous. I won't think any less of you for doing what I'm prepared to do. Will you?"

"Think less of you?" He thought his heart might explode with love. "Of course not."

"Then stop arguing and let's go. It is in the hands of *HaShem*."

"*Baruck HaShem*." It was indeed in God's hands, although God could be whimsical. He hoped this time that God would be on their side.

* * * * *

Kolya struggled awake as Lisette parked the car at the Parkhaus Adlon, a three-minute walk from the Brandenburg Gate. The Reichstag was just a few minutes farther.

"You were having a nightmare. At least that's what I gathered from what you were muttering."

"It happens. Not that often these days." There was an inch of coffee left in the cup in the cup holder. He drained it.

She unbuckled the seat belt. "Are you going to tell me what happened to you? Why you have trouble in dark cellars? And those scars?"

He opened the car door. "Afterwards. Perhaps." She did deserve something of an explanation, but he hated talking about what had happened to him. Anyway, this wasn't the time. He needed to focus on the task at hand. He swung out of the car, opened the back door, and from the seat picked up the duffle bag that contained two HK-91s.

He'd sent Alex a brief text earlier. *Will be out of touch for the day. I love you very much.*

She'd responded. *Love you more. Don't get killed.*

His text had tipped her off that something was about to happen. He regretted that she'd worry, but he needed to send the text, in case he was killed. In any event, the worry would be of short duration. One way or the other, everything would be over within a few hours.

From the Parkhaus, they walked along the Berenstrasse. On either side of the street, groups of people, mostly young, but some middle-aged, all white, mostly male but with a few women, also carrying duffle bags, hurried. Lisette had wrapped a scarf around her head and turned her collar up. Kolya wore a cap and sunglasses. Not much of a disguise, if Frederick spotted either of them. But Frederick was waiting for the arrival of his militia at the Brandenburg Gate, and the

318

mass of people thronging in that direction didn't pay any attention to Kolya or Lisette. They were intent on the path forward.

Kolya and Lisette crossed the Ebertstrasse into the Tiergarten, avoiding the Brandenburg Gate, where members of Germany Now were heading.

In the park, they walked under trees turning to gold.

Near the Memorial to the Roma and Sinti—who had also been murdered en masse by the Nazis—another crowd was gathering. To his surprise, Kolya estimated that it was at least a thousand people, and growing by the minute. This crowd was different from the groups traveling towards the Brandenburg Gate: there were women and men, white, brown, and black. Some wore white baseball caps. Some wore dried white flowers. Some wore white T-shirts; others, white hoodies. Young and old. They carried tire irons, hammers, sticks, and bats. A few, like Kolya, carried duffle bags that Kolya hoped contained guns.

He searched for a familiar face and saw three near the edge of the crowd. He motioned to Lisette. "Come on."

Teo and Frick stood on the edge of the growing crowd. Teo caught sight of Kolya and grinned. Frick nodded a brisk hello. And next to Teo, another familiar face, Tehila. Teo and Frick wore white caps. Tehila, a white hoodie.

"Everyone, this is Lisette. Lisette, my team. Frick. Teo." He paused and then shot a glance at Lisette. "And my victim—Tehila. Tehila, I thought you were back in the States."

She shook her head. "France. I decided to return to Berlin for Day X. Can't resist the lure of killing Nazis."

"Me neither," Lisette said.

All three of them eyed Lisette.

"Didn't she poison you?" Teo was always blunt.

"I'm a Nazi hunter. And he was playing a Nazi," Lisette said. "Very convincingly, too."

Tehila surveyed their dirt-stained clothes. "And what have the two of you been up to since?"

Tehila and Alex were good friends. Kolya decided to answer the question but not the insinuation. "Digging out of a barn cellar where some of Bauer's men trapped us. Barely made it out before they set the barn on fire. Jonathan?"

Frick shook his head. "In surgery. Won't know for hours. Elizabeth's there. You can check on him after we deal with today's shitstorm. By the way, there have been attacks in Bonn on the Ministry of Defense. In Berlin—on the police headquarters."

"Do you have a picture of Arnold Shafer?" Kolya asked.

Teo pulled out his phone and handed it to Kolya. Kolya studied the image, and then he showed it to Lisette. "Is this the man who shot your father?"

She took the phone. "His face has changed, but I think so."

He could hear the uncertainty. "You may never know for sure either way."

"I know." She handed the phone back to Teo. "I still want to be the one to kill him, but if I can't, one of you…"

"Agreed." Frick nodded.

Kolya heard an amplified voice from the front of the still-increasing crowd. Ben Rosenberg, wearing a white baseball cap instead of a yarmulka, stood on a bench, an electric megaphone in his hands.

"Thank you for coming. People will be circulating to answer any questions and to hand out white flowers if needed. In fifteen minutes, we're going to move."

Kolya looked at the crowd and turned to Teo and Frick. "White flowers?"

"Gotta know who's who," Frick said. "Trying to minimize the chances that our side will attack the wrong people. Assume anyone wearing white is one of ours."

"White in honor of White Rose," Teo said. "Ben has dubbed this the White Rose Mob. Kind of catchy."

Kolya nodded approval and accepted a white flower from a woman circulating through the crowd, pinning it to his shirt. It felt odd, as if he were about to join in a wedding party instead of a deadly fight.

"What's the plan?" Kolya asked.

"Not sure of all the details," Frick said. "But generally, they're going to try to stop Bauer's people by following Germany Now supporters to the Reichstag and attacking from the rear. Meanwhile, the three of us, now the five of us, will maneuver through the crowd to get a crack at Shafer and Bauer. We're all wearing vests, so we have a little extra protection."

"You don't happen to have two extra vests?" Kolya asked.

"Sorry," Frick said.

"You can have mine," Teo said.

Kolya shook his head. He wasn't going to protect himself at Teo's expense.

"Rosenberg's people don't have enough guns," Lisette said. "They're armed with shovels and bats. A lot of people are going to get killed."

"Possibly. But hopefully the White Rose Mob will wreak sufficient havoc for one of us to eliminate Bauer and Shafer," Tehila said.

Kolya hoped so.

67

BERLIN, GERMANY

ARNOLD SHAFER PAUSED ON the steps leading into the Reichstag. It was an impressive building, majestic with its pillars, the front offering a view of the traditional, and the glass dome, suggesting modernity. He'd keep the building in use in some capacity after he consolidated power. Downgrade the powers of the Bundestag so that it only passed legislation he approved of and fill the seats with his own people, of course. It wouldn't be hard to do after the events of Day X—politicians who opposed him would mostly be dead. And keeping the Bundestag in some form would still offer the vague appearance of democracy without the annoying opposition of an actual democratic system.

From where he stood, he could hear murmurs of sound from the crowd that he knew was gathering at the Brandenburg Gate and that within minutes of his entrance into the hall would begin its march on the building. He'd checked and double-checked the timing with Frederick. He'd be inside the Reichstag, giving his speech, when everything began.

The checkpoint to enter the Reichstag was guarded by a few bored police officers who barely gave Arnold a glance. They would pose no threat to the three-to-five-thousand armed militia that would be arriving. Everything was going as planned. As directed, the head of the *Bundestagpolizei* police force guarding the Reichstag had done nothing to reinforce the few security officers at the door. The attack on the Berlin police had begun. The attack in Bonn would have the military concentrating on Islamist extremists and would put a supporter in charge. Hopefully, throughout the German states, the attacks on pro-immigration and anti-Germany Now politicians would have also commenced.

But his immediate focus was here, on the Reichstag. There would be no police and no military opposition to the oncoming storm.

He stepped past security and was greeted by one of the five vice presidents of the Bundestag, Petra Huber, a young attractive woman with wrong political views from the state of Hesse who regarded him with an expression of anxiety. "What's happening? There are rumors of attacks."

"It's why I'm here."

He followed her towards the grand chamber where the elected members of the Bundestag, and Chancellor Jung, waited.

* * * * *

Frederick basked in the energy emanating from the crowd. It was hard to make out individual faces, but it wasn't necessary. The crowd belonged to him—and he would have the glory of leading them into battle. His closest allies stood next to him. He'd have liked Hans and Gunter to be up there with him as well, but Gunter was sacrificing himself for the greater cause. Hans, his family and his followers, had to be out there somewhere, and they too would be part of history.

He raised the electronic megaphone to his mouth for his final exhortation. "This is OUR country. We are taking it back. Now and forever. Germany for Germans! Follow me." He heard the echo of the chant, Germany for Germans, rumbling through the crowd, growing in intensity.

He started for the Reichstag, Heinrich next to him, and the crowd flowed behind them like water seeking lower ground.

* * * * *

Ben Rosenberg walked hand-in-hand with his wife. The twins were somewhere behind him. Behind them, the crowd had swelled to somewhere over fifteen hundred, but still outnumbered by Germany Now.

He knew that Tehila, Frick, Teo, Lisette, and Kolya were somewhere in that crowd. Theirs was the real job—the best chance of stopping Day X. His job, and that of everyone following him, was to give them that opportunity.

A calm descended on him. *What would happen, would happen.*

68

BERLIN, GERMANY

CHRISTINA JUNG, A SHORT stout woman with unnaturally red hair, welcomed Arnold warmly, in keeping with an acquaintance that dated back ten years. "I should have listened to you," she told him. "Thank you for coming all this way to speak. I'm naming you acting president of the BfV by the way."

"I'm honored, Chancellor." Arnold felt a twinge of sympathy for the Chancellor, but only a twinge. What had happened to Germany was her fault, and the fault of so many seated here inside this impressive chamber in the heart of the Reichstag. On the other hand, she'd given him a path to power.

He followed her to the podium past rows of purple seats filled with 598 elected representatives from the sixteen German states. The mass of the Bundestag was seated in a semi-circle in front of the podium, with three rows of seats facing the body of the chamber and flanking a raised seating area for the Bundestag President. A podium was situated immediately in front of the raised seating area, and a curved table in front of the podium.

Most of the seats were filled. The president and two vice presidents were seated behind the podium, waiting. As was the rest of the body. The Chancellor nodded to the president as she took the podium, Arnold at her side. She spoke first, introducing Arnold and, her voice breaking at times, informed the assembly of an attack at the BfV that had cost the life of Hannah Abt, and attacks by jihadists on the Berlin police. "Acting President Shafer saw the danger, and unfortunately our security people failed to act. He has important information to share about this crisis." She stepped aside and seated herself at the curved table in front of the podium.

Then it was Arnold's turn. He stood in front of the Bundestag, looking out at the semi-circle of seats and the balcony, filled with 598 members, savoring the moment, thinking of what this moment meant to him and to the German people. Then he began.

"We are faced with an unprecedented terror attack from within— from the immigrants we welcomed into our midst. From officials who should have been safeguarding our country but who have betrayed it."

He heard mutterings.

"Just this morning, I faced down a German who had converted to Islam and who had wormed his way up to the vice presidency of the BfV and then murdered both the president of the BfV, Hannah Abt, and a dear American friend while shouting *Allah Akbar*. He tried to kill me as well, but I managed to get the gun from him."

More horrified murmurs.

He took a deep breath and continued.

"The plot is massive and requires a massive response. Jihadists have attacked the Berlin police. The military headquarters. And, despite my warnings, nothing has been done." He then pointed to the Chancellor. "She has done nothing to safeguard this country from Islamic extremists. To the contrary, she has welcomed them."

He could hear them now, the shouts of Germany Now. Then gunshots. The members of the Bundestag, alarmed, stood, and turned.

He raised his hands.

"Stay in your seats. Our people, the true German people, are angry. They are willing to die to preserve Germany, and yet this body has failed to do just that."

The president banged a gavel and ordered him to sit. He ignored her.

The Chancellor stood and moved towards him. "Arnold, what are you doing?"

He needed the members of the Bundestag to believe that if they voted as he asked, they would survive. "Saving Germany."

* * * * *

Heinrich was the first up the steps of the Reichstag and into the building, followed closely by the rest of the Berlin group and Frederick. Trailing behind were thousands of Germany Now supporters, many of them openly carrying HK-91s.

Four officers of the Bundestagpolizei tried to block the doorway, while one called for help on his phone.

Frederick was the first to shoot, killing three of the officers standing in the doorway.

The last officer fled. Heinrich and the others opened fire, and the fleeing officer went down.

* * * * *

Ben Rosenberg grimly noted that there were at least twice as many people in Germany Now as there were in the White Rose Mob. Many of the neo-Nazis had unpacked guns as they walked. Most of Ben's people were armed with blunt instruments, with only a few carrying guns. But as he and the rest of the White Rose Mob fell in behind the trailing members of Germany Now, he put those disadvantages out of his mind.

The neo-Nazis were focused on the path forward, on breaching the Reichstag and taking the Bundestag. They were not checking who was directly behind them. And if any of them had looked behind, it hadn't yet registered that the men and women wearing white caps, white shirts, and white flowers were against them.

Ben scanned his people on the left side flanking Germany Now members and finally located the American agents. They were, in turn, watching him and waiting for his signal.

Shots from inside the building. It was time.

He glanced to his right. Rachel kept pace with him, her face determined. Next to her, the twins, Ahmet and Hasan.

He wanted to grab her hand, to tell her to go back, but she was right. There was pain but also comfort in having her at his side.

"I love you, Rachel." He thought she couldn't hear, but he was wrong.

"I love you, too. *Baruch HaShem*, may we triumph."

"*Baruch HaShem*. Now!" Ben snatched the baseball cap off his head and waved it three times.

The White Rose Mob surged forward, and he charged with them. He hit a man directly in front of him in the head with the bat he was carrying. Rachel next to him struck with a golf club. Ben hit a second man and then a third. Blood spurted. The men fell. The last row of Germany Now members crumpled as the White Rose Mob struck at heads with bats, tire irons, golf clubs, and with shovels. Nazis deeper into the crowd were shoved forward by those behind them.

Ben grabbed a gun from a man writhing on the ground. Out of the corner of his eye, he saw Ahmet do the same. He hesitated. *Thou shalt not kill.* But Germany Now was here to do just that—to kill members of the Bundestag. They would kill him, his wife, and his children without hesitation.

He raised the gun and fired at a man climbing the steps of the Reichstag, waving the Imperial Flag. The man fell forward, the flag dropping to the ground.

Ben felt both horror and elation.

Then he fired again, this time shooting directly in front of him, hitting several men. One in the head. Two in the back.

He saw heads shattering, more blood, a river of blood.

Next to him, he heard the explosion of gunfire as Ahmet and Hasan also fired guns, aiming at the men on the steps. As were other members of the White Rose Mob on either side of him. The sound was deafening.

And a dozen men dropped.

Ben and the others continued to fire.

Men ahead on the Reichstag steps turned around and shot back.

But with the White Rose Mob now intermingled with the Germany Now, the return fire downed neo-Nazis as well as Ben's people.

Neo-Nazis deeper in the crowd and unaware of the assault from behind assumed that the Germany Now supporters on the steps were firing on them. They raised guns and shot back, downing their fellow members. Then the neo-Nazis on the steps began to shoot at the neo-Nazis who were firing at them.

More people fell, dead or injured. Others pushed their way out of the crowd and ran.

The sound of the gunfire and the screams of the injured grew louder. The smell of blood was overwhelming.

Ben pressed forward, still firing.

69

BERLIN, GERMANY

LISETTE HEARD SHOTS INSIDE the Reichstag but waited until she saw Ben wave his cap. Then simultaneously with the charge of the White Rose Mob, she and the agents near her dashed towards the neo-Nazis climbing the stairs of the Reichstag.

Lisette raised the HK-91 to her shoulder.

"Don't shoot anyone who isn't a threat," Teo said.

"Fuck that," Frick said. "Shoot everyone."

"They're all threats." Lisette aimed her gun at a large man with the flag of Imperial Germany imprinted on the back of his jacket and fired. He went down.

Next to her Kolya shot anyone who turned in their direction. He grabbed Lisette's shoulder and pointed to a gap in the mob, up the far-left stairs into the Reichstag. She nodded her agreement.

Get to the Wolf. Arnold Shafer.

She headed for the gap in the mob with Kolya close on her heels. She assumed the other agents were following Kolya, but she didn't stop to look.

* * * * *

Frederick cast a glance over his shoulder to see chaos. His people on the steps were shooting down into the crowd. People in the crowd were shooting back. Dozens were on the ground. The air stank of gunpowder and blood. Many of the militia members who had followed him from the Brandenburg Gate to the Reichstag were no longer focused on moving forward but on the people behind, and the people behind were focused on those ahead, both groups firing almost blindly. He couldn't tell who was attacking and who was defending.

He'd figure it out. Whoever had attacked his force would pay dearly. After.

Unlike the fools who were now shooting each other, he and those closest to him remained intent on the goal. He still had close to a hundred men around him—not distracted by the chaos—and they were enough to do the job. They were armed, and the members of Bundestag were not. The police and the military weren't coming to the rescue. He sent twenty armed men to the balcony seating of the Bundestag on the second floor. He ordered another two dozen to follow him, and the rest to guard the hall should the attackers get too close.

If it was only a few of Germany Now who took over the Bundestag and forced the vote making the Leader into the Chancellor, the greater the glory to those who succeeded.

* * * * *

A few Bundestag members tried to block the doors to the chambers, but they were shot as the doors were forced open. Arnold shouted, "Quiet!" He could barely hear himself above the screaming, both inside the chamber, and from outside. No one else seemed to hear him either.

As Frederick and his followers spread out around the chamber, marching down four different aisles, pointing guns at the representatives, the vast room fell silent. At Frederick's order, his men confiscated phones. Then they positioned themselves to watch the representatives. In the balconies, his men also stationed themselves. Frederick joined Arnold in the front.

The legislators shrunk down in their seats as Arnold's gaze roved over the assembly.

"These people are angry that our country hasn't been defended, and they demand a leader who'll do what is necessary. It's time for a motion of no confidence in Chancellor Jung to remove her from office and to install someone who will put the interests of the German people first."

"You can't do this." A young woman from Lower Saxony with short black hair and a determined expression stood in protest. He knew who she was—a prominent gay rights and global warming activist.

"Sit down, shut up." Frederick aimed his gun at her.

She sat.

"Arnold, this is treason." Chancellor Jung, who still sat at the curved table in front of the podium, spoke in a low voice. "Stop before this goes too far."

"One more word, and you're dead."

She folded her arms.

Arnold pointed to a tall thin man, one of the representatives from Mecklenburg-West Pomerania, who he knew was a secret member of Germany Now. "Would you like the honor of making the motion?"

The man hesitated, then stood and in a loud voice offered a motion of no-confidence in Chancellor Christina Jung and to install Arnold Shafer in her place.

"Second?" Arnold asked.

The young woman from Lower Saxony remained in her seat, but her words were audible. "This is wrong!"

Frederick shot her in the chest. She slumped in her seat, blood spurting over her neighbors. Arnold waited until the screams died down. Then he asked again.

"Second?"

70

BERLIN, GERMANY

THE CHAOS ON THE steps of the Reichstag and on the pavement below continued to spread. Dozens lay on the ground, shot, or trampled. Sporadic shooting continued. Others fought with fists and blunt instruments. Other Germany Now supporters were fleeing. Kolya gave Ben Rosenberg credit. His plan had succeeded.

Kolya followed closely behind Lisette. Despite the increasing pain in his leg, he kept up the pace.

Apart from being randomly shot, the greatest danger would be from anyone who recognized either of them. But no one looked closely enough to pose a danger, and his team shot anyone who swung a gun even vaguely in their direction.

No sign of the police or the military.

His personal demons were quiet. Hopefully, they'd stay that way for the duration.

They skirted through gaps in the crowd as they climbed the stairs to the front of the Reichstag. To get into the main chamber was a little trickier. It required passing through the now unattended security gate, a narrow entrance.

Between the security gate and the door to the legislative chamber, there were several dozen armed men, stepping over and around bodies of dead security officers.

Lisette, ahead of him, pushed through the security gate. Kolya followed.

Frick and Teo followed Kolya. Tehila was behind Frick, the hoodie obscuring most of her face. The neo-Nazis didn't seem to notice them, intent on the door of the chamber. Kolya and Lisette would have to pass the men to get to Shafer.

Kolya heard shots and then screams coming from inside.

"The two of you. Go," Frick spoke behind Kolya. "We'll cover."

Kolya doubted that three agents could hold off so many, but he didn't have any other ideas. *Get inside. Kill Shafer and Bauer.*

"Better idea. I know them," Lisette spoke quietly. "Let me try to get us past."

It was very risky. If Bauer had disclosed that Lisette was a traitor to the cause, then his followers would kill both of them immediately.

But she didn't wait for his opinion. She approached a muscular man wearing a T-shirt with the numbers 14/88. "Anton?"

He swung his gun in her direction. It took another second, and then his expression changed to recognition. "Lisette? Frederick's inside."

"We got separated. He wanted me there for the big moment. Along with his new bodyguard." She indicated Kolya.

"You're lucky. We have to guard the hall and won't get to watch the Leader become Chancellor."

He signaled the other men, and they formed a corridor to the door. Getting through was the next challenge. If Frederick spotted them on entering, the game was up.

Kolya pushed the door open just enough for Lisette to slip through and then followed her. There were two bodies on the floor near the entrance. But inside, the armed men's attention roamed from the seated members of the Bundestag to whatever was happening on the podium, where a booming voice demanded a second. No one was watching the door.

They quickly took cover: Lisette crouched down in the open space behind the last row of seats. Kolya joined her. They cautiously raised their heads, peering through gaps in the seats. Arnold Shafer stood at the front, and next to him, Frederick Bauer cradled an HK-91 in his arms. Armed men, dispersed around the chamber, guarded legislators.

"We have a motion and a second on the floor," Shafer's voice thundered. "All those in favor of the motion of non-confidence in Chancellor Jung, raise your hands."

Five hands went up.

Frederick shot a grey-haired man who had not raised his hand.

"Let's try again," Shafer said

"Are you confident that you can kill Shafer from this distance? Remember—head shot. He's wearing body armor." Kolya spoke in an undertone as the screams rose again. He knew he could hit either man. Shafer, the Leader, had to be the first killed. But once he shot Shafer, Frederick would have a chance to take cover. Best to take both out simultaneously.

Lisette had dedicated her whole life to this moment. He was fine with her taking the shot. If she could do it.

"I won a gold medal for marksmanship. In Texas."

"Fine. You're on Shafer. I'll take Frederick. Then be ready. Frederick's men will come after us. Good chance neither of us makes it out."

"I know." She gripped the weapon hard. "It's worth it."

"Together. On three." Kolya raised his gun and aimed.

* * * * *

Frick, Teo, and Tehila puzzled the men guarding the hall. And that was even though they couldn't see Tehila face. Anton directed a question at Frick.

"What district are you from?"

"We're members of the Brooklyn Bund."

"Brooklyn Bund?"

"*Ja, ja.*" And Frick spewed out an explanation in German—that they were American supporters of the movement.

But he could feel Tehila's impatience behind him. "They're not completely stupid," she hissed in his ear.

"We're going to die," Teo mumbled.

"Maybe. Maybe not," he muttered under his breath. Other members of Germany Now were pouring into the hall through the security gate.

Were they all stupid enough not to notice that a Black woman with a gun was standing directly behind him? Even though her face was mostly obscured?

Anton narrowed his eyes. "Is that a Black woman with you?"

"Of course not." Frick raised his gun, shot Anton, and sprayed the men around him with bullets. Teo and Tehila fired with him. The three dropped to the floor and continued firing as all hell broke loose.

71

BERLIN, GERMANY

GUNTER AND HIS MEN made it into the headquarters of the Berlin police where they continued to shoot anyone who showed his face. He estimated they'd killed or wounded at least thirty officers. Some lay unmoving, others moaned and called for help. He didn't bother with them. If they were down, they weren't a threat. His orders were clear. Hold for at least half an hour, longer if possible, to prevent the Berlin police from sending help to the Bundestag, at least until the Leader was voted in as Chancellor.

Berlin police officers were no longer showing themselves. He and his men had control of the lobby. But he heard the sirens increasing in intensity.

Gunter checked his watch. Twenty minutes.

He'd done the job. Unless he or his men were captured, and any admitted the truth, the public would blame Islamic jihadists for the attack. They would rally around the new Chancellor.

He signaled a retreat.

They raced outside where a hundred police officers opened fire.

BONN, GERMANY

The three soldiers tasked with assassinating the Federal Minister of Defense made it to the corridor where her office was located. They shot two secretaries, before bursting through the minister's door.

She wasn't there. Neither was the chief of defense.

They retraced their steps but didn't even make it to the elevator before being surrounded by dozens of soldiers. They raised their arms and surrendered.

* * * * *

The bands of assassins in towns all around Germany had mixed success. They killed one or two local officials in half a dozen towns. In others, the police were waiting.

BERLIN, GERMANY

The head of the *Bundestagpolizei* looked at Hermann Beck, his second-in-command, and at the pistol in his hand. He listened impassively as Beck placed him under arrest. He knew that Beck would send *Bundestagpolizei* officers to the rescue of the Reichstag. But he'd done what he could for the Leader. If Chancellor Jung was voted out of office, and Arnold Shafer was voted in, it would be complicated to undo. Maybe even impossible. Especially if the only surviving members of the Bundestag were those who supported the action and would claim that the Bundestag had not been coerced.

* * * * *

The White Rose Mob surged forward as the shooting continued. Most of the causalities were other Nazis, shot by their comrades higher up on the stairs. But the ranks were thinning as guns were tossed down and men began to run. The effort to escape resulted in people on both sides falling.

Ben, with Rachel next to him, reached the bottom of the steps. He still held the gun, but he was no longer firing. Rachel also held a gun, which she'd also grabbed from a man who'd fallen, but she hadn't fired it.

The twins, on the other hand, were deadly shots, downing anyone in their way.

There were bodies and blood everywhere. Stumbling over a man who was still alive, moaning in pain, Ben could barely keep down the nausea.

The sea of white caps, white T-shirts, white hoodies, and white flowers was slowly gaining ground. But the most fanatical members of Germany Now remained in position at the top of the steps and had realized that the attackers wore white. They began to target the White Rose Mob.

Ben saw Ahmet fall and his secretary Lena shot in the arm. He aimed at the man who'd shot Lena and pulled the trigger. More people were being shot on either side of him. He felt like he was in a slow-moving nightmare filled with the smell of blood and the screaming of the injured.

A new sound joined the sounds of battle—sirens—a cacophony of sirens. The cavalry had arrived.

He removed his white cap and waved it. "Drop guns," he shouted.

He felt a blow in the middle of his chest, and then without knowing how he got there, he was on the ground, cradled in Rachel's arms. It was hard to breath. He moved his lips. "*Shema...*" but was having trouble with the rest of the prayer. He heard Rachel speak the ancient words for him. Overhead, the sky was an intense blue, and he felt himself melting into it.

* * * * *

Lisette took a deep breath, let it out slowly, and then took another and held it. In a perfect world, she'd have liked to be the one to kill Frederick as well as Shafer, and in a perfect world she'd have liked to kill them both face-to-face, telling them who she was as they died. But it was not a perfect world. If she didn't get to kill Frederick, she was glad that Kolya would do so.

"Three," Kolya said

She squeezed the trigger just as a fusillade exploded in the hall outside the legislative chamber.

The burst of gunfire startled Frederick and Shafer, and both men fell to the floor as she and Kolya fired. Both shots missed.

Next to her, Kolya muttered unintelligible words in what she assumed was Russian.

She hoped the gunfire outside the chamber had covered their own failed attempt. But her round had hit the high rise of seat directly behind where Bauer had been standing.

Kolya's round had hit a concrete wall.

Frederick was shouting. "Someone shot at us. Find them and kill them."

She remained in position, gun aimed in case Shafer poked his head up again. He didn't. But the armed men who'd followed Frederick into the chamber began to search through the aisles. She ducked down.

"They'll find us eventually," Kolya said. "Stay low and shoot anyone who rounds the corner on the left. I'll take the right."

"*We* could rush *them*."

"Good way to die."

Just waiting wasn't her preference. She poked her head up to see whether she had a possible shot at Frederick or Shafer. But she couldn't see either of them.

A moment later, the game changed.

"This will take too long, Frederick," Shafer's voice. "And you're putting your people at risk. There's a better way."

"Men of Germany Now—stay in position." Frederick issued the order. "The Leader is in charge now."

What now?

Shafer shouted loudly. "Whoever is out there. Throw down your gun and surrender, or we will begin executing people, beginning with Christina Jung. You have two minutes."

Chancellor Jung sat facing the Bundestag. At this distance, Lisette couldn't see her face but could hear her words, spoken loudly for the entire assembly. "The police will be here any minute, Arnold."

"The police are not coming," Shafer's voice. "They have other worries right now."

He was insane. But he was right. The police wouldn't arrive in time to save Chancellor Jung. It was up to Lisette—and Kolya—to stop this. She peered over the edge of the seats again. Did she have a shot?

No.

She glanced over at Kolya. He was taking deep breaths and exhaling slowly. Then he looked at her. "You really were a gold medalist?"

"Of course."

"Good." He began to move, staying low. "Don't miss."

She seized his arm. "What are you doing?"

"If I surrender, Shafer and Bauer could show themselves. They may not realize that there's two of us. You may have a shot at killing them."

"They'll kill you." She kept a firm grip on his arm.

"Possibly. Maybe not if you shoot first." He gently put his hand over hers and removed it from his arm. "Other people are going to die if I don't risk it."

Tears rose to her eyes. And yet she barely knew him. Only a day ago, she'd tried to kill him. He was barely a friend. Still, she felt a profound and deep sadness at the thought of him dying.

"Don't cry." He smiled at her. "Harder to aim when you're crying."

Somewhere in front of the almost six hundred members of the Bundestag, Shafer announced: "One minute until I shoot the Chancellor."

"I don't even know your name," Lisette whispered.

"It's Petrov. Kolya Petrov. My fiancée is Alex Feinstein. If you make it out, tell her..." he hesitated "tell her that I'm sorry. I'm going to try to get closer before I surrender so they won't know that I was hiding back here and possibly check it. Shoot Shafer first, then Frederick."

She willed the tears away and hardened herself. This was what she did. She killed people who deserved it. "Agreed."

Then crouching, he moved to the end of the aisle and made his way several rows forward before standing, dropping the gun, and raising his arms.

72

BERLIN, GERMANY

KOLYA FLASHED BETWEEN THE current situation and the gunfight where he'd been taken prisoner and a friend murdered almost exactly a year earlier. Maybe that was why his hands were shaking as he raised them. And maybe because he knew the odds against surviving.

But if he was about to die, he preferred not to do so while in the middle of a flashback.

He focused on sensory details. The row after row of purple seats, filled with the terrified members of the Bundestag. The flags at the front of the hall. The smell of blood and gunpowder. The sound of gunfire in the hall outside the chamber had eased, and it was quiet enough that he could hear his own breathing. The heavy feel of the HK 9mm gun tucked into his belt and hidden under his sweater. The ache in his leg as he limped forward. As usual, focusing on the immediate senses brought him back.

The shaking eased, even as two of Bauer's thugs crowded in, guns pointed at him, even as they hustled him to the front of the chamber. But they didn't search him. If they had, they would have found the pistol. The pistol wasn't much, not against men holding assault weapons, but it might give him a chance—a very small chance—to kill either Shafer or Frederick—if Lisette missed.

"You!" Frederick stood and pointed his gun at Kolya. But Lisette didn't shoot. Probably because Arnold Shafer was still hiding, and he had to go first. For some reason Frederick didn't shoot immediately either. "Michael. You fucking bastard. Hold him." He gave the direction to the two men flanking Kolya.

They grabbed his arms. Still didn't notice his weapon. *Amateurs.* But he was grateful for their lack of professionalism, even with his arms pinned.

"Hello, Frederick. Is this the peaceful political takeover you were planning?"

"You're supposed to be dead. Along with that whore."

Maybe that was why Frederick hadn't immediately shot Kolya, because he wanted to know what had happened to Lisette.

"She sacrificed herself to save me. Hans killed her, and I killed Hans," Kolya said.

Frederick slung his gun over his shoulder and hit Kolya hard and repeatedly in the midsection. "And now I'm going to kill you."

When Frederick stopped punching, Kolya took a moment to get his breath. "You don't want to kill me. You're already in trouble with the American government. My superiors don't appreciate their agents being shot."

"So you admit to being an American agent." Frederick smiled thinly. "The old man thought you were a Jew." Then he hit Kolya in the jaw.

Kolya spat out blood. He considered remaining silent, but the longer he could keep Frederick talking, the longer he would stay alive. And the greater chance that Shafer would offer himself as a target. "That crazy old bastard was haunted by the Jewish children he'd murdered. I killed him too, by the way. You were right. Time to put him out of his misery."

"You fucking bastard. Are you a Jew?"

"I'm an intelligence officer for the United States, and my country will be angry enough about Jonathan Egan. Shoot me and even if you succeed here, you'll have to watch your back for the rest of your life."

"Who is Jonathan Egan?" Frederick asked.

But Kolya's words weren't meant for Frederick.

Arnold Shafer, the "courageous" leader, finally rose from hiding on the floor. "Jonathan Egan—the American agent I told you about. It wasn't me who shot him. It was a jihadist."

Lying to the end.

As Shafer rose into view, Kolya thought of Lisette. *Take the shot.* But the men holding him had hustled him into the line of fire, and he couldn't shift his position to give her a clear target. She was probably waiting because she was worried about hitting him.

She needed to shoot, even if he were at risk.

Maybe if she knew the answer to her lifelong quest. Speaking loudly enough to be heard throughout the chamber, Kolya asked the question for her. "And the lawyer you killed in Hamburg fifteen years ago? Back when you were called Wolf after the tattoo on your arm. Was he a jihadist?"

"*How do you know about that?*" Shafer demanded.

"I met his daughter. Lisette. Frederick's former fiancée. She grew up very lovely but very angry. It's why she killed six of your people."

Shafer turned on Frederick. "Did you tell Lisette about me?"

"Of course not. Anyway, the whore's dead, and so is he." With the butt of his gun, Frederick struck Kolya again, ribs and stomach. But for the men holding him, Kolya would have fallen.

There were murmurs of dismay from the legislators watching.

Frederick slung his rifle back over his shoulder and removed a hunting knife from his belt.

"Shooting is too easy, Michael, for a spy. Too quick. Cutting your head off isn't quite as good as feeding you to hogs, but it'll have to do. Get him on his knees."

The men on either side of Kolya pushed him down, hands holding his shoulders and arms.

Frederick grasped Kolya's hair in his left hand, pulling his head up, and placed the knife against the side of Kolya's throat with his right.

Kolya resisted the urge to close his eyes. He felt the life pulsing in him—his heart racing, the hard floor against his knees, and everything that he regretted, everything that he'd failed to do or failed to say, flashed through his mind. The blood trickled down his shirt as the knife cut into his skin.

Shoot, Lisette. Goddamnit.

Then she did. Four shots rang out. Arnold Shafer toppled backwards, a third eye oozing blood from the middle of his forehead. The two men holding Kolya's shoulders released their grip and toppled, one shot in the back, the other in the head. Frederick, shot in the shoulder, dropped the knife, and fell to the floor.

Frederick, from his downed position, tried to swing his assault rifle into position, as Kolya pulled the HK from his belt.

He shot Frederick in the head and then answered the question that Frederick had asked although Frederick could no longer hear the response. "And, yes, Frederick, I am a Jew," before collapsing himself. Taking shallow breaths—deep breaths hurt—he pressed a hand to his neck. Cut, but not deep enough to hit the artery.

Then the doors at the back of the room burst open, and police in riot gear flooded inside.

73

COLOGNE, GERMANY

JONATHAN EGAN CRACKED AN eye open. The ceiling looked unfamiliar. He tried to sit up, only then realizing that he had an IV in his arm and various wires and sensors attached to his body. As he became more awake, he remembered being shot by Arnold and being treated by the EMTs—and then nothing until now.

At least there was no pain. Just a vague floating sensation, which probably meant a lot of drugs. He tried to sit up again.

"The bed's electric, and there's a button to move it up or down. I can do it for you if you don't have the technical expertise."

A familiar voice. He turned his head. Elizabeth sat next to the bed, wearing an expression that he couldn't quite identify, although her tone had been as mocking as ever.

"Hey." It wasn't a particularly clever or witty response. "I guess I'm not dead."

"An astute observation. You should be, though. I should kill you myself for not waiting for me before confronting Arnold."

He found the button on the side of the bed. He pushed it and raised himself until he was almost on eye level with her. Now that he could see her more clearly, he could identify her expression. She looked tired and strained, and her eyes were red as if she'd been crying. A pleasant thought.

"Sorry I worried you." He tried to reach for her hand, but she folded her arms.

"You worried everyone. I've been fielding the calls. Petrov. Bradford. Even your mother."

But not his father. That was okay. He didn't particularly care whether his father called or not.

"Kolya's okay, then."

"He has some bruises and a couple cracked ribs, but he survived. It's over. Arnold is dead. As is Frederick Bauer, along with a lot of his followers. Most of the others are in custody. What's left of Germany Now has gone underground."

"And our people?" He tried to pull up the pillow that had slipped down to his back.

She stood and helped rearrange blankets and the pillow. "Everyone survived from our team. I'll fill you in on everything later."

But good people hadn't survived.

On reflection, he was okay with her waiting to brief him. With the drugs coursing through his system, he might not remember anything. Still, her tucking the blanket around him gave him the chance to snag one of her hands. "Think we could try again, Elizabeth?"

"You're always trying, Jonathan." But she didn't pull away.

BERLIN, GERMANY

It hurt to breathe with the broken ribs. With the mission over, his exhaustion would take at least a week to clear, and he'd have to resume physical therapy for his leg after what he'd put it through in the past few days. Worse, the PTSD, which Kolya had barely managed to keep at bay through the events leading up to the attempted coup, had come roaring back in nightmares and flashbacks.

But none of it seemed even worth mentioning. Compared to others, he'd emerged relatively unscathed.

Rosenberg's wife Rachel stood at the side of the grave, clutching her two little boys, as she spoke the words of the Kaddish, the prayer recited by Jewish mourners for hundreds of years, a prayer that did not mention death.

Yesgadahl vavesgaddash smeh rabba. Exalted and sanctified be his great Name.

Standing near Rachel Rosenberg and her boys, the surviving twin, Hasan, wept openly. The funeral for Ahmet had been earlier in the day. Hasan and Ahmet had been Ben's employees—and then his friends. Now, Hasan had become something closer. Ben's Jewish family and Ahmet's Moslem family were united in grief and sacrifice.

Kolya was flanked by Tehila and Teo, who had miraculously escaped the carnage of the attempted coup with minor injuries. Teo had his arm in a sling, a minor wound that had avoided any arteries. Tehila had again suffered bruising to her torso from gunshots but thanks to her Kevlar vest, nothing more. Frick was still in the hospital, shot multiple times, but his vest had also saved his life.

Ben Rosenberg, and at least fifty members of the White Rose Mob, had not been so lucky. At least three hundred supporters of Germany Now were also dead, most of them shot by other neo-Nazis, a few shot by the White Rose Mob.

Kolya felt no sympathy for any of the neo-Nazis.

He felt guilt and sadness for Ben Rosenberg and his friends.

It was a large crowd gathered in a circle around Ben Rosenberg's open grave. Uninjured members of the White Rose Mob. Representatives from the Bundestag. The Chancellor herself would have come, cognizant that Ben's efforts had been critical in thwarting the coup, saving her life and Germany's democracy. However, observant Jewish funerals were held the day after death. In the immediate aftermath of the coup attempt, she was swamped, working with the new president of the BfV to weed out members of Germany Now from posts in the security services. But the vice chancellor attended in her absence.

None of them seemed to recognize Kolya as the man who'd surrendered to Frederick Bauer. Fortunately for Kolya's continued intelligence career, his identity and that of his team had been concealed from the press and the general public, although the story had not. It made for great copy: unknown hero risked his own life to save others, including the Chancellor, from neo-Nazis terrorists, and then an unknown woman shot the would-be killers before the Nazis could kill the hero.

He hated the word "hero."

Members of the Bundestag had told the story to the press. The Chancellor had confirmed the story but claimed that she had no idea of the identity of either of them—that they had slipped away in the chaos. Another lie. The police had helped Kolya to an ambulance without taking his name on the direct order of the Chancellor. None of the Bundestag members had seen his face up close, and all of their phones had been confiscated during the coup attempt, so there were neither photos nor video.

The injuries which might have given him away were not visible at a distance. The bruises on his face and the cut on his throat were toned down, if not concealed, by make-up.

In the appropriate spot and prompted by Tehila, Kolya murmured the Congregation's part of the Kaddish that was printed in a pamphlet handed out by the funeral home. Despite his lack of Jewish education, he had a cursory knowledge of Hebrew from his work as an intelligence operative, enough that he could at least follow the words.

He hadn't known Ben Rosenberg very well, and he didn't believe in God, but he felt an obligation to their shared heritage.

Lisette stood nearby, head bowed.

The service ended, and Rachel picked up a shovel to drop the dirt onto Ben's coffin. The shovel passed from hand to hand through the crowd, with every person stepping forward. Kolya stepped up and took his turn. Then Teo, Tehila, and Lisette.

Two bearded young men filled in the grave. It didn't take long.

"Why don't they leave it to the gravediggers?" Lisette asked.

"It's considered a mitzvah, a good deed, not to leave the dead uncovered," Tehila said.

Then it was over, and the crowd began to disperse, although Rachel and her sons lingered at the site.

"What about going back to Ben's house for the after-funeral service?" Teo asked Kolya.

He shook his head. "This is a time for family and close friends. We are neither."

"We should pay our respects. His wife will want to know that he's honored and remembered," Teo said.

"She knows." Kolya waved a hand at the departing Bundestag representatives.

"Later in the week would be better," Tehila said. "They'll be sitting shiva for seven days. Usually, towards the end, there aren't as many people. Drop by early one morning, Kolya. The mornings are the hardest time to get a minyan."

Most branches of Judaism required a minyan, ten Jews, to say the required prayers twice a day during the seven-day mourning period immediately after the death while the family sat shiva. Orthodox Judaism restricted minyans to men. Kolya noted the absurdity that he, a secular Jew who knew none of the prayers, would be welcomed to form a minyan with the orthodox, but Tehila, who knew the prayers and was religious—albeit in her fashion—would not, because of their respective genders.

Still, while he didn't believe in God, he was a little interested in learning more about the traditions. And he wanted to honor Ben Rosenberg. "I will. I'm going to see Jonathan in Cologne, then I'll go to the shiva when I'm back in Berlin for a few days."

"I thought you were planning to stay for a few weeks."

"In Europe, but only a short time in Berlin. Then Paris."

He was taking three weeks off to recuperate physically and mentally, and he always enjoyed Paris. Good food. Good music. Almost as importantly, Alex, who would be spending his vacation with him, loved Paris, although she was interested in spending a few days in Germany.

"I was thinking of going to see Frick in the hospital today," Teo said. "Maybe I'll go with you to Cologne tomorrow."

"That's a negative, Teo," Tehila said. "At least for today. You are still recuperating. I promised your doctor I'd get you back in bed as soon as the service was over. Let's go. Need a ride, Kolya?"

Kolya indicated Lisette, who stood a little to the side. "She's giving me a lift to the airport to pick up Alex."

Tehila glanced from Kolya to Lisette then back again. "I like Alex a lot, Kolya."

"I'm glad. And she has nothing to worry about. Lisette is a friend. That's all."

"Good. Make sure it stays that way." Tehila's tone held just a touch of warning. Kolya found it both infuriating and endearing. Then she turned to Teo. "Emma made you some nice kosher chicken soup back at the apartment."

Teo rolled his eyes and followed Tehila to her car.

"Emma?" Lisette asked.

"Tehila's wife."

He thought about telling Lisette that but for Alex, he would have wanted to explore possibilities with her, both physical and otherwise. But there was no reason to say anything. Best leave things unspoken—the possibilities that are never acknowledged, never have to be explained.

They walked in silence to Lisette's car.

* * * * *

Before starting the car, Lisette glanced over at Ben Rosenberg's grave. Rachel and the two boys had finally left. "I'm sorry for Ben's children. I hope they don't take my path."

Her grandmother's funeral would be in a few days. Her mother had sent flowers but wasn't flying over. To be expected—after all, her grandmother had hated all of them. And Lisette had returned the feeling, even if she had paid for her grandmother's care and her funeral. She assumed that either Frederick or one of his followers had killed both her grandmother and her caregiver. She felt sadness and not a little guilt that Helen, a kind woman, had been murdered—because of her. But as to her grandmother, she felt nothing. Ironic, wasn't it, the outpouring of love and sympathy for Ben Rosenberg, her own deep sadness in thinking of his death—and of Helen's, while she felt no grief for her own kin. But she'd attend the service. She'd also go to Helen's—which would be more difficult.

"Your path wasn't that terrible. I personally am very glad that you became an expert shot." Kolya snapped the seatbelt into place. "Although I would probably not mention to anyone else that you killed a number of Frederick's people before Day X. The authorities might not be as forgiving."

The authorities had been very forgiving about the events at Hans' farm and about the Germany Now supporters killed by her, by Kolya, the team, or by the White Rose Mob during the attack on the Reichstag. Everything had been categorized as self-defense or defense of the government. If anyone suspected that Lisette was the anti-Nazi vigilante who had killed seven men, no one mentioned it. The only people who knew or suspected—outside of Kolya and his team—were dead.

"Wasn't planning on telling anyone. I'm used to being alone."

"I understand there are openings at the Equality Institute. Hasan will still be working there. It might be pleasant to not be constantly worrying about someone killing you."

She snorted. "That's good, coming from you. You're going to some other dangerous assignment after your vacation, aren't you?"

"It's what I do. I tried being a lawyer. I hated it."

"And your fiancée?"

"She hated me being a lawyer as well."

"Well, there you are. I'd probably hate being a lawyer, too. I may be like you—not suited for the mundane."

"Maybe not. But if you're going to live this kind of life, having friends, having someone you care for, makes a difference. You don't have to be alone."

She wanted to tell him then, that for a brief moment she'd had a fantasy of not being alone, of being with him. But she didn't. What was the point? The fantasy was over. "I'll think about it."

He was at least correct about one thing. She'd done what she'd set out to do fifteen years earlier; she'd killed the man who'd killed hobbits and Santa Claus, along with her father. She should feel completed, but in some ways, she just felt empty. She had to figure out what her life would be now—and she had no idea where to start.

She planned a trip to Austin to see her mother and stepfather, but after that she would need something new to do. Maybe the Equality Institute wasn't a bad idea. Or hiring herself out to worthy causes. *Maybe captain a pirate ship.*

Meanwhile, she would find other passions, starting with riding horses again. But one of the passions would not be Kolya Petrov.

"Just a suggestion. By the way, thanks again for the airport run." He was on his phone, now, smiling down at it as he texted.

"It's the least I can do after trying to kill you."

"You made up for it." His phone beeped as a new text came in. "Alex is looking forward to meeting you, by the way."

"What did you tell her about me?" She was looking forward to meeting Alex as well.

"What was not classified. Which wasn't a lot. Mostly that you have become a good friend."

She liked that. Kolya as a lover would have been nice, but after all the years alone, having a friend was almost as good. Maybe better.

* * * * *

The baggage terminal was crowded. Men and women in business suits. Students in jeans. Europeans. Asians, Africans. They crowded around rotating conveyer belts, snagging suitcases decorated with ribbons and painted designs. Others piled luggage and backpacks on carts and wheeled them through the doors towards waiting busses and cars. It took a minute, then Kolya spotted Alex, a carry-on bag over one shoulder, grabbing a large suitcase from the conveyer. He increased his speed. She set the case on the ground and turned towards him, as beautiful as ever, the dark unruly hair falling below her shoulders, the warm intelligent eyes. He wrapped her in his arms and felt her lips on his. For a moment, the shadows fell away. The world felt right again.

Then she stepped back and surveyed him, her gaze lingering on his throat. "Cut yourself shaving?"

"Razors can be tricky."

"So I hear." She gently touched a bruise on his face. "What else hurts?"

"Not much." But there was no point in hiding it. "Two cracked ribs."

"You're going to run out of body parts sooner or later." Then she looked past him. "Is that Lisette?"

Lisette had trailed him from the parking lot, and discreetly remained at a distance while he greeted Alex. Now she stepped forward and offered a hand. "Nice to meet you, Alex. Kolya's told me a lot about you."

"Has he? That would be very unlike him." Alex smiled at Lisette and accepted the handshake. "He hasn't told me very much about you, although I understand you and Kolya took down a Nazi coup attempt together."

No one was close to them, and the din from the crowd was so loud that their conversation couldn't be overheard.

"I didn't tell you that," Kolya said. "Our involvement is classified."

"The story was all over *The Washington Post* and *The New York Times*. Mysterious man saves the German Chancellor and members of the Bundestag by surrendering to Nazi terrorists, only to be saved in turn by mysterious woman. Beyond the fact that I *know* you—you have bruises on your face and a cut on your throat consistent with injuries suffered by said mysterious man. And I have other means of information."

"Tehila?" Kolya asked. "Or Teo?"

"I don't squeal on friends." Then she turned to Lisette. "Thank you for saving his life." Alex picked up her carry-on bag, and Kolya took her suitcase. She linked her free arm in his. He pressed her arm close to his body.

During the drive back to the city, Lisette pointed out the sights, recited the history of Berlin, much as she had on that first day when Kolya had to fake shooting Tehila. Then she parked near his hotel and stepped out of the car to say goodbye.

"I've wanted to go a Jewish wedding since I was Hodel in our tenth grade *Fiddler on the Roof* production," Lisette said. "Don't forget to invite me."

"Of course," Alex said. "He needs a few people on his side of the aisle. But don't expect a *Fiddler* type wedding. We're not orthodox."

"Disappointing," Lisette said. "Always wanted to dance to Klezmer music, carrying the bride and groom around on chairs."

"Well, I'm open to being carried on a chair." Alex glanced at Kolya. "He may not be, and we still have to fight about the music. It's not going to all be Goddamn jazz."

"Klezmer music would be okay. Carried on a chair—no," Kolya said.

Lisette and Alex exchanged amused glances.

"You have my email address," Lisette said. "Stay in touch."

"When I can." Kolya gave her a hug goodbye. "Take care of yourself."

"You too," she said, with a smile in Alex's direction. "Don't do anything stupid." Then she was gone.

He watched her car disappear and then turned to Alex. He could see a question in her eyes. "What?"

"I think she's into you."

"Possibly," he agreed. "She did try to seduce and poison me when she thought I was a Nazi."

"Obviously she didn't succeed with the poison."

"She didn't succeed with the seduction either." He recalled having a conversation to that effect after he was poisoned, but it had been a hallucination.

"Good. I'd hate to ask Tehila to kill her," Alex said. "I like her."

"So do I. But I *love* you. Anything else?"

"Just this: I know you're not okay. I'm here for you. If you want to talk about what happened, or if you don't. Whatever helps."

What helped was being with her, knowing that she loved and trusted him, and that she accepted who he was, even if she would have preferred him in another profession.

He folded her in his arms for a long and deep kiss.

Acknowledgments

MY CONTINUED GRATITUDE TO Encircle Publications for the support and encouragement, and to the Encircle writing community for welcoming me into your midst. I am honored to be an Encircle author.

Thank you to my husband Jim for listening to my ideas, for multiple readings, for days of editing, and for his patience with my single-minded obsessions. You've made me a better writer, if not a better person.

Thank you to my beta readers, Matt Cost, Cari Davis, Kevin St. Jarre, and Debbie Burke, for reading and offering notes on the draft of *Bloody Soil*.

And as always, a huge thank you to my entire family—Jim, Jenny, Joseph, Dean, and Penelope—for their love and encouragement.

Author's note: *Bloody Soil* is a work of fiction. Names, characters, and story are the products of the author's imagination, and any resemblance to persons living or dead is coincidence. The existence of the far right and plans for a Day X in Germany have a basis in fact, but the individuals, groups, and execution of Day X as mentioned in this novel are fictitious.

About the Author

AN AWARD-WINNING WRITER, **S. Lee Manning** is the author
of international thrillers, *Trojan Horse*, *Nerve Attack*, and *Bloody
Soil*. She spent two years as managing editor of *Law Enforcement
Communications* before embarking on a subsequent career as an
attorney that spanned from a first-tier New York law firm, to working
for the State of New Jersey, to solo practice. In 2001, Manning
agreed to chair New Jerseyans for Alternatives to the Death Penalty
(NJADP), writing articles on the risk of wrongful execution and
arguing against the death penalty on radio and television in the years
leading up to its abolition in the state in 2007.

After taking a class in stand-up at the Vermont Comedy Club,
she was a semi-finalist in the 2019 Vermont's Funniest Comedian
contest, and she still performs stand-up on occasion. Manning lives in
Vermont with her husband and very vocal cat, Xiao. She is currently
working on the next Kolya Petrov novel. For the latest updates, follow
S. Lee Manning on Facebook and visit sleemanning.com.

If you enjoyed reading this book,
please consider writing your honest review
and sharing it with other readers.

Many of our Authors are happy to participate in
Book Club and Reader Group discussions.
For more information, contact us at info@encirclepub.com.

Thank you,
Encircle Publications

For news about more exciting new fiction, join us at:

Facebook: www.facebook.com/encirclepub

Instagram: www.instagram.com/encirclepublications

Twitter: twitter.com/encirclepub

Sign up for Encircle Publications newsletter and specials:
eepurl.com/cs8taP